Charles Towne

KEEPERS
OF THE RING
5

CHARLES TOWNE

Angela Elwell Hunt

Tyndale House Publishers, Inc.
WHEATON, ILLINOIS

Visit Tyndale's exciting Web site at www.tyndale.com

All Scripture quotations are taken from the *Holy Bible,* King James Version.

Designed by Catherine Bergstrom

Edited by Rick Blanchette

Library of Congress Cataloging-in-Publication Data

Hunt, Angela Elwell, date
    Charles Towne / Angela Elwell Hunt.
       p.   cm. — (Keepers of the ring : 5)
    Includes bibliographical references.
    ISBN 0-8423-2016-4 (soft)
      1. United States—History—Colonial period, ca. 1600-1775—Fiction. I. Title. II. Series:
Hunt, Angela Elwell, date
Keepers of the ring ; 5.
PS3558.U46747C48   1998
813'.54—dc21   97-32270

To relive the relationship between owner and slave
we can consider how we treat our cars and dogs—
a dog exercising a somewhat similar leverage on our mercies
and an automobile being comparable in value to a slave in those days.
—Edward Hoagland, U.S. novelist

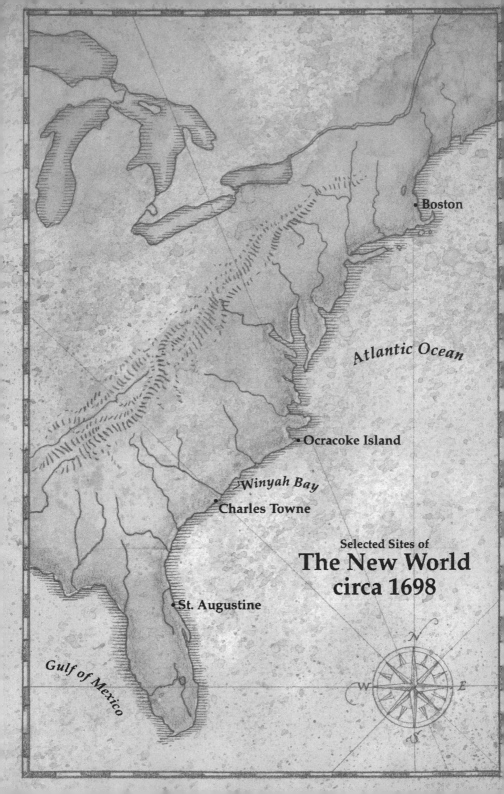

Atlantic Ocean

• Boston

• Ocracoke Island

Winyah Bay

• Charles Towne

Selected Sites of
**The New World
circa 1698**

• St. Augustine

Gulf of Mexico

N

W   E

S

AUTHOR'S NOTE

The earliest settlers of the New World never intended to become slaveholders. As early as 1614, ministers like Reverend Samuel Purchas believed that "the tawny Moore, blacke Negro, duskie Libyan, ash-coloured Indian, [and the] olive-coloured American" should be one "sheepfold" with the English and other Europeans, "without any more distinction of Colour, Nation, Language, Sex, [or] Condition."

But by the close of the seventeenth century, another clergyman, Morgan Godwyn, painted a picture of the reality in the New World. Godwyn observed that in English America, the two words *Negro* and *slave* were "by custom grown Homogeneous and Convertible; even as *Negro* and *Christian, Englishman* and *Heathen,* are by Custom and Partiality made Opposites."

By 1730, when rice cultivation soared in Charles Towne, sixty-six percent of Carolina's inhabitants were of African descent—and enslaved.

Trace Bettencourt's opposition to slavery would have been truly unusual in 1698. Libertalia, the colony on Madagascar where all men were to be equal and free, either did not exist or was destroyed by marauding natives, depending upon whether its history was penned by a historian or a novelist. The story of Libertalia is found in *A General History of the Robberies and Murders of the Most Notorious Pyrates,* credited to a Captain Charles Johnson. Some experts believe this Captain Johnson was novelist Daniel Defoe; others believe Captain Johnson himself wrote a true history.

In any case, America did not seriously consider abolishing

slavery for nearly one hundred years after Trace and Rachelle returned to the *Jacques*. On February 11, 1790, a group of Quakers submitted to Congress the first emancipation petition. Over seventy years later, Abraham Lincoln issued the Emancipation Proclamation, declaring that on January 1, 1863, slaves within all areas still in rebellion would be declared free forever. But not until December 18, 1865, did the Thirteenth Amendment to the U.S. Constitution prohibit slavery once and for all.

But, as Trace Bettencourt would attest, not all men are held in *physical* bondage. . . .

TABLE OF CONTENTS

PROLOGUE

December 9, 1680

Horror snaked down Bertrand Fortier's backbone and coiled in
his belly as Babette's rasping scream filled the house. Lifting the
crystal glass to his lips, he closed his eyes against the sound of
his daughter's cries. The peach brandy swirled warmly in his
mouth and burned his esophagus, but after a moment Bertrand
felt the golden liquid numb his raw nerves.

The minister was right—there was altogether too much alcohol in the Carolina colony, and an overabundant use of it. But the
Scriptures did say, "Give strong drink unto him that is ready to
perish, and wine unto those that be of heavy hearts."

I am both. Bertrand lowered the glass onto the polished mahogany of the huge dining table before him. A flurry of footsteps
thumped on the ceiling overhead, and Babette's latest scream
died away into a long, heartrending moan.

Bertrand clenched his fist until the nails dug into his palm.
*God, where are you? I entrusted my son and my daughter to you. Why
have you returned pain, death, and suffering in exchange for my faith?*

The susurrant sounds of feminine whispering echoed in the
hallway outside the dining room. Reflexively, Bertrand stiffened.

"Monsieur Fortier?" The maid's voice was high and thin, a
mere squeak in the room.

"Enter, Fala."

The ten-year-old Indian slave came forward, just far enough
for him to see her without turning his head. She bobbed in a
quick curtsey but did not meet his eye. "Virtue says it will not be
long now. We can see the head."

Cursed thing.

"Humph." Too distressed to speak, he sent the slave away with a wave of his hand. He knew he ought to inquire about Babette, but the sound of her screaming told him more than he wanted to know. The sight of the child might reveal even more horrible truths.

A cold wind blew past the window with soft moans. Sighing, Bertrand leaned forward and splashed another dose of brandy into his glass. It was because of the thing Babette carried in her womb that they had fled to Charles Towne, away from the prying eyes of those who had sailed with them from Paris. Charles Towne was a fledgling city, a place of tolerance. The eight English Lords Proprietors encouraged settlement by offering all free immigrants one hundred fifty acres of land and an additional one hundred acres for every able-bodied servant they brought with them. Bertrand had sailed from France with his son, Aubrey, his daughter, and her betrothed, Pierre. Only Babette and nine newly purchased slaves accompanied Bertrand when he arrived at Charles Towne port. By that time Pierre and Aubrey were dead and Babette was . . . ruined.

He lifted his hand in a stiff, practiced gesture, tossing the drink down. He had heard Babette's story on two different occasions, and it had differed dramatically in each telling. Only the beginning remained the same: While Bertrand conducted business with his associates in New France, Aubrey, Babette, and Pierre set out with a company of French trappers to spy out the new land. They hadn't gone far, according to Babette, before a fierce group of savages attacked. Pierre and Aubrey were killed—though Babette was never very clear about *how* they died—and Babette was held prisoner for nearly six months until another group of French trappers rescued her.

The doctors warned him not to press her for details, so for three months Bertrand mourned his son and studied his fragile daughter. When she returned to his arms, she cried hot, noisy, pulsing tears—of relief, he thought. But though she mourned her brother and her betrothed, Bertrand thought it odd that Babette did not cease to weep. For an entire summer she walked like a zombie through the inn where they were lodging, silent, steady tears streaming over her cheeks, now gaunt with sorrow. Bertrand studied her from beneath lowered brows, batting away the recurrent gnat of worry that would not let him rest.

When she could no longer hide the truth, Babette came to him with dry eyes and a different story of her ordeal in the wilderness. An Englishman living with the savages saved her life, she explained, and out of gratitude she had married him. But during another attack the Englishman was killed, and Babette escaped with the French trappers. As proof of her story she pulled a slender gold band from her pocket and held it up before his eyes. "See, Papa," she whispered, speaking calmly but with that eerie sense of detachment that boded impending disaster. "His family charge is inscribed inside: *fortiter, fideliter, feliciter.* He and his people strive to live boldly, faithfully, and successfully."

Bertrand had turned his eyes away, unable to look at his daughter and the telltale swelling of her belly. It was all too convenient, this suddenly remembered marriage to an English husband. Bertrand knew that his associates in Montreal would find Babette's story unbelievable; indeed, he could not believe it himself. The ring proved nothing. She could have found it among the Indians; many a dead English settler had been stripped of his jewelry in King Philip's War.

His heart pounded heavily now; he could feel each separate thump, like a blow to the chest. The brandy? Perhaps. Or perhaps his heart rebelled at the thought of the illegitimate cur coming into the world upstairs. It was far more likely that Babette carried an Indian brat than an English child, and he did not even want to *think* about how the child might have been conceived. While living with the Indians, Babette had played the part of a strumpet or a victim, and a thunderbolt jagged through him if he imagined her as either.

Unable and unwilling to remain in Montreal, Bertrand had gathered his household and sailed south to Carolina. A group of planters who had originally settled on Albermarle Point was in the midst of transferring to a small peninsula bordered by the Ashley and Cooper Rivers. A colorful mix of adventurers populated this raw settlement called Charles Towne: Barbadian planters from the West Indies, French merchants, English planters, and a host of wayfaring seamen. Unlike the pious Puritan settlements of the north, life in the port town was fast and easy. Bertrand could smell mischief on Charles Towne's inhabitants as strong as cheap perfume.

He swirled the remaining liquid in his glass and stared out the tall window that looked out onto the street. A knot of seamen had gathered on the dirt road before the house, their tanned faces slack with awe as they gawked. The house was still new, larger and far grander than any other dwelling on the Cooper River. "They say it's all for one man," one of the seamen shouted, his arm swinging wide to encompass the entire lot, "although he has a widowed daughter, I hear tell."

The sailor winked and elbowed his companions, then pretended to flick dust off his shoulders as though he would approach the house to go a-courting.

Bertrand turned his eyes away from the ridiculous spectacle and pressed his lips together, grateful that at least the local gossip had not failed. For Babette's sake, he had pretended to believe her story. She was known in Charles Towne as the genteel widow Babette Fortier Bailie, and as soon as she was rid of the child he would reintroduce her to society and find her a proper husband. There were widowed planters aplenty in Charles Towne, successful men with money and more land than they knew how to farm.

"Push, Madame Bailie, it is time!"

The cry echoed from upstairs, and Bertrand closed his eyes and pressed the smooth coolness of the glass to his throbbing temple. Bailie—why had she settled on that name? And what had possessed her during that savage interval? Why had she allowed herself to be placed in this unthinkable position?

Another shriek rent the air, and Bertrand felt his lips pucker with annoyance. Why did the cursed baby take so long? With any luck, the child would be stillborn and the past could be forgotten. Without the child, Babette could return to Montreal and begin again.

Another scream clawed in Babette's throat and raked Bertrand's heart, building until Bertrand thought he must scream himself or die. But then Babette's shriek dissolved into hysterical laughter, and the shrill cry of a baby filled the air.

Bertrand dropped his glass onto the table, watching numbly as it tipped and rolled slowly across the polished surface. A baby with lungs like that wouldn't die. Such a savage, lusty cry! The child had to be Indian.

Gritting his teeth, he pushed his chair back, then stood. Time to go look the devil's own in the face.

"Friday!" he bellowed, turning toward the hall.

The black slave appeared almost instantly, anticipating his master's call. "Yes, Monsieur Fortier?"

"Fetch the wet nurse. Tell her the babe is born, and she is to take it away immediately."

"Yes, sir." Friday ducked his head, then disappeared like a shadow in the hallway.

Bertrand moved toward the stairs, his hand choking the railing as his heavy feet carried him upward.

Babette Dominique Fortier Bailie

And ye shall know the truth,
and the truth shall make you free.

— John 8:32

December 24, 1682

A most solemn and joyous day! For not only is tonight
the commemoration of our Lord Christ's birth but Papa
has said that I might bring my baby home today. She has
been with her wet nurse for these two years, out of my
sight but always in my heart.

Will she know that I am the one who bore her?

Will she know that I have yearned to hold her since
the day she was born?

Papa does not love her, I know. And though he refers
to me in public as "Madame Bailie" and defers to me as
to a married woman, I fear he holds no great respect
either for my marriage or my child.

But he cannot deny her. She is flesh of my flesh, blood
of his blood. I named her Rachelle Fortier Bailie as she
slid from my womb, and from this day forward she shall
be in my charge.

The clack of hooves upon cobblestone broke the stillness of
the winter afternoon. Dropping her pen upon her writing table,
Babette gathered up her gown and hurried toward the window.
A small wagon stood outside in the gloom of twilight, a dark-
haired peasant woman upon the seat, a squirming bundle in her
arms.

Rachelle.

Dropping the lace curtain, Babette turned and braced herself
against the wall of her bedchamber, swallowing the excited

laugh that threatened to rise from her heart. Her father had managed to keep her from Rachelle for these two long years, but finally the last of his excuses had faded like a cloud that has outwept its rain. The child was weaned from the wet nurse and was past the sickly time when so many babies died. According to the nurse's last report, Rachelle was healthy and active, walking and talking with abandon.

In a flurry of sudden nerves, Babette ran her hands over her gown, then tentatively touched the single ringlet upon her neck. Her mouth twitched with amusement even as her eyes filled with tears. What was she thinking? A child so young would have little appreciation for the niceties of dress and adornment, but Babette wanted her daughter's first impression of her mother to be a good one.

A bell rang from within the depths of the house. Babette drew a deep breath and dashed the tears from her eyes, waiting for the servant to summon her. Her feet itched to ignore protocol and rush downstairs, but her father already thought her disastrously uncivilized. For the sake of keeping peace in the household, she would have to wait until Virtue or Friday summoned her, and then she would have to wait for her father.

"Madame Babette." Virtue, her maid, appeared in the doorway and dipped in a quick curtsey. Her grin flashed briefly, dazzling against her dark skin. "You have a visitor in the parlor."

"Thank you, Virtue." Babette swallowed hard. "Has Monsieur Fortier been informed?"

"Yes, madame." The slave dipped again, her smile fading a little. "He is waiting for you on the landing."

"Well then." Babette wiped her damp palms over the billowing silk of her gown, then lifted her chin. "I shall go to him at once."

Virtue said nothing but moved out of the way as Babette left her bedroom and hurried to meet her daughter.

Her father had not waited on the landing, and Babette flew down the stairs, afraid he might enter the parlor before her and manufacture yet another reason to send the child away. Her fears melted in relief, though, when she looked down the hall and saw him standing stiff as a poker outside the parlor, his hand on the heavy doorknob, his brows set in a straight, unwavering line.

She glided toward him, easing into a smile. *"Bonjour,* Papa." She tilted her head to look up at his imposing sternness. "This is a happy day."

His mouth spread into a thin-lipped smile. "We shall see," he said, turning the doorknob and pushing the door open.

Babette rushed forward, then stopped in midstride. A rather plain serving woman, dressed in a neck-to-heels coverall with a plain cotton shirt underneath, waited upon the sofa. But upon her lap, like a priceless jewel in an austere setting, sat the most beautiful, adorable child in all of Charles Towne.

Babette stared wordlessly across the room, her heart pounding. The child was plump and pleasant, with rounded arms crowned by ten dainty fingers. A wealth of dark, lustrous hair covered her head, and bright eyes black as ink gleamed above her rosy cheeks. Soft color marked those sweet rosebud lips; her nose was straight, short, and running from the cold. She wore a plain dress of cambric over gray cotton stockings, but from this hour forward she would wear nothing but satins and silks, the best Charles Towne could offer.

"Rachelle," Babette breathed, feeling blissfully happy and fully alive for the first time in nearly three years. A hot, exultant tear trickled down her cheek.

The child, playing happily with a sort of wooden doll, made no move to stir from the nurse's lap. Babette moved slowly to the divan across from the sofa, her arms suddenly heavy with emptiness. Did she dare take her?

"Humph."

Reminded of her father's forbidding presence, Babette glanced back at him. He stood behind her, his hands laced behind his back, his eyes fastened to the child in a piercing stare.

"Does she speak English?" he asked, his eyes flitting toward the nurse for a fraction of a second.

"Yes, sir," the woman answered, her eyes wet and bright as

she gently bounced the baby on her knees. "I don't know no French."

"Humph."

Ignoring her father's growl of disapproval, Babette thrust out her hands. "Come, darling," she whispered, clapping her hands lightly, then extending them to the baby. "Come to Mama."

The clapping sounds caught the toddler's attention, but she only squirmed and nestled close to her nurse's bosom, a stubborn expression filling those dark eyes.

"Go to your mother, child," Bertrand commanded, and at the sound of his rough voice the baby screwed up her face and began to howl.

"I'm sorry, Mistress Bailie," the nurse said, turning the child and pressing her to her chest. With a familiar ease she gathered the child in her arms and stroked the baby's back. "But there's been no man around the house since my husband died, and I'm afraid she ain't used to booming voices."

The sight of the baby—*her* baby—taking comfort from another woman was more than Babette could bear. "Give her to me," she exclaimed, determination overriding her caution as she stood and held out her hands.

A suggestion of doubt flickered over the nurse's face, but after an instant's hesitation she held the child toward Babette. At the sensation of being thrust away the child began to scream again, but Babette took the baby and awkwardly gathered her in, amazed at the power in the stubborn creature's flailing arms, curving spine, and powerful lungs. Warm, fleshy scents filled Babette's nose, unfamiliar odors at once repelling and attractive. Tears of relief came in a rush so strong her body trembled.

"There, there, *tais-toi*," she murmured, tenderly stroking the baby's back the way the nurse had. "Quiet now. You are with your mama."

Without looking behind her, she knew her father's expression had darkened like an angry thundercloud. "Babette," he said, his voice tight with irritation, "you do not have to do this. The child could stay with the nurse—whom she obviously prefers—for a few more years, then you could send her to school. We will see to her needs, and even at school she will be better equipped than any other—"

"*Ferme-la!*" Babette snapped, her temper rising. Her father blanched and took a step backward, apparently unable to believe that his daughter had just told him to shut up.

Shushing the child, Babette cut a look toward the nurse. The young woman had lowered her head out of deference, but Babette knew she listened to every word. By sunrise on the morrow every household in Charles Towne would know that Bertrand Fortier did not want to raise his granddaughter and would then speculate about his reasons. The next five minutes might seal the child's social standing for years to come.

"My husband," she told her father, taking pains to speak clearly so the nurse would catch every word, "was an esteemed clergyman, a man of God. And he would want me to remain close to our daughter, to be certain she was cared for and well loved. She *shall* have everything she needs, Papa, including a mother's affection."

Her father did not answer, but for a moment his eyes darkened dangerously. *This is new,* she could almost hear him saying. *Another chapter to your fantasy? Now she is the daughter of not only an Englishman but an English clergyman. Next you'll be saying this brat is the spawn of King Charles himself.*

Babette turned her attention back to the weeping child in her arms. Bertrand Fortier was not a man who accepted second best in anything, but he would have to accept this baby. She was his granddaughter, after all.

"That will be all, thank you," Babette told the nurse, moving the crying child to her hip. The nurse stood, paused for the briefest instant at Babette's side, then hurried out of the room without looking back. As the woman left, the baby stretched out her arms toward the retreating figure, her piteous wail tearing Babette's heart.

"Shhh," Babette whispered, pressing the child to her shoulder. "I am your mama, *comprends-tu?*"

Bertrand stepped forward, his mouth dipping into an even deeper frown as he regarded the baby with impassive coldness. "I had hoped she wouldn't look so dark. If she had blue eyes, I might have believed you."

Babette's glowing happiness faded as his words lacerated her. He meant that he might have been able to tell her story with more credibility, for he had never believed her. She pressed her lips together, stifling the bitter words on the tip of her tongue.

"Excuse me, Papa," she said, avoiding his eyes as she stepped past him and into the great hall that bisected the house, "but I have clothes for Rachelle in my bedchamber. She must be bathed and taken out of these dirty things."

"I'll leave you to her, then." Without another word, he followed her from the parlor and turned into his study, the door slamming behind him with an emphatic boom.

Babette carried her weeping bundle upstairs, where doting servants immediately surrounded her. Twelve-year-old Fala stared at the baby with reserved interest while Virtue, Cookie, and Friday clucked and cooed and shushed the bewildered baby.

Relieved to place the child in Virtue's more experienced hands, Babette retreated to her bedchamber and sank into a chair. As she reached for a handkerchief to wipe her streaming eyes, she wondered what Mojag Bailie would say if he knew she had just welcomed his daughter home.

▼▲▼▲▼ Fala felt her heart twist as she stared at the crying child in Virtue's arms. A memory, a safe one, flitted past her face like moth wings, and she remembered the babies who had lived in her own village before she was taken. Like those babies, this one had dark eyes and hair as black as the inside of a chimney.

Long ago, in another place, Fala had been entrusted to care for the toddling little ones . . . until the white men came and scattered the tribe. That life had ended when she was eight; Fala had hidden behind a tree and watched while her parents and baby brother were killed. Numb with shock and terror, she had not resisted the invaders and so had been spared—for slavery.

Fala had lived through dark days, but since coming to this tall house she had learned that the whites were haunted by dark days, too. After Madame Babette's baby was born and went away, Madame Babette wore black and did nothing but weep for several months. Friday turned away guests with the simple announcement that the Fortier family was not receiving visitors, and most people left after murmuring something about "great sorrow for your loss." Everyone knew that Aubrey Fortier and Madame Babette's husband had been killed in the north nearly a year before, and for a while Fala heard people in the marketplace wondering aloud if Madame Babette's baby had died, too. But the servants discreetly spread the word that the child lived with its wet nurse—an ordinary arrangement that explained the absence of an infant but did not account for the general attitude of mourning that persisted inside the house.

Yesterday Madame Babette had told Fala that her baby would be coming home. "You will be her maid, dear, as Virtue is mine," Babette said, gently resting her smooth hand upon Fala's cheek. Fala frowned in confusion—how could a mere baby be a mistress? But later Virtue explained that Fala would command the little girl until Rachelle grew to maturity; then their roles would be reversed. The arrangement pleased Fala—this task would almost be like her duties in the village.

Madame Babette's baby was hiccuping now, one shiny wet finger in her mouth, her eyes wide and glistening with spent tears. Her hair, damp and disheveled, stood out from her head in great shiny waves.

"Here, honey." Virtue lifted the chubby baby and handed her to Fala. "She's yours now. Take care of her. Madame Bailie has set out a wee dress on the tallboy."

Fala took the whimpering child and carefully lowered her to her own bony hip, then walked into the mistress's chamber. Babette sat in the chair by the window, her eyes following the baby, a faint flicker of unease in the depths of her teary blue-green gaze. Upon the tallboy Fala saw a miniature gown, tucked at the waist and with delicate detached sleeves, just like Madame Bailie's. The dress was ill proportioned for a baby, but Fala did not think Madame Bailie would want correction now. She wanted her child cleaned up, pleasant, and no longer wearing the scent of another woman.

"Hush, hush," Fala crooned as she placed the baby on Madame's bed. She unfastened the loops that held the baby's shift at the neck. "Let us get you into something clean. Something your mama will like."

At the sound of Fala's voice, the little girl stopped sniffling. She looked up with wide and trusting eyes, and something in the child's expression tore at Fala's heart. She had managed to keep her distance from these people, white and black, not risking her heart or her mind to their ways. But from this one, this small one, Fala might not be able to remain aloof.

"You're my mistress, did you know that?" Fala asked, running her hand over the baby's tummy. The little girl smiled at the warm touch of flesh upon flesh, and Fala smiled in response.

Days melted into weeks, weeks into months, months into years. Bertrand minded his business and his family as Charles Towne grew, watching with amusement and pride as his export business became one of the most successful in the settlement. Indian slaves, virgin timber, white rice—Carolina was replete with these goods, and Bertrand was savvy enough to recognize which European and Caribbean ports needed what products. His fortune grew like summer grass while, with something less than pride and absolutely no trace of amusement, he watched his granddaughter grow into a graceful and winsome creature, a rare and exotic bird that could have sprung only from the wilds of the New World.

Before the child's third birthday, he realized that she stood firmly in the way of a proper loving relationship between himself and Babette. He wanted to love his daughter as he had in her younger days, to be the sunlight of her life and her comfort in sorrow, but she kept herself at arm's length, often literally placing the child in the space between them when they stood in front of the house waiting for the carriage. "Rachelle," she had named the child, the lilting name meaning "sweet lamb." It was obvious Babette saw the toddler in that light, but Bertrand saw nothing but darkness when he looked at that raven hair, those oval eyes. Black was the color of sin, of evil, of violence, and God had marked this child with blackness even as he had taken Aubrey. Babette's curly hair was honey brown, her slanting eyes blue-green like the sea. Bertrand could see little of Babette in Rachelle.

Two months before the brat's fifth birthday, King Louis XIV of France revoked the Edict of Nantes that had guaranteed the rights of Protestant Huguenots in his country. No longer able to worship freely, the largely Presbyterian Huguenots fled to Charles Towne in such numbers that Bertrand's decidedly French household was no longer an oddity. Hearing of the toleration practiced in Charles Towne, other religious groups joined the settlement as well—from England, Scotland, and Ireland, gaggles of Quakers, Presbyterians, and Baptists swooped down in noisy and sundry flocks.

The port of Charles Towne, which had been prosperous and active when Bertrand Fortier first brought his daughter to live in the city, now bustled with ships and commerce at all hours of the day and night. Because the streets teemed with swaggering sailors, backwoods trappers, Indians, and merchants, home builders erected piazzas and porches along the southern or western sides of their houses. While this odd position was ostensibly designed to provide protection from the hot sun, no one could deny that the side-facing porches also managed to shelter women and children from the disorderly riffraff in the streets.

In 1686, when Babette's child lost her first tooth and began instruction with her tutor, the French Huguenots had established their own congregation on Church Street, while the Baptists talked about founding a church a few blocks away. Any Catholics in town kept their religious preferences to themselves because in the public eye Catholicism was inextricably linked with hostile Spain, and Spanish Florida lay only a few miles south.

The dreaded Spanish attack nearly materialized during that hot, stifling summer. In August 1686, a greedy fighting force of one hundred Spaniards, blacks, and Indians fell upon a small settlement to the south, then moved to within twenty miles of Charles Towne, looting and burning every plantation in its path. As the women of Charles Towne boarded the windows of their houses and hid the family silver, Bertrand joined the militia and marched to one of the watch houses. To protect his daughter and his estate, he crouched behind the walls, soaked in his own sweat, fearing the battle to come.

Deliverance came from an unexpected source. A mass of dark clouds, stirred by howling winds, rose from the Atlantic. A wonderfully horrid and destructive hurricane pounded the Carolina coast, sending the Spanish attackers scrambling back to Florida. Charles Towne was thoroughly wet and blown about but was spared serious damage.

The inhabitants of Charles Towne, even the covert Catholics, joined together in various houses of worship and thanked the Almighty for his protection. God's hand, it was commonly agreed, had stayed the Indians, the Spanish, the blacks, and the storm. If it had, Bertrand could not stop himself from pondering why God hadn't prevented tragedy from striking his family.

As Babette's child learned to read, sing, play the harpsichord, and write (an unheard-of skill for elegant young women who had secretaries to write for them, but Babette insisted that the child study penmanship), Charles Towne kept pace with the girl, growing from infancy to saucy, bold adolescence.

In the year of the child's birth, Henry Woodard, a Charles Towne planter, had obtained a bag of Madagascar rice, and his experimentation with the seed resulted in a crop that looked promising for the colony. As Babette's child celebrated her tenth birthday, Bertrand bought five hundred acres of prime land at Waccamaw Neck and established his own rice plantation. All the necessary ingredients for prosperity were at hand: a high demand for the product, adequate slave labor, and the proper natural resources. No longer would Bertrand have to rely on the exportation of deerskins, Indian slaves, and lumber. Rice had become the king crop, and Bertrand felt his smile broaden in approval every time he heard a merchant complain that there were not enough ships to export the rice England demanded.

Now he was chief among the exporters of Charles Towne, Bertrand thought, gazing across his garden as he sat on his piazza in the dense shade of an October afternoon, but he and Babette were still at odds over the girl. His rice empire had blossomed into profitable maturity, and so had Rachelle. At sixteen, Babette's daughter stood ripe for marriage. She was old enough to be betrothed, married, and sent away.

Babette could not say that Bertrand had hindered the child in any way. He had provided whatever moneys were necessary for her upbringing and outfitting (an extravagant and horrid expense but worth every shilling as long as Babette remained happy). He had never once lifted his voice to scold the child. He had never confided to anyone his suspicions about her conception or her parentage. And he had good reason to believe that his own reputation, fortune, and social standing had covered the girl in social glory. He had already seen evidence of it—she shone as the belle of every Charles Towne ball, and several wealthy merchants had already approached Bertrand and offered to discuss a possible betrothal for their eager sons.

The cool afternoon air carried faint hints of coming winter days. In some ways, Bertrand thought, stroking his chin, the child's birth had not been the tragedy he had first feared. With every day that passed, the girl looked less Indian and more like her mother. She had acquired Babette's grace and knack for fashion, and her dark hair shone with coppery sparks when the sun flamed upon it. It would be simple to arrange a good match, but thus far he had not been able to convince Babette that Rachelle was mature enough for marriage. Babette had been sixteen when betrothed, and if Pierre de Gua de Monts had not been idiot enough to get himself killed by a group of mindless savages, Babette would have been happily married by seventeen. But Babette seemed intent upon keeping her daughter by her side, like a pet—forever unsullied, naive, and dependent.

Bertrand sighed. As much as he wanted to have the child gone from his house, he was reluctant to press Babette. She seemed to find joy in her daughter alone. She routinely shunned all social activities and invitations unless they specifically included Rachelle; she entertained no male visitors unless Rachelle was present. She never went out unless Rachelle accompanied her—followed by that skinny, crafty Indian maid, of course. Though Babette had surrendered her black mourning garments after Rachelle came home from the wet nurse, in rare moments when Bertrand caught Babette alone, her face seemed shadowed by some hidden grief.

He had to sheathe his inner feelings every time he saw pain in her eyes. He knew its source, of course. The ambush. Aubrey's murder. The vicious attack upon her person. The loss of her virtue, and the shame she must have endured. Why, then, did the fruit of that shame bring her such joy? For only the sound of Rachelle's laughter could lift the shadows from Babette's delicate face, and only when she knew Rachelle slept safely could Babette be convinced to seek rest herself.

And yet she did not cease to cry. Sometimes her tendency to weep embarrassed him, for the sight of an Indian, a deerskin, or a baby could reduce her to sniveling into his handkerchief. Virtue assured him that Babette's constant overflow of emotion was nothing but evidence of a tender heart, but she had never been so tenderhearted before the Indian attack.

Parking his cheek in his palm, Bertrand leaned hard upon the arm of his chair, his mind filling with sour thoughts. Babette's unusual devotion to her daughter had produced one unexpected benefit—no one in Charles Towne suspected that the girl might be of Indian ancestry. They ingenuously accepted Babette's pitiful story about a murdered English husband, and though the child's hair and eyes were as dark as her Indian maid's, no one remarked upon the resemblance. Instead they praised her pale skin, her grace, her fluent tongue, her delicate features—all gifts she had inherited from her mother.

During moments like these, when Bertrand looked over the avenue of his life, he considered that both he and his daughter had faced the worst life had to offer . . . and survived. He had lost a wife and a son; his daughter had seen her brother and fiancé murdered. From a terrifying captivity, she had emerged with a will of iron, a hard-fought wisdom, and a little scrap of a child in whom she found delight. Why, then, could he not be happy for her?

Like the dainty trilling of a silver bell, Rachelle's laughter floated on the breeze through the garden, followed by Babette's warm voice. Bertrand closed the ledger book in his lap and let his mind curl lovingly around memories of similar bright autumn afternoons in France, when Aubrey's and Babette's laughter had filled a different garden and warmed a different heart. . . .

No. He grasped at the strings of reality and held them tightly. He could not go back to the man he had once been; he could only go forward with Babette. Her happiness was all that mattered. Once the child was married, Babette would be lonely, and he'd introduce her to Thomas Moody, the wine merchant near the wharf. Though Moody was considerably older than Babette, the man was wealthy and still had his own teeth, an impressive accomplishment for a man of over fifty years.

He could not look back. Some terrible event had stolen the innocent light from his daughter's eyes and exchanged it for a granddaughter with dark hair and lithe grace, as quick as a shadow and as silent as an Indian. She probably *was* an Indian, but this suspicion could never be voiced aloud, and Bertrand could not bring himself to press Babette for the terrible truth. A half-breed child would never prosper in Charles Towne. The Lords Proprietors of Carolina granted the colonists permission to enslave any and all hostile Indians and sell them in the Caribbean slave trade. This broad brush of approval resulted in a situation where any Indian, by so much as a lifted eyebrow, might be declared "hostile" and manacled on the spot.

Bertrand didn't trust Indians. Unlike the blacks, who had nowhere to run in this foreign land, the Indians knew the countryside and had friends and family out in the dark woods. Sometimes Bertrand thought they could read the weather on the wind. He had purchased the child Fala from a slave mart because he thought Babette's spirits might be brightened by a youngster in the house, but now he regretted his decision. The Indian girl was usually aloof and reserved, yet a crafty intelligence lay behind her dark eyes, and he feared he might yet awaken one night to find her standing over him with a hatchet, ready to part his scalp from his head—

"Monsieur Fortier?"

Bertrand jumped in his chair, startled by Friday's deep voice. "Yes?" He glared at his valet, frowning. "What is it?"

Friday smiled and inclined his head. "Your new slaves are outside in the street, sir. What shall I do with them?"

Bertrand ran his hand over the back of his neck, thinking. There were days when he'd like to send his whole lot of slaves out to the rice plantation, but no self-respecting family could manage a town house without a staff of at least seven. Friday now served as butler and valet, Fala tended Rachelle, Virtue looked after Babette, and Cookie kept the kitchen. He still needed a gardener and a stable boy, and Friday had been broadly hinting that he needed someone to help him tend the house. Dusting and sweeping, the regal African insisted, were beneath him.

"I'm coming." Bertrand set the ledger book aside and rose from his chair. He'd look at this bunch, see if any had an aptitude for housework, and send the rest out to the plantation. The rice furrows needed strong hands and supple backs—aptitude didn't count for much out in the flooded fields.

If only his slaves would have babies, he mused. He'd be lining his own pockets with gold instead of providing so handsomely for the slave trader Ashton Wragg.

▼▲▼▲▼ From her hiding place in the parlor, Fala peered around the edge of the window casing. A line of shackled slaves waited in the dirt at the side of the road, their faces wiped clean of any emotion. She counted three black men, four black women, including a young girl still in pigtails, and an Indian man whose back was striped with vicious red welts.

A sudden swell of compassion lifted in Fala's heart. She knew what had happened—forty lashes were the prescribed punishment for any slave who attempted to escape the barracoon, the large jail built to contain slaves who awaited auction. The law allowed forty lashes for a first attempt, branding for the second, and mutilation or execution for any habitual runaway.

Fala shrank back against the wall as the front door opened. Friday led the way out, then ceremoniously stepped aside as Monsieur Fortier walked down the front path and stepped up onto the carriage block in order to survey his slaves.

"Have any of you experience in a garden?" he asked, raising his voice as if the strangers before him were deaf.

The Africans gave him blank looks; the Indian lifted his chin in silent pride.

"Beggin' your pardon, sir, but these Negroes are right off the boat," the slave handler said, touching the rim of his cap in respect. "They speak very little English, so they're not understanding you at all."

Monsieur Fortier shrugged in mock resignation. "Very well, then, I don't suppose any of them will do for housework." His steely gray eyes fell upon the Indian. The slave stood facing Monsieur Fortier, so the worst of his injuries were hidden, but his chest was blue with bruises, and a few telltale welts marked the sides of his exposed rib cage. Monsieur Fortier stiffened as if in shock, then stepped from the carriage block and walked round the Indian, gaping at the man's ferociously wounded back.

"Sir!" A thread of exasperation lined the master's voice. "Why did Mr. Wragg send me an injured man when I paid for a healthy one?"

"Beggin' your pardon again, sir, but you're getting this one as a bargain. He's strong as an ox, Mr. Wragg says, and would cost more, but as he's stiff from the whipping he'll go for the standard price." The slave handler gave the master a cocky grin. "He tried to escape, so Mr. Wragg bade me give him forty lashes. Took the fight right out of him, I declare. You'll not be having any trouble with this one."

The master's eyes ran up and down, eyeing the Indian's chest and scarred arms. "I was hoping to purchase a healthy male. I've

a female of childbearing age, you see, and had hopes for a breeding pair—"

Fala gasped audibly, then stepped back from the window. He
could only mean her. A breeding pair! Like they were horses or
cows or dogs!

She took a deep, quivering breath to quell the leaping pulse
beneath her ribs, then clenched her fists and let her head fall
back against the plastered wall. She could taste hate in her
mouth—acid and foul. She was no dog! She was as much a
woman as Mademoiselle Rachelle and Madame Babette, albeit a
different kind of woman.

Her anger abated in a sudden rush as the old feelings of aban-
donment surfaced into her consciousness like a powerful under-
tow that pulled her under against her will. Within an instant she
was drowning in the deep well of memory and loss, questioning
the God who guided her days.

Why had her parents died and left her alone? Why hadn't the
elders of the tribe moved away from the whites? Her people had
been debased, debauched, and destroyed, all within one generation. Were they so evil that God almighty had to wipe them from
the earth? And what had *she* done to deserve a life of slavery?

"Fala? Where are you?"

Madame Babette's gentle voice drifted down from above. Fala
took a deep breath, wiping her face clean of all emotion, before
she moved toward the staircase. "Yes, Madame Babette?"

The lady appeared at the upstairs railing, her complexion
gray and pink in the dappled light from the tree-shaded window. "Rachelle would like to swing in the garden. Would you
see to her?"

Fala stiffly dipped in the curtsey with which she had been
instructed to answer every command. "Yes, madame."

▼▲▼▲ The day was a delightful combination of a
brisk wind and warm sunshine, and Rachelle shivered slightly in
the October breeze as she lifted her face to the sun. The sky was

a faultless wide curve of blue above her head, the ground a patched carpet of green grass and orange-brown mud. Cookie's garden had already yielded the last of the summer vegetables; nothing remained but a few spindly gray stalks.

Friday had hung Rachelle's swing. Dangling from a lower limb of the sprawling live oak that stood like a sentinel at the back of the house, the swing marked the boundary between the white Fortiers and their colored slaves. The kitchen had been built directly behind the live oak, and the small, ramshackle slave cottage stood behind the kitchen.

Rachelle glanced back at the cottage. *Grand-père*'s new slaves— a string of fierce-looking blacks and one terrifying savage—had just been ushered into those cramped quarters, but they would stay there only until *Grand-père* could transport them to the rice plantation.

Rachelle stirred uneasily on her swing, then looked away. She had nothing to do with the plantation slaves. They were like wild animals—savage, barbaric, uncivilized. They frightened her, but *Grand-père* would not let them remain near the house for long. Already there had been talk of a slave revolt, for there were now nearly as many blacks and Indians in Charles Towne as whites. Gentlemen like *Grand-père* worked hard to keep their slaves under control.

Rachelle felt the grim line of her mouth relax as Fala stepped out the back door. She had never felt afraid of Fala—or Virtue, Cookie, or Friday, for that matter. They were thoroughly tame and content, happy in her grandfather's service, comfortable in their roles.

She idly ran the toe of her slipper over the fallen leaves at her feet, then smiled as Fala drew nearer. "There you are," she called, a gentle chiding note in her voice. "I'd like to swing but mustn't get my gown mussed up. Mama and I are invited to tea at Mistress Wragg's house this afternoon."

Fala did not answer but woodenly took her place behind the swing. Rachelle felt the woman's strong hands grip the ropes, then Fala pulled back and released.

The cool air brushed Rachelle's cheeks as the swing carried her up and back again. Immediately Fala's hands centered upon Rachelle's back; then the maid pushed with surprising force.

"Not so hard," Rachelle protested, feeling her stomach drop as the ground flew by in a dizzying rush. "What are you doing, Fala?"

Rachelle swung back, but this time the slave did not touch her. Puzzled, Rachelle turned as much as she could without losing her grip. Fala stood behind the swing, her gaze downcast, her arms crossed against her chest in a defensive posture.

Something was wrong. Fala was often as indifferent as rain, but this attitude was unusual. Something had upset her today.

"Stop the swing, Fala," Rachelle commanded, tentatively lowering her foot so her slipper could catch the ground. The swing completed two more passes; then Fala thrust out her hand and caught the rope, jerking Rachelle to such an abrupt halt that she nearly spilled onto the ground.

Rachelle bent down and checked the hem of her gown to be certain that no mud had stained the silk fabric. She knew she ought to rebuke the woman for her abrupt action. Fala had probably just indulged in a small display of temper, and temper, Rachelle had been told over and over again, could not be tolerated in a slave. "A slave must be docile, gentle, and know who his master is," *Grand-père* had repeatedly told the women of his household. "If you let them have the upper hand even once, you have established a dangerous precedent. Tolerate no outbursts of stubbornness or temper, and allow no fits of passion."

Rachelle glanced up at her maid's face, trying to discern whether the smoldering look in Fala's eye was temper or stubbornness. "Fala," she said, twisting the ropes as she turned in the swing to face the slave, "something is bothering you. Tell me what it is."

Cold dignity created a stony mask of Fala's face. "Nothing is wrong, Mademoiselle Rachelle."

"Speak the truth," Rachelle answered, lowering her head as if she could peer up into the woman's conscience. "Do not lie to me, for that would be a sin. Did Cookie scold you? Did Friday rebuke you for something? Surely my mother did not say anything harsh."

"Nothing is wrong," Fala repeated again. Her lids came swiftly down over her eyes. "No one has troubled me." With an obvious effort, she lowered her thin arms to her sides. "Would you like me to push you again, Mademoiselle?"

"No." Rachelle folded her hands in her lap and decided to try another approach. She offered the woman an understanding smile. "Why won't you speak freely with me, Fala? I have known you forever, and you are my personal servant. You can tell me anything, and I will keep your secret. I will not tell Mama or *Grand-père*—"

"You have not known me forever." Fala ground the words out between her teeth, each word a splinter of ice. Rachelle blinked in surprise. The slave had never spoken in that tone before.

"'Tis true, I did not speak literally." Rachelle lifted her hands to the twisted rope, then rested her cheek upon her hands, prodding the ground with her toe and gently moving the swing. "How could I have known you forever?" She softened her voice. "I was not even born when you came to this house. But I've known you all *my* life. Surely you can forgive my thoughtless remark and tell me what troubles you."

Fala turned her eyes away, her dark hair glistening like polished wood as she stared toward the lowering sun. "Nothing troubles me," she repeated, her stirring eyes giving lie to the words. "And if you do not wish to swing, I should go in. Cookie wants help with dinner."

Rachelle frowned in exasperation. Of all her grandfather's slaves, Fala was the most stubborn and taciturn. Virtue would talk for hours about anything, and Cookie churned out rumors like a waterwheel, eager to circulate all the gossip she'd scooped up at the market. But Fala was a deep lake, filled with secrets that never saw the light of day.

"Go, then." Rachelle's lower lip edged forward in a pout. "But do not say that I did not try to be your friend, Fala."

The maid did not answer but squared her shoulders as she walked toward the house, her stubborn strength and stamina at odds with the delicate slenderness of her body.

"Go away, and see if I care," Rachelle muttered under her breath. She kicked at the dead leaves beneath the swing, grimacing in pleasure as dirt covered the toe of her satin slipper. Mama would be displeased, and Fala would be to blame.

Ashton and Cambria Wragg lived less than a mile away from the Fortier mansion. Though Babette and Rachelle could have walked the distance in less than a quarter hour, no respectable woman would have dared sully her slippers in the dusty road with passing servants and seamen. The Fortier carriage gently deposited Rachelle, her mother, and her maid upon the carved carriage stoop before the Wraggs' gray three-story house. Rachelle looked up, admiring the black shutters that framed tall windows bordered in white. A sweeping piazza edged the south side of the double house, its delicate wooden railings like frosting upon a wedding cake, and an ornately carved door peered forth from a thin beard of tangled ivy clambering round the front steps.

The Wraggs' silent butler admitted the Fortier women into the ornate parlor, and within a few moments Cambria Butler Wragg entered the room in a cloud of lemon sachet. "Welcome, darling Babette and Rachelle," she cried, her birdlike arms outstretched to greet them. "I am so delighted to have you take tea with me today."

As Cambria herself led the way to the drawing room, Rachelle flinched and retreated a step before the massive African butler's outstretched arm. The man was huge, his hands big and square, his profile rugged and somber. Of course she would have expected the town's leading slave trader to have exceptional slaves, but didn't Mistress Wragg worry about her safety with such a gigantic African in the house?

"Don't mind Ulysses," Cambria Wragg murmured, apparently reading Rachelle's thoughts. "He looks fierce, but he's been gentled."

Gentled? Rachelle's mind bulged with the unasked question, but she bit her tongue and moved quickly past the butler. She turned in time to see him look at Fala and point toward a narrow hall. Fala promptly disappeared through the hallway, and Rachelle knew the maid would spend the next hour or more sitting with the Wraggs' slaves, alert to the ringing of a bell that might summon her if Rachelle needed something.

Rachelle moved forward, feeling instantly out of place in the Wraggs' elegant drawing room. The room undoubtedly reflected Cambria's tastes—the furnishings were as delicate as a magnolia blossom and about as useful. A gilded music box sat on a table next to a spindly chair; a ridiculously large vase decorated with tulips held nothing but air and a thin layer of reddish brown dust.

Cambria urged her guests to take a seat, then draped herself over her own couch, tucking her legs up under a lap blanket.

"Madame Bailie, I am so pleased to make your acquaintance," she said, her fair skin magnifying the inky depth of her blue eyes. "Mr. Wragg is quite convinced that we should spend more time together. Of course I'd love to spend more time with female friends, but owing to my ill health, I don't visit as much as I ought. Church on Sunday mornings, you know, and dinner with the minister when we can." She sighed heavily, her thin bosom rising and falling; then she pressed her slender hand over the lace at her throat. "I have a *condition*, you see. All of the Butler women have it. Frail as lilies, we are, and the least little sun is likely to make us droop with enervation."

"We are pleased to accept your kindness," Rachelle heard her mother murmur. "My father deals so often with your husband, it seems only natural that we should be friends."

Cambria Wragg's blue eyes now fell upon Rachelle, who automatically set her lips in a polite smile. "I have heard many good things about *you*, dear girl," Cambria said, a sweet edge to her voice. "I am told that you speak English *and* French and that you play the harpsichord."

"Only adequately, I'm afraid," Rachelle said, lowering her

head. "I had a good teacher, but I fear my temperament does not suit long hours of practice."

"Ah? That is a shame." The warmth in Cambria's voice faded somewhat, and Rachelle bit her lip. Her grandfather would not be pleased. *Grand-père* had dispatched Rachelle and her mother with express orders to charm and disarm the Wraggs. Though Rachelle wasn't certain what lay behind his command, she had the distinct feeling that if Cambria Wragg wanted Rachelle to be a harpsichordist, a harpsichordist is what she must be.

"I'm afraid my daughter is altogether too modest," Babette said, tenting her gloved hands. "She plays as well as any girl in Charles Towne."

"Humility is certainly a worthy virtue in a young woman." Cambria's smile offered tentative approval. "And I would love to hear you play."

Rachelle swallowed hard, trying to manage an answer. "I couldn't—"

"Please." A note of command rang in Cambria's voice, and Rachelle gripped the fabric of her gown, knowing she must obey. The harpsichord stood in the opposite corner of the long rectangular room, near the window. Rachelle rose and slowly crossed over to it, then seated herself upon the low stool. In truth, she hated the harpsichord and had taken lessons for only two years before begging that she might be allowed to give it up. Her repertoire consisted of two simple songs, a dance and a hymn, and she hoped one or both might be enough to slake Mistress Wragg's odd interest in her musical ability.

She wiped her hands on the dark silk of her gown, then placed them on the keys. Biting her lip in concentration, she began to play the dance, mentally counting the beat and praying that her fingers would not lose their way. When she had finished, her mother broke into an enthusiastic pattering of applause.

With renewed humiliation, Rachelle pushed back the stool, ready to return to her chair, but Mistress Wragg had other ideas. "There is a sheet of music on the instrument before you," she said, pointing delicately toward the harpsichord. "Could you play a bit of it for me? I have been intending to sound the piece out, but—" she pressed her hand to her forehead and weakly batted her lashes—"I have not felt strong enough to undertake it this week."

Silently wishing that it were considered socially acceptable to tell Mistress Wragg to go kiss a toad, Rachelle blew out her cheeks and looked at the piece. Someone had roughly transcribed a popular English melody on the parchment. Rachelle grimaced when she read the key signature. The tune was set in the key of E, and four sharps were not at all to her liking. She had always been able to manage flats, but sharps were another problem altogether.

She couldn't play it. On her best day, when she wasn't worried about making a good impression for *Grand-père*'s sake, she would mangle it. Today her trembling fingers would annihilate whatever good impression Mistress Wragg might have gained thus far. She glanced at her mother, silently pleading for help, but Babette's eyes were on the carpet, her posture tense with waiting.

"Can you make it out, my dear? The piece is original, and the writing a bit messy, I know."

Original? Someone had completely fooled Cambria Wragg, but Rachelle wouldn't be the one to shatter the woman's illusion. "It's fine," she said, draping her fingers over the keys. Her thoughts raced. Once, with her teacher, she had been in a similar situation, ordered to play a piece she hadn't prepared. A childish ruse had worked then, and it might work now.

She lifted her brow, looked toward her audience with a confident glance, then placed her fingers over the notes of the first chord. She held to the keys, allowing the music to ring in the air, then took a theatrically deep breath. But the tightly laced stays of her garment prohibited deep breathing, so the effort instantly launched her into a coughing fit.

"Dear girl!" Cambria Wragg straightened, concern in her eyes. "Are you well?"

"Excuse me," Rachelle managed to reply between gasping coughs. She stood to her feet, clinging to the harpsichord as if she were the invalid Cambria Wragg pretended to be. "But I just need a drink of water."

"I'll ring." Cambria reached for the bell to summon the servants, but Rachelle waved her concern away and darted through the doorway leading to the main hall. Coughing conspicuously, she caught sight of the butler. "Water," she croaked, one hand going to her throat.

He did not speak but lifted his hand and pointed to a corridor at the end of the hallway. The kitchen and pump lay outside the main house, and Rachelle followed the butler out into the sun, grateful for a chance to be away from the older women's stilted conversation. She had nothing in common with Cambria Wragg and no real desire to sip tea with women twice her age. She had done her part for *Grand-père;* it was now her mother's turn to shower social graces.

The butler worked the pump handle, splashing water into the waiting bucket, and Rachelle pushed up her sleeve, then dipped her hand in and took a token sip. "You may go. I can find my way back," she told the butler, slinging excess water from her hand as she calmed her breathing. Through the open doorway of the kitchen house she spied a teapot and teacups laid out upon a silver tray. She lifted her hand and gestured to it. "They will be ringing for tea soon, don't you think? You will want to go back in to answer your mistress's bell."

The butler lifted a brow, undoubtedly seeing through her ruse, and Rachelle smiled at him and lowered her voice. "I'll just be out here a few minutes; then I'll creep back in time for tea. By then they will have forgotten all about the harpsichord."

Something like a smile twitched upon his dignified face; then he turned and headed for the house. Watching him go, Rachelle exhaled in relief, then lifted her hands to her arms, rubbing the light layer of goose bumps that had lifted on her arms as she stared at the silent black man. She didn't know how he'd been "gentled," but just thinking about the concept sent anxiety spurting through her.

The sun was sinking toward a living purple cloudbank piled deep on the western horizon, and Rachelle shivered in earnest, knowing that evening's chill would soon be upon her. She ought to go back inside, but she didn't want to face Cambria Wragg's frigid blue eyes. She glanced around. The garden behind the Wraggs' house wasn't nearly as nicely kept as Cookie's, which was surprising, considering that the Wraggs probably owned ten slaves for each one of the Fortiers'. But a small garden bench squatted in a patch of sunlight in front of the kitchen house, the perfect place to be still and let time slip away.

A pair of slave boys ran across the pathway, rakes slung across their shoulders like muskets. Rachelle smiled at them as they went past, but they kept their eyes carefully averted from her gaze. They wore white cotton shirts, clean, if not perfectly ironed, and uniform navy breeches. Both skipped along without shoes, apparently not feeling the autumn cold, and Rachelle frowned as she noticed a peculiar pattern of raised red welts that covered the backs of their calves and vanished beneath the edge of their breeches. A disease? She frowned, considering the possibility that some strange African malady might descend upon her, then shrugged as the boys moved out of her sight. Ashton Wragg's slaves were none of her concern.

She moved to the garden bench and sat down, feeling herself relax almost immediately. The autumn afternoon hummed with the sound of insects, and the sound of slaves' voices was impersonal, no more than an accompaniment to Rachelle's thoughts. Hugging herself, she leaned her head back against the wall of the kitchen house and felt the warmth of the brick seep through the fabric of her bodice. She'd have to be careful, for in this restful silence a girl could fall asleep. . . .

The sound of Fala's voice brought Rachelle instantly awake. "My master bought a new group of slaves today," Fala was saying, her voice calm and clear through the open window. She was in the kitchen house with the Wragg slaves, probably sweating in the heat of the ovens. "Three men, four women, a girl about the age of my mistress—" she paused—"and an Indian."

"Did you know him?" a deep, guttural voice asked.

Fala didn't answer verbally, and Rachelle twisted on the bench, seized by a sudden terrible curiosity. The small window was above her head, but if she stood and thrust her face through it, she'd certainly be seen. And if Fala wouldn't talk to Rachelle in the privacy of her own home, she certainly wouldn't talk to her here.

"I fear the Indian will not last long on the plantation." Fala spoke in the low voice reserved for dreaded things. "He had already tried to run once, and they gave him forty lashes. He will run again."

"Where will he go?" The cook's rough voice dropped in volume, and Rachelle strained to hear it. "There ain't no place round here to hide."

"The land will hide him." Fala spoke with conviction. "The white men have not followed the setting sun. There are other tribes who have not felt the sting of the white man's disease or his long gun, and they will welcome a brave warrior."

Silence reigned in the kitchen. Rachelle could hear nothing but the faraway clop of an ax as some slave prepared wood for the fire. She pressed her back to the kitchen house and concentrated on the murmur of voices within. Why did Fala feel free to open her heart to these slaves and not to her own mistress? These slaves were virtual strangers, whereas she had passed practically every night of her life in Fala's presence.

"Have you ever done it?" The cook's voice was suddenly breathy and filled with wonder. "Tried to escape?"

Rachelle's heart battered against her ears. Why would Fala want to escape? *Grand-père* was a kind master and a wealthy man. More important, Rachelle and Fala were friends.

"I have not tried," Fala answered. Rachelle breathed a small sigh of relief, then tensed as her maid continued. "But I would if I could be sure of my escape. Today I heard my master say—" Her voice broke off, and Rachelle lowered her head, pressing her ear to the brick in an effort to listen. What had *Grand-père* said to upset Fala so?

The silence stretched for a long moment; then Fala finally finished her thought. "My master bought the Indian man . . . for me. He wants us to have children."

The old cook made quiet sounds of sympathy. Rachelle listened with bewilderment, unable to understand the reason for Fala's distress. Why would the idea of babies upset Fala? She was a grown woman, and what woman did not want children? If *Grand-père* was kind enough to find Fala a fine Indian husband, why couldn't she be happy about it?

"In my tribe," Fala went on, her voice trembling with a depth of emotion Rachelle had never heard before, "women choose the man they want. If I had not been taken, if my father had not been killed, I would have chosen my man from all the suitable warriors in my tribe." Fala's voice, so flat an hour before, was vibrant with restrained fury. "I would have chosen a man with great heart and great skill. He would be a good hunter and one who would be kind to his children and the elders."

"Go on, honey," the cook urged.

Fala needed no encouragement. "And yet, here among the whites, I have no choices. My master would give me a man—a wounded, angry man—and treat us with less dignity than one of his hunting dogs."

The cook was sobbing now, her snuffling cries serving as an accompaniment to Fala's impassioned tirade. Fala's voice fell to a weak and tremulous whisper. "And when—and if—I had a child, he would send it away with a nurse and bring it back only when it could serve his family. My child would not know his history, his people. I would tell him he was one of the Yamassee, but he would never know how it feels to stand free beneath the trees with the wind in his hair; he would never hunt or dance or join with the other warriors in songs to the Great Spirit."

"But what are we to do?" the cook exclaimed as Fala paused for breath. "What am I to do? I ain't like them; I ain't even like you. I don't know these woods, and I'm scared of what's hiding out there. My master says I'm safer here with him than in the wilderness with the wolves and the savages."

"Never believe him," Fala answered, her tone juicy with contempt. Without rising at all, her voice took on a subtle urgency. "If you are willing, I will help you escape. I will talk to the Indian, for I am certain he will not remain at my master's house. And when he leaves, I will go with him, and we will come for you." Her words hung for a moment in the silence. "If you are willing, I will see to it."

Insects whirred from the dying garden, and Rachelle strained to hear the old slave's response. "Yes, I'm goin' with you," she finally answered, her voice thick and unsteady. "No matter what lives in those woods out yonder, I'm goin' with you."

▼▲▼▲▼ As Rachelle had suspected, Mistress Wragg and her mother had forgotten all about the harpsichord by the time she returned to the drawing room. The two women were deep into a discussion about the virtues of Chinese silk when Rachelle slipped into the room and perched on the edge of her chair. A steaming cup of tea sat on the table next to her, and she lifted it, sipping carefully while her thoughts chased each other in a confused tumble. Would Fala really try to escape? All because her grandfather wanted her to have a baby?

What was so troubling about a baby? Lots of women had them. Rachelle had never actually seen a pregnant white woman, since all respectable ladies were carefully cloistered away as soon as the impending birth was evident, but behind bars in the barracoon she had seen black women with bulging bellies. One or two, she recalled, had been auctioned in the street, bringing a high price because the auctioneer assured the crowd they would get "two for the price o' one."

Reconsidering Fala's outburst, Rachelle frowned into her teacup.

"You are quiet, my dear." Cambria Wragg gently placed her cup on her saucer and gave Rachelle a wan smile. "Are you quite recovered from your coughing spell? I hope the water from our well does not disagree with you."

Rachelle shook her head. "Your water is as brackish as ours," she remarked offhandedly, turning her gaze toward her mother. Babette was lifting a tiny scone to her lips now, nibbling daintily at the edge, like a mouse.

"Mother," Rachelle said, shifting in her seat to face her mother directly. "I overheard the servants talking. Fala is upset because she thinks *Grand-père* wants her to have a baby."

The scone flew from her mother's hand. All traces of color faded from Babette's cheeks as her wide eyes turned toward Rachelle. From the opposite sofa, Cambria Wragg made a soft choking sound.

Babette closed her eyes and pressed her hand to her throat. "Rachelle," she said, her voice fragile and shaking, "we do not discuss such things in other people's drawing rooms. Such topics are best limited to occasions when you and I are alone together."

Rachelle cut a look to the sofa. For the first time, Cambria Wragg looked truly ill. Her nose quivered, and her mouth had taken on an unpleasant twist.

"I beg pardon if I have offended," Rachelle recited the words *Grand-père* had forced her to repeat on a thousand different occasions. "But I need to know. Fala is very upset. She and the cook outside would like to run away."

If possible, Cambria Wragg went a shade paler. "Run away?" she whispered, drawing a ragged breath. "You're quite sure you heard correctly?"

Rachelle turned to her mother. "If I may explain, Mama—"

"Go on," Babette answered in a strangled voice. Her eyes were shiny with impending tears.

Rachelle turned toward Mistress Wragg. "Fala says *Grand-père* wants her to have a baby with the Indian slave he bought today. But Fala says she knows the Indian will try to escape. So she wants to go with him, and she has promised to stop here and take the cook with them into the woods."

She looked back to her mother, baffled by Mistress Wragg's

horrified attitude. "I don't understand why having a baby would upset Fala so. After all, you had a baby." She glanced again at her hostess. "Mistress Wragg, surely you are a mother?"

"Yes," the lady answered, looking up with a cold and piercing eye. "I have a son." Her brows rose, graceful wings of scorn. "In fact, it was his piece you were about to play on the harpsichord."

Rachelle lifted her hand, not wanting to continue upon *that* particular topic. "You see? What is so upsetting about having a child? Why would Fala want to run away? I thought we were close; she's been my maid since I was small. I was certain she would never want to leave me."

"Listen, dear girl." Cambria Wragg folded her hands in her lap, then stared across the space between them with burning, reproachful eyes. "I know you are young, but you must understand this—the Indians are savages, no more, no less. They are inferior, a fallen race, a nation of hostile heathens who deserve the captivity so many have fallen into. The Africans are equally repugnant. They are the sons and daughters of Ham, a cursed race. Almighty God himself decreed that they serve us, and for slavery they were designed. They would not be happy in the woods, and you can be sure they would die if we did not care for them and put them to useful service."

An edge of desperation lined Mistress Wragg's voice, but so strong were her words and her expression that Rachelle could only nod. The gesture seemed to calm Mistress Wragg. "The Indians and Negroes should be grateful that we are willing to take care of them and set them to useful work," she went on, lifting her teacup again. She paused with it before her nose and gazed at Rachelle over the rim. "Too many of them are barbarous, wild, savage creatures. They require patience and a firm hand, mind you."

"Indeed," Babette echoed from her place. Rachelle saw that her mother's hand trembled in her lap, but her eyes were busily searching the carpet, probably looking for the pastry she'd tossed in the excitement.

At that moment from the hallway came a barking, a masculine voice, and the vigorous stomping of boots. Rachelle tensed as two huge mastiffs appeared in the drawing-room doorway; then a voice ordered them away, and they slunk away into the hall. An instant later the doorway filled with the broadest pair of shoulders Rachelle had ever seen upon an Englishman.

"Excuse me, Mother." The young man who stood there inclined his sleek golden head in a salute. "I didn't know you had guests."

This timely interruption filled Mistress Wragg's face with much-needed color. She leaned forward, her face blooming with pride and tenderness. "Come in, Son, and allow me to introduce you." She turned a dazzling and proud smile upon Babette and Rachelle. "Mistress Bailie, Mistress Rachelle, I'd like you to meet my son, Lanston."

The young man walked with nonchalant grace through the drawing room and gallantly made a leg before the assembled ladies. Rachelle felt her own hand begin to tremble at the sight of the devastatingly handsome man; she quickly returned her clattering teacup and saucer to the table by her chair.

A bright shaft of sun from the window struck his hair and set it to gleaming like dark gold, and though it was probably immodest to notice, Rachelle observed manly wisps of the same golden hair curled against his neck where his shirt parted in a V.

"Ladies, it is a very great pleasure." He straightened, his hat in his hand, and Rachelle felt a blush stain her cheek as his blue eyes roved over her, flickering with interest. "I have often seen you—" he nodded toward Rachelle—"at the balls, though I never thought to find you in my own house.""Lanston." His mother's voice lifted in a teasing rebuke. "I told you not to wear those filthy boots in the house. The servants have more to do than clean up after you."

"I apologize, Mother." Lanston turned the force of his smile upon his mother, then gestured to the hall, where a slender black boy waited, his hands wrapped around the huge dogs' collars. "I'll have Caesar clean up. Is there anything else?"

"No, darling." She twinkled responsively as he bent to kiss

her cheek. "Just try not to be late for supper, please? You know how your father hates tardiness."

"Never fear, Mother. I will be on time."

As handsome as the devil and kind to his mother, too. Rachelle felt her heart flutter wildly as she studied Lanston Wragg. *And they say a man who is kind to his mother will be kind to his wife. . . .* She lowered her gaze, afraid her thoughts were showing on her face. She had glimpsed this handsome man at many of the Charles Towne balls and soirees, but he had avoided the ballroom, preferring to linger in the smoky drawing rooms, where men discussed business. But he had noticed her! The thought left her feeling surprised and more than a little addled.

Turning toward Rachelle and Babette, Lanston bowed again, the warmth of his smile spilling over Rachelle like rays of sunshine. "Ladies, your acquaintance is a veritable delight. I hope we meet again."

"Au revoir," Rachelle whispered, stunned for a moment into her grandfather's tongue.

"Ah." The smile in his eyes contained a sensuous flame now. "Au revoir, mademoiselle. Till we meet again."

All too quickly, he was gone. Rachelle sat in stunned silence for a moment, wondering why in the world they had never visited the Wraggs before today.

After a discreet pause, Babette set her teacup and napkin aside, then looked at Rachelle. "We must thank you for a delightful afternoon, but we should be going." She met Mistress Wragg's gaze and smiled. "There is dinner to oversee, and my father does not like to be kept waiting."

"Of course, my dear." Mistress Wragg smiled, but her smile held only a ghost of its former warmth. "And I hate to bring up an unpleasant subject, but you will see to this escape rumor, won't you?" She lifted a delicate blond brow. "As much as I respect you, my dear, I cannot have your Indians coming here to steal away my cook. I have spent months training the woman— she would be an incalculable loss."

"Have no fear; nothing shall happen to your cook." Babette

rose to her feet and folded her hands prettily at her waist. Taking her cue from her mother, Rachelle stood too as Babette continued. "I shall speak to my father. Rest easy, Mistress Wragg; none of our slaves will run."

"I am glad to hear it, but I think I shall have my husband call upon your father to lend a hand in the matter." With that Mistress Wragg rang the silver bell at her right hand; the butler immediately appeared and escorted the Fortier ladies to the front door. Rachelle walked behind her mother, lost in a confusing rush of thoughts. As they neared the carriage block Babette turned and fixed Rachelle in a frightened stare. "I hope you know what you have done, *ma petite cherie*," she whispered, wringing her hands.

"What have I done?" Rachelle asked, folding her arms. "I only wanted to prevent Fala from leaving us. Perhaps I can convince her that babies are a good thing."

"No, no, say nothing!" Babette hissed as the carriage came round the corner. Fala stood on the back bumper, her hair whipping over her face, her expression as immobile as it had been this afternoon when she would not speak to Rachelle.

Rachelle stared at her maid, baffled. How could a woman be so passionate in one moment and so granite faced in the next? If she hadn't recognized Fala's voice, she would almost have believed that it had been some other Indian woman talking in the kitchen.

The carriage slowed to a stop, churning up the dust of the road. The Wraggs' groom stepped forward and helped Babette up onto the carriage block and into the vehicle, then held out his gloved hand for Rachelle. She took it and followed her mother, more confused than she could recall being in a very long time.

After helping Cookie serve the Fortiers' dinner, Fala stepped outside to eat her own supper with her fellow slaves. Above her, the thickly clustered stars hung so low they appeared to be tangled in the branches of the live oak, but tonight Fala felt no inclination to ponder their beauty. The darkness seemed to press down upon her, drawing down like a black cowl that would suffocate her if she remained in this place another night.

The mood in the slaves' quarters was no less grim than her own. The African newcomers ate ravenously, their eyes darting from the stewpot to their bowls as if they were afraid the food would be snatched from their grasp at any moment. Friday, who had been an adult when captured by Dutch traders and brought to the colonies, spoke to them in a halting African dialect and learned that the three men and four women were all part of the same family. A warring tribe had turned them over to slave traders four months before. Although they had been terrified on the sea journey and in the holding pens of the barracoon, at least, one of the women told Friday, "here we have food."

The Indian, Fala noticed, sat on the ground away from the others, saying nothing and eating little. Despite the initial revulsion Fala felt when she overheard her master's plan, her heart moved with pity toward the man who sat against the wall of the slave cottage, as if to hide the sight of his wounded back from the others. He was not Yamassee, she knew. The tattoos on his arms and shoulders were unfamiliar to her, and yet he was more like her than any of the other slaves in this house.

She ate her stew slowly, reserving the choicest bits of meat. While Friday, Virtue, and Cookie joked and tried to put the newcomers at ease, Fala slipped away from the others and made her way to the warrior's side.

The firelit shadows of the night rippled over him like water over a sunken stone. He showed no more expression than a stone, either, as she knelt by his side.

"Eat." She placed her bowl by his side, then lowered her eyes in order to preserve his dignity. Unable to see him, she studied the play of his shadow upon the ground. He sat as still as a statue for a long moment, then slowly turned his head toward her.

He spoke softly in his native tongue; it was a dialect she did not know or could not remember. Perhaps her people had spoken it, but she remembered so little from her childhood.

Taking courage, she lifted her head and looked directly at him. His face, while not old, was like a stretch of sunbaked earth, seamed with deep-cut lines—a map of violent passions and indomitable pride. The wind and sun had bronzed his face, and the set of his chin suggested a stubborn streak. His golden skin stretched taut over high cheekbones, and his eyes glowed with a passionate intensity she could not recall ever seeing in any man's gaze.

"If you want to live, you must eat," she said, speaking slowly and distinctly. She had no idea how much he understood, but he slowly dipped his hand in the dish, his eyes not leaving her face until he had emptied the bowl.

Reverting to some custom she had forgotten, she bowed her head before him and lifted the empty bowl with both hands, then rose to take it away. Her mother had probably served her father in just this way, as her grandmothers had served the old ones.

The other group had broken up. The house slaves moved away from the stewpot and hurried to complete their daily duties. The new Africans huddled together as they retreated into the sanctuary of the cottage, their arms about each other, the stronger ones supporting the weaker. The Indian sat alone in the starlight, his arms at his sides, his legs bent and crossed in front of him.

Fala returned her bowl to the wash barrel, then wrapped her arms about her middle and turned to watch the Indian. He had expressed no thanks, no curiosity, no anger. He probably wanted to be left alone; he might be planning his escape right now. But if she was to go with him, she would have to gather enough courage to speak.

She stepped forward, then winced as a light flared in the window of Rachelle's bedchamber. Did she really want to do this? Master Fortier probably did think of her as a trained animal, but she had resided in this household for nearly twenty years. She remembered little of her old life. And the man before her bore the marks of grievous suffering, a visible reminder of what could happen if she tried to run—and failed.

Still—what Master Fortier planned was insufferable. She had learned that word from one of Rachelle's lessons; it meant "not to be borne." She could bear hard work, mindless tasks, ingratitude, deliberate slights, unprovoked insults. But she would not couple with a man she did not know in order to create more slaves to feed the insufferable system the white man had designed.

She padded silently to the Indian man, then knelt again, facing him. "Fala," she whispered, touching her chest. He turned his gaze upon her, his eyes as dark and powerful as his scarred body, and she floundered before the brilliance of his look. "I am of the Yamassee tribe," she whispered again, looking at the cottage wall, the ground, anywhere but his face. "I have been at this house since I was eight summers, but if you want to go, I will help you leave."

His gaze raked boldly over her, and Fala shrank back, afraid he had misunderstood her intention. A muscle clenched along his jaw; then he spoke: "Dustu," he said simply, his voice a deep, tobacco-roughened whisper. "Of the Santee. I was taken ten moons ago."

Fala relaxed a little; he obviously understood more English than she'd thought. Carefully, she shifted her weight from her legs and sat on the hard-packed ground. "The first time—or the second?"

He grunted and rested his wrists atop his bent knees. "The first. My tribesmen were trading upriver. The white man at the trading post said we cheated him, but he lied. He took all our skins and gave us nothing; then other whites came and took us to their jail. We waited there until they moved us to the cage near the water. My brother and I climbed the wall. My brother escaped."

I did not. The words did not need to be said; he bore the evidence of his failure upon his back. But his eyes glowed with a hot and awful joy, and Fala knew he considered his escape attempt worthwhile. His brother had succeeded.

His eyes narrowed, the black pupils within them glowing fiercely. "A slaver beat me until the white man was unable to throw another blow. I bore the pain with the courage of a bear, but in the end I could not win. And now my wife and son have no one to defend them."

"Speak no more," Fala begged, a flash of wild grief ripping through her. She had buried her past, her sorrows, her memories, and yet in the space of five minutes this stranger had brought them all to the surface. She swallowed hard, pushing down the memories of the musket flash that had torn open her father's bare chest and of the eternal scream that had poured from her mother's throat.

"If you want to escape, I will help you," she repeated, closing her eyes lest his gaze open her wounds again. "They trust me. I can help you."

"Why?" His brows lifted the question, and the mere fact that he had to ask proved he had spent time among the white men. If she had been of his tribe he would have taken her help for granted; she would not have had to offer it. But he had seen the way white men treated one another, and Fala had lived among them for a lifetime.

"I will help you." She pressed her hand to his knee for an

instant, sealing her promise with a touch, then rose and went into the house, ready to put her mistress to bed.

▼▲▼▲▼ Rachelle drifted in placid, dreamless sleep, troubled only by a rhythmic flat sound, as though someone in the cookhouse were scraping a bowl with a wooden spoon. A meowing wail rose to accompany the sound; then the roar of absolute silence brought Rachelle fully and completely awake.

Her own room, the real world, slowly made its way back into her consciousness, and she looked at the plastered walls, trying to remember why she had awakened. She had been dreaming of a kitchen and a kitten wailing for milk—

No. The sound had been real, and there were no cats in the Fortier household, for they made her mother sneeze and weep even more than usual. Rachelle swung her legs out of bed and gasped at the first shock of the cool wooden floor, then gathered her wrapper from the foot of the bed. Quickly covering herself, she padded through the doorway toward the stairs. A light burned from the attic, where Virtue and Fala usually slept, but the space overhead seemed as silent as the grave. Another light moved in the stairwell below, and Rachelle instinctively pressed her back against the wall. The muscles of her throat moved in a convulsive swallow as she stared down. Had some thief broken into the house? Was she the only one aware of the danger?

Slow, trudging footsteps creaked the stairs, and Rachelle held her breath, releasing it in explosive relief when Virtue appeared, her cheeks wet with tears and her eyes red-rimmed in the light of the candle she carried.

"What is wrong?" Rachelle stepped forward to the stair railing and looked down at her mother's maid. "Virtue, why are you crying?"

Virtue's expression of grief vanished, wiped away by astonishment. "Mademoiselle Rachelle," she scolded, her voice rough with anxiety, "you should be in bed. Your mama would not be happy to find you out now."

"What happened?" Rachelle persisted, glancing down the dark staircase. There was no activity below, but now she could hear sounds from the yard—a man's gruff voice and a woman's cries.

Virtue pursed her lips together and stared straight ahead toward the attic ladder. "Mademoiselle," she insisted, her mouth dipping into a frown, "I am going to bed. You should go to bed, too, before your mama wakes and finds you out here."

Why were slaves so stubborn? Ignoring the woman, Rachelle slipped past Virtue and descended the dark staircase, turning toward the backyard. In the glow of moonlight she saw a stranger standing by the live oak. Tall and dressed in a white shirt and breeches, he held a whip in his hand.

Rachelle's gaze moved past the stranger. Two human forms were strung from the oak branch that had, until tonight, supported Rachelle's swing. The first dangling shape, a woman, appeared unconscious as she hung by her wrists. Her dark head lolled against her chest, her hair spilling like a tide of black ink over bare skin. The second puppet, a man, still stood erect, but his back gleamed wet and black in the moonlight.

Rachelle took another step, sudden recognition congealing her heart into a small lump of terror. "Stop!" she screamed, scarcely aware of her own voice. "What are you doing to Fala?"

The tall stranger turned toward her, his eyes gleaming wild in the night. "Go inside, missy," he said, coiling the wet whip in his hand. "You shouldn't be out here."

"Fala is my maid," Rachelle insisted, taking a step forward. "What right have you to treat her like this?"

The man glanced at his handiwork again; then, apparently satisfied, he turned to face Rachelle. Thrusting his thumbs into the waistband of his breeches, he gave her a slow smile. "These two slaves were planning an escape. Mr. Wragg sent me to fulfill the law before they could run."

"Fulfill the law?" Rachelle's mind spun with bewilderment. "But my grandfather would never allow this—"

"Mr. Fortier gave his permission," the man answered, straightening. He paused for a moment and wiped a trickle of sweat from his brow—apparently beating two slaves nearly to death was demanding work. "The slave law, missy," he went on, a trace of condescension in his voice, "says that up to forty lashes can be given any slave who runs away. And we have it on good authority—"

"But they *didn't* run away."

"They were aimin' to, and that's the point." The man turned blank eyes upon her, then spat on the ground. "Better to flog 'em now and spare ourselves the trouble of traipsing through the woods with the hounds. An' this way they'll serve as an example to the others."

Rachelle stared at Fala's limp form, her own blood running thick with guilt. *Her* words were the "good authority"; *she* had set this event in motion. But she had never dreamed Mistress Wragg would send someone to beat Fala.

She didn't know what went on at the rice plantation, but she was sure *Grand-père* had never beaten any of the house slaves. But now—because of her—things would never be the same. Her eyes roamed over Fala's limp form. The Indian woman would never be the same either.

Rachelle looked up at the stranger. "Who are you?" she asked, addressing him with all the dignity she could muster.

"Why, Devin Garr, of course," he answered, smiling at her as if the answer should have been obvious. "I work for the Wraggs down at the barracoon." With no small amount of pride he added, "I'm the best slave handler in Charles Towne. A slave has but to lift his head in rebuke and people call for me. I fix 'em like no one else."

She suppressed a shiver. The barracoon was little more than a prison, and she felt the wings of tragedy brush lightly past her each time she passed the place.

"Thank you, Mr. Garr, you may go now." She lifted her head. "You have done what you came to do."

"Aye, that I have. You tell Mr. Fortier that if he has any more trouble just to send for me." His gaze dropped from her face to the thin ribbons that held her wrapper closed. "I'll come running if you call, missy." He grinned at her then, and Rachelle felt a shudder of humiliation, aware that she stood before him in her bare feet and nightgown—hardly proper attire for a gentleman's granddaughter.

"Go now." Rachelle nodded curtly and looked toward the beaten slaves, not moving until she heard the latch of the gate and knew Devin Garr had gone. Then she whirled and ran into the house, flying up the stairs like a silent ghost, hurrying to fetch Virtue and Cookie. They were waiting in the attic, still dressed, and came willingly when Rachelle summoned them.

Back out into the night the women hurried, the three of them moving in silent camaraderie. Rachelle led them to Fala, then wrapped her arms around her maid and supported Fala's weight until Virtue cut the ropes. Fala fell, moaning, into Rachelle's embrace.

Friday appeared from nowhere. He lifted Fala's limp body in his arms and carried her into the kitchen, where Cookie kept a supply of healing herbs. Watching them go, Rachelle turned next to the Indian man who had waited for help in silence. She halted, her hand rising defensively before her face when she saw his expression.

"I'll—I'll get someone else to help you," she murmured, backing away from the storm of hate in his eyes.

▼▲▼▲▼ *Cold.* Fala lay upon the chilly board of the kitchen table, her bruised cheek pressed to the wood, her bare back exposed to prying eyes. Strong, capable hands were caressing her body, running over her tender skin, pressing some cold and creamy substance into the hot ribbons of torn flesh on her back and arms. At first she had refused to cry out under the slave handler's blows, preferring to lock her screams inside her teeth until she fainted, but the pain had become *insufferable* . . . not to be borne.

Now, her defenses shattered, she shrieked in dazzled agony.

She should have known the stranger's intent when he came to the kitchen house after dark. The Fortiers were all safely abed inside the house, tucked away from the brutality—even Monsieur Fortier had retired unusually early, taking his pipe upstairs with him. The stranger had appeared at the slaves' cottage without warning, and his baleful eye singled out Fala and Dustu with an impartial expertise. With a deliberate snap of his fingers he ordered Friday to take the savages outside and bind them to the big oak, and Friday had been too shaken to disobey.

"Easy, child, rest easy," Cookie crooned, her warm hands as smooth as satin on Fala's skin. Fala bit her lip until it throbbed like her pulse, then closed her eyes and wished to die. Why hadn't she been killed with her parents? She would not have known length of life, but her life would have been happy. The ache she felt over the people she had lost had never really left her, and tonight her rash words had caused another human to suffer. She barely knew Dustu, but he did not deserve this fate.

He didn't even know why he had been singled out, but Fala understood the situation all too clearly—someone at the Wraggs' house had overheard her talking to the cook, or the cook herself had been frightened enough to confess the plan. Mr. Wragg, fearful of losing either his cook or his reputation as a dealer in steady, submissive slaves, had sent his handler to deal with a potential problem. But though Fala had been certain Dustu would eventually try to escape, he had not uttered a word to deserve this exquisite pain.

"Hold still, child." Virtue's husky voice fanned the hair near Fala's ear. "You've had a rough whipping, to be sure, but things get easier after the first time. Shame to ruin your pretty skin, though, but it will heal in a few days, and then you'll be tougher for it. I's had four whippings myself, all before I ever left the slave yards."

Fala smelled bitter herbs and moist clay, and her hand reflexively pressed against the table as if she could push away the events of the last hour.

"Sit up now, honey, and I'll bind you." Fala flinched at Cookie's unfortunate choice of words, but her meaning became clear when the woman unrolled strips of washed cotton and proceeded to bandage Fala's back.

"Take care not to let the wounds show on the morrow," Virtue went on, her voice a comforting whisper in the semidarkness. "The white folk don't like to be reminded of what the slave handler does. Why do you think they were all abed? Just go on about your business as if nothing happened, and all will be well."

Fala pressed her lips together, steeling herself against the outrage in her heart. How could she pretend nothing had happened? Oddly, an image of the towering magnolia tree near the Fortiers' piazza flashed through her mind. Two summers ago lightning had struck the trunk, splitting the tree nearly in two. The magnolia survived, but now it grew in a different direction, forever marred by the storm.

"I know what you're thinking, honey. I see it on your face," Cookie said, winding the strips with patient endurance. "And you've got to bear up. Not all the Fortiers were abed—Mademoiselle Rachelle is outside now, waiting to bring in that Indian. She's upset, and she'll be wanting to—"

"I know," Fala interrupted. Rachelle would want to help. The girl did have a tender heart—she had wept over one of the hunting dogs that had to be shot last year, and the sight of a fallen baby sparrow could make her lose her appetite. Fala's pain would also make Rachelle cry, but on the morrow she'd still be wanting her gown laced and her hair arranged.

Someone rapped on the door. "Come," Cookie called, pulling a threadbare blanket over Fala's shoulders. Taking Fala's hands, she helped her slide from the table, and just in time. The kitchen door swung open. Friday and Moses, one of the new arrivals, staggered in through the opening with Dustu draped between them. Fala quickly drew the blanket tighter round her neck, then moved toward the hearth to give the men more room. She would have to leave—Cookie needed the space to doctor someone else.

Fala stepped out of the kitchen house, her movements stiff and awkward. Lifting her eyes, she gazed at the sky occupied an hour before by thousands of diamond stars. It seemed to her that the sky now contained nothing but a dark and palpable sadness.

"Fala?"

She turned slowly. Rachelle stood in the shadow of the big house, a small vision in white. A tremor passed over her delicate face, and a sudden spasm of grief knit her brows. "Fala, I'm so sorry." Hesitating within the circle of lantern light, Rachelle twisted her hands and tiptoed on the dividing line between the Fortier house and the darkness of the slave quarters.

Though she wanted nothing more than to find a quiet spot to lie down and sleep, Fala walked toward her mistress, knowing that Rachelle would not leave until she had done whatever she felt was the proper thing.

"Go to bed, Mademoiselle Rachelle," Fala answered. The girl wanted to hear that Fala was fine, that everything would be all right. Rachelle always wanted people to be happy; she lived in a tidy, perfect world where no pain had been allowed to enter.

"Are you all right?" Tears gathered in the corners of Rachelle's dark eyes and slowly, delicately spilled from the fan-shaped ends of her long lashes.

Fala bit back the words she wanted to say and glanced over at the kitchen house. Virtue stood in the window, her eyes flashing a warning.

"I'm fine, Mademoiselle Rachelle," Fala answered, shivering with chill, pain, and fatigue. "I will wake you in the morning."

Fala turned toward the slave cottage, hoping Rachelle would take the hint and go into the house, but the girl would not leave. "Fala, I never knew this would happen." Her words came out at double speed, as if they'd been glued together. "I heard you talking to the Wraggs' cook and told Mistress Wragg, but I only wanted to know why you'd be so upset about having a baby." Her jaw tensed in frustration. "And I was angry. You wouldn't tell me why you were so upset with my grandfather, but you had no trouble telling another slave. I just wanted to know. I just wanted you to be my friend."

Fala turned slowly, unable to believe what she was hearing.

Rachelle had not moved, but she lowered her gaze as tears slowly found their way down her cheeks. "Fala, I never thought Mr. Wragg would send that man. We have never beaten our slaves. I am so sorry."

Fala swallowed a hysterical surge of angry laughter. She would never have dreamed that Rachelle might be the source of this agony.

Rachelle looked up, probably hoping for quick and easy forgiveness, but something had gone hard in Fala's soul with the first stroke of the whip.

"She says they never beat their slaves." Virtue was speaking to Moses, but her voice carried through the night well past Fala and Rachelle. "But that child don't know what goes on out there at that plantation. Moses, you listen to me—things is nice here in the city when all goes well, but if the master sends you to the plantation, you'd better toe the line. 'Cause the foreman out there is as bad as old Devil Garr, and I've heard the story straight from those who been there."

From outside the kitchen, Friday snapped, "Hush, woman!" as his brows drew together in an angry frown. He turned toward his young mistress with a delicate smile. "Mademoiselle Rachelle, we thank you for your help, but you'd best get to bed now. Monsieur Fortier won't like hearing that you were out here. You let us tend to these folk, and you get your little feet up to your room where you belong. Run along now, mademoiselle."

A dim flush raced across Rachelle's pale face. Friday had just administered the sternest rebuke a slave might give his mistress, and Rachelle was savvy enough to realize she'd been dismissed. But she was proud and would not go easily.

"Promise me, Fala," she said, her voice edged with command. "Promise me you'll never think about running away again."

"Go to bed, mademoiselle," Fala replied in a low voice taut with anger.

Rachelle hesitated, shifting indignantly from foot to foot, then turned and ran toward the house.

"That girl will be the death of us," Virtue called out the window.

Troubled by her own guilty conscience, Fala walked slowly to the kitchen house, then peered through the open window and looked at Dustu. She waited until he opened his eyes, then held his gaze through the sheer force of her will. "This is my fault," she whispered, hoping he would understand. "I thought you would run again . . . and I hoped you would take me with you."

His olive black eyes were unfathomable in their murky depths, but with a great effort he extended his hand through the empty air toward her.

Leaning back in his chair, Ashton Wragg propped his ankle upon his knee. "So I take it," he said, smiling at Bertrand around the edge of his pipe, "that the ladies' meeting went well?"

"Very well," Bertrand replied, returning his gaze to his host's face. They sat in the library of the Wragg house, and everything Bertrand had seen thus far delighted him. Ashton Wragg's wealth and good taste were evident in everything from the gilded mirror above the fireplace to the silk carpet on the floor. "My daughter," he went on, running his hand over the polished satinwood of his chair, "was enchanted with your wife. And my granddaughter, Babette tells me, was most fascinated with your son."

Wragg chuckled. "Yes, Mistress Wragg told me that Lanston stopped by for a proper introduction. He was likewise taken with your Rachelle. She is a lovely girl and a talented one. Cambria was particularly struck by her proficiency upon the harpsichord."

Bertrand covered his mouth with his hand, suppressing a guffaw. Babette's brat was many things, but she was not a musician. She must have made a *very* good impression for her halfhearted pluckings to be counted as proficient.

"Your business is good, I presume?" Wragg asked. "Those slaves I sent last week—will they suit your purposes?"

Bertrand looked down and swirled the rum in his glass. They were talking about everything but what he had come to discuss.

"Very well." He transferred his gaze back to his host. "Shadow Grove is producing even more than we hoped; my foreman expects to export double the rice we harvested last year."

"You'll be needing more slaves, then."

Bertrand nodded. *"Oui.* And I expect you'll be needing your usual ten percent commission."

The slave trader drew his lips into a tight smile. "But of course, my friend. Do not forget, I hope to bestow a generous wedding gift upon my son in this coming year. The more extravagant I can be, the more secure will be your lovely granddaughter."

There—the man had finally come to the point. Bertrand smiled and rolled his glass between his hands, staring down into the shimmering liquid as though seeing in it the fulfillment of their plans. "My daughter has agreed to Lanston—she was most impressed with him. Though she still feels Rachelle is too young, she has agreed to let them be betrothed for a year, in which time the girl will certainly mature." His mouth curved in a mirthless smile. "But we have yet to arrange a meeting between Rachelle and Lanston. This betrothal cannot be negotiated further unless both young people are agreeable."

Wragg's tight smile relaxed measurably. "How could they not agree? Lanston is a fine young man, and your granddaughter is a jewel, truly the pride of Charles Towne. Her reputation precedes her, my esteemed friend. There is but one thing. . . ." He paused, fretting with a button on his coat for a moment, then looked up, his eyes deep-set and gleaming beneath crepey lids. "My dear wife, Cambria, wishes she knew more about Rachelle's father. Bailie is not a well-known name in these parts."

"The late Reverend Bailie was from Boston," Bertrand answered, straightening himself with dignity. With a perfectly composed expression, he parroted Babette's lies. "He was a clergyman, as was his father before him. Babette knows his family history, of course, but I have never pressed her because her grief is still very near the surface. One does not lose a dear and honorable husband without mourning him commensurately."

"Of course, she has our sympathies," Wragg murmured, bowing his head.

"If you would like references, I could write to Reverend Bailie's associates in Boston." Bertrand spoke in a quiet voice, yet with an undertone of cold contempt, hoping to end the discussion of Rachelle's paternal lineage. He had no intention of writing anyone—the mythical Reverend Bailie could not possibly *have* associates—but Bertrand had won many a card game bluffing men far more cynical and sophisticated than Ashton Wragg.

His disdain had the desired effect. "What more could I want than the girl herself?" Wragg lifted his hand and smiled in delight. "She is charming, lovely, skilled, and moreover, she is a Fortier. My son will be delighted with her, and I look forward to joining our houses in more than friendship."

"Then it shall be done." Bertrand lifted his glass and held it up for a toast. "Mr. Wragg, you and yours are invited to my house tomorrow night for dinner."

"We shall be there," Wragg answered, lifting his glass in acceptance.

The crystal clinked in agreement, and the men drank to their futures.

▼▲▼▲▼ "Hurry, Fala!"

Fala smothered a groan and looked at her young mistress, wondering if the pain of another whipping might be worth the pleasure of slapping the girl silly. Rachelle stood in the center of her bedchamber, half-dressed in silk stockings, pettipants, corset, and chemise. There remained only the farthingale and the gown itself, but neither could be managed without a maid's help.

Moving stiffly, Fala lifted the awkward farthingale and clasped it around Rachelle's waist, then stooped to fasten the hooks that held it in place. Rachelle impatiently batted the fabric-covered frame, glancing at the new gown the sempstress had delivered earlier in the afternoon. It was an elegant creation of deep pink, heavy silk, complete with the longest train Rachelle had ever worn. Embroidered braid and lace trim surrounded the square neckline of the bodice; lace cuffs and a pleated hem on the petticoat provided the finishing touches.

"There." Rachelle pointed impatiently at the pink silk mound on the bed. "I'll put it on; then you can dress my hair. I want tight curls all about my face, do you hear? And that little lace-and-ribbon cap with the pink ribbons and rosebuds. They'll match the dress, no?"

"Yes, they will match." Moving slowly to the bed, Fala gritted her teeth as the dressings around her wounds stretched and chafed against her broken skin; then she gathered the silk petticoat into her arms. She stretched on tiptoe to drop the heavy overskirt over Rachelle's altered shape. The creation fell prettily over the farthingale that extended Rachelle's hips, narrowing her waist to nothingness.

"He's coming tonight," Rachelle trilled. "Lanston Wragg will be seated at our dining table!"

Fala didn't answer but held up the bodice, into which Rachelle joyfully thrust her arms. She waited while Fala fastened the row of hooks down the left side of the bodice, then impatiently pinned the bodice's front hem to the petticoat's waist while Fala struggled to pin the back. The sleeves followed—why did Rachelle wait until the last minute to dress?—then Rachelle danced lightly toward her dressing table. She seated herself on the stool, careful not to disturb the overskirt's pleating.

"Don't you think," she said, eyeing her reflection in her looking glass, "that Lanston is the most handsome young man in Charles Towne?"

Fala said nothing but removed the blue ribbon from her mistress's dark hair. Rachelle was in one of her giddy moods, and Fala had learned it was best not to comment on the girl's foolish prattling; she needed only to listen. The girl probably imagined herself in love with this young man, though Fala knew they had met only once. Rachelle said he was handsome and charming, and from Cookie's market gossip, Fala knew the Wraggs were nearly as wealthy as the Fortiers.

But all the wealth in the New World could not protect Rachelle from her grandfather. *Poor child*, Fala thought, carefully smoothing one of Rachelle's natural curls around her finger. Rachelle would be trussed up and delivered to young Wragg whether she liked it or not, though they'd probably do all they could to present the slave trader's son in a pleasing package. In one way, Fala mused, Rachelle was as much a slave as Cookie and Virtue, but she would never know it. She didn't even seem to realize that her grandfather despised her, though the disdain in his eyes when he looked at her was as obvious as rat droppings in the sugar bowl.

"Did you happen to catch a glimpse of Lanston while we were at the Wraggs' house?" Rachelle asked, catching Fala's eye in her looking glass. A blush rose upon her cheeks, and Fala wondered if the girl's heightened color resulted from thoughts of Lanston Wragg or the trouble that had erupted after that visit. If it was the latter, at least Rachelle knew she might be dredging up an unpleasant memory.

"No, Mademoiselle Rachelle," Fala answered, her tone dry. "I didn't see him. I was in the cookhouse with the other slaves."

A wounded look filled Rachelle's dark eyes, and Fala turned her gaze away. She was treading on dangerous ground. Virtue had warned her that no slave should get too close to one of the white folks, for the hand that petted you one night could turn and slap you the next. It was better to keep a safe distance.

"Lanston is quite handsome and charming." The light note had vanished from Rachelle's voice. "If you have an opportunity, you should peek at him while we are at dinner."

Fala resisted the urge to roll her eyes. She cared nothing for what might happen in the Fortiers' dining room tonight. She wanted nothing more than to get her mistress ready, wish her well, and then retreat to the slave quarters, where the Fortier slaves would entertain the Wraggs' coachman, maid, and whoever else had accompanied them out into the night. Dustu would be there, and under the noise of the others' merrymaking, she would continue the language lessons she had begun the night before. If he was to survive until he could escape and return to his wife and son, he would need to speak English and understand enough French to comprehend the master's bawled orders.

Despite her pain and annoyance with Rachelle, the beginning

of a smile tipped the corners of Fala's mouth as she thought about the hour to come.

▼▲▼▲▼ Rachelle gave just enough thought to the dinner to assure herself of its perfection; the rest of her attention she devoted to Lanston Wragg. What his parents discussed or how her mother or grandfather behaved, she paid no attention to, but she noted every blink, smile, and breath that proceeded from Lanston Wragg's perfectly shaped face. He sat across from her at the table, and on one occasion she thought it possible—even likely—that his boot actually brushed her slipper. Unfortunately, a respectable young lady had no way of discerning whether or not such a forward act had actually occurred—or if it was committed on purpose.

After the dessert of flaming peaches had been served and devoured—heartily by Lanston, daintily by Rachelle—her grandfather's voice broke into her concentration.

"Mr. and Mistress Wragg, my daughter, Babette, begs your pardon. She is not feeling well and wishes to retire, but I would be honored to entertain you in the drawing room."

Rachelle felt her heart sink at the announcement. With her mother gone, she would undoubtedly be expected to entertain Mistress Wragg. While she was prepared to enjoy the lady's company for Lanston's sake, the harpsichord stood in the drawing room—and music was not the after-dinner entertainment she had in mind.

"Mistress Bailie." Lanston stood and bowed to her in a gracious and noble gesture. "I could not help but notice that your grandfather has a most beautiful garden outside. Since the night is young and the moon full, could I ask you to show me the fragrant beauties yonder?"

She caught her breath, surprised that he had asked so boldly. She was about to protest that the garden was far from lovely— autumn winds had already stripped much of the greenery—but then she realized that Lanston may not be particularly interested in plants after all. So, that *had* been a boot upon her slipper.

A blush of pleasure burned her cheeks as she turned to her grandfather. "Could I, *Grand-père?*"

She expected an outright refusal, but her grandfather's stately face rearranged itself into a rare approving smile. "Yes, of course, child, show him everything. Friday will go before you to light your way."

"It is settled, then," Lanston said, giving her a smile that reached clear to her heart.

▾▴▾▴ A circumspect chaperon, Friday moved slowly and deliberately along the garden path, holding a lantern aloft and leaving the two young people to follow behind. Lanston said little as they walked but carried his hands behind his back, eyeing the well-trimmed hedges, the bare rose beds, and the flowerless oleanders as if they were the most interesting plants in all the earth.

"I'm afraid, Mr. Wragg, that I bored you terribly at dinner," Rachelle said, linking her own fingers together as she matched her steps to his. "You have traveled to so many interesting places, while I have never been outside Charles Towne. I must seem terribly provincial and unsophisticated to a man like you."

"My dear Mistress Bailie," Lanston answered, one corner of his perfect mouth twisting upward as he stopped in the garden path. "Haven't you heard that homegrown beauties are the dearest? In all of Virginia, Maryland, New England, or Barbados, no girl could compare to your loveliness."

Rachelle's breath quickened, and she lifted her hands to cover her suddenly warm cheeks. "Now I know you are teasing me, for I've seen girls far prettier than I right here in Charles Towne." She lowered her eyes, aware that his gaze had fallen to the creamy expanse of her neck, and she pressed a hand absently to the lace above her bosom. "Mama says I am too boisterous and

independent to be feminine. I love to talk—too much, I fear—
and my thoughts often wander where they should not go."

"I have the same problem." Lanston reached for her hand,
pulling it from the security of her throat, and Rachelle felt herself
blushing again when she noticed that Friday had discreetly
halted on the path.

Lanston's gaze traveled over her face and searched her eyes.
"I have heard nothing but good about you, Rachelle Bailie. If you
will forgive my directness, I would like to come quickly to the
point."

"The point?" she echoed, trying to throttle the dizzying current racing through her.

"I am twenty-five, already a full partner in my father's business, and anxious to expand his work beyond its present capac-
ity. I am dependable, not overly given to emotion, and I believe
life is a system of challenges to be mastered and overcome."

"Those—those are admirable qualities," Rachelle answered,
wondering what had spurred such a confession. His galvanizing
look sent a tremor through her. "My mother and grandfather
speak very highly of you, Lanston. Your reputation is quite flaw-
less—"

"I will need a wife—and soon," Lanston interrupted, increasing his gentle pressure on her hand. "You would do me a very
great honor, Mistress Bailie, if you would consent to be my bride.
I expect we shall be betrothed for about a year, unless your
mother will allow us to be wed sooner. Your family can arrange
the wedding, and mine will see to our future home. I will build
you a house grander than anything Charles Towne has ever
seen."

"Mr. Wragg!" Laughing, she pulled her hand away, then
pressed her palms to her cheeks again.

His brows drew downward in a sudden frown. "Have I said
something to displease you?"

"No." She lowered her hands, feeling her heart turn over the
way it had the day he looked at her in his mother's drawing

room. "You please me very well, Lanston Wragg. But this is so sudden!"

Without a moment's hesitation he reached for her hand again, then fell to one knee on the path. As the molten orb of the moon hung low over the garden wall, he pressed his free hand over his heart and gazed at her with determination in his eyes. "Mistress Bailie, my heart will beat for you alone if you agree to become my wife. Will you, Rachelle, agree to unite our families and our fortunes as we face the future?"

He raised his eyes to her face in an oddly keen, swift look, and Rachelle felt her mind empty of all protestations and considerations. Why shouldn't she marry him? Her mother and grandfather had obviously approved the match. Lanston Wragg was charming, and she found his direct approach rather appealing. The hand that gripped hers was strong and firm; the face lifting toward her in the moonlight radiated a vitality that drew her like a magnet.

"Yes, Mr. Wragg," she whispered, smiling down at him. "I would be honored to be your wife."

He lowered his head then, pressing his lips to her palm, and her entire body tingled from the contact of his flesh upon hers.

Surely this was love.

"Bless you, Mistress Bailie." Lanston's breath softly warmed her hand. Turning his head, he pillowed his cheek lightly upon her palm for an instant, then looked up at her with a smile in his eyes. "Shall I call tomorrow? We could ride along Oyster Point and watch the ships come in."

"That would be lovely," she answered, releasing his hand as he stood. He paused before her for a moment, his blue eyes gleaming black and dangerous in the lantern light; then he gestured toward the house. "I suppose we should go in and tell our families," he said, his smile matching hers in liveliness. "Shall you tell them, or shall I?"

"We'll tell them together," Rachelle answered, turning back toward the house. She felt the pressure of his hand at the small of her back as they walked, and she smiled, liking the sensation.

▼▲▼▲▼ The next three days passed in a flurry of carriage rides, long walks, and candlelit suppers with either Mr. and Mistress Wragg or Bertrand Fortier. Rachelle's mother, who had taken to her bed with a fever, sent congratulations from her bedchamber and wished the couple every happiness.

Rachelle was astonished at the sense of fulfillment she felt. The years of enduring tutors, dancing teachers, and even those frustrating harpsichord lessons had prepared and molded her to become Lanston Wragg's wife. Within twenty-four hours of Lanston's proposal, congratulatory cards and letters began to arrive at the house. The grim line of her grandfather's mouth eased almost to a smile.

"During the year there will be a series of balls, of course, my dear," Cambria Wragg told Rachelle one morning as she dropped by the Fortier house to reiterate her best wishes and inquire after Babette's health. Her pale hand floated up from beneath her cloak and touched Rachelle's cheek with tenderness. "Already the governor's wife has contacted me about hosting a soiree for you and Lanston. As soon as your mother has recovered from this dreadful ague, we will have tea and discuss our plans."

Rachelle nodded dumbly, her heart too full for words. She had known that her grandfather was a leader in the city, but she had had no idea her wedding would be touted as the social event of the season. But at least the excitement had done Mistress Wragg some good. A glowing picture of good health, Cambria drew Rachelle into a fierce embrace, then walked briskly to the door, delivering orders to her coachman in a voice of velvet steel.

An hour later, Friday announced that Lanston himself waited in the parlor. Rachelle snapped her fingers at Fala, urging the woman to hurry with her toilette. Rachelle had risen early, had Fala dress her in a proper afternoon frock, then had visited briefly with her mother and Mistress Wragg. Now Fala was struggling to pin a tall headdress of looped ribbon amid Rachelle's curly hair.

"Don't bother," Rachelle snapped, yanking the silly headdress from her head. "I'll wear a bonnet—we'll be outside riding in the wind." She held up the looking glass, pinched her cheeks and bit her lips, then lightly squeezed the tip of her nose, uselessly wishing it were a tiny bit more narrow. But Lanston loved her anyway, and as long as he did nothing else mattered.

As far as Rachelle could tell, Lanston adored her. Unlike most Charles Towne men, who kept their women safely hidden away behind lace curtains and high walls, every day he linked her arm through his and took her from merchant to merchant, calling upon prospective customers. Encouraged by his somewhat unconventional attitude, Rachelle followed at his side, her eyes intent upon her surroundings, feeling a wee bit like a prize pony on parade.

She had not spent an hour on the docks when she realized that she had been truly sheltered from the harsh realities of life in Charles Towne. Before venturing out with Lanston, she had never visited the wharf. Prior to her betrothal she had ventured only across the safe, sheltered thresholds of the Bay Street merchants who displayed barrels of sugar, rum, and molasses, along with neat stacks of woolens, silks, and calico. On the docks of Charles Towne, however, Rachelle saw variations of men and lifestyles she never knew existed. The wharf teamed with sunburned sailors, polished navy officers, black and Indian slaves, disgruntled passengers, peevish customers, cursing loaders, and merchants of all sorts.

The Wragg family business, she knew, dealt in slaves. Each day Lanston checked the docks to see what ships might have arrived in the night; then he hurried aboard to check their cargo. Lanston promptly greeted any Dutch captain who carried a cargo of slaves and escorted him to the nearest tavern to discuss business. Even pirates, Lanston told Rachelle, had to be treated with respect, for most of them had valuable goods to sell and were not overly particular about their profit.

Slaves—whether black or Indian—were in high demand. The rice planters, many of whom had immigrated to Carolina after fleeing overpopulated Barbados, eschewed indentured servants in favor of African and Indian slaves. The Barbadian sugarcane growers had been forced to stop using free servants when they could no longer promise land and freedom at the conclusion of a term of indenture. In time, the sugar planters learned that enslaved West Africans could be fed and clothed far more cheaply than indentured Europeans. In addition, sugar produced enough profit that the planters could afford to literally work Africans to death and replenish them as the need arose.

Slaves, Lanston told Rachelle, could be sold nearly as quickly as they were unloaded from the slave ships. Part of his job was to acquire them in his father's name, transfer them to the barracoon, where they could be inspected for disease and disability, then see that they were auctioned properly. Carolina rice planters, desperately in need of hands to work the fields, were willing to mortgage their acreage and their present slaves in order to buy more.

"Negroes," Lanston remarked as he and Rachelle stood on a dock and watched a line of manacled slaves being led up from the bowels of a recently arrived ship, "are the bait proper for catching a Carolina planter, as certain as beef to catch a shark."

Rachelle frowned as she watched the seaman's whip fall rhythmically and indiscriminately upon the emaciated slaves' backs in an effort to keep the line moving. She turned away, shriveling a little at the memory of Fala's recent whipping.

Lanston himself had referred to that occasion the day before. "Slaves are a cunning lot when they want to be," he had told her as they walked along the beach at Oyster Point. "That's why I sent Devin Garr to your house the night we heard about your slaves' planning to escape."

Lanston sent Garr to whip Fala and Dustu? Rachelle was too surprised to do more than nod. She had blamed Mr. Ashton Wragg for that trouble.

"I thought you might be a bit upset," he had gone on, apparently taking her silence for understanding, "but you've got to learn how to be firm with your slaves, Rachelle. As my wife, you'll have more slaves than anyone else in town, and you can't let them walk over you. They outnumber us—always remember that."

She had nodded weakly, trusting in his maturity and experience.

Now she tucked her sour thoughts away. Though she found violence distasteful, she trusted Lanston implicitly. Sometimes whipping was necessary, he told her, much as a parent found it necessary to discipline his children or the groom his horse. Did not the Bible itself say that a slave would not be corrected by words alone? The whip reinforced proper behavior, and as long as a slave obeyed, he proved that he had learned his lesson. The whip, the brand, the chain—these were only tools, much as Babette's hickory switch had taught Rachelle not to play near a dangerous open well.

Lanston possessed such wisdom! A feeling of glorious happiness sprang up in Rachelle's heart whenever he walked through the door, and she loved every moment spent in his company. He talked incessantly, filling her imagination with stories of his travels in Boston and New York and Virginia. He had even completed one voyage to Africa and had shot a lion with his musket.

"Truly?" Rachelle gasped in amazement. She smiled and gently put her hand upon his, thoroughly enjoying the danger-excitement his presence elicited. He was a wonder, and he was hers.

The house echoed with silence when Lanston said his farewells after their third day together. Rachelle grappled with sudden guilt as she crept quietly up the stairs to see her mother. The doctor had visited Babette the day before, and his report had not been encouraging. The physician had taken a pint of blood and urged Babette to keep to her bed.

"Oh!" Rachelle stopped on the stairs, stunned by the sight of the dour little physician outside Babette's door. Her grandfather stood there, too, his face dead white, unshaven, and sheened with a cold sweat.

The physician looked through Rachelle as if she did not exist. "It is the pox," he said, his expression and voice tight with strain.

"I have bled her again to drain her body of morbific matter, and she may recover, being that she is a white woman. But if you have Indians about, keep them out of the sickroom or you are likely to lose them. The pox kills them straightaway."

The pox. Rachelle clung to the stair railing, then sank to the steps, melting in grief against the banister. The pox had swept through Charles Towne earlier in the summer, killing over two hundred people.

Mon Dieu, please help my mama. This cannot be true.

The doctor moved past her, a grave look on his lined face as he descended the stairs. Rachelle felt a little spasm of panic shoot across her body like the trilling of an alarm bell; then she rose to face her grandfather. He would know what to do. Bertrand Fortier always knew what to do.

"*Grand-père?*" She moved slowly toward him, hearing her own voice through a fog of confusion. "*Grand-père,* what will happen to Mama?"

She reached out, but his hands were cold and lifeless in her own, his eyes as distant as the stars. She saw a tremor run down his throat and heard a soft sound as he swallowed his fear. He trembled, then looked at her, his blue eyes sparking.

"Leave me." He ripped his hands from her grasp and pushed past her, leaving her in the hallway. He had spoken without heat, but his words fell with the weight of stones in still water, spreading endless ripples of pain and confusion through Rachelle's heart.

Gasping at the deep, unaccustomed pain in her breast, Rachelle sank into the chair outside her mother's door and burst into tears.

▼▲▼▲▼ Bertrand Fortier sat silently upon the small chair at Babette's secretary. How dainty were the objects she had spread upon the desk. There was a small porcelain vase, as fragile as a moonbeam, a tiny basket filled with letters she had yet to answer, a tray filled with quills, and a bottle of ink. A great writer, his Babette. A great reader, too, though Bertrand himself had never held a great love for books. That trait had come from her mother, dead these many years.

Sighing, he turned away and considered the form on the bed. The windows were closed tight against any contamination from the nighttime air, and the air in the sickroom was thick and sour with the smells of illness, sweat, and something else . . . the faintly sweet odor of impending death. Bertrand had smelled it before, in his beloved wife's chamber. He had been helpless then, and he was helpless now.

He had kept watch over his wife, too, on a Parisian evening much like this one. Sometimes Bertrand felt trapped in an endless night—as if the stars above him were locked in place and sunrise would never come. Occasionally he thought he might catch a glimpse of light, of life, but then darkness descended again. His beloved Claire had died, and he and his children had journeyed to New France to begin again. Then he had spent six horrid months in darkness, thinking his children dead, but the sun had risen again with Babette's return.

But God had not returned the same Babette. This one was more somber, more sorrowful, and a mother. After lying down with the Indians, Babette had risen and returned with an Indian's child.

He snorted softly. Ironic that she should now be dying of the disease that killed Indians like flies. Europeans died of pox, too, but Indians fell before it like grain before a scythe.

As Babette was falling now.

From her bed, she moaned softly, and Bertrand tensed at the sound, afraid his thoughts had somehow awakened her. A silence settled upon the room, an absence of sound that had almost a tangible density. It was in moments like this, the minister had recently told Bertrand, that we could feel the presence of God, that we could know his power.

Bertrand licked his lower lip, managing for a moment to quell his anger. He had known nothing good from God's hand. God had taken his wife, his son, and soon his daughter. The Almighty had left him a girl with eyes as black as pitch and a soul surely as dark, but the child would never compensate for the loss of the mother. *But still,* an inner voice reminded him, *Babette loves the child. Provide for her.*

The wind outside rattled the windows; stark white bones of lightning cracked through the black skin of the sky. Bertrand tilted his head toward the window, then blinked slowly as the heavy skies opened and seemed to weep. As the October rain poured over the dying earth, a roar of thunder shuddered in the air like a bellow of rage.

Resigned to the storm, Bertrand let his head fall to the back of the chair and closed his eyes.

The duties of nursing Babette fell to Virtue, and each morning she sternly turned Rachelle away from her mother's door. "Your mother's none too pretty now. She's covered in spots," Virtue explained, standing before the door with her arms folded tight as a gate across her chest. "She sends her love, and she has me to care for her, so you stay away, Mademoiselle Rachelle."

Rachelle paused in the hallway, hearing the soft moans of sickness from behind the closed door. As desperately as she wanted to see her mother, Rachelle knew the pox was terribly dangerous. She would only add to her mother's pain if she took sick, too, so she slowly nodded and moved away.

Lanston curtailed his visits when he heard that Babette was gravely ill, though he sent regular letters and promised to pray for Mistress Bailie's recovery. Rachelle assumed her mother's responsibility to oversee the household, and she noticed that her grandfather moved about the house as though permanently distracted, his head tilted slightly toward Babette's upstairs chamber. She would have done anything to alleviate his distress, but when she tried to speak to him, he only stared through her with eyes clouded with visions of the past.

On the tenth day of Babette's illness her grandfather abruptly summoned Friday and Rachelle into the library. "I am riding out to Shadow Grove," he said, running his hand over the folds of crepey skin at his throat. "If there is any change in Babette, send word to me at once."

Rachelle wondered why Bertrand Fortier would leave in the midst of a crisis, then decided that he simply could not bear the suspense of not knowing whether his daughter would live or die. She stood on the piazza with Friday and watched her grandfather ride away, then turned back into the house, feeling the heavy burden of responsibility fall squarely upon her shoulders, lessened only by the faith that had supported her since childhood.

As a Huguenot, Rachelle had been taught to accept Jesus as her Savior and Lord, and in the days of her mother's illness she began to experience God as her comforter. With no one else to turn to, she spent hours in prayer, her eyes wide and unseeing, her heart overflowing with emotions and concerns she could not voice. A feeling of resolute calm—she could not quite call it peace, for her own spirit was too restless—descended upon her, giving her the strength to endure another day.

Virtue spent her days with Babette, and *Grand-père* sat with her during the night. The doctor had banned Rachelle from the sickroom, but since *Grand-père* had gone, Rachelle could not allow her mother to suffer alone. Gathering her slippery courage, Rachelle climbed the stairs and pushed open the door to Babette's bedchamber. What she found in the sickroom chilled her blood to the marrow.

She had heard that death from smallpox was a torturous and repulsive affair, but hearsay had not prepared her for the gruesome reality. Her first thought was that the skeletal figure on the bed did not look human. Babette's once-curvaceous figure had evaporated; she seemed a chain of bones poorly encased in broken skin. Though Virtue changed the bedding every day, the suppurating sores soon soiled the linens again. Virtue was in the midst of tending Babette when Rachelle entered, and Rachelle gasped in horror when she realized that Babette's skin was literally glued to the linen. To keep from prolonging the painful ordeal, Virtue tugged quickly on the linen, flaying off another layer of broken skin and leaving Babette's flesh bloody and oozing worse than before.

"Mademoiselle Rachelle!" Virtue snapped, a thrill of alarm in her voice when she looked up. "You shouldn't be in here!"

Rachelle shivered through fleeting nausea and stepped closer, silencing Virtue's sudden protest with an uplifted hand. The ravages of the disease had not even spared Babette's lovely face. She appeared to be sleeping, for her eyes were closed and her mouth relaxed, but Rachelle saw the telltale clenching of her mother's fist when Virtue turned her in order to smooth a clean sheet over the mattress.

"I'm going to stay, Virtue." Rachelle lifted her head, daring the maid to contradict her. "*Grand-père* has gone to the plantation, and I will stay with Mother when you need rest. Do not argue with me."

Virtue sighed heavily. The thin line of her mouth clamped tight for a moment, and her dark throat bobbed once as she swallowed. "Very good, mademoiselle," she murmured, turning her attention back to the woman on the bed. She continued to work, alternately lifting Babette and positioning the sheet, but glanced occasionally at Rachelle as she talked. "It started with just one or two spots," she said, taking care to keep her voice pleasant and light. "And then there were a hundred. The spots turned into sores on the sixth day, and now her entire body is covered. She cannot rest, poor thing; she can't sleep."

"Isn't she asleep now?"

"Fainted, I expect. She can't stand the pain when I have to move her." Virtue straightened Babette's thin legs, then moved to the end of the bed and snapped the sheet taut beneath them. As a final ministration, she shook out a light summer blanket and laid it gently across her mistress.

Until that moment, Rachelle had been praying for her mother's recovery, but as she sank into the chair by the bed she lifted her eyes to heaven and begged God to take her mother quickly. This death was worse than torture, more terrifying than anything Rachelle could imagine. Bertrand Fortier's beautiful and charming daughter had become a living corpse, a seeping, moaning specter.

Except for brief moments, Rachelle did not leave her mother's room for nearly two days. She sat silently, watching death bear down upon Babette with a slow and stately deliberation, knowing she could do nothing to stop it. Fatigue settled in pockets under her eyes; her nerves throbbed with exhaustion, and yet she did not dare leave the sickroom. She had prayed that God would take Babette home. How could she leave until that prayer had been answered?

Babette moaned throughout the second night of Rachelle's watch, but as blue-veiled twilight crept into the room, she grew silent, the only sound her labored and irregular breathing.

Rachelle stirred from her chair, listening. Last night she had sent Friday to bring her grandfather home, but as of yet there had been no sign of the slave or his master. *If Friday has run away, I'll let him go,* Rachelle thought, her mind thick with fatigue. *Just like I'm letting Mother go.*

"Rachelle?" Babette's voice, cracked with disuse and weakness, broke the silence. Her head lifted slightly from her pillow, and her open eyes sought Rachelle's.

"Mama?" Rachelle leaned forward and stifled the urge to reach for her mother's hand. Babette could not be handled; the pressure of another's touch brought her nothing but agony.

"Darling *cherie,* I must tell you something." Black circles ringed Babette's eyes; her cheekbones rose like tent poles under a slick canvas. Her once-full lips had shrunk to thin lines of pale blue, but for once her eyes were dry, with no sign of tears.

"Shh, Mama, don't talk. Rest."

"No." Babette struggled to lift her head. "I want you to know . . . the truth."

Rachelle shook her head, wondering if this was the delirium of impending death. "It's not important, Mama. Lie back and rest. *Grand-père* will be here soon."

"No!" Babette's faded eyes stirred with agitation. "I have to talk to you alone. Your father, Rachelle—I want you to know about him. There is more to the story . . . than you know."

Stunned, Rachelle took a quick, sharp breath. "What story, Mama?"

A hint of tears glistened in the dim wells of Babette's blue-green eyes. "His name was Mojag Bailie, and I—" She paused and licked her broken lips, marshaling her strength, then looked at Rachelle with something very fragile in her eyes. "I did not know I was carrying a child when I left him. But I did not want to live among the Indians forever."

"Live among the Indians?" Rachelle hesitated, torn by conflicting emotions. Babette was confused; these were the ravings of a diseased mind. "Mama, my father was *captured* by the Indians, like you. Reverend Bailie was an Englishman."

"He had English ancestors." Babette's wounded hand clawed at the sheet that covered her, but her voice was calm, without even a thread of hysteria. "But he had Indian ancestors, too. And he lived with the Indians. It's all there . . . in my journal."

Her trembling hand lifted for an instant toward the tall secretary where she usually sat to record the household accounts.

"Your grandfather," Babette whispered when Rachelle turned toward her again, "would not understand. So I could not tell him . . . the entire truth. But Mojag was a good man. You need not be ashamed of him."

"Shh, Mama, don't talk." The words rose automatically to Rachelle's lips, but her mind reeled in wonder. Was her mother telling the truth or wandering in the fog of impending death? She shook her head, turning away from the unsolvable question. It didn't matter. The past was history, dead and buried. Rachelle had only to consider this painful present.

But still—*he had Indian ancestors, too.* Rachelle sank back, searching anxiously for the meaning behind those words. If her father had been part Indian, then she was Indian, too. She sat still in her chair, blank, amazed, and very shaken by the idea. The Carolina colony considered Indians of no more significance or value than Africans. She shuddered, considering the implications. No wonder her mother had hidden the truth!

"Rachelle?" Babette spoke in an aching, husky voice Rachelle scarcely recognized.

"Yes, Mama?" Tears clotted Rachelle's throat now; she couldn't suppress the well of emotion rising inside her.

"My wedding ring—your father would want you to have it. It has been in his family . . . for generations."

Rachelle bit her lip, fighting back tears. "Yes, Mama."

Babette's frail hand trembled above the bed. "Take it now."

Weeping freely, Rachelle reached out and slipped the gold circle from her mother's finger. Though the ring was dirty and smeared with blood, Rachelle could see an inscription on the inside of the slender band.

"The words are Latin," her mother said, her cracked lips curving in an expression that might have been a smile. "I don't remember what the words are, but they mean *boldly, faithfully, successfully.* That was how Mojag lived. That would be his wish for you." Her voice fell to a thin whisper. "It is my wish for you, too. May you be more . . . than I have been. I am such a coward, but you are much like your father."

Rachelle dropped the ring onto the bedside table, unwilling and unable to consider the wishes of an Indian father she'd never known. The father of her imagination was a reserved and proper English clergyman who had been dead and buried these seventeen years.

Babette's eyes widened with pain at the sound of the metal clattering against the table. "No, Rachelle—"

"Mama, don't—" Words of protest welled in Rachelle's chest, but her throat closed up, choking them back.

"Rachelle, it is right . . . that I go first." Babette paused, clearing her throat of rumbling phlegm. Then the tip of her swollen tongue clumsily swept over her cracked lips. "I leave you . . . to carry on. You have made my life worthwhile. Worth something. Find your father . . . so he can see."

Her mother's voice faded away like the morning mist. Rachelle's clamped lips imprisoned a sob as she heard the absolute finality in her mother's dying gasp. Babette's chest heaved toward the ceiling as she struggled to breathe one final time; then she relaxed . . . and was gone.

Rachelle sank back into her chair, her gaze clouding with tears as ice spread through her stomach. Babette Fortier Bailie, who never did what anyone expected, had spent her life giving Rachelle a happy home. In dying, Babette had presented her daughter with a father who might well prove to be Rachelle's undoing. Why?

Rachelle picked up her mother's wedding ring and held it in her open palm, staring at the gold band as if it might suddenly metamorphose into one of the tiny African vipers Lanston had told her about, the kind that could sneak into your coat pocket and inflict a fatal bite when you least expected it.

Boldly, faithfully, successfully. *Mon Dieu!* How could she think of a father when she had just lost her mother?

Hoarsely, she called for Virtue.

The sweltering humidity of Charles Towne mandated that citizens who died in the summer be buried hastily, but the relative cool weather of late October granted the Fortier household a measure of grace. Rachelle moved through the household with wooden solidity, arranging for the hearse, the burial space in the churchyard, the satinwood casket.

Her grandfather had arrived back at the house an hour after Babette's last breath. Overflowing with grief, Rachelle rushed forward and threw her arms around him, only to be rebuffed with hands that did not lift to hold her. When she lifted her streaming eyes to study his face, she saw that his eyes were as glassy and blank as windowpanes, as though the soul they housed had long since flown. She stepped back, chilled in the icy silence that surrounded him; then Bertrand Fortier turned and climbed the stairs to his bedchamber, leaving Rachelle to do as she pleased.

On the thirty-first of October, three days after Babette Fortier Bailie's death, the funeral hearse pulled up to the house, and slaves bore out the black-draped casket. Dressed in black from head to toe, Bertrand and Rachelle trailed the hearse on foot, followed by the remaining Fortier slaves and a collection of friends and acquaintances. The funeral procession moved slowly toward the French Huguenot church, where the minister led the gathering in prayer and committed Babette's body to the hallowed ground of the cemetery.

As the minister's words droned on in the thick silence of the churchyard, Rachelle stared at the casket and idly fingered the golden band on her right hand. The day after her mother's death, she had scrubbed the ring with hot water until she could

clearly see the engraving: *fortiter, fideliter, feliciter.* Latin for
"boldly, faithfully, successfully."

Within the scope and meaning of those three words a ghostly
likeness of Mojag Bailie had begun to take shape. She cast aside
the one-dimensional image she'd imagined, dismissed the dour
garb and somber English face she'd visualized as Mojag Bailie's.
With her dying breath, Babette had shattered all of Rachelle's per-
ceptions. A man who *boldly* lived in the wilderness was clearly
adventurous and no coward. A man who proclaimed *faithfulness*
among the Indians could not be halfhearted or dour. And one
who strove to live *successfully* could not be complacent or weak.

The minister's voice cut into her thoughts, and Rachelle lifted
her head, her gaze meeting Lanston's. He stood next to her, his
eyes studying her with a curious intensity. She managed a tremulous smile, wanting to assure him she had found peace. So many
had died of pox in Charles Towne—she could not complain
because the dread disease touched her household as well. And
once her mother had succumbed to it, Rachelle could not rightfully beg God to prolong her suffering.

"Forasmuch as it has pleased almighty God in his great mercy
to take unto himself the soul of our dear sister here departed, we
therefore commit her body to the ground; earth to earth, ashes to
ashes, dust to dust." The minister paused as the pallbearers
began to lower the casket into the ground. When he was certain
the casket moved smoothly downward, he continued, his voice
ringing with finality: "In sure and certain hope of the resurrec-
tion to eternal life, through our Lord Jesus Christ, who shall
change our vile bodies that they may be like unto his glorious
body, according to the mighty working whereby he is able to subdue all things to himself."

Swallowing the sob that rose in her throat, Rachelle's eyes followed the dark box until it settled with a soft thud upon the
orange-tinted earth.

Lanston Wragg

I pity them greatly, but I must be mum,
For how could we do without sugar and rum?

—*William Cowper, English poet*
"Pity for Poor Africans," 1788

Standing amidships on the deck of the *Jacques*, Captain Trace
Bettencourt crossed his arms behind his back and studied a
sleepy line of gulls squabbling languidly over a ripple on the
approaching sea. The port of Charles Towne lay upon the western horizon like a gleaming crown, its tight rows of stately
houses rising up behind the warehouses and shanties that bordered the docks. The calm water of the harbor steamed as the
cold February air pressed upon the warmer surface of the sea.

Trace resisted the shiver that threatened to course through his
body. While Carolina was the southernmost English colony, even
this comparatively mild winter weather was a shock to his system after a month of basking in the tropics.

"By the deep eight, by the deep eight," the master called, judging the depth of the channel they had entered. "By the mark
nine, a quarter less nine, by the deep eight."

"Monsieur MacKinnon?" Trace called over his shoulder without looking, knowing his first mate stood nearby.

"Aye, Captain?"

Trace turned just enough to see the tall man's blond beard,
then nodded toward the horizon. "Bring us in gently, *s'il te plaît*,
and take care not to upset any of the English captains. We must
not make waves in an English harbor, no?"

"As you wish, Captain." MacKinnon turned to bellow the necessary commands, and the *Jacques* woke to urgent life. At
MacKinnon's call seamen rolled from their hammocks and
spidered up through the ropes, furling the sheets that had
brought them across the Atlantic to Carolina.

Trace walked slowly toward the forecastle, considering the

harbor before him. Carolina was an English colony, but owing to the number of foreigners who had flooded Charles Towne, the port had a decidedly less English flavor than Boston or Jamestown. The harbor also had a reputation among seamen—a captain could unload his cargo at the dock and sell it with little trouble and no questions asked. Few officials even asked to see the ship's bill of lading. If Trace and his crew were to encounter trouble, the odds of finding it in Charles Towne were less than in any northern port.

The Treaty of Ryswick, enacted in September of the previous year, had officially ended the Anglo-French hostilities known as King William's War, a pointless series of battles that raged on the sea and throughout New England for eight years. News of the treaty, which had not reached the *Jacques* until late October, had marked a turning point in Trace's career. During the time of war the naval vessel had been legally entitled to prey upon English warships and merchantmen, but under the treaty of peace the *Jacques* could no longer continue to follow such orders. Unfortunately, due to the criminal action that had taken place aboard her decks, she could no longer return to France either.

The *Jacques* had been uncommonly successful. In a mere twelve months at sea her crew had captured over thirty English vessels, taking aboard enough goods to sustain the ship and ensure a goodly portion to each seaman aboard her. But she sailed now as an outlaw ship, operating outside both the French navy and maritime law.

The night after receiving news of the treaty, Trace had climbed into the forecastle and spoken to his assembled crew. "You know what we have endured together," he said, his unspoken words carrying far more weight than the speech that spilled now from his tongue. His eyes scanned every face for any sign of reluctance or misgiving. "And you know what awaits us if we return to France. So I ask you now—shall we continue at sea? Or shall we put back into port and face whatever fate King Louis decrees?"

There was no sound for a long moment, save for a pair of

gulls shrieking among the masts, their voices as raucous as squabbling seamen. Finally Duncan MacKinnon cried out, speaking for the others: "A gold chain or a wooden leg, Captain!" The others raised their arms and voices in assent. "Whatever lies ahead, we'll stand with you!"

"Hear, hear!" Cries of support wrapped around Trace like water around a rock, and he knew his men would remain faithful unto death.

Now the muddy, dimpled waters of the Cooper River slid by, and Trace turned, parsing the hot scent of the sea as he looked toward Charles Towne harbor. The only question remaining was whether he and his men would meet death via a mutineers' guillotine or a pirates' noose.

For pirates—he gripped a rope, steadying himself as the ship entered the wind-whipped waters of the harbor—was what they had become. Instead of legally preying upon English ships, now they illegally accosted any ship that suited their purposes. It was not a particularly virtuous life, but it was tolerable. They had chosen to remain alive and free, and if that meant they would walk the rest of their lives on the knife-edge of danger—so be it.

The late afternoon sun streaked the water crimson, and Trace watched in approval as his men sent the *Jacques* gracefully winging toward an empty berth at the dock. Fully loaded with rum, sugar, and molasses—the cargo of the last English merchant ship they had plundered off the coast of Barbados—Trace fully expected that this night he would have a decent bath and a meal of something other than hardtack and dried beef. If he was extremely fortunate, he might even enjoy a woman's smile—a rare pleasure after staring at blistering ocean and ragged seamen for days on end.

Cries of welcome rose from the men on shore, and as the *Jacques* moved into her place, loaders swarmed over the docks like bees around a hive. Thoughts of business at the wharf brought Trace back to present realities, and he sent another command over his shoulder. "Monsieur MacKinnon, bring up the men from the cargo hold."

"Aye, Captain."

"And arm each of them with a sword or blade—whatever you have, but no pistols. I will speak to them when they are assembled."

"Blades, Captain?" MacKinnon's voice rose in surprise. "You want me to arm them?"

"Unless the cannons have deafened you, Monsieur MacKinnon, yes, you have heard me correctly. Now bring them up, and quickly. We are soon to be met by those cursed traders."

MacKinnon's eyes darkened in sudden understanding; then he darted down the companionway and disappeared into the hold.

Trace thrust his hands behind his back again and stared at the bustling dock. He looked forward to enjoying all the comforts the port had to offer, but first he must endure a necessary bit of unpleasantness. Aggravation was the price he would have to pay in Charles Towne, yet the cost was far less than any he'd have to pay in a French port.

▼▲▼▲▼ From his desk at the wharf office, Lanston Wragg looked up in time to see the elegant blue-and-gold frigate glide by on her way to a berth at the docks. The *Jacques!* The French privateer had not been sighted in these waters since the trouble with the French and the Indians broke out in New England. Small barges manned by French sailors often brought in goods under the cover of darkness. Though they knew full well they were buying goods from pirated English ships, Lanston and several other merchants had been pleased to barter for sugar, cotton, rum, and whatever else the seamen had to offer.

Lanston left the pirates to worry with their own consciences; his was perfectly clear. He had never stolen from any man, living or dead. If others happened to ply a bit of thievery on the high seas, well, Lanston made it a point never to ask. He didn't want to know where the valuable goods originated, and unless cargo had been stolen from a ship operated by Ashton Wragg & Son, he didn't care. He was content to follow his father's instructions and bring buyers and sellers together. The merchantmen and slavers brought in badly needed goods; the plantation owners and merchants of Charles Towne had money to spend and a hankering for luxuries.

Pulling on his frock coat, he stood in the open doorway and studied the *Jacques*. A truly majestic ship, she moved with slow grace through the water, her hands expertly tossing the heavy hawsers over the huge posts on the dock. Lanston took a quick breath of utter astonishment as the *Jacques* drew nearer, for *black* men moved about on her decks. They did not move with any purpose, but at least a dozen stood there, apparently healthy and in good condition.

Lanston reached for his hat and dropped it on his head, closing the door behind him with a slam. He'd be the first merchant to welcome the captain of the *Jacques* to Charles Towne and also the first to make an offer on the Africans. The price for black slaves had been rising steadily since the pox had carried away so many of the Indians, and it appeared that this French captain had several fine specimens on board.

Humming to himself, Lanston straightened his coat, pulled the lace of his cuffs from beneath the sleeves of his frock coat, then strolled toward the ship.

▾▲▾▲▾ "Captain Bettencourt a merchant alongside begs permission to come aboard."

Trace stiffened slightly, then turned his eyes from the wide horizon at the taffrail to the midshipman who'd brought the news. "Is he drunk," he remarked softly, "or can the man walk the gangplank?"

A grin played briefly on the midshipman's lips, then vanished. "He seems sober, sir. He's standing straight enough."

Trace nodded. "Wait for about five minutes, then lower the plank and let him come aboard."

Turning from the boy, he faced the twenty Africans his ship

had taken from a Dutch slaver they'd met off the shore of St. Kitts. The men stood blinking in the bright sunlight, tentatively gripping the weapons they'd been given. Most, Trace noticed, wore grim, uncertain expressions.

"Monsieur Severin," Trace called to a seaman scrambling down from the mizzenmast. "Your assistance, *s'il vous plaît.*"

The seaman dropped to the deck like a monkey, his ruddy face brightening at the prospect of an unusual development in his day.

"At your service, Captain."

Trace jerked his head toward the slaves on deck. "Monsieur Severin, you speak a little African?"

The man blanched, then gave Trace a lopsided grin. "I don't really know that I'd call it African, sir. But I have spent a bit of time with these men and have managed to make myself understood. To be sure, most of them have picked up more French than I have African."

"It will have to do. Tell them that today they must choose between three options. First, I can sell them to the Englishman who will shortly come aboard. If they leave with him, however, they will remain in slavery for the rest of their lives, and any children born to them will be enslaved as well."

Severin flushed. "That's no choice, Captain. They'd have to be fools—"

"Not fools," Trace contradicted. "It is possible some of them have family members who have already been brought here. If they are seeking family, they may wish to remain in Charles Towne. We must give them that opportunity."

The sailor nodded. "I understand, Captain."

"Tell them now, please."

In a mingled flow of French, English, and sign language, Severin presented the men's first choice. Trace felt a grim smile cross his face when the Africans began to murmur among themselves.

"Now give them their second choice," Trace went on, gazing impassively at the startled men before him. "If they like, they may journey to an island called Madagascar and a city called Libertalia. I have heard stories of a settlement there where all men are equal, and no men are slaves. I would be pleased to take them there, if any wish to go, but I cannot promise when we will arrive—or that the place even exists."

Again, Severin translated. Trace wasn't at all certain whether or not the men understood, but they seemed to grasp the idea of travel and freedom, for several eyes lit in anticipation.

"Finally," Trace continued, "they can choose to remain on board the *Jacques* and join this crew. The *Jacques* is a pirate ship, they should make no mistake about it, but we are not slave traders or cold-blooded murderers. We are wanted men, shunned by the world and welcomed only in ports where men are more greedy than scrupulous. But we can always use strong hands and willing backs, and though we are a disciplined ship, we share our work and our rewards equally."

Several of the men nodded as Severin offered his tortured translation of Trace's offer. When he had finished, Trace walked forward, looked directly at the first man in the group, and extended his hand toward the gangplank lowering toward the dock. "Do any of you wish to disembark in Carolina?"

As if they were of one mind, the body of Africans involuntarily shuffled backward. Trace was about to ask how many of them might be interested in journeying on to Madagascar when a boisterous voice interrupted: "Captain Bettencourt! It is my very great honor to make your acquaintance. The *Jacques* is a fine ship, sir, a most beautiful vessel!"

Spinning neatly on his booted heel, Trace turned. A tall, straight young man, clad in colors that would put a peacock to shame, was approaching along the gangway. The interloper carried himself with a commanding air of self-confidence, accented by the condescending way he tapped his walking stick over the deck as if testing its strength. Thick, golden hair curled from beneath his fur-trimmed tricorne and framed a boldly handsome face.

"*Je suis désolé.*" Trace inclined his head in a small—very

small—measure of respect. "I am sorry, sir, but I have not had the honor of making your acquaintance."

"Lanston Wragg, sir, forgive me." The young man lifted his free hand and made a leg, a ridiculously inappropriate posture for one who stood amid roughened pirates and armed African slaves. His bow complete, the young man looked up, his face shining with steadfast and serene confidence. "At your service, Captain Bettencourt. I have heard of you, of course, and feel as if I have already made your acquaintance, so please pardon my assumption."

Trace noticed that the hands on Wragg's hat fairly trembled with eagerness.

"Undoubtedly you know my father, at least by reputation, for Ashton Wragg is the foremost slave merchant in the Carolina colony."

Trace listened to the young man's babbling through a vague sense of unreality. He had a feeling that he should never have allowed the man aboard, but he did have goods to barter and a fierce need for provisions.

"It is my honor to make your acquaintance." Trace managed a polite smile. "How can we help you, sir?"

Wragg's young face opened in astonishment. "Why, I presume you are eager to sell your cargo. And as a duly empowered representative of Ashton Wragg & Son, I'd like to be the first to inspect and bid upon the goods you have to offer."

The Englishman's eyes turned greedily toward the Africans, and Trace noticed that most of the men immediately donned blank, stony expressions. Undoubtedly they had learned, long before he met them, that a wise man did not readily reveal his thoughts upon the canvas of his face.

"*Bien sûr*, I would be pleased to have you inspect my cargo once my men have unloaded it," Trace answered, the tightening muscles in his cheek turning his smile from a social grace to a rictus of necessity. "We have several hogsheads of fine rum, sugar, and molasses."

"Very good, of course," Wragg answered, his eyes still appraising the group of Negroes, "but I am primarily interested in these blacks, Captain. How many have you and—" his brows rose in obvious surprise—"why in God's name have you given them weapons?"

Trace laughed to cover his annoyance. "All of my men are armed, Mr. Wragg, particularly when we put into port. And since you asked about blacks—well, sir, I don't truly know that I have any aboard. There are a few chocolate-hued men among the crew, as well as a pair of brothers I'd describe as coffee colored. There are a couple like bronze, one or two I'd paint as buckskin or chestnut, and a string of older men who might qualify as cinnamon. We picked up a Spaniard in the Red Sea who has tanned to the hue of a nice sorrel pony, and a young cabin boy whose neck retains the color of mud because he never bathes. My first mate is a foul-tempered Scot whose mood is ofttimes more black than his skin, but as to honest black men—"

"How many Negroes?" Lanston snapped, a critical tone to his voice. He paused a moment, clasped his arms across his chest, and gave Trace a calculated smile. "Your humor is very clever, Captain, but you must know I speak of the Africans. How many are you willing to sell?"

Trace looked across at the knot of former slaves. "It is not my place to sell any of them," he said, his words as cool and clear as spring water. "They are free men, after all. What right have I to sell them?"

"Captain, how many?" Wragg insisted, bridled anger in his voice.

Trace lifted his head, addressing the Africans. "How many of you wish to depart the ship here in Carolina?" he asked, raising a brow. Not a man stirred in the silence; even the seamen in the ropes grew still, watching the deck below. After a long moment, Trace turned and faced the slave trader.

"As I told you, Mr. Wragg, I have no men for sale, black, brown, or beige." He forced himself to smile, though his breath burned in his throat. "The goods I do have—rum, molasses, and sugar—will be brought out onto the docks as soon as my men can unload. At that time, I expect other merchants will want a voice in the bidding as well."

Wragg smiled briefly, acknowledging defeat but not yet ready to make an enemy. "Whether I buy your slaves now or later, I will offer you the highest price. If you are waiting only to collect more bids—"

Trace tempered his anger with amusement at the young man's persistence. "I assure you, Mr. Wragg, I have no intention of entertaining bids upon a human life. I am a privateer, not a flesh merchant. And so I bid you good day."

The Englishman stood there, tall and very angry, as his dark gaze swung over the Africans one final time. "I must warn you to be sure these men do not go about freely in the streets of Charles Towne," he said simply, the insolence in his voice ill concealed. "Slaves are not allowed out after dark. And since your brown men are as dark as night itself, I would hate to see any of them mistaken for a runaway and flogged."

"I, too, would hate to see the officials of Charles Towne guilty of such malfeasance," Trace answered, a silken thread of warning in his voice. "It would not bode well for your city council if any of my men were harmed. We men of the sea are united, Mr. Wragg, and we do not suffer fools gladly."

"Then we are agreed," Wragg answered, bowing stiffly. "And I beg your leave until we meet again."

"*Au revoir,*" Trace answered, his voice soft and mocking. "Farewell, Mr. Wragg."

Rachelle leaned her forehead to the windowpane and felt the sting of its icy touch. The air outside the house seemed lifeless, the winter light melancholy and filled with shadows. The lady of the house had been dead for nearly four months, yet still the mansion echoed with the preternatural silence of mourning.

Rachelle felt as if there were hands on her heart, slowly twisting the life from it. After spending nearly a month locked in his bedchamber, her grandfather had resumed his usual activities, none of which included Rachelle. Apparently those activities did not satisfy or comfort him, for in January he and Friday journeyed to the plantation house. He had been gone for over a month, and Rachelle feared he might not come back.

He had gone away to escape—that much she understood without being told. The Charles Towne house whispered of Babette. Her taste was evident in the furnishings, the paintings, and the carpets; the scent of her delicate perfume lingered in every pillow and drape. Sometimes when the winter wind blew down the chimneys, Rachelle thought she heard her mother's soft moans. But it was only the wind. Nothing else.

Lanston still dropped by on occasion, but the pleasure Rachelle had found in his company seemed strangely muted. Her feelings about her mother and her absent grandfather were much too raw to discuss, and so, respecting her grief, Lanston withdrew from her presence, though he continually sent her little notes to remind her of their upcoming wedding. He thought she needed time alone, Rachelle realized, but how could complete and utter loneliness heal her aching heart? Perhaps when the earth had shaken off the mantle of winter, Rachelle could shake off her own mourning. Until then, there was nothing to do but move woodenly throughout the household, overseeing servants who had no one to care for and a house that seemed as empty as a dry shell on the beach.

Rachelle felt more alone than she ever had in her life. Fala, who had always been a willing companion, if not a friendly one, remained aloof, and Rachelle realized that her maid would never forget the occasion that had led to her flogging. Though the Indian woman's eyes never lifted in recrimination or blame, an air of remoteness clung to her, a barrier no one could penetrate. Fala did not even talk to Virtue, as far as Rachelle could tell, and the other Indian, Dustu, had been transported to the rice plantation.

And yet one presence grew more real with each passing day—the fuzzy, ill-defined image of Mojag Bailie. Rachelle had seen a dim outline of his face in church this morning every time she closed her eyes to pray. She tried to put his name out of her mind, for he was as dead as her mother and much less precious to her, but as silence sifted down like snowfall in the empty house, she felt herself drawn to know more about him.

Her mother had mentioned a journal. Rachelle had never intended to read it and doubted if it still existed, but searching for the book was a mindless activity that might help camouflage the deep despair of her loneliness.

Leaving the narrow window at the front of the house, Rachelle climbed the stairs, then hesitated at her mother's door. Entering this room was like bathing in grief afresh, but Rachelle tossed her head and moved forward. Consciously averting her eyes from the empty bed, Rachelle walked straight to the tall secretary and turned the tiny key in the locked doors.

Her mother, Rachelle realized anew, had been a great reader. Many books crowded the lowest shelf, among them *The Excellent Privilege of Liberty and Property,* by William Penn; Francis Bacon's *The Essays; The Pilgrim's Progress,* by John Bunyan; Mary Rowlandson's *The Sovereignty and Goodness of God, Together with the Faithfulness of His Promises Displayed, Being a*

Narrative of the Captivity and Restoration of Mrs. Mary Rowland-son; and a collection of Anne Bradstreet's poetry, *Several Poems Compiled with Great Variety of Wit and Learning.*

Rachelle frowned and ran her hand over the spines of the books. She had thought Babette looked directly toward this shelf when she mentioned the journal. Though such a book might be hidden among her papers and correspondence, *Grand-père* often rummaged through Babette's letters, and it seemed likely that she would have hidden her journal from his prying eyes.

Rachelle ran her hands over the upper shelves, then opened the doors and rummaged through the secretary. Nothing. Her mother had been out of her mind with fever, travailing to enter heaven and mightily confused about earthly matters.

Rachelle stepped back and tugged on the curl dangling over her shoulder. Babette might well have been delirious, but a sheen of purpose had lit her eyes. And deathbed charges were supposed to be heeded at all costs. . . .

Obeying a sudden impulse, Rachelle ran her hand through the empty space between the row of books and the secretary's wooden back. Almost at once her fingers felt the brittle edge of old leather, and she caught her breath as she lifted a dusty black volume from the space.

A journal. So Babette had not been deranged.

Settling into her mother's chair, Rachelle gently opened the book. An exuberant girlish hand had inscribed the first page: *The Adventures of Three Young People, Sent into the Wilderness to Explore and Learn.*

Rachelle thumbed through the scrawled pages. Babette had filled the entire book, carefully dating each entry. More than three full years had been faithfully recorded.

A pain squeezed Rachelle's heart as she thought of her mother, young and beautiful, writing in this journal. What had happened in the wilderness that would compel her to hide this book and the truth about Mojag Bailie?

Rachelle ran her hand over the textured leather, then tucked her legs under the chair and opened to the first entry.

October 10, 1679
Montreal

I am so thrilled to be included in the expedition southward to explore the dominions of New France! I can
scarcely believe that Papa has trusted my health and welfare into my brother Aubrey's hands, but Pierre, to
whom I will be married in the spring, will travel with
us. If either one of them fails to guard me, Papa will
have his head!

But I should not jest about matters so horrible and
serious. Though heathens known as the Iroquois have
grievously cut down the Algonquin and Huron, our
allies, danger from an Indian assault has ebbed. Governor Frontenac promises that our colony's strength has
intimidated the savages and that we will be safe on our
journey to explore the frontier.

Aubrey, Pierre, and I are traveling with a group of
coureurs de bois, traders and trappers who know the
woods like the palms of their hands. They trade often
with the Indians and are not afraid of the fierce creatures
that dwell in the shadows of the forest.

For two weeks Babette wrote every day about life on the trail:
the strange creatures she encountered, the miles she endured on
horseback, the startling sounds of the forest night. Then Babette
left a blank page, and Rachelle bit her lip when she saw the jerky,
stilted handwriting of the next entry.

October 24

Oh, will my heart never stop this pounding? How can a
heart broken by grief beat so strongly? I thought yesterday that my life was over, and now I wish it had been
taken from me! For yesterday was Pierre's time to die.

I shall try to still my heart long enough to record this,
for if Aubrey and I do not make it back to Papa—

It happened this way. Yesterday, the trappers moved away to set their traps, leaving Aubrey, Pierre, and me sitting by a brook to eat our meager dinner. I had just begun to enjoy my share of the food when I heard a snapping sound in the brush. I screamed, thinking a bear had come upon us, and Pierre laughed at my fears. He stood, taking his musket, and said, "Let me show you there is no danger." To assuage my fears he fired into the brush, then gaped in horror as a red man fell forward, shot most grievously through the forehead.

The thought that Pierre had committed murder had no sooner taken hold in my brain than a great swarm of Red Indians burst in upon us. Their leader, a tall, muscled man who wore nothing but a loincloth, even in the cold of October, walked at once to my Pierre. With fire in his eye, he struck my betrothed upon the head with his ax. Pierre did not have time even to cry out but fell forward, his blood staining the earth at my feet.

I could do nothing but scream for God's mercy— mercy for myself, for Pierre, and for Aubrey, who scrambled to his feet to enjoin the enemy, for such these savages surely were. But one of them stepped forward and spoke rapidly to the others, his hands pointing first to Pierre, then to the dead savage. I am not certain, but I believe he saved our lives. At his urging, the savages took my arms, then held Aubrey. We are their captives! They allowed me to take my gunnysack but bound Aubrey about the arms. After placing us upon our horses, they led us a great way through the forest until we came to their village.

Now Aubrey and I are kept inside one of their wooden houses, and I do not know if we shall live to see tomorrow's sunset. Oh merciful God, if you care for your children, send aid to us now! Keep my dear Pierre's soul in heaven, and comfort his father, who will surely

be heartbroken when he hears that his son has entered
eternity through an act of savagery in the wilderness.

Rachelle felt herself begin to tremble as fearful images built in
her mind. How terrified her mother must have been! She had left
the genteel comforts of home and a fine family and found herself
thrust into an Indian camp with only her brother for comfort.
But, Rachelle thought, recalling her own loneliness, at least
Babette had a brother.

Her breath quickened as she skimmed the next few pages.
Babette wrote of spending a sleepless night as the tribal leaders
debated what to do with the prisoners and of how the "reason-
able" savage who had restrained the others from bloodshed
entered the longhouse and spoke to Babette and Aubrey in perfect English.

> I have never been so astonished in all my days. *Non de
> nom,* what a gentle man! He did not seem at all savage as
> he sat before us and apologized for our captivity. He
> said that our friend—meaning Pierre—was foolish to fire
> blindly into the woods, and the murderous Indian had
> reacted in just anger and a desire for vengeance. But the
> Indians were content now, he said, and we were free to
> move around the camp.
>
> I asked, of course, when we might return to New
> France and our father. The man looked away for a
> moment, then confessed that it might be many months.
> Winter was fast approaching, he said, and the men of the
> tribe were intent upon gathering meat. The snows were
> nearly upon them, and no one could be spared to escort
> us back to some civilized settlement. But in the spring,
> when the snows melted, more trappers would come,
> and we could go back to New France with them.
>
> Aubrey, kind soul that he is, thought to ask our new
> friend's name. "Mojag," he answered, a strange and
> beatific smile upon his face. "I am called Mojag Bailie."

Rachelle shivered, her pulse rate increasing as she recognized the name. Her father! Half in anticipation, half in dread, she smoothed the page and continued reading.

Aubrey and I shook our heads in amazement. How did a savage come by an English surname? Mojag explained that his grandfather had been an Englishman, and his father a missionary to the savages involved in the war they credit to the heathen King Philip. His eyes darkened as if with sorrow when he confessed that savage's name, and I wondered what pain tore at his heart. But then he excused himself, his manners unfailingly polite, and asked if we would come out to dine with the Indians. And so we did, both of us wary, both of us as pale as ghosts against the dark brown floor of the forest. We felt as out of place as laughter in church, but no one seemed to notice.

October 26

An Indian family has invited us to sleep in their warm longhouse. We share freely of their food and seem to be expected to share in the work as well. I do not mind, for the women are pleasant and content to have me work with them—they laugh at my mistakes and clumsiness. But Aubrey is not faring as well, for he has developed a cough and tires easily. The hunters went out this morning and left him behind, for though the wind is cold and sharp as a knife, Aubrey wore great drops of perspiration upon his brow and lip. He is sleeping now as I write, and his face is pale and damp. I pray he has only overexerted himself with concern for our trials.

October 27

Today Mojag brought a wise man, a healer, who painted Aubrey's chest with colored clay and offered a cup

steaming with herbs. The man—a very old, stooped, and
wrinkled fellow—sang strange songs and brushed a
feather over Aubrey's chest for nearly a quarter of an
hour, I expect. And then, when he was finished, I was
astounded to see the wise man bow his head and pray
just as we do. Mojag translated the prayer—in English,
for he speaks little French—and together we prayed that
Aubrey would recover speedily.

As he left the longhouse, Mojag remarked that he
would continue to pray for my husband. "Oh," I
answered, blushing like a schoolgirl, "Aubrey is not my
husband—he is my brother."

Mojag said nothing, but my heart thundered in my
chest when he smiled at me. He is, I think, a very good
man.

October 28

Aubrey seemed better this morning, but by afternoon his
fever had returned. For fear of spreading the fever,
Mojag has moved Aubrey from the family's longhouse
to another small house, much like the one in which we
first found ourselves. Only Mojag and I are allowed to
tend Aubrey now, for Mojag fears that the Indians will
not be able to resist this ague, whatever its cause.

As Aubrey slept, Mojag and I spent several hours talking together—how grateful I am to have a companion
with whom I can talk freely! He speaks the savage
tongue with an ease that belies his English ancestry, but
he is a thoroughly civilized man. If ever one man knew
how to be at home in both the savage and civilized
worlds, I suspect that man is Mojag Bailie.

He is a quiet sort, unless I address him directly, and
then I feel as if I have uncovered a deep well brimming
with the purest, most refreshing water! He is a godly
man—not even the minister back home could find fault

with his character or convictions—and yet he is singularly charming. Tenderly he cares for Aubrey. Gently he cares for me. The savages look after only their families, so Mojag alone has made certain we have food enough and warm clothing. Tonight he has promised to bring me deerskins cut in the fashion of an Indian woman's dress—he says I will be much warmer in them than in the gown I wore from Montreal.

Fascinated, Rachelle continued reading. The next week was recorded in bits and pieces. Aubrey continued to languish in the mysterious fever. Babette worked alongside the Indian women and learned to speak a few words in the language. And Mojag Bailie, the mysterious English Indian, kept her company and continued to tend Aubrey.

A blank page followed the scattered entries; then Rachelle read a page where the ink had been blurred as if with raindrops:

November 7

Aubrey died yesterday. I can scarcely bring myself to record this terrible reality, but if I do not survive this journey, I want my father and any who would come after me to know the truth. The Oncida—the tribe with whom I am living—treated Aubrey with nothing but compassion. And Mojag Bailie tried desperately to save Aubrey's life.

I do not know how I could have stood the horror of losing my beloved brother without Mojag. Yesterday when Aubrey breathed his last, Mojag took me outside and pointed to a great spruce tree outside the camp. He said these Indians believe the great spruce communicates with the Master of all life. The tree symbolizes the sisterhood of all people, while the roots represent the five tribes that make up the Iroquoian confederacy.

"Just as the tree lifts your eyes to heaven," he told me, his words falling like healing rain upon my broken heart, "know that a man's death brings him closer to God. Your brother was a Christian, and today his soul is higher than the treetops, for it is with God."

While Mojag spoke, the elders of the tribe came round to wrap Aubrey's body in deerskins. They sang, chanted, and prayed over him while the women placed furs around my shoulders and comforted me. And then Mojag took my hand. We led the procession through the village, then took Aubrey's fragile earthly shell into the forest and left him upon a platform, sleeping forever beneath the spruce trees and the heavenly stars.

As we walked back to the camp, I must confess that I wept bitterly, feeling forsaken, fragile, and frightened. But Mojag drew me under his arm as a mother hen gathers her chicks, and I was comforted.

Several weeks passed without an entry; then Babette resumed writing.

December 10

I have hardly been able to bring myself to write since poor Aubrey's death. In past weeks I have lost my brother and my betrothed, but life here amongst the Red Men has taught me that the Scriptures are true: Life is but a fleeting vapor. Since I have lost the two men I loved, the Indians have lost five of their number—one young boy was mauled by a very big bear. Another died as he slid from his mother's womb. One of the elders lay down in his house and gave up the ghost while the others chanted around him, and two warriors have disappeared in the woods. Mojag fears these two have met with some mischief from trappers or another tribe.

And what shall I say of Mojag? I know as certainly as

I live and breathe that God sent him to these people, for he has brought the light of the gospel into a dark and heathen world. Their worship is unlike anything I have ever seen in one of our stone churches, but many of them speak of the Great Spirit and his Son who died. Upon their deathbeds, they do not trust in their works or good natures but in the Son of God. If that is not true faith, what is? They do not all have faith—no more than all the men in New France walk close to God. But many of them do.

And I am beginning to believe that as God has brought Mojag to these people, surely he has brought me to Mojag. Feeling so bereft myself, I never dreamed that such a capable and godly man might feel lonely until Mojag confessed that truth to me. At midday, while we sat outside under an empty pewter sky, Mojag confessed that he had loved but one woman in his life but lately had begun to love another. I smiled and tried to guess which of the Indian women had captured his affection, but he took my hand and said, "Upon my honor, Babette Fortier, I speak of you."

I could not answer—what could I say? I owed my life to him and probably my peace of mind and spirit. In this foreign place I would have been helpless and completely frightened without him, but he has sheltered me and brought me peace.

Frightened, I looked up—his entire aspect seemed to be filled with waiting. I felt my cheeks burning even in the cold, and then his rough hand cupped my cheek and his face drew nearer to mine. "Babette Dominique Fortier," he whispered, heartrending tenderness in his gaze, "do you think God could lead you to marry me?"

My lips could frame only one answer: Yes. My mind did not pause to consider my father, my home in Montreal, Pierre's parents, or anything of my past life. Those things are a limb that has been cut off; they are only a distant memory. My mind, my heart, my soul are filled with Mojag alone, and I trembled as I gave him my answer and a kiss.

With the Indians there is little ceremony about such common things as marriage. Certain of my willingness and my heart, Mojag took my hand and led me into the center of the camp. Drawing me to his side, he announced in a loud voice that I had consented to become his woman before God (at least such was the effect of his words—I understood little of it, but the Indians had the clear idea). The tribe gathered around—some coming out of their longhouses and others looking up from their cook fires. We stood in a circle of warm smiles. The sachem, an elder with a most benevolent aspect, stepped forward and chanted a blessing in our honor; then Mojag turned to face me and took both my hands in his.

"I am a minister of the gospel," he said in English, watching me intently. "And before my Creator and Lord, I promise to love you until death separates us. I will honor you with all my body and mind and soul. I will defend you, provide for you, protect you, shelter you from wind and rain and cold."

He then took a ring from his finger, a simple gold band, and slid it over my finger. "This ring has symbolized the union between many of my people," he said, his gaze locked to mine. "It is inscribed with the Latin words *fortiter, fideliter, feliciter*—boldly, faithfully, successfully. In all these ways I will be true to you. Until death separates us, Babette Fortier Bailie, I will be loyal to you and I will love you."

I was not certain how to respond, but I drew a deep breath and tried to echo the sentiments he had expressed. "Mojag Bailie," I said, studying his lean, dark face, "I promise to love you always, until my dying day. I will be true to you and love you until I draw my last breath."

And there in the center of the camp, before the bright
and smiling eyes of the Oneida, Mojag drew me into his
arms and kissed me. Though it may be immodest to
record and scandalous to read, honesty compels me to
write that his kiss left me weak, confused, and happy,
buffeted by the winds of a savage harmony.

While the Oneida yipped and howled in celebration,
Mojag took my hand and led me back to the longhouse
we would now share as husband and wife.

Rachelle sat back in her chair and smiled as a warm glow
flowed through her. Her mother truly had been married! Though
Bertrand Fortier had never openly disapproved of Mr. Bailie,
Rachelle had heard scorn in his voice every time he pronounced
the man's name. But her mother and Mojag had truly loved one
another. Though this marriage had taken place in the wilderness,
they had traded vows before witnesses, one another, and God.
What could be more honorable?

The next several pages were scrawled with the delirious
ramblings of a love-struck newlywed. Babette wrote of loving
her husband's handsome face and thick black hair, of his skill
with a knife, his wisdom, his gentle strength and power. She
described their daily routine in the village. Every morning she
rose early to help the women prepare a morning meal while
Mojag dressed in buckskin and went out to check the snares
and traps outside the camp. And then, later in the day, while
the elders and the unmarried youths gathered around the fire
to exchange stories and gossip, Mojag and Babette shyly
retreated to their house. There they reveled in the delights of
love and the sheer miracle that they had found love and each
other in the wilderness.

March 29—late winter

Oh, I am so lonely! A great sourness has filled the pit of
my stomach, for Mojag has gone with a group of hunters

to look for deer. He says the leaves will burst forth from the trees soon and the deer will be harder to find. So the tribe prepares for a great feast when the hunters return, and soon I must go outside and help the women prepare the herbs for cooking.

I do not feel quite so alone as I might have, though. A group of French trappers has descended upon us from the lake region. They brought whiskey to share with the Indian men—abominable stuff, and I fear for our warriors when they drink it. Mojag has warned the Oneida about the evils of liquor, and he told the trappers that our men are unused to it and therefore susceptible to its dizzying effects. But the Frenchmen laughed and offered the sachem a bottle, and 'twould have been inhospitable of him to refuse the gift. Mojag watched, standing as tense and quivering as a bowstring just fired, but his voice was calm as he rebuked the trappers for bringing whiskey.

I have not drunk of the whiskey, but lately I am feeling as dizzied as if my water were laced with spirits. Oh, how can I write what is on my heart? I fear I have not counted the cost of my marriage, but Mojag would not understand my feelings. Sometimes I am a little afraid of him—not that he would hurt me, for I know he would not, but I fear the powerful potential of his love. Tonight he was angry with the trappers about the whiskey, and his eyes burned with fire so bright I felt a shiver pass down my spine. He is such a man. . . . I cannot bully him, I cannot control him, but what frightens me most is the knowledge that I could hurt him.

And how he could hurt me! He often goes out hunting with the men, and yet sometimes they do not return—or they return bearing the scars of a bear or other fierce creature. What if he goes away and does not come back? How could I live if I lost him? I would be

left here, a stranger among strange people, with no one
to call my own.

I have asked him if we might live in Montreal some-
day, and he quietly told me that his place is with the
Indians. He used to live among white men, he says, and
was so sickened by their attitudes and ignorance of the
Red Men that he abandoned their company forever.

And yet my sleep of late has been troubled by images
of Pierre and Aubrey and Papa. They are weeping for
me, shedding tears for the life I forfeited in a moment of
reckless passion, for the books I will never read again,
the harpsichord I will never again touch, the banquet
table where my chair stands empty. I see Papa in my
dreams nearly every night, and an aura of melancholy
radiates from his pale and noble features.

What have I done? I have married in haste—shall I
repent at leisure? I feel like Lot's wife, who turned to
look back and changed into a pillar of salt. Perhaps I am
the farmer who put his hand to the plow and cannot
complete the furrow. To confuse me further, one of the
trappers pulled me aside today and asked if I wanted to
journey away with them. I am sure he thinks it odd that
a civilized white woman would desire to remain among
savages, but he does not know Mojag. . . .

April 5

What shall I say? My life has become a bitter battle.
Tomorrow the trappers are leaving, and I have secretly
planned to go with them. Mojag will be heartbroken, but
I have come to believe we were wrong to allow passion
to rule uppermost in our minds. He is a godly man and
a virtuous one, and I shall probably be stricken with
divine punishment for deserting him.

I promised to love him until I died. I promised to be
true. But I did not promise to live in the woods and sleep

in flea-ridden skins in a house frequented by Indian curs and stray children. Tonight I shall love him well and hold him close through the night so he will know my love is true. My spirit is indeed willing, but my flesh is false. May God strike me for it—I shall answer to him alone.

"Mademoiselle Rachelle?"

Lifting her gaze from the journal, Rachelle came back to reality, blinking in surprise as Virtue's voice and the objects in the room reminded her where she was. The maid dropped a curtsey from where she stood in the doorway.

"Begging your pardon, mademoiselle, but Mr. Wragg and his son are waiting in the parlor. Will you receive them?"

"Receive Lanston?" Rachelle shook her head, scattering the intriguing images of her mother's surprising past. "*Oui, bien sûr.* Please tell them I'll be right down."

Virtue nodded and stepped away. Rachelle closed the journal, then dropped it back into its former hiding place. Ceaseless inward questions whirled in her brain— she had always heard that the Reverend Bailie died in the Indian camp, but unless he had died later, Babette had lied. Why? And why had her mother abandoned Mojag Bailie if she loved him so deeply? Was love not enough to ensure a happy marriage? That thought had barely crossed her mind before another followed: Had her mother ever regretted leaving her husband?

"*Non de nom,*" she whispered, standing. "So much to think about!" She had never before considered that love might be a complicated matter. Marriage had seemed simple enough to her—she met Lanston; she liked him; she felt her heart flutter when he took her hand and pressed his lips to her palm. All the potentially tricky matters of dowry and money and housing would be settled between Lanston's parents and her grandfather, so she hadn't even bothered to consider those details.

But now she had to contemplate another issue before she

could stand beside Lanston Wragg and promise to be faithful unto death. She would have to be certain she could tolerate whatever lifestyle he planned for them. She would have to count the cost. By her own admission her mother had failed to do so, and so had made a mistake.

Rachelle paused before her mother's looking glass and gave her reflection a quick glance, pinching the high ridge of her cheeks to restore the rosy glow that had vanished in the last hour. Her black mourning gown did nothing to enhance either her complexion or her figure, but she was not shopping for a husband. She would soon have one—a wonderful young man who planned to build her a fine house and provide for her every need. She and Lanston had been born to the same lifestyle. Unlike her parents, Rachelle and Lanston were well suited for one another.

She hesitated at the doorway, her hand on the smooth knob. Should she tell Lanston what she had discovered? A wife should have no secrets from her husband, so perhaps she should tell him. But his father was another matter. Ashton Wragg would probably be horrified to hear that Babette Fortier had married amid the squalor of an Indian camp and then abandoned her husband. He might even suspect that marital unfaithfulness ran in the family.

Better to conceal the truth, at least for now.

Lifting her chin, Rachelle stepped out into the silent hall and went downstairs to greet her guests.

▼▲▼▲▼ "Make your case plainly. Do not dither about it," Ashton Wragg told his son. He sat back in his chair, a frown puckering the skin between his dark eyes into fine wrinkles. "The girl's mother is dead, and Rachelle is now the old man's only heir. So if the marriage takes place while his heart is still soft with grief, he may double or triple the dowry he originally intended to bestow."

"I am more than happy, Father, to move the wedding date forward." Lanston's sharp eye roved over every item of bric-a-brac in the parlor. Like most wealthy women, Babette had decorated the room with accessories that brazenly called attention to their costliness. His gaze swept over the room with approval, then returned to his father. "But women can be difficult about such things. She will want to mourn her mother. She may want to assemble a trousseau. And I have promised to build her a home before the wedding."

"I'll purchase a lot before the week is out," Ashton answered, his voice heavy with irritation. "And I'll speak to Fortier. In his present state he can't be thinking clearly—the old fool was besot-ted with the dead daughter. I hope he will be agreeable, but there is no predicting what his mood will be."

"He's always been most polite to me," Lanston said, shrug-ging.

His father gave him a quick warning glance. "Be careful, Son. A Frenchman will be polite until he is angry enough to kill you. Then, for the least little offense, he'll call you out and shoot you dead."

At the sound of footsteps, Lanston stood and turned. The black maid opened the door; then Rachelle entered, her pale beauty momentarily causing a crisis in Lanston's vocabulary. The black silk of her mourning gown heightened the golden translucence of her face and neck, and Lanston drew in his breath, wishing for an instant that he might skip the marriage ceremony altogether and take her in his arms immediately.

At last he found his voice. "Rachelle, my dearest!" Aware of his father's critical gaze, Lanston took her hand and gently planted a chaste kiss upon her knuckles.

His father stood, twirling his hat in his hand, then cleared his throat. "Mistress Rachelle, my son and I have come again to express our sincere condolences. Your mother was a charming woman, and our hearts are broken with yours."

Rachelle's lovely face darkened with unreadable emotions, but she lowered her head and cast a quick glance at Lanston's father. "Thank you very much, Mr. Wragg," she murmured, blushing prettily. "My grandfather and I could not begin to thank you for your kindness over these past few months."

"Actually, you could," Ashton answered. "Let my son explain."

Lanston felt his father's prodding gaze upon him again, and he steeled himself against it.

"I believe Lanston has a request," Ashton went on blithely, "but if you'll excuse me, I'll let him speak with you privately. I have urgent business on the docks."

Rachelle's brows lifted in faint surprise, but she stepped back without a word, allowing Ashton Wragg to pass. As he moved through the doorway, Ashton fitted his hat over his wig, then turned and called out a last command: "Make your request, boy," he called, trying, as always, to manipulate his son like a puppet. "And make it well."

The parlor door clicked shut, and Rachelle turned to Lanston, her brow high and rounded. "You have a request?" she asked, a gentle softness in her voice.

"Only this." Lanston opened his arms to her. "Come to me, love, and let me comfort you."

For an instant her eyes widened in surprise; then she crossed the room and entered his embrace. Wrapping her arms about his waist, she rested her cheek upon the lapel of his frock coat. *"Excusez-moi,"* she whispered, clinging to him as if he were the only substantial structure in the room. "I'm sorry, Lanston, but I have experienced so many emotions this morning! I felt so melancholy when I awoke, and then I found the journal my mother kept while she was traveling in the northeast—"

"Shhh." Running his hand over the lustrous curls of her dark hair, Lanston quieted her, then lifted her chin and nodded toward the sofa. "Let us sit, all right? We will put all thoughts of the past away, for I wish to speak to you of the future."

She pulled away, a bit of uncertainty in her expression, but she took his hand and allowed him to draw her to his side on the sofa. He waited until she sat still and quiet beside him; then he released her hand and slipped a protective arm about her slender shoulders. Lanston saw that she had flushed at his touch and had trained her eyes upon the floral carpet at her feet.

"Rachelle," he said, injecting a note of compassion into his voice, "my father and I have been talking. After so much sorrow, why should you wait to know the fulfillment of joy? We would like to move up the date of our marriage. Why should we wait until October when we could be married in May—or even April? I know I have promised you a home, and you shall have one. I shall buy a lot next week. But we can live with my parents until our house is finished."

He placed a hand on her forearm, noting that her skin was cool and dry. "Rachelle," he murmured, staring at her until she blushed, "I love you. And I cannot bear to think of you alone here with no one to comfort you."

She tilted her head toward him, her eyes wide and seemingly far away. "I have *Grand-père*," she whispered, an inexplicable look of withdrawal falling upon her face. "And the servants. Fala is with me, and Virtue and Cookie—"

"Slaves are not family," Lanston interrupted, daring to take her hand. "And your grandfather has been living at Shadow Grove for weeks." Carefully he curled his hand until his fingers entwined with hers. "Slaves cannot comfort you like someone you love, for God did not give them human feelings."

She hastily drew her hand away. Lanston removed his hand to his knee, cursing his impatience. What had he done? He had moved too quickly; perhaps her mother's death had deadened the flame of desire. But he had felt its pulse within her; he had seen it sparking in her dark eyes. And any ember, no matter how long asleep, could be awakened to new life if prodded gently.

Ignoring her withdrawal, he drew her closer with the arm he had slipped around her shoulder. "Rachelle," he whispered, whimpering in pretended hurt. "I am to be your husband, and yet you draw away from me as if I were a monkey—"

"*Je suis désolée*," she whispered, managing a trembling smile. "I am sorry, Lanston. But I am a bit discomfited; my mother's journal has sorely affected me. She wrote of my father, things I have never heard—"

Lanston waved her words away. "Your father is dead and buried, so he is of no consequence."

"But he was Mama's great love," Rachelle went on, stubbornly lifting her chin. "And he was English, but—" She hesitated, then turned to him with two deep lines of worry between her eyes. "He worked with the Indians. What think you of that, Lanston?"

She seemed to want an answer, and from the serious expression on her face he knew she considered the question important.

"I think," he said, drawing her closer yet, "that you are worrying about nothing. Years ago everyone who came here had contact with the Indians, for this was a savage land without proper cities." He reached up to lightly finger a loose tendril of hair upon her cheek. "Association with the Indians does not mean your father was a savage, only that he lived in a savage time."

"I have reason to believe," she went on, a lovely musk-rose flush rising to her cheekbones, "that my mother deserted him. I had always thought him dead, but . . . what if he is not?"

The question abruptly broke his concentration on her beauty. What *if* her father still lived? There was no risk, surely, as long as the man remained in the northern colonies. But if he somehow discovered that his daughter was the sole heir to the greatest fortune in the richest colony of the Americas . . .

"Your father," he said, his voice cold and exact, "is a devil and deserves nothing of your love or your thoughts. Don't even think of him, Rachelle. Wherever he is, dead or alive, let him rot."

Her face twisted in an expression of horror. "But my mother loved him! I read her own words. She said he was an honorable and godly man!"

"If he was honorable," Lanston went on, bending closer to look her directly in the eye, "then why did he let your mother leave, and her with child? Why didn't he follow her? Search for her? Go to the ends of the earth, if necessary, until he found her?"

He took her hand and held it tightly, feeling her pulse race at the commanding pressure. "If he had loved her as I love you,

Rachelle, he would never have let her go. If you were to disappear tomorrow, I would follow you to hell and back before I would give you up. Neither oceans nor savages nor poverty nor sickness nor pirates could keep me from your side."

A look of intense, clear light poured through her eyes, and he pulled her roughly, almost violently, to him, hoping the force of his embrace would convince her of the passion in his heart. He heard her gasp in surprise, then felt her arms slide willingly around his neck.

Ah, the flame was relit. "I would never let you go, Rachelle," he whispered into her tumbling hair, her breath hot against his cheek. Then, handling her as if he owned her already, he kissed the pulsing hollow at the base of her throat, certain he had won the point he had come to debate.

▼▲▼▲▼ Rachelle heard the front door close as Lanston left; then she slowly pushed herself up from the sofa, her hand going to the fevered flesh of her neck. Thus far in their courtship Lanston had behaved as the soul of propriety, but in that flash of an instant he had given her a glimpse of—what? Of the kind of passion her mother had shared with Mojag Bailie?

Somehow Rachelle didn't think so. Babette had written of feeling cherished and loved, and Lanston's kiss left Rachelle feeling . . . *conquered.* Passion aplenty burned in his eyes and in his lips, but after he kissed her he stood suddenly, bowed with the seriousness of a court attendant, and took himself away to the door.

Perhaps he had been embarrassed at his lack of restraint. Perhaps he had feared that one of the servants would walk in on the intimate moment. No—her mind rejected those suppositions. Lanston had been deliberate and careful in his movements, and they were betrothed. The servants might have been surprised, but they would never have been shocked at the sight of their mistress being kissed by her fiancé.

Moving slowly, like an old woman, she climbed the wide staircase and went back to her mother's room. The morning sun had abandoned the chamber, leaving it shadowed and cool, and Rachelle fumbled among the books again until she found the journal, then curled up in her mother's chair to read.

As much as she hated to admit it, Lanston's words had aroused certain suspicions. Why *hadn't* Mojag followed her mother when she left with the trappers? A man who loves a woman would not let her walk away without at least a confrontation.

Opening the book again, Rachelle skimmed the entries until she found her answer.

April 7

It is done. Though I have wept copious tears for the last half of the day, I have left the Oneida. Mojag will return from the woods and find the trappers and his wife gone.

Will God forgive me for this? I think not. I think I shall mourn until I draw my last breath, for Mojag is a good man and loving, and I am the weaker vessel who could not keep my promise to remain at his side.

I shall tell Papa about Pierre and Aubrey—I can tell God's truth about those two and feel no sorrow in my heart. And I can publish the news that I lived with the Indians for months and found my way home with the trappers. Perhaps Papa will be so pleased to have his daughter restored that he will ask no more questions.

But I shall wear mourning for Aubrey, Pierre, and Mojag . . . until my heart is no longer broken. And I shall not allow Papa to arrange another betrothal for me, for though I cannot tell him of my marriage, I have a husband. To marry another would be a sin in God's eyes.

Poor Mojag! He has done no wrong, and yet he will suffer grievously. If he would put on a coat and breeches and tie back his hair, if he would live in Montreal and travel to the Indian villages once a year, we could be happy. I did him a great injustice to marry him, but I was lonely and sorrowful. I was weak, and I am still weak, may God forgive me.

But do not think me completely heartless. Before leaving, I wrote Mojag a letter and confessed my terrible wrong. Though we have been married only a short while, I know him completely, and I fear he will risk his health and his life trying to find me again. So I piled another sin atop the ones I have committed thus far, and I lied to my husband. I told him I did not love him. I wrote that if he sought and found me, I would not return with him to the Indians no matter what he might say or do. I wrote that I married him only because I feared for my life in the Indian camp.

He is an honorable man, as I have said. And I know he will not follow me, for he is a gentleman and would not force his love upon a woman who will not have him.

May God forgive me for the wrong I have committed this day.

Rachelle pressed her hand to her throat as understanding dawned. Lanston had been right: A man who truly loved a woman would pursue her, and her mother had known that Mojag would not let her go unless she lied and denied the love that had brought them together.

"Mama, how could you?" Rachelle whispered, grief and despair tearing at her heart. If Babette had remained with Mojag, Rachelle would have known a *father*. She would know the sensation of climbing aboard a man's broad back and giggling in the wind, the touch of a father's proud eyes, the feel of velvet stubble of a daddy's beard beneath her questing fingertips. Growing up, she'd known none of those things.

Through *Grand-père* she'd learned about men's rough voices and their varying moods; she'd learned the scents of tobacco and alcohol and firearms. But Bertrand Fortier had never been a *father* to anyone but Babette.

The thought left her with an inexplicable feeling of emptiness, but she turned back to the journal, hoping she'd discover that her mother had at least experienced second thoughts.

Babette had continued to record entries as she traveled through the forest and arrived with the trappers at the outpost at Quebec. From the fort she was able to dispatch a letter to her father, and within the month Bertrand Fortier arrived to take his daughter home.

But by the time she arrived back in Montreal, Babette realized that she carried a child. And by the time her belly had begun to bulge through her chemise, her father had moved his household to the fledgling English settlement at Charles Towne. There, Babette wrote, she was quietly accepted as Mistress Bailie, the widow of an Englishman, the mother of a baby destined never to know an earthly father.

With growing fascination, Rachelle read of her own birth, her grandfather's insistence that the baby be sent away with a wet nurse until the time of weaning, and Babette's rejoicing when Rachelle finally came home. In an entry dated January 1, 1683, Babette had written:

> Now I am finally free to put off the clothes of mourning. For my darling daughter is home with me, and there is much of Mojag in her face and features. How I wish he could know that she lives and bears his name! But as much as I still love him, I would not allow her to go to the Indians to live with him, nor would I join him there. And so I must remain, selfish and false, until my dying day.

One page remained, and water sprang up in Rachelle's eyes as she read it.

> If God has been merciful and I have been granted a death at home in my bed, surrounded by my loved ones, then it is you, Rachelle, who are reading this, for I would willingly entrust this journal to no one else. If you are

able, dear one, and if you are willing, find your father and make his acquaintance. Though I have kept you in ignorance of him for many years—however many, only God knows—I would like you to find him if you can.

He is a good man, Rachelle, most worthy of having a daughter like you. And if you find him, tell him that I have departed this life and that he is free to love another, if he so chooses. And then, dear daughter, allow him to know who you are so I can return the love I unfairly stole from him so long ago.

You should be proud of him—I know he will rejoice in you.

There is one final thing I must tell you, and I would have you remember it always. Do I regret my journey into the wilderness? Even though it cost me dearly—I lost Pierre and Aubrey—I cannot say that I regret one moment. God worked in the wilderness. He gathered in my loved ones . . . and he helped me find my heart.

I pray you will seek your father, *cherie* Rachelle. God will go with you if you do.

The journal ended there, and Rachelle sat in silence for a long time, her hand pressed to the yellowed pages, a world of strange and troubling thoughts skittering through her brain. She had a father—Mojag Bailie—who, if God was merciful, still lived somewhere in the wilds of the north. At one point in the history, her mother had written that Mojag worked with a Puritan minister, John Eliot, who lived in Roxbury, a small settlement outside of Boston. Eliot had ordained and supported Mojag in the early years of his work with the heathen tribes and was quite renowned in Massachusetts for his evangelical efforts with the praying Indians.

Rachelle pressed her fingers to her lips, an idea slowly germinating within her. It would not be hard to find the Reverend John Eliot in Roxbury, particularly if he was well known. Boston was the largest city in the colonies; ships regularly sailed from Charles Towne for that port.

It was a far-fetched and outlandish idea, but she *could* take Fala and journey to Boston alone. She could go before the wedding and take a few weeks to find her father. And after finding him, she would relay her mother's message. She might even give him the journal so he could understand her mother's reasoning and be comforted by the knowledge that she had never stopped loving him . . . or weeping for him.

Rachelle sighed softly. Her mother had been loving and faithful, but she had never been strong.

Pressing the journal to her chest, she wrapped her arms around it and wearily looked out the window. Gusts of winter wind blew through the street outside, rippling the puddles and shaking the rain from the trees. A journey north at this time of year would not be pleasant, and if Lanston truly wanted to be married as soon as April or May, she'd have to go right away.

If I want to find my father.

Did she want to find a perfect stranger who just happened to share her blood? One who might have another family of his own? A man who lived a lifestyle completely foreign to Rachelle's?

She let her head fall against the back of the chair, astonished again by the thought that her father, God willing, still lived. And he was an honorable man, one who knew how to love.

Rising slowly, Rachelle dropped the journal back into its hiding place, then moved out onto the piazza. Calling for Fala to bring her a shawl, she settled into a sheltered chair and watched the wind.

The Boar's Head Inn, the pub closest to the dock where the *Jacques* lay at anchor, buzzed with sailors, loaders, and merchants. In order to escape the briskly cold breeze, Trace Bettencourt stepped into the tavern, crinkling his nose at the mingled odors of beer and human sweat. Accustomed as he was to the wide expanse of the salt-scented sea, most crowded buildings proved distasteful to his eyes, his ears, and, most particularly, his nose.

Behind him, Trace heard his first mate snort in disgust.

"I'll fetch us two mugs, Captain," MacKinnon said, shouldering his way through the milling crowd. Trace turned, grateful that the big man was willing to venture into the mob, and spied an empty spot at a corner table. He walked stiffly toward it, aware that the crowd parted like the Red Sea as he approached.

"That's him—the pirate Bettencourt! His ship's crawling with armed Negroes!"

"Can he really intend to let them keep their blades?"

"The man's a fool—but I'd not be saying so to his face."

"I hear he's wanted for piracy—the Boston folks say they'll hang him if he shows his face in that port again."

Trace sank into the empty chair, gallantly pretending deafness to the comments around him. A moment later MacKinnon approached with two large pewter mugs and set them on the table with an attitude of grave dignity.

"'Tis the best they had, though I'll warrant the stuff in our cargo hold is finer," MacKinnon said by way of apology as he lowered his bulky frame into an empty chair. "But it's wet, and that's all that matters, aye, Captain?"

"Very good, Monsieur MacKinnon," Trace answered automat-

ically, his eyes strafing the gathering to be certain no red uniforms of His Majesty's Royal Navy were present. Though the
war was over, the buzzing rumors in the tavern just might tempt
an English loyalist to draw a sword and attempt a bit of valiant
stupidity. Trace had no doubt he could dispatch anyone who
tried to accost him, but he hadn't left the *Jacques* to fight. He
wanted a change, a brief respite from the duty of command, a
moment's peace. As much as possible, he wanted to relax.

He saw a flash of red in a Scotsman's plaid and another in the
bright gown of a strumpet, but no uniforms. Carefully, he
brought the mug to his lips and sipped the ale, dropping his
guard a bit. He'd spent the entire morning bargaining with tight-
fisted merchants along the wharf, and his money purse bulged
with more gold than it had carried in a long time. In addition, he
had bartered for several pounds of indigo. Those dusty dried
bricks would fetch a great price in England—if he could safely
unload it.

He let the warm ale run over his tongue, then made a face. It
was terrible stuff, meant more for deadening a man's senses than
imparting any sense of delight. *"Oui,* it's wet," he told
MacKinnon, setting his mug back down on the table.

A familiar voice caught his ear, and he turned his head in time
to see the slave merchant Lanston Wragg pinch the red-dressed
strumpet's petticoat. She squealed in pretended insult; then, as
her earrings swung back and forth in a gay rhythm, she leaned
over the table and whispered something in young Lanston's ear.
He laughed, his eyes slipping down to ogle the creamy expanse
of the woman's ample bosom. The man seated next to Lanston
placed a warning hand on his arm and jerked his thumb toward
the door.

Interested in spite of himself, Trace followed the man's gaze.
A graceful, elegant young woman had just entered the tavern,
and Trace recognized the expression of distaste on her face—he
had worn it himself a few moments before. She and her maid
hesitated upon the threshold as if uncertain about entering; then

her searching eyes fastened upon Lanston Wragg. Relief flooded her face, and her generous mouth lifted in a smile.

"Are you thinking, Captain, that we'll be sailing on tomorrow's tide?" MacKinnon asked, his voice hoarse in Trace's ear.

"Be silent for now, Monsieur MacKinnon," Trace answered quietly, crossing his arms while he kept his eyes locked on the fascinating tableau before him. Lanston had risen at the sight of the young woman, practically pushing the harlot out of the way as he hurried toward the tavern door. He took the woman's gloved hand with an ease that spoke of familiarity, then led her back to his table, which his companions had hastily vacated in order to make room. The Indian slave, Trace noticed, retreated to the wall just inside the front door, where several black men and women waited without a word, their faces wiped clean of expression. Like a line of statues, they stood as still as stone, awaiting their owners' pleasure.

"Monsieur MacKinnon," Trace said, glancing at his first mate for an instant, "you are from Scotland, no?"

"Of course, Captain, you ken that verra well."

"And you know the English?"

MacKinnon's voice hardened. "Better than I'd like to."

Trace lifted an eyebrow, then smiled in understanding. "I see. Well, if you know the English, do you think you are skilled enough to interpret the words of an Englishman across the room?"

"I beg your pardon, sir?"

Trace nodded toward Lanston and the woman. "Yonder sits the froward slave merchant who sought to take our men."

"Aye, I remember him." MacKinnon frowned. "What's he up to?"

"That, Monsieur MacKinnon, is what I'd like to know." Trace folded his hands. "An experiment, *s'il vous plaît*. What do you think our friend Mr. Wragg is telling the lady at yonder table? Keep in mind, Monsieur MacKinnon, that I just saw him pinch the hindquarters of the hussy in the corner."

"Ah." MacKinnon's eyes lit in comprehension. He leaned forward, his eyes intent upon the couple across the room. "Well, sir, obviously he's fond of this gentlewoman. Look how he's holding her hand and keeping his other arm across the back of the bench, as if to protect her."

"Yes." Trace lifted a brow. "Do go on."

The first mate frowned. "Well, she came here to tell him something verra important, 'cause the color has risen in her cheeks. She's a wee bit determined—see the lift of her chin? But he's having none of it. His shoulders are movin' as if in laughter, and unless I miss my guess, he'll be shakin' his head in a moment— there! Now he's rebutting whatever she said."

"I do believe you are correct, Monsieur MacKinnon," Trace drawled, lifting his mug again. "Keep watching, and tell me what you see."

He took a quick sip of the loathsome brew, then replaced the mug on the table, holding his gaze to it for a moment. He'd been gazing at the young woman with such concentration that a ghostly image of her loveliness still floated faintly across the surface of his vision. He wasn't certain why she had attracted his attention; perhaps it was her obvious gentility. In a rough tavern like this one, she stood out like a lightning bug against a black velvet sky.

The girl's image wavered against the dark ale, and Trace frowned. The image shouldn't have wavered—nor should the ale, for it had been firmly seated on the table, which neither he nor MacKinnon had moved. For a moment he felt as if he were at sea, where perpetual motion was the rule rather than the exception, but the tavern stood on firm land.

From the fireplace came the sharp sound of splintering wood. Trace turned quickly to investigate, but the fire burned steadily, the only sounds now the normal crackle and pop of flaring, fatty pine knots.

"Something wrong, Captain?" A trace of concern lined MacKinnon's voice. "You look like you've seen a wee ghostie."

"I'm fine, Monsieur MacKinnon," Trace answered, his tension slowly altering into relief. He lifted his gaze to Lanston and the young woman. She had fallen silent, and her faint smile held a touch of sadness.

Trace felt the corner of his mouth twist upward. He'd be sad, too, if he were sitting with Lanston Wragg.

"But, Mr. Wragg—," Rachelle protested, trying to make her point.

"Call me Lanston, please." His golden eyebrows arched mischievously. "After all, we're to be married in only two months."

"That's what I must discuss with you." Rachelle took a deep breath, preparing to launch again into the topic she'd come to address. It had taken nearly all her courage to venture into a disreputable dockside tavern, and she felt a little unsteady on her feet, owing to the fact that she'd scarcely slept the night before. Thoughts of her father and her mother's plea that Rachelle find him kept her awake until a faint glow low on the eastern horizon assured her that the sun would bring her an opportunity to locate Mojag Bailie.

"Lanston," she began again, "I'd be pleased to marry you anytime you wish, but there is something we must discuss first. I think I might like to travel to Boston."

"What on earth for?" His surprised expression held a note of mockery. "What does Boston have that Charles Towne does not?"

"Old family friends," she whispered, choosing her words carefully. "Friends of my mother's. It's only right that I visit and tell them of her death. She would want me to go, and as soon as possible."

Lanston frowned into his tankard. "Let your grandfather go for you. You are a bride. There is a wedding to plan. My mother says there will be at least a dozen balls in our honor—"

"Oh no!" Aghast, she abruptly pulled back from him. "No balls, no parties, not so soon after my mother's death! That would not be respectful." She cast her gaze downward. "And I haven't the heart for celebration right now."

Lanston observed her with a sweet, musing look. "I'm sorry, my dear. Of course I'll respect your feelings. But what matters more, public opinion or your own happiness? Why should you spend the next few months mourning your mother when you could spend that time preparing for our marriage?"

For an instant wistfulness stole into his expression. "I love you, Rachelle Fortier Bailie, and I want you to be my wife. I'd marry you tomorrow if I could. If your grandfather would allow it, today I'd carry you out of this tavern and into the church, then home to my father's house where we could be alone—"

Rachelle held up a hand to cut him off, glad of the semidarkness that hid the flush in her cheeks. Lanston had a tendency to turn the conversation toward matters of the flesh whenever she wanted to talk, and she knew he was no longer listening. She had followed him to a tavern because she urgently wanted to discuss the contents of Babette's journal, but Lanston's cavalier attitude convinced her that he could not be trusted with the entire truth. He seemed to think the matters troubling her heart were as trivial as a parrot's prattle.

"Lanston, I really think I ought to go to Boston." She tried to catch his eye, to make him understand, but he had picked up her hand and was now nibbling gently at her knuckles. "Lanston—"

A row of glasses fell from a shelf behind the bar, the loud crash triggering an oddly primitive warning in her brain.

▼▲▼▲▼ Trace jerked forward at the sound of breaking glass. "Monsieur MacKinnon, go at once to the ship," he commanded. He did not need to turn to be certain the first mate heard the order. Long experience had taught him that MacKinnon heard everything and obeyed instantly.

A murmur of voices and a palpable unease washed through the tavern, and Trace glanced toward the door. MacKinnon vanished through the opening in a blue blur, and another pair of seamen from the *Jacques* followed him, doubtless anxious to know why he'd left in such a rush. The slaves by the door looked at each other with wide eyes, and Trace silently willed them to run for their lives. The doorway was narrow, barely a yard across, and there was no way the hundred or so persons inside the tavern could exit in time.

"What the—?" the dim-witted barkeep shouted, scratching his head as he eyed the sprung shelf from which the glassware had spilled.

As if in answer, a row of pewter plates on another shelf began a slow rat-a-tat-tat, like the chattering of a skeleton's teeth. Trace slipped immediately to the floor and crouched beneath the table, his whole being concentrated in his ear for the sound of impending disaster.

Within a heartbeat, a ripping mayhem of noise made the very air vibrate. Trace heard the whip and snap of weathered timbers, the scraping of a picture tilting on the wall. The table above him bounced as if a giant had seized it in his hands; the mortared stones around the fireplace shot from the wall as if thrown by demons. As women screamed and men shouted, the crack of destruction ripped through the building like the thunder of war.

Those who could stand surged toward the door. Trace ducked as a shower of plaster, dirt, and wood rained down from the edge of the sheltering table, and through the confusion he saw Lanston Wragg take the lady's hand and pull her toward the mob at the door. *The fool.* The brick floor rippled and undulated as if a giant serpent writhed beneath the ground, and the resulting rise tripped Wragg so that he lost his balance and pitched forward. He released the girl's hand but barreled through the doorway on the momentum of his fall.

Left alone, the woman spun like a bewildered child in the midst of the surging crowd, her face a mask of horror. Fighting the panic rising in his brain, Trace rose on his hands and knees and launched himself forward, reaching out until he caught her arm, then unceremoniously pulled her through the press of people. When she stood next to the table, coughing and strangling on plaster dust, Trace grabbed her hand and crouched down, pulling her beneath his shelter.

"*Je m'excuse vous avoir dérangé,*" he murmured, scarcely aware of what he was saying.

"What?" she yelled, cringing as a huge timber from the roof creaked and fell onto the table. She screamed in earnest when another falling beam cracked a man on the head and sent him crashing to the floor at her feet, his face marred by a bloody gash.

Grasping her shoulders, Trace pulled her farther back under the heavy oak table. "I said I'm sorry for having disturbed you," he said, capturing her wide eyes with his. "But you were about to be knocked by the same beam that felled yonder drunk."

She ducked her head and screamed again as yet another timber broke and crashed downward in a cloud of dust and dirt. Trace gallantly fished a handkerchief out of his pocket and extended it to her. "With my compliments, mademoiselle," he said, breaking into an open, friendly smile. "It appears we will be sequestered under this table until the earth stops shaking."

She did not answer but looked at him with eyes as vulnerable as a baby's. After a moment woven of eternity, while the earth trembled and the Boar's Head Inn tumbled in upon itself, Trace lifted his head. The silence that ensued was like the hush after a thunderstorm, when the leaves hang limp in the quiet air and nature seems to catch her breath, but Trace knew the silence would not last. An injured man trapped near the door was beginning to moan, and above those low sounds Trace heard the steady crackle of flames hungry for the unexpected offering of weathered timber.

"Excuse me, mademoiselle," he said, leaning forward to crawl over the voluminous mound of her petticoats. A faint shower of white powder rained down upon his face, and he shifted his hat forward to catch the dust so he could see out from beneath the table. To his right, heavy timbers held a mound of dusty bodies in a death grip, blocking the opening that had once been a doorway. To his left, where stones had once framed the tavern's fireplace, greedy flames inched steadily forward, licking at the fallen timbers and devouring the spilled liquor. From where he stood he could hear a whispering, crackling noise as though the fire were talking to itself.

He extended his hand to the girl under the table. "Mademoiselle, we must be away at once."

"My maid," she whispered, her face pale with plaster dust.

"If she was near the door, she is likely waiting outside." Trace took her hand and drew her out forcibly. "I suggest we join her before this place goes up in flames." Struggling to find firm footing in the rubble, he glanced around, searching for a way of escape. The door was totally blocked, and there were no windows, but a patch of blue sky showed at a corner of the building where the roof had fallen away.

"Lanston." The girl turned toward a heap of rubble in the center of the room. "He's my betrothed."

"Mr. Wragg escaped." Trace drew his lips into a firm line. "I myself saw him slither out the doorway after he fell. You will find him outside."

The thickened air had begun to cloud with smoke, and Trace felt his eyes sting. Still holding tight to the girl's hand, he began to climb up and over shattered chairs and broken beams, testing each foothold to be sure it would support his weight, pulling his reluctant companion.

"Sir," she protested weakly, indicating her wide gown through a tangle of debris, "I cannot climb over tables and chairs in this gown. Perhaps I should sit and wait for help."

"You will come with me, mademoiselle, if you wish to live," Trace answered, pulling hard on her arm. She whimpered in a sharp exclamation of pain but did not protest. They stood only a few feet from the opening in the roof, but she would have to trust him if he were to hoist her upward.

"Mademoiselle," he turned to look her squarely in the eye, "I must lift you up. I trust you have no objection if I attempt to save your life?"

A blush burned through her pallor, but she did not flinch before the directness of his gaze. "I will trust you, sir," she whispered, moving closer to him. "I understand—and I will take no offense at whatever you may have to do."

He nodded, then let his eyes rove over her slender figure. She was small but not short, graceful and willowy in that ridiculous dress through which he would never gain a firm handhold. . . .

"The petticoat," he said, frowning. "You will have to remove it."

"Sir!" Her flush deepened to crimson. "I cannot. I am Bertrand Fortier's granddaughter, and I will not parade about the wharf in my pettipants—"

She bit her tongue, probably embarrassed that she had dared to speak of undergarments to a stranger. Ignoring her discomfiture, Trace looked up toward the roof, scarcely two feet away. "Leave on the petticoat, then, but remove that enormous farthingale," he said, placing his hands on her waist. He moved her forward until she stood in front of him. "Look up at the size of yonder hole, and consider the width of your hips in that contraption. Unless you remove that birdcage from beneath your petticoat, you will stick in the opening like a cork in a bottle, smothering me in the process."

She glanced behind her as if looking for some other chivalrous knight to defend her honor, but nothing moved below but the rapidly encroaching flames. "All right," she said, modestly lowering her head. He averted his eyes while she lifted her petticoat and jerked at some fastenings; then the whalebone-and-linen apparatus fell away.

"*Dieu merci!*" Trace breathed, fitting his hands around her waist again. The flames were much closer now. The smoke rose to clog his lungs, and the voice of the fire had grown from a whisper to a self-satisfied, chuckling roar. Refusing to look behind him, Trace lifted the girl toward the roof and heard her grapple for purchase on the rooftop.

"Test the tiles—make sure they will hold you," he called as he shoved her weight up and forward. Her booted feet disappeared through the opening, and an instant later he heard her triumphant cry. Sweat beaded in hundreds of tiny pearls on his skin, and he jumped upward, caught the edge of the roof, and hoisted himself up. An instant later, he saw her slide down the newly lowered roofline and land in a heap upon the ground, disheveled but apparently unhurt.

Following her example, Trace scooted down the tiles and jumped to the ground at her side. A crowd was scrabbling at the door, trying to dislodge timbers and bricks to rescue the men caught in the rubble. Lanston Wragg, if he searched for his betrothed at all, was undoubtedly among those at the door.

Trace turned to the girl and took advantage of the confusion outside to hold her in a silent scrutiny. A blush like a shadow ran over her cheeks, but she smiled and held up her arms as if to prove she remained in one piece. "I am quite all right, monsieur. And I must—"

"Mademoiselle Rachelle!"

She looked away, distracted. "Fala!"

Running forward from a knot of bystanders, the Indian maid took her mistress's arm and helped her stand upright. The young woman actually laughed as she wiped dust from her collapsed gown, her natural feminine form a thousand times more appealing than that artificial farthingale—

Abruptly reining in his thoughts, Trace stood and brushed himself off, grateful that he'd had the forethought to order MacKinnon back to the ship. A ship might ride out an earthquake with no damage, but if the dock to which it was tied toppled into the sea, a set of mooring ropes might well pull the ship onto its side.

"Sir?" The young woman stood before him now, blocking his path.

"Yes, mademoiselle?"

She gazed at him intently for a long moment, then stepped forward and gently took his hand with a lingering smile more warming than the feeble February sun. "My name is Rachelle Fortier Bailie, and I owe you my life. You are French, are you not?"

He stiffened, momentarily abashed at her display of gratitude. "*Oui*, mademoiselle, I once was. But we all belong to the colonies now, no?"

For an instant she wore a look of puzzlement; then her eyes cleared and she laughed. *"Oui*, monsieur, we belong to Carolina. But today you have saved my life, and my grandfather and I would be honored to offer you the hospitality of our home. If I might have your name?"

Her gentle, grateful tone made him flush in shame. She thought he was noble and honorable, someone she might bring home for dinner! This hothouse flower would not appreciate the man he truly was.

"Enchanté, Mademoiselle Bailie," he answered, bowing stiffly from the waist. "I am not unaware of the honor you have bestowed upon me by this introduction, but, gentle lady, I am afraid I will not remain in Charles Towne after today. You see, I am a seaman, and my ship sails tonight. But I thank you for your graciousness."

"But—" The gentle appearance was deceiving; she clung to his hand with the tenaciousness of a bulldog. "But you must allow me to show my gratitude!"

"Another time, perhaps," he answered, nodding formally. He caught the maid's dark glance before he moved away, and the Indian's impassive, knowing gaze gave him pause.

She knows, he thought. *And if she is any sort of guardian, she will take pains to keep her mistress away from me.*

Sighing, he moved away toward the docks, where the *Jacques* lay at anchor.

The earthquake that rocked Charles Towne on February 24, 1698, destroyed more than the Boar's Head Inn. Rachelle and Fala returned home to find the Fortier house in flames. The earthquake had shaken the house to its foundation, and the flames from fireplaces and lamps quickly set fire shadows to dancing upon the cracked walls of what had been the finest house in town. Virtue and Cookie had barely managed to escape with their lives.

After waking from the stupor into which he had been knocked by a blow from a falling tavern beam, Lanston walked to the Fortier mansion and collected his weeping fiancée and her servants. Mumbling through her tears, Rachelle kept murmuring that it was all gone, every trace of her mother, but Lanston shushed her with steady pats and gentle words. Lanston's father immediately dispatched a letter to Shadow Grove, but Bertrand Fortier sent word that as long as Rachelle was safely in Lanston's care, she could remain where she was. "If the house is gone," he scrawled across the bottom of the letter that returned to Ashton Wragg, "it is just as well. Babette is gone, too."

The Wragg home had been shaken, but the stout building rode out the quake with only minor damage. The slaves had already picked up the broken china and bric-a-brac by the time Lanston arrived with Rachelle and her servants, and Lanston noted the triumphant look in his father's eye when he announced that Rachelle had nowhere else to go.

Ashton Wragg promptly opened the guest rooms on the second floor, giving Rachelle the finest room at the front of the house. Once the shaken girl had been tucked into bed with

warm bricks and several comforting blankets, Lanston met his
father and mother downstairs in the drawing room. After assuring his mother that the knot on his head caused him little pain,
he sank into a chair by the fireplace and stared moodily at the
flames.

"This has been a terrible day for the city," Ashton said, pour-
ing himself a drink from a crystal decanter on the mantel, "but a
wonderful day for you, Son. What do they say—a bird in the
hand is worth two in the bush? And today we have welcomed
your bride into our house. The old man will doubtless remain on
his plantation until the town house can be rebuilt, so why
shouldn't Rachelle marry you now?"

"Propriety would seem to demand it," Cambria echoed from
the sofa where she reclined. She lifted an elegant hand toward
her son. "In a time of tragedy, the rules of society are easily bent
and forgiven. We can have the wedding here, in the drawing
room. The minister would be happy to perform it as soon as the
guests can be summoned."

"We should wait at least two months—no, one would do,"
Ashton said, cupping his hands around the crystal glass in his
grasp. "I will ride out and speak to Bertrand Fortier as soon as
the girl has sufficiently collected her wits." He drew his lips in
thoughtfully. "Perhaps I may even suggest that Bertrand rebuild
the burned-out house as a wedding gift to you and Rachelle. The
lot is superb, and the foundation already laid. I have slaves
aplenty to do the work and expect a new shipment from Barbados next week."

"Father." Lanston extended his hand. "Let me speak to
Rachelle. She is eager to wed, I know, but must be persuaded to
be wed so soon." He tented his hands at his waist. "She still
mourns her mother, and today she kept insisting that she must
travel to Boston."

"Of course. The girl wants a trousseau," Cambria spoke up,
her voice dry. "Everything she owned was lost in the fire. She is
a proud little thing, and evidently our Charles Towne merchants
cannot satisfy her. Well, if she wants to go to Boston, let her go

next week." She waved her hand and managed a tremulous smile. "I'd go with her myself, the darling, but my frail constitution could not stand the trip. With one look at those waves—" She pressed her fingers to the bridge of her nose and shuddered slightly.

"No, Mother, I would not expect you to go." Lanston reached toward the sofa and took his mother's frail hand in his own. "I will go with her myself. I'll let her shop or do whatever she wants to do; then I'll bring her home for the wedding." He tossed a grin toward his father. "Surely by then you will have her grandfather's approval."

Ashton lifted his glass in salute. "Give me the old man, a week, and a bottle of rum, and I could have Bertrand Fortier agreeing to anything."

▼▲▼▲▼ "Marry so soon?" Rachelle grasped the porch railing to steady herself, so shocked was she by Lanston's announcement that they would marry as soon as she returned from Boston. "Lanston, I don't think you understand."

"I understand that I love you," he answered, sinking into a chair on the wide piazza. He crossed his legs and folded his arms at his waist. "And the sooner we are married, the better off we will all be. Your grandfather has so much on his mind since the tragedy of the earthquake. Why not relieve him of the burden of caring for you?"

Rachelle stared wordlessly out at the gardens. The bright, sharp morning air was wind-whipped and bitter cold, but she thought the chilly piazza a great deal more comforting than the oppressive atmosphere inside the Wraggs' house. She had never thought of herself as a *burden*, but perhaps Lanston was right. If her presence was burdensome, a journey to Boston might relieve her grandfather, the Wraggs, and Lanston, too. She would move out of the way and let them make their plans while she sought her father.

"Lanston," she began, knowing she could not forever postpone telling him the truth, "I have not fully explained why I want to go to Boston."

He lifted his index finger, interrupting. "Mother says you need to shop for a trousseau. I'm sure the sempstresses of Boston are quite skilled, so you may gather whatever you need. And do not worry about money." He smiled indulgently at her, like a parent amused by the worries of his child. "I know your grandfather lost his house, and you lost everything. Whatever you need, I will provide."

"I'm not interested in Boston dressmakers." She turned and leaned on the rail, flattening her palms against the dark silk everyday gown Mrs. Wragg had been generous enough to provide for her. If his parents wanted to believe she preferred to shop in Boston, she would let them, but as her future husband, Lanston deserved the truth.

"Lanston, I'd like to find my father. I believe he may still be alive, and if he is, I would like to know him before I marry." She gave him a one-sided smile. "Perhaps we could invite him to the wedding."

Her eyes clung to his, waiting for his reaction, which followed swiftly. "Your father?" His eyebrow arched in humorous surprise. "We have discussed this before, Rachelle. Your father is dead. If he is not, he ought to be dead to you. You owe him nothing."

"I think I may owe him . . . a lot." She looked away, casting about for a way to help him understand without divulging too many of her mother's secrets. Babette Bailie had suffered enough in life; there was no need to tarnish her reputation now that she lay in the grave.

"My father," she began, slowly searching for the right words, "was involved in missionary work on the uncivilized frontier, and my mother did not care for the roughness of that life. She left him a few months after their marriage. To spare my grandfather's feelings, she told him—she told all of us—that her husband, Mr. Bailie, had died. But it was not the truth."

Lanston's lips twisted into a cynical smile. "How do you

know she lied? That was many years ago, Rachelle, and the frontier is far away."

"She told me about her journal the day she died." Rachelle swallowed hard, hot tears springing to her eyes. "And when I read it, I learned that Mr. Bailie was alive when she left him. He worked for a clergyman who lived in Roxbury, a town outside Boston. Mama bade me find my father. She wanted me to tell him of her death and give him her apologies."

"Well." Lanston thumped the arms of his chair, his brows pulling into an affronted frown. "Can this not wait? We could be married and take a voyage together."

"No." She felt a momentary panic as her mind filled with visions of what she might discover in Boston. She could not tell Lanston that she suspected her father was Indian, for then he would run from her as if she had the pox. But there was always a chance that her mother had been confused, that Mojag Bailie was truly an Englishman and that Rachelle's lineage was pure enough to be joined in a holy marriage with a civilized man.

"This is something I want to do alone." She turned again toward the winter-bare garden, unwilling to face the denial upon his face. "I know that what I am suggesting is unusual, but I will ask *Grand-père* and Fala to go with me. 'Twould not be fair to detain you, for if I find my father I may want to spend a few weeks with him. After all, he knows nothing of me, and I want to learn all I can about him."

"This is crazy, Rachelle." Lanston sounded as if he were strangling on repressed epithets. "You cannot go to Boston with only an old man and an Indian slave. If your mother wrote the truth— which is surely a point of debate—this man could still be living among the savages. Are you up to a journey into the wilderness? You are as innocent as an angel. Do you really believe you can manage such a journey? How do you intend to find this man? And what will you do with him once you find him?"

"I don't know!" she cried, flashing into sudden fury as she whirled round to face him. "But I have to try!" She gulped down her anger, trying to control herself, but her chin quivered and her eyes filled in spite of her efforts. "Lanston, you *know* your father. You have a mother. And now I have no one but *Grand-père*. My mother gave me a precious gift before she died, and now that I have no home and no mother, I want to find my father!"

"Your father has done nothing for you. He means nothing to you, and you mean nothing to him." Lanston's blue eyes darkened like angry thunderclouds. "Forget the past; forget him. What could knowing your father possibly do for you?"

"That," she said, turning away from him again, "is what I must discover."

▼▲▼▲▼ A week later, Bertrand Fortier paced in the Wraggs' splendid drawing room, carefully eyeing the expensive carpets, the imported chandelier, and the hand-painted wall coverings. Everything in this house, as in his, had been selected and designed to impress the visitor with the owners' wealth, but what did it all matter? The two-headed monster of earthquake and fire had devoured his precious possessions, and suddenly Bertrand Fortier found himself virtually naked in Charles Towne, stripped of his fine house, his glorious possessions, and even his beautiful daughter. Of course, he still held a prosperous rice plantation, one hundred slaves, and a fortune safely deposited in the Bank of England. He also had a granddaughter, but that girl was a stranger to him, as remote as a time before birth.

It was on Rachelle's account that he had returned to Charles Towne. Three days before, she had written to him with an unexpected request—she wanted to visit Boston, she said, before she married. "Of course, *Grand-père*," she had written, her hand spidery and delicate on the page, "I want you to come with me. A trip would be good for you, would take your mind off things here. You can appoint an overseer to rebuild the town house, and by the time we return it should be well under way."

"Boston?" he had muttered stupidly after reading her letter. Since Babette's death he often felt that half his brain lay somnolent and heavy under the effect of strong grief. But Boston struck a familiar chord in his memory; he had visited the place and liked it in his younger days, when Aubrey and Babette were still children.

"*Grand-père*, it is good to see you!" Rachelle's face was pink with eagerness as she stepped into the drawing room and smiled a welcome. As direct as a bullet, she came toward him. "Shall I arrange our trip, then?" she whispered, standing on tiptoe so the words flew to his ears alone. "We will take Fala and Friday on the boat with us. Fala and I will shop in Boston while you look up old friends."

Bertrand shrugged. He did not know that many of his friends remained in Boston, but it would be a blessed relief to leave Charles Towne; the town held nothing but bitter memories for him now.

"I'll arrange it, then." Rachelle reached out to pat his shoulder, the rustle of her gown painfully reminding him of Babette; then a fingertip of her dainty hand gently traced the line of his jaw. The look on her face mingled eagerness and tenderness. "Dear *Grand-père*, things will be better soon. I promise."

Without another word she turned and disappeared into the hall, her light tread mocking his memories of Babette. Bertrand closed his eyes against the welling grief in his heart and fought hard against the tears he refused to let fall.

▼▲▼▲▼ "Fala!"

With a cold chamber pot in her arms, Fala stiffened at the excited tremor in Rachelle's voice. A moment later her mistress entered the Wraggs' guest chamber, her eyes bright as clear black glass.

"Yes, mademoiselle?" Fala asked, looking up. Rachelle had not been herself these last few days, and Fala suspected there was more to Rachelle's uneasiness than the obvious explanation of disaster. Though the earthquake had been a traumatic experience for Fala and Rachelle, so many people in Charles Towne had been left homeless and bereft that the Fortiers were blessed by comparison. The plantation house had not been damaged, they still had slaves to care for them, and they had friends willing to extend hospitality.

"Fala, put that pot down. I need you to pack two trunks and a valise," Rachelle said, stepping into the room. She pressed her index fingers to her lips, thinking. "Warm clothing, I think, but simple. My riding boots. And *Grand-père* will need a trunk. Tell Friday to pack his best frock coat—"

"Mademoiselle—" Fala lowered the chamber pot and turned toward her mistress, daring to interrupt—"your riding boots are gone. Everything is gone in the fire."

Rachelle swatted Fala's protest away. "Fine, we shall not need much. We will take valises only, with a change of clothing. 'Tis better if we travel with few encumbrances. We may have to venture into the wilderness."

A bubbling excitement rose in Fala's chest. "Travel, Mademoiselle Rachelle?"

"We're going to Boston." Rachelle laughed in sheer joy, then reached out and took Fala's hands. "You are to go down to the wharf this afternoon, Fala, and find a ship bound for Boston. We'll want to leave immediately; tomorrow is not too soon. Find a ship with room for a gentleman and his granddaughter, and two slaves, of course."

"I am going with you?" Fala burst out, shocked. She had not been outside Charles Towne since before Bertrand Fortier bought her at the slave auction on Chalmers Street.

"But of course!" Rachelle's smile was eager and alive with delight. "Have you ever been away from me?" She released Fala's hand and pointed toward the door. "Now you have an errand to run. Go to the wharf; see to our journey."

"The wharf?" Fala's delight vanished, replaced by a sense of unease that gelled in the pit of her stomach. "Mademoiselle Rachelle, I can't go down there alone. They'll think I'm a runaway. I've heard stories about slaves being picked up at the docks and taken to the Indies for sale."

Rachelle looked up, her eyes flashing with quick anger, but

after an instant they calmed. "You're right." She crossed her arms and tapped her toe, thinking. "All right, take *Grand-père*'s Indian slave with you—he's returned from the plantation. You'll find him with Friday out at the slave quarters. And I'll write a letter explaining your errand so no one will accuse you of running away." She walked to the small desk in the corner, pulled a sheet of parchment from the drawer, and sat down to scratch out a message.

Fala hesitated, her mind reeling. This demand was totally unexpected and quite unlike Mademoiselle Rachelle. Women did not go about in public without an attendant, preferably a male escort, but last week Rachelle had bade Fala accompany her to that tavern to speak with Mr. Wragg, and now she wanted Fala to go to the wharf with only Dustu as her guide.

"Fala, *je suis pressée*, move along! I want to leave Charles Towne as soon as possible!"

Spurred to action by the sharp tone in her mistress's voice, Fala turned and moved through the doorway, her heart in her throat.

▾▲▾▲ They found a Boston-bound ship without too much difficulty, though more than one man lifted a suspicious brow at the sight of two Indians moving freely about the wharf. Fala had to present Rachelle's letter to the harbormaster before he would give her the information she desired, but at last she learned that the *Fitz James*, captained by Henry Lodge, would be sailing for Boston on the morrow.

"Has the captain room for four passengers?" Fala asked, wiping her hands over her petticoat. She had hoped that her neat gown, apron, and cap might assure the man of her civility, but he stared instead at Dustu, who bore a look of savage wildness even in canvas pants, stockings, and a frilled shirt.

The harbormaster checked the passenger list for the *Fitz James*. "Four?" he asked, crinkling his nose. "I'm not certain. So many are fleeing northward on account of the earthquake. Captain

Lodge has a full complement of passengers, but if these are people of influence—"

"Two people of influence," Fala interjected, feeling the burn of a blush upon her cheek. "And two slaves."

"Well now, that'd be different." The master lowered the parchment to his desk and scowled at her. "I thought you said four *passengers*. There's always room for slaves—they ride below in the cargo hold."

Fala breathed an exasperated sigh. "My mistress begs you to add her and her grandfather to the passenger list." She spoke softly, her voice as tattered as her nerves. "Monsieur Bertrand Fortier and Mademoiselle Rachelle Bailie."

"Ah! Monsieur Fortier! Of course we will find a place for *him*," the master said, the tip of his quill pen driving furiously across the page. "So be it. Tell the honorable Monsieur Fortier and his party to arrive early upon the docks. Captain Lodge will sail before noon, I expect."

Fala nodded and turned to leave, holding out her hand as a sign that Dustu should follow. She did not dare look back, but she had the uneasy feeling he had remained in his place to glare at the harbormaster. Though his English was not quick enough to grasp all that had occurred in the office, she was certain his intuitive nature had enabled him to discern the gist of the exchange.

The afternoon was asleep under a clouded molasses-colored sky, the air heavy with impending rain. The two slaves walked for five minutes without speaking, silently dodging seamen, slaves, and worried merchants; then Fala deliberately walked past the tall marble statues that marked the carriage entrance to the Wraggs' house. If Dustu noticed her mistake, he gave no sign of it but remained doggedly at her side, his rugged face like stone above her.

Fala turned the corner, willing to walk a few moments more in the hope that she could speak to Dustu. Because he'd been out at the plantation with the master, she had seen him only twice since that dreadful night when they had both been whipped.

Guilt still hung like a cloud over her, threatening to choke off her words before they would come. The whipping had been her fault—if she hadn't spoken to the Wraggs' cook, that horrid Devin Garr would never have been dispatched to the Fortiers' house.

But how could she begin the conversation? How could she help him cope with his new situation? She had been living with the Fortiers for years; she knew them better than they knew themselves. But Dustu was still a stranger to the people he served and was hampered by the bitter pride dwelling inside him.

As they passed the small building where the French Huguenots worshiped, Fala grasped Dustu's arm and pointed toward the church.

"The Fortiers go there to worship the Great Spirit," she said, noticing that his muscles tensed under her fingertips.

An expression of surprise flitted across his chiseled face. "The Great Spirit listens to them?"

Fala tilted her head and nodded. "They believe he does. They call him God the Father and tell of how he sent his Son, Jesus, to earth. But evil men captured Jesus, bound him, and beat him." She caught sight of the small wooden cross above the door and pointed to it. "And then the Son of God died upon a tree."

Dustu grunted as he studied the cross. "If they enslaved God's Son, why does he still hear them? I would not listen to people who did that to a child of mine."

His question hammered at her, and Fala hesitated, not certain how to explain the God she herself had accepted but did not fully understand. "He loves them anyway," she said simply, pulling her cloak more closely about her as a sudden gust of wind blew down the street.

They walked a few moments more, turning up the block that would bring them again to the Wraggs' house. Time was short. She must speak, but what could she say? Suddenly she whirled, blocking Dustu's path, and lifted her hand. Reaching up, she touched his cheek, his skin cold beneath her fingertips.

"Brother," she said, "Mademoiselle Rachelle and I are going away. Master Fortier will leave his slaves in the hands of his overseer, so you will be returned to the rice house." She looked up at him with an effort. "The overseer is not a gentle man."

Dustu's jet black eyes regarded her impassively.

"Friend," she went on, angry with herself for feeling helpless, "we may be gone for many days, but promise me you will not run away. I know the work at the rice plantation is difficult, and I know the woods will whisper your name. But if you want to see your wife and son again, do not run. I speak this warning as a friend, as a sister."

His dark eyes took her in, reflecting glimmers of light. "Why do you tell me this?" His voice was velvet, yet edged with steel.

Fala's blood pounded, her face grew hot with humiliation. "Master Fortier," she whispered, "bought you for me. He thinks we are like animals, that we will have young ones."

A flash of cold filled his eyes, and a dark flush mantled his cheeks. "I have a woman," he said simply.

"I know," Fala whispered, fighting a momentary surge of jealousy. In this respect, he was more fortunate than she, for she might never know the joys of having a mate, of belonging to a man. She dismissed the thought and held Dustu in a steady gaze. "But if we pretend to go along with his plan, the master will leave you alone with me, and he trusts me. I could help you escape then. I know the roads and the places where the city walls have not yet been finished."

She looked away, her emotions bobbing and spinning like a piece of flotsam caught in the harbor tide. "I know you have a woman," she said, an odd wave of warmth trembling along her pulses, "but if the master tells you to go with me, do not argue with him. And then, if you would go home to your wife and son, take me with you. I will return to my people—if I can find them."

His gaze rested on her, remote as the ocean depths, but he nodded.

Lanston paced back and forth in the great hallway, mentally
checking the list of things he'd meant to do before this morning.
The servants avoided him, reading his impatience in his posture,
and even the dogs slunk away, preferring to lie down in the
drawing room rather than in the path of Lanston's restless feet.

He paused at the bottom of the staircase and glanced upstairs.
Sunlight from an east-facing window bathed the area in dazzling
light, and tiny motes of dust floated in the air. But there was yet
no sign of Rachelle.

There. He smiled, hearing the sound of a door opening and
closing followed by the murmur of a feminine voice in the
upstairs hallway. Another door closed, and Bertrand Fortier's
baritone grumbled in greeting.

Summoned by the sound of voices, Ashton Wragg stepped
out of the drawing room and lifted a brow toward his son. "You
could not convince her to stay?"

"No, Father," Lanston ripped out the words impatiently and
looked up the stairs. He forced a note of calm into his voice. "But
I have handled the situation. Never fear—she shall not escape."

From the corner of his eye, Lanston saw his father sneak a
quick look up the staircase. "I have heard from Hawkins this
morning," Ashton murmured, after assuring himself they were
still alone. "The Fortier fortune is not depleted in the least. The
rice crop this year alone will provide enough to rebuild the
house, and still Fortier will make a tidy profit."

"I said," Lanston insisted with returning impatience, "that
you should not fear."

Amid the rustling of petticoats, Rachelle appeared at the top

of the stairs, neat and tidy in her gown and his mother's traveling cloak. Behind her, Bertrand walked stiffly, leaning hard upon
his cane. Friday and Fala completed the procession, each of the
slaves carrying a small valise.

Rachelle moved gracefully down the stairs, her long lashes
shuttering her eyes as she navigated the steep steps. When she
reached the bottom, she lifted her gaze to Lanston's father, as
was proper. "Mr. Wragg," she said, an uncommon delicacy and
strength mingling in her face, "I don't know what we would
have done without you, but we will not intrude upon your family any longer. And you must allow my grandfather and I to
repay you for your hospitality."

"I wouldn't hear of it," Ashton blustered, bowing with a rictus of embarrassment. "'Tis no more than one gentleman does
for another."

"All the same, when we have returned to Charles Towne we
shall extend the best hospitality of our house to you and your
wife," Rachelle answered, reaching back for her grandfather's arm.

Bertrand moved forward unsteadily until he stood at her side.
"Farewell, Wragg," he rumbled, clapping Lanston's father on the
shoulder. "*Au revoir*, my friend."

Rachelle remained at the foot of the stairs while Friday
escorted Monsieur Fortier to the carriage waiting outside. When
the two slaves and the old man had moved away, Rachelle
turned her black satin eyes upon Lanston. "I will return soon,
Lanston," she murmured, timidly placing her hand upon his
arm. "And then I will tell you all I have learned in Boston. And I
promise, as soon as we are settled, I'll be happy to set the date
for our wedding—"

"My dear Rachelle," he interrupted, taking her hand in his
own, "what would you do without me to take care of you? Do
not worry, dearest. I have considered your needs already. The
wedding date has already been set, and the minister has been
consulted."

"Already?" Lanston saw the tiny flicker of shock that widened her eyes and the sudden panic, swiftly quelled, that tightened the corners of her mouth.

"One month from today, Saturday, April fifth," he said, warmly sandwiching her hand between his palms.

"April fifth!" She shook her head in disbelief. "But, Lanston, that gives me very little time!"

"That's plenty of time to prepare for a wedding." He lowered his voice to a sympathetic tone. "Since your mother has passed on, my dear, my mother will attend to the guest list and all the arrangements while you are traveling. And just to be certain you do not find a more suitable husband in Boston—" he smiled playfully—"I have booked passage to Boston as well and will sail with you on the *Fitz James.*"

"Lanston!" His father exploded in a brief burst of astonishment, but Rachelle merely gaped in surprise.

"Yes." Lanston lifted his gaze to meet his father's startled eyes. "The Indian slave gave me the information last night. We are sailing this morning to Boston—together."

"Dear me," Ashton murmured, casting his son a look of doubt behind Rachelle's back.

"The Indian slave?" Rachelle tilted her head absently and frowned. "Fala told you which ship we had secured?"

"No, the man." Lanston looked over at his father and sent him a wry smile. "He is not one for words, but eventually I got the truth out of him."

"*Mon Dieu!*" Rachelle's hand flew to her mouth. "You didn't beat him again!"

Lanston shrugged and picked up his own valise, which the butler had left behind the staircase railing. "That one is beyond beating." He held out his arm to Rachelle and gave her his warmest smile. "Shall we go, my dear?"

Tentatively Rachelle placed her hand upon his arm and allowed him to lead her outside. He helped her up to the carriage block and into the carriage, then handed his valise to the black man sitting on the back of the buggy.

"Lanston," his father called, coming down the front steps of the house. He walked slowly toward his son, his hands behind his back, his lips pursed suspiciously. "Just for my curiosity, Son—what did you do to make the Indian talk?"

Lanston turned his back on the carriage and its occupants, then gave his father a casual smile. "Do you remember, Father, what happened last year when Gabrielle Glaze's three Negroes tried to run to Florida?"

Ashton's face emptied of expression. "Yes, Son. I do."

Lanston shrugged. "The law allowed for their emasculation. So I took the law into my own hands and had Garr castrate the savage. The Indian wasn't going to talk for a mere beating."

Lanston saw the Adam's apple bob in his father's throat as he swallowed. "But one of Glaze's slaves died."

"Aye," Lanston agreed, turning to the street. He moved with a quick, light step toward the carriage block, then tossed his final farewell over his shoulder as he poised himself before the open buggy. "But the city council paid him sixty-five dollars in compensation, didn't they?"

▼▲▼▲▼ Lanston kept up a steady stream of bright conversation as they rode to the wharf, but Rachelle scarcely heard a word, so shaken was she by the thought that Lanston had done something to Dustu. Whatever had possessed Lanston to interrogate another man's slave? And why in the world had he decided to journey to Boston with them?

She turned slightly, trying to glance at Fala, who rode with Friday on the back bumper. Fala had slept last night on a cot in Rachelle's room in order to facilitate their preparation for the journey, so it was entirely possible that Fala knew nothing of the encounter between Lanston and Dustu. And there would likely be no opportunity to question the other slaves, for Friday had slept in her grandfather's room, and over the last week Mrs. Wragg had practically adopted Virtue, claiming that her regular maid was completely incompetent. Virtue, it had been decided, would remain with the Wraggs until Rachelle and Lanston returned from Boston, while Cookie would be sent to the rice plantation.

Rachelle turned forward again and pressed her gloved hand to her lips, thinking. Her grandfather often said that slaves were like animals—they could hold a place in a white man's affections, and certain of them were loyal, useful, and intelligent. But they had none of the higher emotions—neither shame nor a conscience nor the ability to reason beyond the most simple problems. But Virtue had wept with real grief when Babette died, and Fala's eyes had blazed with the same excitement Rachelle felt when she realized they would be going to Boston.

Rachelle leaned back and crossed her hands in her lap. She couldn't worry about Dustu. Friday, Fala, and Virtue were house servants and therefore set apart from the slaves who did mindless drudge work out in the fields. After all, at one end of the gamut of dogs were tiny companions who seemed nearly human, and at the other end hounds who did little but roll in mud and scent squirrels.

The secret to happiness in a home, Rachelle decided, hearing Lanston's voice as nothing more than annoying background noise, was knowing where one's place lay . . . and then being content in it.

▼▲▼▲▼ The wharf buzzed with activity even at this early hour, Rachelle noticed with some surprise. Deep-tanned seamen marched over the docks that jutted into the sea at regular intervals like the teeth of a gigantic curving comb. Other sailors literally swung from the yardarms of tall ships that glistened in the gilding sun of the morning. Lanston knew, of course, exactly where the *Fitz James* was berthed, and it was with mixed feelings that Rachelle followed him over the docks.

The gangway had been lowered by the time they arrived at the *Fitz James*'s berth, and Rachelle frowned as Lanston moved onto the gangplank. She had hoped his announced intention to accompany her to Boston was merely a joke or an attempt to dissuade her from the journey, but he led the way onto the ship's broad deck as if he'd been anticipating this voyage for years.

Sighing, she followed. He might be sorry he had come, and sorrier still that he had already set a wedding date with the minister. If she found Mojag Bailie living in an Indian camp, dressed in Indian clothes, and staring out at the world through Indian eyes, Lanston might run back to Charles Towne as if the hounds of hell were giving chase. He would spread tales of what he had seen and heard, and soon Rachelle Bailie would not only be minus a fiancé but she'd be a social outcast as well.

No wonder Babette had buried the truth about her wilderness marriage! Few Europeans had any understanding of the Indians; even fewer wanted to learn anything about them. In fear they waged wars and passed laws, ultimately taking the liberties of life and free will from those they called savages.

Ignoring Lanston, who moved to the center of the deck and called for the captain, Rachelle stepped toward the stout railing and studied the water, fascinated and repelled by the sight. The sea was a fierce and threatening body, holding myriad terrors, yet its steady rhythm was soothing. Beards of algae adorned the pilings of the dock, lifting and swirling in the tide, alternately revealing and obscuring the gray patches of barnacles that clung to the wood.

Rachelle turned from the railing and leaned back upon it, eyeing the other passengers. Most of the men and women coming aboard with great noise and bluster were not emigrants in rags. In one swift appraisal of their clothing and manner, Rachelle knew them to be wealthy planters and merchants, off to Boston to do a bit of business. One man, dressed in a black frock coat and hat, came aboard alone, his somber face announcing his role as a Puritan minister as effectively as if he had worn a placard across his chest.

One family—a father, mother, and two children—stood at the far railing with the shell-shocked look of those who had lost everything in the earthquake and fire, but they disappeared quickly into the steerage, the space belowdecks near the forward hold. Looking around, Rachelle saw that Fala and Friday had vanished, too, no doubt to the hold where they would travel with casks of rum, passenger trunks, and whatever livestock the captain had put aboard to feed his crew.

Two apparently wealthy women stood at the forward railing. Dressed like a pair of bouquets, one in a dress and hat of tulip pink, the other in a complicated outfit of periwinkle blue, they held their parasols high to guard against the sun. The older woman, in her late thirties and working hard to stay there, kept glancing nervously from right to left, her eyes searching the harbor as if at any moment she expected to see a shark or other bloodthirsty denizen of the deep.

"Mama, I'm sure we won't see him," the younger woman scolded, her cheeks pink with wind-whipped color. "The fierce pirate Bettencourt is quite elusive."

"But he was here," the older woman insisted, one corner of her mouth falling in disappointment. "Mistress Bishop says her son saw him. And Mistress Bishop says he is quite handsome and that we should know him on sight."

"There are other handsome men aboard," the younger woman answered, and Rachelle lifted her brow, stunned to realize that the young woman was staring directly at Lanston, her green eyes fixed on him with obvious longing.

Well. Rachelle straightened and lifted her chin. She'd have to correct this young woman's misconception. Lanston *was* handsome, but he was definitely not available.

Lanston stood near the mainmast amidships, one protective arm through *Grand-père*'s, his face turned toward Captain Lodge, who was pointing out to sea. Rachelle bit down hard on her lower lip, wondering again why he insisted upon following her. From what she knew of him, he was not the sort to keep his wife imprisoned inside the house, but this unwillingness to let her travel to Boston smacked of distrust. But why in the world wouldn't he trust her? There were no other suitors in her life, no one of whom he could possibly be jealous. She had never ventured beyond the protective hedge of her grandfather's guardianship, her mother had been her constant companion in public, and Virtue or Fala had always accompanied them, as close as shadows. Until the day of the earthquake Rachelle had never dared to go out with only a maid for companionship.

With a shiver of recollection her mind drifted back to that afternoon in the tavern. Every sort of bedlam had broken loose. She couldn't blame Lanston for getting knocked on the head and barely making it out alive, but he had been completely ineffectual in protecting her.

She dimpled, remembering the keen probing eyes and inscrutable expression of the French gentleman who had shared his shelter with her. If Lanston wanted to be jealous, *that* was the kind of man he should be jealous of. Though the man was reserved and as cool as a cucumber on ice, she would have found his charm and striking good looks terribly alluring if she had not been so frightened. Capable, too, he was—and courageous. Though the world had literally fallen in upon them, she had not seen one flicker of fear in those blue eyes or felt one quiver in his strong arms. "A definite gentleman," she murmured, noticing that Fala had come up from below, her face seeking Rachelle like a plant seeks the sunlight. "And he was humble— not even wanting to accept my thanks and my grandfather's hospitality."

"Do you need anything, Mademoiselle Rachelle?" Fala asked, dipping in a low curtsey as she halted before her mistress.

Turning out of her thoughts, Rachelle studied her maid's face. Fala had probably come up in order to escape the confines of the dark and dank cargo hold, but she could not be faulted for wanting to serve. "I need nothing, but you may stay here with me," Rachelle answered, feeling generous. Turning again toward the sea, she held tight to the railing and leaned backward, relishing the scent of the salty sea. "Isn't it wonderful, Fala? I feel—free. For the first time in my life, I'm leaving Charles Towne. Though I am a bit nervous about all this water. How rough can the seas be?"

Fala said nothing but stared out at the crushed-diamond water, her brown eyes as flat and unreadable as stone. Did her Indian blood account for her aloofness? Rachelle wondered. Or was she distant because she was a slave and Rachelle her mistress?

Rachelle turned toward her maid, regarding the older woman with somber curiosity. "Fala," she said, lowering her voice to a conspiratorial whisper, "I am nervous about meeting my father. He is part of me, and yet I've never known him. What shall we talk about? Will we be able to talk at all?"

A pair of loaders walked by, leaving a trail of ribald laughter along the docks, but Fala said nothing.

"Tell me," Rachelle persisted, finally daring to voice the question uppermost in her mind, "if you could return to your tribe tomorrow, could you start over again with your people? Could you be *Indian* again, after being with white people all these years?"

For an instant Fala's countenance seemed to open, and Rachelle saw bewilderment, incredulity, and a quick flicker of humor cross her maid's face. "Could I be an Indian?" she asked, her voice cracking with sardonic weariness. "After being with *white* people?"

She bit her lip and looked away, her shoulders shaking. For an instant Rachelle thought the maid wept; then she leaned forward to catch a glimpse of Fala's face and saw that the woman was laughing. "Could I be an Indian?" she whispered hoarsely, dashing a tear from the corner of her eye. "Mademoiselle Rachelle, Indian is what I *am*. And I have never *been with* white people, not the way you mean. I am a slave; I am your servant."

Rachelle nodded back without speaking, suddenly aware that those were the most sincere, heartfelt words she had heard her maid utter in months. Through a small tear in the tent of grimness that enclosed Fala, she had caught a glimpse of the woman.

"What would you think," Rachelle said, determined to press forward in this unusual thawing of Fala's reserve, "if I were almost as Indian as you?"

Fala closed her eyes and opened her mouth—her signal that Rachelle had stepped past the boundary of human logic. "Mademoiselle Rachelle," she finally said, holding her head back as though she would sniff Rachelle's breath, "have you been nipping at your grandfather's brandy bottle? What has come over you?"

Rachelle smiled, then leaned her arms on the railing. "Freedom, I suppose," she murmured, studying the glassy surface of the heaving sea.

Trace Bettencourt

*Talk about slavery! It is not the peculiar
institution of the South.
It exists wherever men are bought and sold,
wherever a man allows himself to be made
a mere thing or a tool,
and surrenders his inalienable rights
of reason and conscience.
Indeed, this slavery is more complete than that
which enslaves the body alone.*

—Henry David Thoreau
Journal entry: December 4, 1860

The *Fitz James* quivered beneath Bertrand Fortier's feet as if
eager to untie her square sails and turn them to the distant
winds. As he walked slowly over her deck, Bertrand wished that
his heart might fly away, too. His grief was overwhelming, like a
heavy body strapped to his back.

Stopping at the railing, he stared out at the sea and pushed a
thin sheet of sweat up into his white hair. Babette's eyes were
like the sea—pale blue with a splash of green. He saw her eyes in
every little cat's-paw the wind ruffled up on the surface of the
sea, heard her voice in the soft murmuring from the hold
beneath his feet, in the musical humming of the lines and hawsers singing in the breeze.

He turned his eyes into the bitter March wind, feeling the
sting of tears. He was not crying now, though his eyes watered in
a simple overflow of feeling. His heart had not ceased to weep
since she died; perhaps his eyes would never cease to water.

He had built the house in Charles Towne for Babette; for her
he had established the rice plantation, bought the slaves, built up
a trade with the merchants in Charles Towne and those infernal
English Lords Proprietors in England. For her security he had
amassed a fortune; for her reputation he had ingratiated himself
with the English; for her happiness he had endured her child.

And now she was gone. It was fitting, in a way, that the house
and all her belongings had been devoured in that fiery blaze. The
house had haunted him after her death. It was more than he
could bear, having to walk past her room and breathe in the
aroma of the lemon verbena that always scented her hair, her
clothes.

The soft lap of oars pulling against calm water broke his concentration, and Bertrand looked down as a small barge rowed past, its oarsmen looking up and nodding in a silent salute. Bertrand lifted two fingers in a feeble gesture, his thoughts drifting away.

At one point after the funeral, Ashton Wragg had tried to console Bertrand by reminding him that he still had a granddaughter, but Bertrand only laughed at that insipid remark. He had tolerated Rachelle only for Babette's sake, and he looked forward to her wedding with a sense of relief. With her dark hair and eyes, the child and Babette were as different as mustard and custard. The fact that the people of Charles Towne accepted Rachelle as the daughter of an esteemed English clergyman was testimony to the effectiveness of Bertrand's campaign to salvage his daughter's reputation. Everyone told him the child was a treasure and a beauty, but he could see nothing in her eyes but Indian blackness.

"Excuse me, sir, but you'll have to go below now."

The ruddy seaman who stood before Bertrand did not even doff his cap as he issued this command, and Bertrand turned heavily from the rail, reluctant to part with it. It seemed to him the single solid thing in a world gone soft and nebulous, an empty world in which pestilence and destruction had destroyed everything he held precious.

He moved heavily toward the narrow ladder leading down to the hold, grimacing as his heart squeezed in pain and anguish. This trip made no sense, but he had agreed to go because some fiendish and unholy part of him wanted to stand beside Babette's misbegotten child as she learned that the so-called Reverend Bailie had never existed. Rachelle had insisted that she could find the mysterious clergyman, and so Bertrand had agreed to accompany her on this fool's journey, knowing it would end in the truth. The child would learn that Babette had invented both the man and the marriage.

And then you, Aubrey—he paused on the ladder, clinging to the railing as a wave of nausea washed over him—*you will be avenged. And the evil spawn of the ones who attacked you will feel the same pain you knew, Babette.*

He felt sweat bead on his forehead and beneath his arms as a sense of foreboding descended over him with a shiver. Babette had always been given to white lies and boundless exaggeration, but because he loved her he had accepted and published the story that accounted for the child. The story she told Rachelle before her death was undoubtedly the fantastic rambling of a woman gripped by fever. Rachelle would find the truth soon enough.

He had been a good provider—why couldn't Rachelle be happy with what he had given her? How greedy she was! She had taken Babette's love, and now she wanted the truth. She was welcome to it.

"Excuse me, Mr. Fortier." One of the passengers, an English soldier Bertrand recognized from the markets, tipped his hat and leaped up from his place on a bench by the window, clearing a space in the crowded hold. Bertrand nodded his thanks and stumbled forward, spying Rachelle and Lanston at the end of the bench. Banging his walking stick noisily across the floor, he sighed in gratitude when Friday appeared and took his arm, leading him to the bench where he could sit and rest.

He dropped onto the seat and balanced his hands on the cane, looking around. He was seated between Rachelle and Lanston, haunch to haunch, a rather undignified position for a man of his stature. Closing his eyes, he leaned back, hoping the voyage would pass quickly.

The seamen's footsteps thundered overhead as cries rang out: "All hands to unmoor." "Away aloft." "Step lively there; cast off the gaskets; let fall the sheets."

Opening one eye, Bertrand glanced at his granddaughter. Rachelle had turned toward the porthole, her face an exotic mingling of high cheekbones and a delicate countenance. Next to the window, Fala stood and leaned toward the water, her eyes wide with fascination. Bertrand found himself mentally comparing the two women. Though Fala wore her hair pulled back in a

simple knot at her neck, her hair was like Rachelle's—shiny and
black as a raven's wing. Though he supposed it *might* be possible
that Rachelle's father had been a blue-blooded Englishman, the
girl looked more likely to be half savage.

He looked again at the water, searching for Babette's face, but
saw only the shadowed reflection of the *Fitz James*. The ship
groaned and creaked and groaned again as her sails unfurled.
Then she moved out, the wind catching her sheets, a run of living water at her side.

Bertrand turned his gaze from the window and leaned back
against the ship's ribs, closing his eyes again. Though the ship
had spread her wings like an eager hawk, he was in no hurry to
reach Boston. That city could hold nothing for him but a stark
and terrible confirmation of the truth.

▼▲▼▲▼ Brimming with anticipatory adrenaline,
Rachelle directed her attention to the sights beyond the window,
feeling Fala's excitement across the empty space between them.
She had allowed her maid to remain with her so Fala could enjoy
the sea, for there were no windows or openings in the slaves'
hold. Standing erect and taut, Fala watched the sea with the
same fascination Rachelle felt.

"Can we go up on deck now, do you think, *Grand-père?*"
Rachelle asked, turning to face him. Instantly she regretted her
words, for her grandfather leaned against a wall with his eyes
closed, his long face pale and furrowed with sadness.

"He sleeps," Rachelle whispered to Friday, who stood nearby.
"Pray don't disturb him. But I would like to see if the captain
will allow us to walk about on the deck."

"Perhaps he would rather we stayed below," Lanston warned,
his eyes flashing in the semidarkness of the hold. "I cannot think
that Captain Lodge would enjoy having a woman on his deck."

"Nonsense! We've been at sea for hours, so he cannot mind if
we stretch our legs." With a bit of effort, Rachelle pulled herself
up from the crowded bench, knowing that her gown was likely

wrinkled in a thousand different ways. She smoothed the deep maroon silk as best she could, then rechecked the tension of the bonnet straps beneath her chin. There was bound to be a stiff wind, and she couldn't have her one and only bonnet flying away in the breeze.

"I suppose I'll have to go with you," Lanston answered, sighing as he stood. He gave Friday a stern glance. "Mind your master, slave. We will not be long."

Rachelle climbed the ladder and stepped out onto the deck amidships. The deck stirred with life: the first mate peacocked over the deck, inspecting his crew; the sentinel scanned the horizon from a crow's nest upon the tall mainmast; a knot of seamen plied needle and thread upon a mountain of canvas. And all the while the breeze hummed through the rigging above, the sonorous notes rising and falling as the ship rolled rhythmically, her masts straining their shrouds and braces first on one side, then the other. Rachelle felt the hot gaze of the seamen as she and Fala climbed up onto the deck, but the sailors nodded as she, Lanston, and Fala walked toward the rail.

"You're not going to the side, are you?" Lanston asked, stopping a full ten feet before the railing. "It's very dangerous, I expect. You might get dizzy at such a height and fall overboard."

"If the seamen can walk on ropes out over the water, I think I can manage to stand at the railing," Rachelle answered, glancing back at him. His face had gone pale, and his mouth had thinned with displeasure, but Rachelle was not going to let Lanston's disapproval stop her from enjoying the ship's movement over the sea.

She neared the railing and reached out to grasp it, beaming with approval when Fala came forward and stood by her side. She had not imagined Lanston capable of fear, and it was slightly reassuring to know that her future husband would not always be self-assured and in total control.

She turned her face toward the bow, feeling the life of the ship under her fingers. A strong wind blew, filling the sails overhead until they stiffened. She crossed her arms, the wind caressing her face as she watched sparks of light reflecting off the deep blue of the water. The coastline was visible in the far distance; Rachelle could see white lines of surf purling across a deserted western beach. But to the north, south, and east, nothing but great glassy waves rose and fell, like an undulating plain of slick blue-green grass.

Her gaze dropped downward to the side of the ship, and every nerve leaped and shuddered in response. Standing here, only the rail separated her from the bottomless depths of the churning water below. For an instant her legs went weak, and she understood the fear that kept Lanston at the center of the ship. Looking out at the horizon was one thing; looking directly down into the boiling water was a different experience altogether.

She turned her back to the rail, preferring to watch the play of the ship against the sky, to study the seamen as they scampered along the ropes and yardarms. Two of the men down in the passenger hold had already turned slightly green with seasickness, holding their stomachs and clutching at the walls as if they could still the steady sweeping motion of the ship, but Rachelle found the powerful motion exhilarating. At this speed the *Fitz James* would reach Boston in good time, and she could commence her search for her father immediately after reaching port.

She felt a shiver of anticipation touch her spine. In two weeks, maybe less, she might stand before her father for the first time. Then she would know without doubt that her mother had written the truth.

Her grandfather had surprised her by agreeing to come on this voyage. Of course the trip was in his best interest, for there was no work to be done on the rice plantation that the overseer could not handle. The solitude of that place was not good for a man actively mourning his daughter. In her efforts to convince him that they must go to Boston, Rachelle had mentioned finding Babette's journal, but the old man had shaken his head and released a scornful laugh. "She was a reader, my Babette," he said, his eyes darkening with emotion. "She had a great imagination. She could invent anything."

Had she invented Mojag Bailie? Feeling suddenly chilly, Rachelle hugged herself and ran her hands over her arms. Babette might have had a great imagination, but she wouldn't have invented Rachelle's father. Doubt tore at Rachelle's insides, but she'd know soon enough whether Babette wrote the truth. Within two weeks, God willing.

"Isn't this marvelous?" she called to Fala, yelling to be heard above the roar of the wind. "Have you ever felt anything so wonderful?"

Fala did not answer but kept her eyes turned toward the sea, her face alight like sunshine bursting out of the clouds. Rachelle grinned at her maid, feeling a sudden rush of identification with the older woman. They had experienced so many things together, and now they were both delighting in the sea for the first time. Rachelle leaned back upon the rail, joy bubbling in her laugh.

"I give you good day, my lady." Rachelle jumped as a voice sounded in her ear, then turned to see the captain standing beside her, his hat in his hand. "I trust all is well?"

"Captain Lodge!" She straightened and smiled in pleasure. "All is well; indeed, all is wonderful. I have never been aboard a ship before, and the experience is quite thrilling!"

Clicking his heels together, he bowed sharply from the waist, then turned to Lanston, who still languished in the center of the deck. "Mr. Wragg, won't you join us?"

Rachelle smothered a smile as Lanston bowed, then gravely declared that he should go below, for he was concerned about Monsieur Fortier. "If you are willing to ensure Mistress Bailie's safety—"

"Have no fear for her; go below with the old man," Lodge answered, regarding Lanston with a look of faint amusement.

"The sea affects many men this way," Lodge said, lowering his voice. He reached up to steady himself upon a rope that stretched from the railing to a mast above. "They don't get their sea legs until a couple of days out, if they get them at all."

"I'm certain Lanston will get them." One corner of Rachelle's mouth pulled into a wry smile. "He gets everything he wants."

The captain did not answer but leaned back to study the sails overhead, calling out orders to the seamen entwined in the ropes. Rachelle leaned back and crossed her arms, drinking deeply of the sunlight. Even the air tasted different out on the water—tangier, with a definite flavor of salt and adventure.

"Sail ho," the sentinel above called, and Rachelle turned and shaded her eyes with her hand, straining to look out across the horizon. For a moment she saw nothing but the broad expanse of the deep; then there it was, to the east—a single white fleck on the rim of the world.

She looked to Captain Lodge, who had pulled a spyglass from his coat pocket and now trained it with concentrated diligence upon the heaving sea between the *Fitz James* and the eastern horizon.

"Is it another English ship, Captain?" Rachelle asked, a sense of unease rising into her mood like a snaking wisp of smoke.

He did not look at her but kept his glass pointed toward that tiny white triangle, a watchful fixity in his face. "Probably, my lady, but we'd best get you below while we make sure, eh?"

"I'll go down, sir." Rachelle turned toward the companionway, Fala following like a shadow. As Fala's foot fell upon the ladder rung right above Rachelle's hands, Rachelle heard her maid's frightened voice: "Do you think—could it be pirates, mademoiselle?"

Though the same thought had been hovering in her mind, Rachelle tensed to hear the word spoken aloud. "I shouldn't think so," she whispered, icy fear twisting around her heart. Charles Towne had been horrified by stories of ruthless pirates at sea, murderers who would cut a man's throat as easily as greeting him, thieves so desperate for gold that they would sell innocent English-women and children to the highest bidder in exotic and faraway lands.

"Why have you come down?" Lanston stood in the center of the alarmed passengers, his hands on his hips. Rachelle noticed that Mistress Tulip and Mistress Periwinkle stood by his side, their lashes furiously batting in his direction. "I heard the lookout shout something about a sail."

"I don't know what it is," Rachelle answered, turning to face the room. She felt her face stiffen but forced a smile to her lips and glanced at her grandfather who, thankfully, still slept. "The captain sent us below until he can be sure."

"I blame the merchants," one old man called from his corner, the tip of his white beard wagging like a scolding finger. "They have taken the poisonous pirates to their breasts, eager for stolen bounty. They forget that a viper is always a viper and will bite whoever holds him close."

"I can see the ship!" A little boy's terrified treble cut through the buzz of voices. "Look there! And she's not flying the Union Jack!"

"What is she flying?" Lanston demanded, striding toward the open porthole.

"I cry you mercy, sir, but I think she's flying a square of red!"

Standing on tiptoe near Lanston's elbow, Rachelle craned her neck to see through the small porthole. The approaching ship seemed much larger now and more clearly defined. She rose from the horizon as a triple pyramid of white, her sails full and brilliant against the darkening sky, a moustache of foaming water at her bow to mark how rapidly she came. The little boy was right; a single red flag flew from her forward mast. Every adult in the hold knew what that flag meant—surrender, or blood will be spilled.

The air in the hold filled with the muffled thunder of bare feet on the deck above and the seamen's excited cries. Forcing herself to look away from the threat that bore down upon them, Rachelle listened to the sailors and realized with a pang of alarm that they were shouting commands about *guns*.

"Mon Dieu!" Panic like she'd never known before welled in her throat.

Now a bell was clanging through the cries of "Number seven gun to the bow. Powder boy, grab your cartridge. Level off, there! Let fall, let fall, mizzen tops'l. Sheet home. Hoist with a will now, chaps; hoist away."

The threatening ship stayed on her tack, beating up against the swell, moving steadily closer. Rachelle stared out the window, feeling an icy finger touch the base of her spine. White water swept across the strange ship's forecastle; then, as she crested the next swell, a white puff appeared at her bow, answered an instant later by a dull reverberation of thunder and a resounding splash not ten yards in front of the porthole where the *Fitz James's* passengers watched.

The strange ship was firing upon them.

▼▲▼▲▼ He was dying. The realization came not as a dazzling burst of mental illumination but as a tiny pinhole of light. Slowly it widened, meeting another crack of understanding here, connecting with blinding comprehension there. Here on this bench, with the swell of the sea around him and Babette's child at his feet, Bertrand Fortier was going to breathe his last and meet his Maker.

He stiffened as an even more terrifying realization washed over him. He wasn't ready.

He opened his mouth and gasped, but he had no voice. Words tumbled in his head like bricks in a barrel, inchoate thoughts spurring him to ready his soul for heaven: *Almighty God, Father of my Lord Jesus Christ, Maker of all things, Judge of all men: I acknowledge and bewail my manifold sins and wickedness—*

the child

—which I, from time to time, most grievously have committed by thought, word, and deed against thy divine majesty—

the child

—provoking most justly thy wrath and indignation against me. I do most earnestly repent and am heartily sorry for these my misdoings—

your hatred toward the child

—the remembrance of them is grievous unto me; the burden of them is intolerable—

the child!

Have mercy upon me, most merciful Father, for thy Son my Lord Jesus Christ's sake. Forgive me all that is past, and grant that I may ever hereafter serve and please you in newness of life—

Too late. There would be no hereafter for Bertrand, at least not on this earthly plane. No chance to make up for the years of coldness and hostility, no opportunity to love the girl—for her own sake or for Babette's.

Almighty God.

He stared past the dark-grained wooden beams into the gray stillness of eternity. *Almighty God and Lord, give me a voice again. Five minutes, mon Dieu, that I may speak to her.*

A sudden spasm clenched his chest, and Bertrand blinked in pain, then felt the iron grip around his lungs relax.

▼▲▼▲▼ Rachelle heard one of the women scream; then the little boy's father stood and clumped loudly over the floorboards. "We can't just sit here and let them shoot at us!"

"We won't, sir." Though his face had gone pale and pearls of perspiration gleamed on his upper lip, Lanston straightened himself and walked to the companionway ladder, firmly grasping the rail. "I intend to ask the captain what he proposes to do about this."

A hoarse, choking voice cut short Lanston's declaration. "Mr. Wragg!"

Rachelle turned at the sound of her grandfather's voice. He had not spoken since the strange ship appeared; she had supposed him asleep. He sat next to Friday, his silver brows slanted in a frown, his jaw clenched. A strange livid hue had overspread his face, but he gazed at Lanston with a look of implacable determination.

"You will not disturb the captain now." Bertrand's stentorian voice echoed in the small chamber. "He and his men are trained, and you know nothing about the sea or this ship. You will sit and wait, young man. If you wish to be truly useful, you will pray for our safety."

Lanston took a quick breath as if to protest, but as the enemy ship's cannons thundered again he snapped his mouth shut, apparently reconsidering his usefulness. "Very well," he said simply, then sank into a neat pile by the companionway ladder. "I'll keep guard so no one annoys the captain." His blue eyes flared over the small crowd, shooting sparks in all directions. "No one gets past me."

"Grand-père!" Rachelle hurried to her grandfather's side. His face glistened with sweat despite the cool air from the open porthole, and his eyes peered out from deep sockets like caves of bone. Sinking to the empty spot next to him, Rachelle saw that a muscle quivered at his jaw. She reached gently for his hand. "I thought you were asleep."

"No, child."

She gave him a smile, and he returned it, but with a distracted, inward look, as though he listened to some voice only he could hear.

"My dear." He gasped for breath, then squeezed her hand, his face darkening with the effort. "I've just been having a talk with my Maker. It seems he is done with me . . . and he isn't very pleased with what I've done here."

"What are you saying?" His words set alarm bells ringing within her, and she clung to his hand, refusing to believe that he could be anything but the strong and stalwart man she had always known. "That cannot be, *Grand-père*," she whispered, her voice soft with disbelief, "since I am certainly not done with you. You must have been dreaming."

The ship was turning, she felt the deck shift under her feet. Of course, the guns were along the sides of the ship, not at the bow, and in order to defend themselves they'd have to face the enemy with the *Fitz James*'s broadside exposed. Holding her grandfather's hand, she breathed in quick, shallow gasps and looked up toward the porthole, seeing nothing but blue sky. A moment later, the ship's cannon fired in one great rolling deliberate thunder.

Captain Lodge was fighting this enemy, whoever he was. Her grandfather would have to fight his unseen enemy, too.

She bit her lip to stifle the outcry in her heart. *"Grand-père,* listen to me."* Part of her mind disconnected and wondered at the clear calmness in her tone. "If you're not feeling well, lie down here and rest until we can find a doctor. I'm sure there is a ship's surgeon on board. I will go look for him."

"I think not, my dear," he whispered, his hand closing around her wrist with surprising strength. He lifted his head as if he would straighten himself, then gave up and crumpled like a rag doll, his head and shoulders falling back upon the wall where he had been leaning.

Rachelle felt fear blow down the nape of her neck. She looked toward Lanston, hoping he would offer some sort of help, but his eyes were fastened to the porthole opposite, his face set in fear of the enemy outside. Friday sat beside her, though, one hand on his master's elbow. He gave her a look of understanding mingled with pity.

"'Tis a strange feeling, sitting here," her grandfather said, his face shiny with perspiration. His voice was absolutely emotionless and the sound of it chilled her far more than his usual gruff tone. "With my back to this wall I can almost feel the sea around me. The thought of being only inches removed from the creatures of the deep is a sobering notion, my dear."

"Please, rest now." Rachelle smiled at him, but worry puckered her brows. His hands were cold and clammy, and his breathing had grown alarmingly shallow and quick. She had never known Bertrand Fortier to experience sickness, yet here he was, sprawled before her in a sheen of sweat, his patrician features contorted with pain.

"Grand-père," she whispered, blocking all thoughts of pirates and cannon from her mind, "let me fetch the doctor. You are not well, and—"

"Hush, girl, a battle is raging outside. I'm not so far gone that I can't hear it. Be silent a moment. I haven't much time and would like to . . . collect my thoughts. I'm—I'm going to die."

Rachelle started to quiet him yet again, but a small inner voice spoke to her heart. If this truly was Bertrand Fortier's time to die, shouldn't she do him the courtesy of listening? She had listened to her mother's deathbed confession; she owed her grandfather the same consideration. She looked up at Friday, who caught her eye and nodded silently.

She closed her eyes, feeling utterly miserable, then looked down at the dying man. "I am here, *Grand-père*. I will listen to whatever you want to say."

He closed his eyes, still wheezing for breath. Her heart pounding, Rachelle glanced around for help. Lanston sat abstracted in his position at the base of the companionway ladder, but Fala stood by Rachelle's elbow, her eyes wide with fear and wonder.

Thank God for faithful slaves. "Fala! Ask among the passengers if anyone is a doctor. And tear Lanston away from that ladder—he should know how to help!"

In truth, Rachelle didn't know if Lanston would be able to offer any aid to her grandfather, but she needed someone to stay the death angel until she could make peace with the man who had done nothing but drizzle dour disapproval every time she walked by.

As if he had sensed her unspoken thoughts, her grandfather's eyelids fluttered open. "Rachelle," he whispered, her name sounding strange and unfamiliar on his tongue. She couldn't recall his calling her by name more than five or six times in her entire life. "I have committed a great wrong," he went on, his voice fainter than air. "I have not been fair to you . . . nor have I been the grandfather I should have been. I must beg your forgiveness, *ma petite cherie.*"

My little darling? Only her mother had ever called her that.

"Shhh, *Grand-père*, don't try to speak." His hand was damp in hers, and she closed her other hand around his palm, hoping to hold his spirit by the sheer force of her will. She glanced over her shoulder, searching for help. There was no one—Fala had ineffectually tugged on the coat sleeves of several men near the window, but every pair of eyes was fixed upon the terrible threat approaching from the sea beyond.

"Je suis prêt." Her grandfather's chest rose and fell with the effort of speaking.

I am ready. He opened his mouth as if to speak again, then quivered in a spasm that arched his back and sent his head crashing back against the wall. Rachelle clung to the edges of his coat, crying out his name as he writhed in a paroxysm of pain.

As if in answer to her prayer, a soldier turned at Fala's insistence and rushed to Rachelle's aid. Taking Bertrand Fortier by the arms and legs, he and Friday lifted him from the rough-hewn bench and gently laid him upon the deck.

Rachelle knelt at her grandfather's side, her silken petticoat billowing about her like a pool of blood. *"Grand-père?"* Gently, she placed her hand on his chest. There was no movement, save the brief flutter of his eyelids before he looked up at her. Unspoken pain was alive and glowing in his eyes, but his hand reached up to touch her cheek, then fell to the deck, his face gone blank and empty with heaven's seeing.

Rachelle sat upright, stunned with sorrow. So much grief, so much misery. It was too much, too soon! How could she bear to lose her grandfather? He was all she had left, the only person in the world who had reason to love her, her only link with the life that had vanished in the flames of Charles Towne. All that remained to her was a fiancé who crouched helpless in a corner, an Indian slave who barely spoke, and a father who had no idea she existed.

Above her, footsteps thundered over the deck, accompanied by shouting and shrieking unlike anything she had ever heard. The *Fitz James* resonated like a sounding box to the crash of her cannon, and in the hold Rachelle could hear the enemy ship's rejoinder—a curious dead thump, like a padded hammer a great way off. Wafts of smoke from the guns drifted down outside the portholes; the terrified weeping of other women passengers wound around Rachelle like soft tendrils of sound.

Beneath her hands, her grandfather breathed no more. Quivering silently, Rachelle pressed her hand over his face, closing his eyes, smoothing the distorted flesh. The events of the last few months had been too much for him—Babette's death, the earthquake, the fire, the attack. Even a man as resolute and fearless as Bertrand Fortier could only withstand so many blows to the heart.

"He's gone, Mademoiselle Rachelle." Friday spoke in a hoarse whisper, as though the words were too terrible to utter in a normal voice.

Rachelle nodded stiffly, then placed her hand over Friday's outstretched palm. "We'll keep him with us until Boston," she mumbled, her mind traveling back to the recent memory of Babette's coffin and the funeral hearse. "Perhaps the captain will show us where to put him—when this trouble is done." Mechanically, she considered the steps she would have to take. There were letters to be written, the minister to contact, people who would come to visit—

Where? She gave herself a stern mental shake. Her thoughts were following the old paths, taking the old choices, and none of those applied any longer.

"Mademoiselle." Friday helped her to her feet, his dark, earnest eyes seeking hers. "Mademoiselle Rachelle, he's gone, and you've got to come away from the windows. I can't say of certain, but I think our captain is losing this fight. They are pirates, of certain, and they are hard upon us."

She stepped back, caught up in a curious, tingling shock. *"Mon Dieu!"* she whispered under her breath. "God was good, *Grand-père*, to take you before we are boarded!"

Clinging to Friday's hands, she turned slowly toward the nearest porthole. The ship climbed a swell and fell; then the broadside of the attacking ship came into view, bright against a blue sky and surging sea. Her leeward side was veiled in a cloud that drifted across the intervening sea to join the smoke shot out against the wind by the *Fitz James's* guns. Through the smoke from the other ship she could see the stab of orange flame.

"Are we to die today, too?" she murmured, scarcely aware of

anything but the heavy sense of foreboding that gripped her heart. Strangely enough, she didn't care. God had been merciful to take her grandfather. Perhaps he would extend his mercy and allow all of them to die swiftly. If she walked up on deck, perhaps a cannonball would catch her in the belly and end her distress once for all. . . .

A sudden breeze cleared the obscuring smoke away to reveal the enemy ship, right upon them, her seamen furling her main sail to check her way and come alongside. Rachelle heard the crack of small-arms fire in the pirate ship's rigging, an attempt to clear the *Fitz James*'s deck. Bronzed seamen, laughing with exhilaration, dangled from her yardarms, ready to lash her spars to theirs. A dense swarm of blood-and-sweat-streaked pirates stood at the rail with grappling irons.

Aboard the *Fitz James*, the Puritan minister pulled a prayer book from his coat and began to pray in a loud voice: "Oh most powerful and glorious Lord God, stir up thy strength, O Lord, and come and help us; for thou givest not always the battle to the strong but canst save by many or by few. Make it appear that thou art our Savior and mighty Deliverer, through Jesus Christ our Lord. . . . "

The crowded hold now swirled with acrid, piercing gunpowder smoke, and Rachelle gasped, finding it impossible to breathe. "Friday," she called, reaching out as the black fog at her feet rose up to choke her.

She never knew if he answered, for then darkness claimed her.

▼▲▼▲▼ Crouching in the small space between the companionway ladder and the wall behind it, Lanston saw Rachelle pitch forward in a faint. He started toward her but stopped when he saw the old black valet catch her.

Sighing in relief, Lanston ran his fingertips through the sweat-soaked hair at his temples, then pressed his hands over his ears, resisting the sounds of battle. How could such great luck and grievous ill fortune visit a man in the same hour? The old man had just died; that much was apparent from Rachelle's faint and the mournful look in the old slave's drooping face. That event was an unexpected lagniappe, for now his betrothed was the sole heir to the Fortier fortune. But if they did not survive this attack, if this cursed pirate proved to be the bloodthirsty sort, Lanston knew he might not live to enjoy his blessings.

He felt as though Beelzebub had just handed him the world and demanded his soul in return.

He ran his knuckle across his upper lip, wiping off small sparkles of sweat. Everything—his entire fortune and future—would depend upon the commander who had brought the wounded *Fitz James* alongside his vessel.

Lanston cocked his head and turned an ear toward the hatch above the companionway. More flies could be attracted with sugar than with vinegar, his father always said. And if Lanston could promise a rich reward for sparing his and Rachelle's life, this pirate captain might be easily ensnared.

He ran his hand through his hair in a detached motion, then hugged his knees to his chest and lowered his head. If he had to meet this pirate, he'd promise bribes, gold, or whatever was necessary to purchase his safety. But if he could remain quiet and out of sight, perhaps he wouldn't have to face this pirate at all.

Standing amidships, Trace Bettencourt crossed his arms and stared at his wounded quarry. The *Fitz James*, trailing a curtain of dark seaweed and taking on water through a breach below the waterline, was still seaworthy, but with her torn sails and broken spars she'd be lucky to make four knots, even with her topgallants set. His practiced eye took in every detail of the merchantman. Even if the *Fitz James* hadn't been battered, she wasn't a prize worth capturing. The ship was far too big and slow to be of any use for privateering.

But merchantmen often carried a king's ransom in their holds.

The men of the *Jacques* cheered as the grappling hooks caught the *Fitz James* and held her close. The two ships came together with a grinding thump, the *Jacques*'s larboard side to the *Fitz James*'s starboard; then the *Jacques*'s seamen spilled over the rigging like a flood of determined ants. From the other ship Trace heard cries of "All hands to repel boarders." A handful of stubborn seamen pulled out their blades, ready to engage in hand-to-hand combat. Cutlasses slashed the boarding netting, swords flashed in riotous defense, but it was a token effort at best. The *Fitz James* was defeated, and her captain had to know it.

Trace moved to the larboard railing, his expert eye running over the deck of the English merchant ship. Disorganized gun crews ran about, their match tubs upset; shot, cartridges, swabs, and rammers were scattered about like a child's discarded toys. The *Jacques* had scarcely sustained a blow in the battle—one shot had landed amidships but above the waterline, and another had torn through both topsails before plunging harmlessly into the sea off the starboard bow. The captain of the *Fitz James* had evidently cared more about loading cargo than about loading an experienced crew, and today his crew's inexperience would cost him dearly.

"Surrender!" Trace cried, lifting his sword into the air.

As the cries and snapping small-arms fire died away, Trace leaped up onto the railing and climbed over a plank one of his men dropped over the netting. The crew of the *Fitz James* stood numbly along the starboard rail, bloodied and weary, their faces resigned to defeat. Trace dropped down onto her deck; then her captain, gray and toughened like a dry hide, stepped forward and withdrew his sword with a flourish.

Trace felt the corner of his mouth lift in wry recognition. This was Captain Henry Lodge, an Englishman with a reputation for weak seamanship and unstinting cruelty. Six months before, two seamen had signed on with the *Jacques* after jumping ship from a frigate Lodge had captained. Lodge was all charm, they said, when there were paying passengers about. But amid the silence and loneliness of the sea, he metamorphosed into a quite different animal.

"I'm not quite sure how this is done," Lodge was saying now, his shaggy, soot gray hair blowing in the wind. He stiffly extended the hilt of his sword. "If we were at war, this would be an act of surrender between gentlemen. But since our countries are at peace . . ."

Bowing, Trace took the proffered sword and tucked it beneath his arm unceremoniously. "If we were two gentlemen, Captain, I'd accept your sword in a more dignified manner." He gave the man a bland smile and pulled his shoulders back. "But since I am a pirate and you are a shame to all who sail the sea, let's just dispense with the formalities, *oui?*"

Lodge's nostrils flared with fury, but he bowed slightly and stepped aside, his face red and blotchy with anger. "You have captured this ship. What, exactly, do you hope to gain by beggaring it?"

"That I don't know—yet." Trace lifted his eyes to the tattered sails. Properly patched, they would hold enough wind to see the ship safely into one of the Carolina harbors off the barrier islands or, if managed carefully, back to Charles Towne.

He looked at Captain Lodge again, staring at him with deadly concentration. "What cargo have you?"

"Indigo," Lodge answered, ticking off the list on his fingers. "Rice. A few casks of rum. And passengers—many of them. You can't do us harm, Bettencourt, without expecting retaliation from the citizens of the Carolina colony."

"So you know my name?" A smile ruffled Trace's mouth. "I'm flattered. I know your name, too, Lodge, and I can't say that I've heard much good associated with it." Turning with a quick snap of his shoulders, Trace gestured to his men, who stood waiting and eager to begin the real work of their day. "Monsieur MacKinnon?"

"Aye, Captain." The huge Scot stepped forward. "I'm here."

Trace made a slight gesture with his right hand but kept his gaze fixed upon Captain Lodge. "Secure the prisoners; then load the cargo into our hold. And have the men bring up the passengers, so we can have a look at them—and don't forget the slaves in the cargo hold."

"I wouldna do that, sir." MacKinnon strolled forward, bawling orders and pointing the seamen to one task or another. Trace bowed slightly to Captain Lodge. "Captain, would you be so good as to see yourself to your cabin? I can assure you that we will be quickly on our way."

Lodge's broad-carved face twisted in anger, but after a moment he pressed his lips together and stalked away, disappearing into the tiny cabin under the forecastle. Trace caught the eye of one of his men and jerked his head toward the cabin. The man nodded, understanding the unspoken command. Quietly checking his pistol, he moved toward the cabin door and stationed himself before it.

Whooping in delight and victory, the seamen of the *Jacques* spread out over the ship. The officers began to investigate her holds and cargo while the bosun and his crew herded the defeated sailors together and secured them with rope from the

Fitz James's rigging. They worked quickly, for they drifted in a well-traveled sea-lane, and Trace could not know how long the horizon would remain empty.

While Trace's men conveyed casks of rum, boxes of indigo, and bolts of cloth from the bowels of the ship, a line of passengers ebbed out of the hold. There were several couples, white faced with terror; a whimpering child; a red-faced English soldier; three women, one with an Indian slave; and a Puritan minister. Of the slaves Trace counted a dozen blacks and one Indian.

Several of the women were red eyed from weeping; nearly all clung to their husbands or slaves or escorts as if they thought the pirates were planning to boldly commit some unspeakable horror upon the deck.

Struggling to disguise his annoyance, Trace cleared his throat and stood on an empty box to address them. "Hear me," he called. Like puppets on a string, their somber faces turned to him—all but one. One young woman—tall, slender, and well dressed—stood slightly apart from the others, her hands clasped in front of her, her face hidden by the brim of her bonnet as she turned her eyes to the waters beyond the larboard railing. Perplexed, he glanced past her, half afraid she'd seen a ship that might prove to be his undoing, but there was nothing on the southern horizon but the tarnished silver sea.

Thrusting his hands behind his back, he stepped off the box and moved toward her, determined to know if she was deaf, daft, or just unconscionably stubborn. In three strides he stood next to her.

"Madame?"

"Please, sir," the Indian maid whispered. "She's just had a terrible shock."

The girl herself did not answer. Trace bent slightly in order to see her face, then drew in a quick breath. This was the young woman from the tavern—the one he'd hauled to safety after the earthquake. He looked at the maid, matching the Indian woman's face to the one in his memory. But there was another face he associated with this girl—

He turned and pensively looked toward the darkness of the yawning hold. She did say she was betrothed.

"Monsieur MacKinnon." His voice startled the passengers; they fluttered like a flock of nervous birds. "Have *all* the passengers come up?"

"I'll check, Captain." MacKinnon disappeared down into the dark, and Trace bent forward, still studying the girl. She had not lifted her eyes when he spoke; her gaze remained upon the sea while her lips moved soundlessly as if in prayer. He had the feeling he could wave his hand before her eyes and she would not even blink.

He looked away, his mind floundering. Had the woman gone soft in the head? He had seen young sailors shocked into a stupor after the fear and heat of battle, but a girl who would argue about the improprieties of removing her farthingale in the midst of earthquake and fire was not likely to faint at the thump of a cannon.

"Up, you bugger," MacKinnon yelled. Stiffening, Trace glanced toward the hold. As he suspected, Lanston Wragg appeared in the opening, his expression hard and resentful as MacKinnon lifted him by the back of his coat, literally hauling him up the ladder. "I found him hiding beneath the companionway," MacKinnon explained, breathing heavily as he struggled with his unwilling burden. "There's naught else below but a dead man."

A dead man? Trace frowned, then steeled himself to the regrettable reality of his work. They had been engaged in a battle, after all.

"Well." Trace lifted his chin and stared at the unpleasant young Englishman. "Mr. Wragg, is it not?"

"It is," Wragg snapped, jerking out of MacKinnon's grasp. He took a moment to straighten his shoulders and adjust his coat, then moistened his dry lips. "Of certain I never expected to meet you on the sea, Captain Bettencourt."

A pair of ladies against the railing gasped, then sent him beautifully bright smiles, their eyes gleaming like brass buttons.

"Obviously not." Ignoring the women, Trace gave Lanston Wragg a brittle smile. "And yet you should not be surprised. You have traded with me in the past—from where do you think I receive my goods?"

Wragg bristled. "'Tis none of my business what you do on the open sea," he said, running a hand through his fair hair. "I'm a merchant, that's all." He smiled in a way that only emphasized that he hadn't been smiling before. "And I'm a *prosperous* merchant, if you take my meaning. If you will let my goods and people go unharmed today, I shall be happy to make it worth your while."

"Why are you concerned with my ventures only when it works to your advantage, Mr. Wragg?" Without waiting for Wragg's answer, Trace glanced at the girl. Her face had turned toward him during this exchange, and a flash of recognition now lit her eyes. Her complexion, always fair, had gone paper white, surprise siphoning the blood from her face.

With an effort, Trace turned to look Wragg in the eye again. "You cannot accept the end result without approving the means. And since you have approved my ventures, you cannot fault me for continuing in them."

"You're nothing but a low-down, stinking, cursed pirate—"

Trace lifted a wagging finger and made soft *tsk*ing noises. "Name-calling, Mr. Wragg, is undignified and quite beneath you. Mind your manners, lest I seriously consider the idea of tossing you to the sharks."

He smiled, finding satisfaction in that thought, and Wragg stepped back, a tremor touching his smooth, marblelike lips.

Trace turned to his prisoners and lifted his chin, offering them the most pleasant smile he could muster. "Ladies and gentlemen," he said, basking in the knowledge of his power, "I am Captain Trace Bettencourt of the *Jacques*. My crew and I were privateers during the war with England—" he paused as a dramatic gasp of horror rose from the group—"and now that the war is done, we do not know any other trade."

His men, busy lightening the ship of its valuable cargo,

laughed, the sound strangely out of place amid so many somber faces.

"First," Trace went on, eyeing the brawny English soldier, "I wish to assure you that no harm will come to you by my hand unless you attempt to harm me or my crew. In that case, your life is forfeit." He hesitated, lifting a brow to see if anyone would step forward and attempt such a brazen act, but not one of the passengers moved. The soldier, who had the craggy look of an unfinished sculpture, stood as stiff as a ramrod, his face utterly blank.

"Very good." Trace nodded in approval and turned toward the slaves from steerage. Two slaves, he noted with curiosity, had come up with the whites from the passenger hold. "Second, to those of you who are slaves—" he turned to include the two who stood with the passengers, an old black man and the Indian woman— "I wish to offer you two options. My crew and I have heard of a colony on Madagascar called Libertalia. It is said that in this place all men are equal; none are slaves or masters. If you choose to go there, you will sail on my ship as a passenger only. No work shall be required of you." He waited, letting the implicit message sink into the wide eyes watching him. He was offering freedom without guilt. No man or woman would have to go a-pirating in order to choose liberty.

"If you'd rather not join those at Libertalia," he continued, taking care to keep his voice level so as not to show partiality and sway some confused soul, "you can join my crew. We sail up and down these coasts in the name of freedom. Our duty is to take cargoes from slaveholders and use the profits from said cargoes for two things only: wages for my crew, for a laborer is worthy of his hire, and provisions for those who choose Libertalia."

"Libertalia!" Lanston Wragg spat the word, a thunderous scowl darkening his brow. "There is no such place!"

"How would you know, sir?" Trace swallowed hard, trying not to reveal the growing anger within him. "Of certain you would know nothing of it, for you are too busy enslaving Africans to listen to those who would liberate them."

"Liberate them?" Wragg's angry gaze swung over the crowd of passengers. "I hope you're not believing him. We all know that the blacks are nothing but heathen, savage animals cursed by God. Look at them! Why else would God give a man black skin? Black is the color of sin, of evil—"

"Black is the color of a sinner's heart and is invisible to another man's eyes, Mr. Wragg. Unless your heart is as pure as God's grace, you should be silent." Trace nodded to Monsieur MacKinnon, who promptly thrust a beefy arm around the foolish Mr. Wragg's neck. "Another word," Trace murmured to the Englishman, lowering his voice, "and you will be sleeping beneath this ship, *comprenez-vous?"*

Wragg shot him a cold look but said nothing as MacKinnon maintained his stranglehold.

▼▲▼▲▼ Fala stared at the pirate captain in a paralysis of astonishment. Freedom! He had just offered to take her to a place where all men were equal, where she might decide for herself when to rise and when to go to bed, where she could choose her own husband and bear children in peace and safety. These were the fantasies that made her life bearable, but they were only fantasies, spirit dreams that vanished in the cold light of morning.

She shook her head and clutched Rachelle's valise closer to her chest, smiling sadly as her dreams disappeared in an assault of common sense. Where and what was Madagascar? And what sort of men inhabited Libertalia? Knowing men as she did, she could not help but believe they would be made of the same stuff as the men in Carolina. Evil natures dwelt even in the most Christian of men. Christ's own disciples, the minister had once told her, fell prey to temptation and sin and trouble.

She lifted her eyes to the sky, studying the wide expanse. Freedom! That was the only dream worth pursuing, and perhaps she would never know it on earth. For freedom meant being able to rise above trouble and temptation and toil. One day she would be free, able to soar like a bird over the things of this earth, free to explore the blue bowl of God's sky, drifting wherever the winds might take her.

But to seek freedom now—her heart began to thump almost painfully in her chest. She knew nothing of life in the air or on Madagascar or in this place called Libertalia. A bird could not settle just anywhere; enemies lurked in the most unlikely places.

Rachelle's unexpected questions rang in the dim recesses of her memory—*"If you could return to your tribe tomorrow, could you start over again with your people? Could you be Indian again, after being with white people all these years?"*

Could she? No, Fala realized with an odd twinge of disappointment, she could not. Though she had dreamed of escaping with Dustu, she had also managed to stall him for months. In truth, she did not have the courage to leave. She had come to depend upon the relationship that bound her to the Fortiers. Cut off from her people, her family, and her traditions, she had embraced the white folks' language, their lifestyle, even their God.

Freedom, with its wide range of possibilities and opportunities, would have to be claimed by someone else. Fala could not— would not—fly away from her mistress and her place.

▼▲▼▲▼ "As I was saying—" Trace turned back to the assembled slaves, wondering which of them would have the courage to step into the unknown—"Libertalia is a colony established by sea captains Tew and Mission. Whether you spend your freedom on that island or upon my ship is immaterial to me, but if you wish to claim it, you must step forward now."

"He's lying!" Lanston Wragg roared, MacKinnon's stranglehold notwithstanding. "How do you know he won't take you to sea and feed you to the sharks?"

Faced thus with a threat and an opportunity, most of the slaves lowered their heads, propelled by force of habit to hide their countenances from their masters. But one by one, they stepped forward—first the small Negress who clutched her mistress's basket in her arms, then the venerable older man who stood beside the Indian woman and Lanston Wragg's lady.

"Friday!" The heavy lashes that had shadowed the girl's cheeks flew up.

"I'm sorry, Mademoiselle Rachelle," the man said, straightening himself with dignity, "but I'm going. My master is gone, and you have no use for me."

The young woman turned abruptly to her Indian slave. "Fala?" A hint of plaintive entreaty filled her voice. "Will you go, too?"

The Indian lifted her head, her profile strong and rigid. "Libertalia is not my home," she said, her voice seeming to come from far away. "I will stay with you, mademoiselle."

The shuffling and movement among the slaves ceased; nine had stepped forward. Trace extended his hand toward the netting and plank connecting the two ships, and at this gesture they whooped and scrambled forward in delight.

"Sir, what will become of the rest of us?" One of the Englishwomen, a young creature beneath a terribly pink hat, stepped forward, her voice brimming with energy. She turned slightly, giving him a slanted brow and a pouting smile. "Are you going to maroon us on an island? If you're taking us away, I'd rather go with you than stay . . . with the others."

Trace ran his hand over his mouth, trying to wipe his smile away. What sort of stories were they telling about him in the taverns and churches of Charles Towne? This woman was practically inviting him to ravish her, yet Trace had never laid a hand on any of his victims, male or female. Other pirates routinely marooned their victims; some thought nothing of forcing themselves upon women or murdering everyone aboard a captured ship. But he could not take life so callously. His past was too much a part of him.

When he was certain his face was suitably grave, he dropped his hand. "I shall leave you as I found you." He shrugged slightly. "The *Fitz James* is not much hurt. I expect Captain Lodge will be able to put you back in Charles Towne in two or three days."

He thought one or two of the women sighed in relief, but the men's faces were too firmly set in disapproval to reflect honest emotion.

Wilson, a vigorous, elfin seaman from the *Jacques*, paced before the passengers, his eyes flitting restlessly over the ladies' fingers and necks. He demanded—and received—whatever jewelry he asked for, then paused before the young woman at the railing. "That's a gold ring on your finger, milady, and I'll be relieving you of it now."

"No!" The young woman, tense and very much alive now, snatched her hand back as if Wilson's touch had burned her. "May God protect us, what are you thinking? No, no, you can't take it!"

"It's gold, lady," Wilson answered, pressing forward until he pushed the girl back against the rail. "If you haven't noticed, this is a raid. So hand it over, and be quick, before I have to get rough about it."

Several of the Englishwomen gasped in delighted horror at the prospect of a scuffle, and Trace stepped forward, his nerves suddenly at a full stretch.

"*Allons, allons!*" he called, urging the seaman to hurry. "What is the problem here?"

Wilson lowered his head slightly, then jerked a thumb toward the young woman who held her hands clasped tight under her chin, her face set in a stern and forbidding expression.

"She won't give me the ring." His smoke blue eyes tilted cat-like as he looked up. "That ring would buy provisions for many a slave, Captain," he reminded helpfully.

"Mademoiselle." Trace bowed, careful to keep both recognition and admiration from his voice. "The other ladies have all surrendered their jewelry. Won't you comply like the others?"

"No." She showed her neat white teeth in an expression that was not a smile. "This ring was my mother's, and I won't give it up. Not under any circumstances."

Trace sighed and looked toward the sky. This was a most awkward situation. He had never harmed or hit a woman, but he wouldn't get the ring without a struggle. That fact was as evident as the sun at noon.

"Mademoiselle," he whispered. He took a step forward, as though his nearness might help her understand his situation. "I have a reputation to maintain. I am the fierce pirate Bettencourt, and I steal things. You must give me that ring, or I shall be forced to do something that might injure both your dignity and your lovely fair skin."

"Captain Bettencourt," she answered, looking up at him with eyes as direct as a bullet, "*you* must understand. This ring belonged to my mother, who is now dead. It is all I have of my father, whom I have never met." Her eyes lifted to his, mute pools of appeal.

"Mademoiselle." He dropped his eyes before her steady gaze and looked away, silently urging his seamen to hurry. "Perhaps you can understand the delicacy of my situation. I have taken the other women's jewelry, so I must take yours. If I allowed you to keep your ring, 'twould show unjust favoritism." His appreciative eye traveled from the hem of her maroon gown to her daintily pointed chin; then his gaze met hers. "And I think, mademoiselle," he murmured, speaking in the low, easy tones of those who have found their way past the early awkwardness of first acquaintance, "that for the sake of your own reputation, you would not want it said that you were a favorite of the fierce pirate Bettencourt." He lifted his chin in an abrupt gesture, then nodded toward Wilson. "I see no other option in this situation. Give him the ring, *s'il vous plaît.*"

With dazzling determination, the young woman thrust her hands behind her back and edged closer to the rail. "You have not given this much thought, Captain." Her voice was soft but filled with a quiet boldness all the more extraordinary for its control. "You are worried about reputation, *no*? You want to safeguard your honor as a ruthless pirate and yet guard my good name?"

A reluctant grin tugged at the corners of his mouth. "Something like that, *oui.*"

"Well, then." She glanced for a moment toward the Indian woman, then took a deep breath and trained the full brilliance of her dark eyes upon him. "In that case," she said, her voice so low he strained to hear it, "I freely sacrifice my reputation and will do more than my part to enhance yours. I will not give you the ring, Captain, but you may take me aboard your ship. Call me a hostage, a slave, whatever, but you must take me off this boat."

Trace blinked, feeling his features harden in a stare of disapproval. A hostage? He'd never taken an unwilling soul in his life, and he wasn't about to begin now. Why did the women on this ship seem so determined to board his vessel?

"*Non de nom!*" he muttered, looking away from her. The other passengers were staring; he could feel the pressure of their eyes upon his back.

"Monsieur MacKinnon!"

"Aye, Captain?" From the corner of his eye, Trace saw his first mate turn, but Duncan didn't release his hold on the obdurate Mr. Wragg.

"Take the passengers below—especially the man in your grasp. Secure him with rope and station a guard until we leave this ship."

"Aye, Captain."

"Wait!" Wragg called, struggling in MacKinnon's grasp. "Rachelle! What are you going to do with her? Rachelle, give him whatever he wants!" His eyes met Trace's. "By all that is holy, you fiend, you will pay for this!"

Wragg's blustering threats gradually receded as MacKinnon pushed the man toward the companionway. Trace turned and bowed formally to the other passengers as they turned, tossing uneasy glances over their shoulders at him—and the girl.

"I'd appreciate it if you'd all go below and remain there until we have departed," Trace called, hearing a note of impatient irritation in his own voice. "I will make certain there is food and water enough remaining for your use."

"God bless you, Captain!" The little boy's voice sang out. His mother promptly clapped her hand across his mouth. Doubtless once they were below the boy would get a stern lecture on the proper disdain that must be paid to one's captors.

Trace frowned, turning again to the girl. Wragg had disappeared into the darkness of the hold, but his shouts and threats continued, muffled curses and screams from the belly of the ship.

"Captain Bettencourt?"

The young woman's soft voice startled him, sending his heart into sudden shock. "What is it, mademoiselle?" he asked sharply. There were still a half dozen passengers on deck, including the brazen woman in pink, lagging behind the others out of mingled fear and curiosity.

"I can't go back to Charles Towne. I have to go to Boston. I'll . . . I'll give you the ring you want, but you must take me to Boston first."

He tilted his head, looking at her with amused wonder. Did this little princess think he was running a passenger service? He couldn't take her to Boston; he had seized a rich merchantman outside that port two months ago, and the word would be out— the *Jacques* would not be able to pass easily through *that* harbor for months to come. But at least he had managed to establish one fact. She would part with the ring, and the terms were negotiable.

"I am sorry, mademoiselle," he replied with heavy irony, "but perhaps you are unacquainted with life upon the sea. I am a pirate, not a nanny. I care not whether you get to Boston, Charles Towne, or Hades, for that matter. I am concerned only for my business, my crew, and my ship."

"I think you underestimate yourself, Captain." A muscle quivered at her jaw. "A man who cares so much for slaves and steals to help them must have a great deal of compassion in his soul. My grandfather—" Inexplicably, her chin quivered. "*Grand-père* always said that God blesses the man who regards the life of his slaves and his beasts."

"His slaves and his beasts," Trace repeated, frowning in exasperation. "And I suppose you must get to Boston to provide for your slaves or your animals."

"No." Twin stains of scarlet appeared on her cheeks. Her eyes were dark and unfathomable as she looked up at him. "Monsieur Captain, have you never wanted to change the past?" The corners of her mouth went suddenly tight with distress, and her eyes shone with a hint of tears. "I have spent a lifetime mourning a father I thought was dead. My grandfather—he's the man in the hold—died less than an hour ago." She clasped her slender hands together and stared at them. "Now I have no one unless my father still lives. And I cannot find him unless I reach Boston."

Trace flinched, a sudden quiver of guilt smiting him in the gut. "Your grandfather—did he die in the battle?"

"No." She shook her head. "It was his heart, I think. He died before your ship came close."

Trace looked away; MacKinnon was gesturing to the last seamen aboard the *Fitz James*. Time to leave.

"When you return to Charles Towne," he said, looking at the girl again, "write to your father. Tell him about your situation, and he will send you aid."

"I can't write him." She reached out in desperation, her hand falling upon his arm even as he turned to go. "He doesn't know me, and I don't know where he is. I must find him, Captain Bettencourt, and that will take a bit of doing."

He hesitated, stunned by the reckless determination glittering in her dark eyes.

"There is one more thing," she whispered, her voice dull and troubled. "If you leave my maid and me aboard this ship, you leave us to Lanston Wragg. He will not be happy that I am talking to you. He is already angry. And as my betrothed, he will certainly feel compelled to demonstrate his displeasure toward me."

Trace frowned, puzzled by new thoughts. The girl intended to marry Lanston Wragg, yet wariness, stark and vivid, glittered in her eyes.

"Will he hurt you?" he snapped, his temper flaring.

"Not me." Her burning eyes held him still as she released his arm. "But he will hurt Fala. He has already had her beaten once before, and I could not stop him."

With a long, exhausted sigh, Trace grasped his hands behind his back. "If I allow you to come aboard the *Jacques*," he said, narrowing his eyes as he peered at her, "I cannot promise to take you to Boston. I may only be able to take you farther north. If we run into the English navy—"

"I'll risk anything, only do not send me back to Charles Towne." She stood as stiffly as a soldier before him, showing no signs of relenting. She was young, naive, and completely unaware of the risks she was asking *him* to assume, but all in all she was, he reflected, really quite remarkable.

"Mademoiselle, you should consider—" He paused, hesitating to approach what might be an indelicate subject. "If you come aboard my ship, your good name might be somewhat . . . sullied. Pirates are not particularly known for manners or modesty with women. Your betrothed, ah, might wish to release you from your promise to him, and you might find the women of Charles Towne guarding their daughters lest they breathe the tainted air in your vicinity."

Her soft mouth split into a smile that lit her eyes like the sun sparkling on water. "My actions have always spoken louder than my words, Monsieur Captain," she replied in a determined voice. "I am an independent woman at the moment, bound neither to family nor husband. If Lanston Wragg should cast me off for wanting to find my father—" She paused, her face softening as she looked away. "He wouldn't. Lanston loves me, and love would understand. And he'll believe me when I tell him that I was not harmed aboard your ship, Monsieur Bettencourt. He will believe in me."

"Well, then." Trace turned and adjusted the angle of his hat, shielding his face with his hand lest she see the mocking light of cynicism in his eyes. She was young. She would learn. And then, God help her, she would better understand men.

"All right then, come aboard, you and your maid." Not daring to look at her again, Trace jerked his thumb toward the plank. "But let me hear nothing from you while you are aboard. A privateer is no place for women."

"A pirate ship, you mean," she answered, moving away.

He was about to dispute her, but she had already taken her maid's arm and darted toward the plank and boarding nets. As he watched her kneel on the plank and crawl clumsily amid a mass of silk and petticoats, Trace tented his hands beneath his chin and lifted his eyes to heaven.

"Mon Dieu," he whispered, staring at the scribbles of clouds above. "What have I done?"

▼▲▼▲▼ "Sit down here, and let me bind you to the mast."

Lanston glared at the huge Scotsman, violence bubbling beneath the surface of his self-control. Nearly all the passengers had filed back into the hold, but still there was no sign of Rachelle or Fala.

"I dinna want to be hurting you, so sit down," the Scot insisted, his voice scraping like sandpaper against Lanston's ears. "Sit down now."

Lanston drew himself up to his full height. "I won't."

"Sit down, mind you, or I'll—"

Not giving the man time to finish, Lanston dove forward, his nails ripping at the Scot's eyes. A shoulder blow sent the muscular pirate crashing to the floor; then Lanston managed a front snap-kick to the groin. The Scot curled around his pain, gasping in surprise, and Lanston turned and flew up the ladder as the stunned crowd of passengers cheered.

As he climbed the ladder his eyes sought Rachelle, but there was no sign of her on the deck. "What is happening here?" he muttered. Slipping past another stinking pirate at the companionway hatch, Lanston stormed toward the confident, cocky captain on the deck. His hand reached out, nearly touching Bettencourt's shoulder; then his eyes caught a glimpse of deep maroon upon the *Jacques.* Rachelle stood there, her gown billowing in the wind, her arm linked with Fala's.

His head spun with disbelief. Rachelle was speaking with one of the pirates, as collected and calm as if she were in church talking to the minister.

The sight lit a hot, clenched ball of anger at Lanston's center, and he rushed toward the railing. Bettencourt must have promised her something extraordinary to entice her aboard his ship. And only heaven knew what evil he intended for her once she was aboard.

"Rachelle!" He cupped his hands around his mouth and yelled, then grunted in satisfaction when her head lifted. "Rachelle, come back this instant! What are you *doing?*"

She came toward the railing, a little hesitantly, and strengthened her voice to be heard above the clamor on the deck. "Lanston, I have to go to Boston. This captain has agreed to take me."

"Rachelle, you can't listen to him!" Lanston yelled, his temper at a flash point. Some sailor reached for his arm, but Lanston snapped his own fist up and out, breaking free. So furious he could hardly speak, he stalked across the deck until he found the pirate captain.

"Bettencourt!" he screamed, his fists clenched hard enough to make his arms quiver. "What are you doing with her?"

Lanston drew back as the pirate turned, intent upon smashing his fist through that handsome visage, but another, heavier hand struck Lanston across the base of the neck. He fell, his muscles suddenly weak and helpless, and heard the Scot's voice rising from somewhere in the darkness above.

"I'm sorry, Captain. I dinna mean to let him go. But he jumped out at me like he had a bee up his buns."

"Indeed, Monsieur MacKinnon." Bettencourt's disembodied voice floated down. "Well, I'm sorry I missed that. But put him back below, will you?"

"No." Resisting the black clouds that threatened to envelop

him, Lanston struck wildly through the air. "You cannot take my wife. Give her back."

A pair of heavy hands grasped his arms, and Lanston heard the creak of boot leather, as if someone had knelt by his side. "*Au contraire*, Mr. Wragg," Bettencourt's voice was closer now, and soft. "Your lady asked to board the *Jacques*. I would not take her unwillingly."

"You cannot," Lanston gasped, fury almost choking him, "take an unescorted woman aboard ship! You are kidnapping her! You will ruin her reputation!"

"That's what I told her, but she didn't seem to care." The pirate's voice held a sardonic note that sent Lanston's temper soaring higher. "If it will put your mind at ease, know that her good name and her virtue are safe with me. And she is hardly unescorted; her maid is with her. And as for being your wife, the young lady assured me that she is not yet married."

Lanston's fury yielded quickly to shock. Why would Rachelle share that particular nugget of information? And why would she want to leave him? Had her grandfather's death been such a blow that the girl had taken leave of her senses? A woman gone numb with grief was apt to make rash decisions and foolish choices. She was likely to get herself hurt, even killed. And if she did, who would control Fortier's money *then?*

Lanston blinked, trying to clear his head of the dark spots that lingered in his field of vision. "Rachelle!" he screamed, a thread of panic in his voice. "Rachelle, come back to me!"

"You'd best tie him up until we are away," Bettencourt said. "Make him fast; then come aboard. We'd best be off."

Unseen villains took Lanston below, their hands tight around his arms and legs, their breath sour in his nostrils. They lashed his hands to the mainmast while the other passengers murmured in pity. Lanston pressed his lips together and forced himself to stop flailing about. He had lost this round, and Rachelle had behaved foolishly, but he would not blame her. She had just borne a devastating loss.

He would go back to Charles Towne and assemble a crew to

find her. His father would give him advice. And on the basis of the public betrothal, Ashton Wragg & Son would take charge of Bertrand Fortier's estate and manage things until Rachelle returned home. And then they would be married, and Lanston would place this entire event firmly out of his mind.

And as my wife, Lanston thought, closing his eyes as if he could hide himself from his curious fellow passengers, *she will not make decisions on her own. She will not leave my sight without permission. She will never presume to act alone. I will be the head of the house; I will be her husband and master. And then I will have no more days like this one.*

Satisfied that at least his future would be assured, Lanston slid down the mast and folded his long legs on the deck. From above, he heard the sounds of falling rope and creaking wood as the *Jacques* moved away.

He smiled faintly as his head slowly stopped spinning.

▼▲▼▲ The ship trembled slightly underfoot, her boards brushed by a light swell that parted her from the *Fitz James.* The *Jacques* moved straight and true toward the north, her riggings and sails suddenly dark with men racing aloft to repair the damage done in the battle. Rachelle had the feeling that she and Fala ought to be down in the hold with the slaves taken from the *Fitz James,* but the open air was so inviting, the sights so interesting, that she felt rooted to the deck. Fala, she noticed, seemed content to stand beside her, her own dark eyes fastened to the sky above as if she had never seen it before.

Trace Bettencourt had called himself a pirate, but how could such a man be accurately described with such a despicable name? The man who had sheltered and saved her from the rubble of that burning tavern had been a gentleman in every sense of the word. And earlier, on the deck, he had seemed honestly unwilling to take her aboard and thus ruin her good name. True, he had emptied the *Fitz James* of its cargo and coaxed away nine valuable slaves, but perhaps they had been owned by cruel masters.

But Friday had been one of the first slaves to step forward, and she knew *Grand-père* had never been unkind to him. Rachelle frowned, thinking about her grandfather's valet. Perhaps he felt bereft and alone. *Grand-père* had just died, and perhaps Friday hadn't the heart to serve anyone else after losing his beloved master.

A lanky seaman hurried by, his arms filled with folded canvas, and she put out a tentative hand to touch his shoulder.

"Excuse me, sir?"

He stopped, a shy smile spreading across his face, and she smiled in return. "Sir, is this attack the sort of thing Captain Bettencourt does often, or did he perhaps hold personal animosity toward Captain Lodge?"

"No seaman is fond of Captain Lodge," the man answered, giving her a gap-toothed grin. "But Captain Bettencourt catches whatever merchant ships he pleases; don't matter who's captain on them."

"I see." She frowned. "So he is, in truth, a pirate?"

The seaman shrugged. "I suppose so, but he's not a bad man. He pays us well, feeds us good as he can, and wins his battles more by careful planning and good seamanship than foolish brawling. I think every man aboard would die for him, and that's the honest truth, ma'am."

He tugged on the brim of his hat, dismissing himself, and Rachelle stepped aside to let him pass. A compassionate and diplomatic pirate—could such a creature exist? And how in the world could a man of violence inspire such loyalty?

Trace closed the door to his small cabin, then leaned back upon it, thinking about the woman he had just brought aboard. Some cynical inner voice assured him that he had just welcomed trouble, though it was hard to believe that eyes as open and honest as hers could bode ill will of any kind. And, Lanston Wragg notwithstanding, she had declared herself an independent woman and able to make her own decisions.

So why, then, did he suddenly feel unstrung, emotionally at loose ends?

He walked to the small window in his cabin, staring past the sea into his own thoughts. He had felt similarly disturbed the first afternoon he had entered this cabin as captain of the ship, for he had neither planned nor anticipated his tragic promotion.

That summer day, nearly eight months ago, dawned bright and blue, just like this one. The late morning air was warm and burnished with sunlight, a perfect day for sailing and scouting for enemy English ships.

As first mate of the French navy ship *Adrienne,* Trace stood at attention on the forecastle, his eyes roving over the men in his charge. The mild wind caressed him through his open shirt and pressed against his canvas trousers; the ribbon holding his dark hair flapped silently against his cheek. A few feet away, red-faced Captain Mariveux paced like a dog on a chain, exuding displeasure like a miasma. Trace felt the muscles of his forearm harden beneath his sleeve. Mariveux was a volcano on the verge of erupting, and whatever happened within the next few minutes would not be good.

"Monsieur Bettencourt!" Mariveux roared.

Trace stepped forward into the silence that loomed like a heavy mist between the captain and his men. The entire ship's company had assembled aft; they stood in the silence with implacable, sweating faces.

"Here, Captain."

"Are all the officers present?"

Trace glanced around. His fellow officers stood along the taffrail, and the anxious looks on their faces told him they knew this would be no ordinary disciplinary action.

"*Oui*, Captain. All present and accounted for."

"Bring forth the accused."

Trace lifted an eyebrow toward the quartermaster, not exactly certain who had been accused of what. Silently the quartermaster jerked his head toward one of the midshipmen, a twelve-year-old who stood at attention and shot Trace a frightened look.

"Monsieur Webber?" Trace asked.

"That's the one." Mariveux nodded abruptly. "See this stain on my coat?" He pointed to it, a satisfied look upon his brick-colored face. "He spilled ale upon me at dinner. For his clumsiness and the price of a decent cleaning, I order you, Monsieur Bettencourt, to bring the cat out of the bag!"

MacKinnon and the quartermaster stepped forward on cue, seizing the hapless Webber by the arms. Without a word they removed his shirt; then MacKinnon pointed toward the mizzenmast. The boy bravely walked toward it, then thrust his thin arms around the beam while the quartermaster bound him about the wrists, effectively locking him against the mast.

Trace moved stiffly toward the box where the cat-o'-nine-tails rested in its bag. It seemed unnecessarily harsh to flog a mere boy for something as accidental as spilling a drink, especially on a day like today, when rough seas made even the most seasoned sailor's steps unsteady. Flogging was usually reserved for theft, disobedience, or dereliction of duty. In all his years in the Royal Navy Trace had never heard of anyone being flogged for something so trivial. But Mariveux ran a strict ship, the sort where men walked on eggshells, afraid to lift their eyes. The captain seemed not to notice that his taut crew was uncommonly resentful and sullen. Frequent flogging, thought Trace, made men unhappy, and an unhappy ship was neither efficient nor useful.

The boy Webber stood silently against the mizzenmast, his hands bound together on the far side, his back as smooth as calm water save for a path of pink pimples lightly sprinkled across his shoulders. There was something in the desperate way he clung to the mast that reminded Trace of a child yearning for his mother's embrace, and he pinched his lower lip with his teeth as he removed the vicious cat from its bag.

"Commence with the flogging, Monsieur Bettencourt."

Trace unfurled the leather strips, flayed and worn from a multitude of previous uses, and felt the smooth wooden handle slide into his palm. He paused, looking round at the officers along the rail behind Mariveux, and he caught MacKinnon's eye.

Don't do it, the Scot's eyes said. *Don't do it, and we'll support you.*

Trace's gaze swept over the other officers. The first lieutenant, the bosun, the master gunner, the ship's surgeon—all looked at him with faintly eager eyes, deepened by a common resolution. He was the first mate of the *Adrienne;* if they were ever to stop this tyrant, now was the time.

Trace looked down at the boy's back, glistening now with the sheen of primal fear. Webber slammed his eyelids shut, but not before Trace caught the expression of frank terror in those blue eyes.

Trace knew that terror. A harsh and punitive father had left his mark on Trace's own back. Several years of frequent beatings were more than enough for anyone, Trace had reasoned, so on his tenth birthday he kissed his sweet mother good-bye and ran to the docks. Within a week he convinced a one-eyed sailor that he'd be useful and quick aboard ship, and so he joined the crew of His Majesty's Ship *Beltone* as a midshipman.

Color rushed into Trace's face; the wooden handle of the cat felt as slick as glass in his damp palms. He had no qualms about dispensing proper punishment when deserved, but a man ought to be able to draw a line somewhere.

He heard the crew's sharp intake of breath as he drew back the whip; then he set the cat's tails flying, the sound of the crackling leather snapping through the stillness of the deck. He deliberately aimed wide, though, lashing the deck, not the boy. The crew erupted in a simultaneous roar of approval, and from the corner of his eye Trace saw Mariveux's crimson face stiffen in a horrifying expression of malignance.

"Monsieur Bettencourt!" The splinters of ice in his voice were tipped with poison. "What is the meaning of this?"

"There is no naval code," Trace answered, the words hoarse and forced through his tight throat, "against a lad spilling ale."

A cold, hard-pinched expression settled on Mariveux's granite face. "There is a code," he answered, his voice rising an octave, "against deliberate and reckless disobedience. Monsieur MacKinnon," he called, staring steadily at Trace. "Take the cat from Monsieur Bettencourt. Messieurs LaSalle and Bonite, release Webber and lash Monsieur Bettencourt to the mast."

Trace's blood slid through his veins like cold needles, but he held out the cat, wordlessly offering it to whoever would come forward to claim it. He saw glances interchanged between Duncan MacKinnon and the other officers; then a glint of sunlight touched the pistol MacKinnon pulled from his belt.

Trace felt a sharp pang of sorrow. He knew the proper procedure for removing a captain from power, and he knew with absolute certainty that Captain Mariveux would not go peacefully. Through his cruelty and stubbornness, this captain would destroy the naval careers of his officers and his crew and perhaps even doom his ship.

"Captain Jacques Mariveux," Trace announced, his voice cutting through the heavy silence, "will you go to your cabin, sir? As first officer, I am hereby taking command of this vessel, under the rules and regulations of His Majesty's navy, section thirty-nine, paragraph two."

"I'll do nothing of the kind!" Mariveux snapped, his eyes flashing like summer lightning. "You, sir, will go to Hades and see yourself to the brig!"

"Captain!" MacKinnon spoke now, stepping round until he stood in front of Mariveux, the pistol leveled squarely at the captain's chest. "Go to your cabin, sir, we urge you. There's not a man aboard who wishes you harm—"

Mariveux moved so suddenly that Trace blinked, uncertain that he'd seen clearly. The captain reached out for MacKinnon's throat, and the bosun reacted instinctively. Trace saw a flash, heard an explosion, then smelled the acrid scent of gunpowder. An instant later Mariveux lay upon the polished deck, a red rose blooming in the center of his spotless linen shirt.

MacKinnon looked at Trace, his terrified eyes like black holes in his pale face, while the men on the deck erupted in an approving roar.

Suddenly they thronged around Trace. A hundred hands slapped him on the back; a dozen or so grateful kisses landed on his hands and cheeks. MacKinnon hung back, slowly letting the pistol drop to the deck, his share of the compliments apparently falling upon deaf ears.

"You are our captain now," LaSalle said, formally stepping forward and extending a hand. "You were first mate, so it's only right that you ascend to leadership."

"We'll be tried for mutiny and murder," Trace murmured, stunned by LaSalle's cool appraisal of the situation. "This is a royal ship—we are part of the French navy. MacKinnon and I will hang by the yardarms for our part in this, and the rest of you will be separated and sent out to serve in some godforsaken place."

"Then we shall not be the king's ship anymore," LaSalle said, lifting his voice so that all might hear. "Let the *Adrienne* henceforth be called the *Jacques*, in honor of the blood we have paid to be free of a tyrant. Let us roam the seas and follow our own hearts!"

The men cheered, their voices lifting in great waves above the softer sounds of straining cordage and the constant brush of the sea. Trace walked forward on legs that felt like wood, cut the bonds that held Webber, and caught a glimpse of gratitude and something like adoration in the young man's eyes.

While Trace saw to Webber, the seamen of the newly christened *Jacques* picked up Mariveux's body and tossed it without ceremony into the hungry sea. Confusion reigned for a long while—the madness of rebellion and anarchy, the hysterical eruption of men too harshly suppressed for too long a time—but before an hour had passed the company of officers banded together, then took Trace by the arm and led him to the captain's cabin.

Trace paused before the door, still reeling from the tragic experience of the afternoon.

"Captain Bettencourt," MacKinnon said, swallowing. His Adam's apple did a dance in his thick neck, and Trace knew MacKinnon was not entirely at ease with the situation, either. Their eyes met and held, and in that moment a compact was given and received. The entire crew had just committed mutiny and witnessed a terrible tragedy, but Trace and MacKinnon had committed a far worse crime. At a court-martial, even the truthful testimony of wee Webber would depict Trace as a mutineer and MacKinnon as a murderer. They had stepped over the line of proper conduct, and only by remaining outside the jurisdiction of the law and the French navy could they preserve their lives.

"I'll be standing with you, Captain," MacKinnon said, with a creditable attempt at coolness, marred only by the thickness in his voice. "No matter what happens or where we go."

"Thank you, Monsieur MacKinnon." A flicker of a smile rose at the edges of Trace's mouth, then died out. This was not a time for levity; this afternoon had changed the course of their lives. As first officer, Trace could still reinstate the captain's authority and arrest Duncan MacKinnon for murder, but the Scottish sailor's faithfulness and warmth had impressed Trace ever since they had pulled him out of a sinking fishing boat off the coast of France.

No—in a contest of character, Duncan MacKinnon would beat Jacques Mariveux by an ocean's breadth.

Trace looked his friend straight in the eye. "And I'll be standing with you, Duncan." He moved his gaze over the half dozen men who had escorted him to the captain's cabin. "And the rest of you?"

"Whether we earn a gold chain or a wooden leg, we'll stand with you," LaSalle answered, speaking for the rest. "From this day forward, you are Captain Bettencourt of the *Jacques*, and we are your crew. Lead us wherever you like. Command us as you will. Anything is better than life under a tyrant."

Though they were now his officers and subordinates, they were also his friends, and Trace knew them well enough to know that disciplined naval officers could not become conscienceless pirates overnight. And so he invited them into his cabin, and together they sat around the table and laid forth new rules of conduct to govern the *Jacques*. Since they had escaped tyranny to find freedom, they would likewise seek to bestow freedom wherever they could.

The French naval ranks were cast aside in favor of simplifying life upon the ship. Duncan MacKinnon was unanimously elected first mate, ranking next to the captain; LaSalle was confirmed as boatswain, in charge of the ship's rigging, cables, anchors, and deck crew. The jobs of gunner, carpenter, and cook were doled out to those best qualified to perform them. The position of quartermaster would be filled by a seaman elected by the crew, since he was entrusted with the duty of settling any disputes that might arise between officers and seamen at large.

The other rules of the *Jacques* were simple:

Every man had a vote and equal right to whatever provisions or treasures were seized or purchased.

Any man caught stealing from a shipmate would have his nose or ears slit. No person was to game at cards or dice for money.

Each man was to keep his pistol, dagger, and cutlass clean and fit for service.

Any man attempting to desert the ship in the midst of battle would be put to death.

No man might strike another in anger on board. If an offense were given, a challenge would be issued and the matter settled on shore, with sword and pistol.

No man was to talk of breaking up their affiliation until they had liberated one thousand slaves.

The fiddler had to rest on the Sabbath day.

Unless she was a slave seeking safe haven, no man was to bring a woman aboard the ship.

The thought of that last rule brought a wry, twisted smile to Trace's face. He supposed the young woman from Charles Towne would say hers was an exceptional case, but if not, he had already broken one of his own rules.

For the short remainder of King William's War, the crew of the *Jacques* had boarded only English ships, but in the last few months they had not been particular. In six months they had removed slaves from the stinking holds of Dutch slavers, English merchantmen, and French frigates. Stolen cargoes provided for the slaves' provision and would serve as the foundation for their new life in Madagascar. Trace planned to sail to Libertalia as soon as the *Jacques* had gathered one hundred slaves, and until then any willing slaves served as extra hands among the crew. As many black bodies as white ones worked in the rigging, and as many black faces as white lay cocooned inside the hammocks that lined the hold.

So why, Trace quizzed himself, turning from the open porthole, had he taken a white gentlewoman aboard?

▼▲▼▲▼ "Mistress Bailie?" Two days later, the seaman Rachelle knew as Duncan MacKinnon climbed down the companionway ladder, then stood before her, one hairy arm bent across his chest in a dignified gesture of supplication. "I'm sorry to seem verra familiar, but your maid told me your name."

"What can I do for you, Monsieur MacKinnon?" Rachelle asked, snapping shut her valise. She had been looking for a ribbon with which to tie back her hair, for the wind had brought it tumbling down around her shoulders. She had grown tired of wearing the same bonnet every day, yet there was no other help for her rambunctious curly hair.

MacKinnon's ruddy face split into a wide grin. "The captain

asks if you would do him the honor of dining with him tonight. His private table will be spread in the captain's cabin, of course."

Rachelle was caught off guard by the unexpected invitation. "Dine with the captain? In his cabin?" She looked at Fala, hoping for help. "I couldn't, sir, not unescorted."

"Oh." The barrel-chested seaman colored fiercely, a sight that startled Rachelle nearly as much as the unexpected invitation. "I assure you, ma'am, there is nothing untoward intended. The invitation is for you and your maid." A deep, painful red washed up his throat and into his face, sudden as a brush fire. "You can be verra sure I will be present as well."

Rachelle glanced toward Fala, noting that one corner of her maid's mouth had twisted in wry amusement. "Then of course, Monsieur MacKinnon, we would be delighted to attend. Tell the captain we thank him very much for his graciousness."

The first mate hurried away, and Rachelle opened her valise again, spilling gloves and handkerchiefs and pettipants as she searched for a ribbon. "*Dépêchez-vous*, Fala, hurry and dress my hair! I'll not go to him looking like a windblown strumpet!"

Fala had managed to subdue Rachelle's curls and restore proper order to her gown by the time MacKinnon descended again to escort the women to the captain's cabin. Rachelle was surprised when they actually reached the place. Beneath the forecastle, the small door required any visitor to stoop before entering, but inside the chamber was unexpectedly commodious. A generous table had been spread with linen, china, and silver—for four, Rachelle noted with surprise.

She glanced around. Captain Bettencourt stood in a corner, his hands tucked behind his back, and Monsieur MacKinnon stood at the door, waiting for Fala and Rachelle to maneuver into their seats. There were no other guests—surely the captain did not expect *Fala* to sit at the same table as her mistress? Rachelle had rather expected that Fala would sit in the corner to await her pleasure as she always did in Charles Towne.

Captain Bettencourt pulled out one chair and bowed gallantly, waving Rachelle into it with a slender, strong hand. "For you, mademoiselle," he said, thoughtfully averting his eyes as she maneuvered her ungainly gown into the narrow space. And then, to Rachelle's interested amazement, MacKinnon pulled out a chair for Fala, bowed, and waited until the slave self-consciously took her seat directly across from Rachelle.

Rachelle could not have been more astonished if Captain Bettencourt had invited a pet monkey to sit at the table with them. Speechless with surprise, she turned toward him, her mind spinning with a dozen questions as he sat down, shook out his napkin, and carefully placed it in his lap.

"I hope you like what our cook has prepared," he said, smiling first at Fala and then turning his attention to Rachelle. "I believe the menu includes a nice lamb stew, cabbage soup, and asparagus."

"With fruit for dessert," MacKinnon added, gracefully tucking his napkin into his collar. "We picked up a load of verra sweet pineapples in the Indies." His dark eyes moved into Fala's. "Have you ever had one? They taste a wee bit like liquid sunshine. I ken there's nothing better on God's earth."

"I've had pineapple," Rachelle answered dryly, more than a little bewildered by the attention MacKinnon was paying Fala. "But our slaves would not know about such things."

"Indeed." The captain's dark brow lifted. "So you do not share everything with your slaves?"

"Of course not," Rachelle answered, feeling strangely uncomfortable. "Not all things are meant to be shared. Even the Holy Bible says we are not to cast our pearls before swine."

MacKinnon made a sharp, strangling sound, then promptly buried his expression in his cup. Rachelle glanced back to find the captain staring at her, lines of concentration deepening along his brows and under his eyes. "Mademoiselle," he said, his eyes not moving from her as he gestured to the cook who stood in the door with a steaming tureen, "I was somehow under the impression that you were a woman of some virtue and great compassion."

The cook came toward the table and lowered the steaming tureen, then lifted the lid. As the mouthwatering aroma of warm cabbage soup filled the tiny cabin, Rachelle peered around the cook's broad back and looked the captain in the eye. "I am a woman of compassion and, I hope, adequate virtue," she said firmly. "My father is a clergyman in New England. My grandfather was a godly man, and my mother a virtuous woman." The cook finished ladling out four bowls of soup and backed away. Rachelle straightened in her chair, her eyes piercing the distance between her and Trace Bettencourt. "I think you are forgetting, Captain, who is the outlaw here. You are the pirate. I am the victim."

"Not a victim." The captain held up a warning finger, his blue eyes sparkling as though he played a game. "Can you have forgotten so soon? You came aboard willingly and begged me to take you north—" his eyes fell upon the ring on her finger— "even suggesting payment. At some risk to my ship, I am taking you as far north as I can, where I must dispatch you with all due haste, for your young man down in Charles Towne will undoubtedly spread the word of your so-called abduction. Do not forget, mademoiselle, that the *Jacques* is engaged in a mission of mercy, to free the oppressed and restore liberty to the captives. You, on the other hand," he went on, his words loaded with ridicule, "are a slaveholder."

"So is every other gentlewoman in Carolina!" The objection fell from her lips without conscious thought. "Why do you single me out for scorn—"

"I do not scorn you." His eyes, darker than midnight sapphires, fastened upon her. "I pity you. You have been misled, my dear. Just because a thing is universally accepted does not mean it is right."

"What?" She stared at him in dazed exasperation. *"Non de nom,* you cannot believe that slavery is wrong?"

She could feel the weight of his gaze, dark blue and restless as the sea at dawn. *"Oui,* I do." Turning to MacKinnon and Fala, Bettencourt lifted his spoon in a silent salute and tasted the soup. Though it smelled heavenly and enticed her ravenous appetite,

Rachelle was too distracted to eat—and more than slightly offended.

Lifting her chin, she assumed all the dignity she could muster. "How can you say slavery is wrong, Captain? Slavery exists in the Bible. Joseph was sold into slavery; the Israelites were slaves; then the Israelites *had* slaves. Did not the apostle Paul tell slaves to willingly serve their masters?"

"The Scriptures also recount tales of murderers and harlots, yet we are admonished not to be like them." The captain stirred his soup, his eyes growing openly amused. "And was it good that Joseph was a slave? God told Pharaoh to let his people go. To release them. To grant them freedom so they could enjoy liberty and a land of their own."

"That is different—the Jews were white people," Rachelle plunged on carelessly, picking up her spoon. "*Grand-père* said that black people were cursed by God. They were the sons of Ham. They looked upon Noah's nakedness, so as punishment they are to forever be the servant of servants—slaves, sir, if you please."

"That is a very pretty explanation, but it suffices not," the captain answered, glancing for a moment at his first mate. Smiling at Fala, the captain continued. "Slavery, as known in the Scriptures, was quite different from that now practiced by the planters on Barbados and in Charles Towne. Murdering a slave in biblical times was a capital offense, and any master who punished a slave so that he lost a limb, or even a tooth, had to set him free." He lifted a brow in Rachelle's direction. "Did not Christ himself say he came to preach good news to the poor and proclaim freedom for the prisoners?"

Rachelle felt a wry smile curl upon her lips. "Then are you saying, Captain," she paused, lowering her spoon in order to fold her hands, "that you, a *pirate*, are a religious man?"

His handsome face suddenly went grim. "I know a thing or two about the Bible," he said. He rubbed a hand over his face, scrubbing violently as though to wipe away all feeling. "I know that men in the Bible showed more mercy than slaveholders of the Carolinas. God commanded that his people should not return runaway slaves to their masters. That's what we do upon the *Jacques*—we take slaves from their bondage and give them the opportunity to find freedom. I am enjoined by Holy Scripture not to return an enslaved man to his captivity."

"Slaves, sir," Rachelle said, her fists clenching beneath the table, "are property, according to the law of the Carolina colony. And you are a thief, stealing them as easily as you steal cotton and indigo."

"A man," the captain countered, his demeanor growing in severity, "is created in the image of God and can never be reduced to the level of mere property, no matter what the law of Carolina says. And because God sees the desired state of man as free, my sympathies are on the side of any slave who wishes to cast his lot with me."

He glanced up sharply, transferring his gaze from Rachelle to Fala. "You, Mademoiselle Fala," he said, his voice oddly gentle, "will you answer one question for me?"

Rachelle blinked, surprised yet again by this unpredictable man. Not only had he spoken directly to her maid, he had called her *mademoiselle* and asked her opinion—as if a slave could have one that mattered.

"A question?" Fala looked out at him from behind her usual blank and bland expression.

"*Oui*, mademoiselle. Tell us, if you please—if you could live your life over again, would you choose to live it as a slave or free?"

Rachelle resisted the temptation to roll her eyes. The captain did not know Fala, whereas she had lived with the Indian woman since her weaning. Fala loved Rachelle, depended upon her, had chosen to remain with her rather than board the *Jacques* alone. They were bound as inseparably as the sun and its light. The idea that Fala yearned for freedom was as unthinkable as a mouse yearning for the love of a cat.

"I think," Fala's voice faded to a hushed stillness, "I would like to be free."

Rachelle was barely able to control her gasp of surprise. Free?

How could Fala say such a thing? She was confused; Betten-court's charm and senseless rambling had muddled the wom-an's thinking.

The captain did not look at Rachelle but smiled at Fala, encouraging her to continue.

"But I could not go with you to that place, that colony," Fala went on, a small faint line between her brows as she felt her way into the conversation. Beneath the cool surface of the wom-an's face there was a suggestion of movement and flowing, as though a hidden spring were trying to break through. "This land—Carolina—is my home. My people are buried here. And somewhere in the west, my aunts and uncles and grandfathers still live."

Rachelle stared at her maid, speechless. "Fala," she stam-mered, searching for words, "you have never spoken of this to me! Indeed, I never knew you even thought about such things."

The woman lifted one slender shoulder in a shrug. "It is not your place to ask. And it is not my place to speak of myself, nor is it wise . . . to speak of the past." She let out a long, audible breath. "We cannot bring it back."

Rachelle stiffened as an unwelcome blush crept into her cheeks. From the corner of her eye she could read Captain Bettencourt's darkly handsome face, see the I-told-you-so in his eyes. She lifted her chin, maintaining her pride, but her spirit whirled in chaos. She could not have been more astounded if her grandfather's favorite hound had opened his mouth and sud-denly declared that he didn't like to hunt after all.

She lowered her eyes, bracing herself for the cutting words that would undoubtedly flow from the captain's lips. Why didn't he just take Fala with him to that mythical kingdom where all men were perfect gentlemen and all women queens? Fala obviously felt no loyalty or fondness for Rachelle, and this was a man who liberated slaves. . . .

"There you have it, mademoiselle," Bettencourt remarked, his voice more gentle than she had anticipated. "Nothing on earth can stop a man from feeling himself born for liberty. It is a God-given gift. Whatever may happen, he will not accept servitude, for he is a thinking creature."

A thinking creature. Rachelle's thoughts, jagged and painful, whirred in her brain, and she knew she would find no rest this night. All her life she had believed herself a virtuous and gentle Christian woman, and yet this man, quoting Scripture, had intimated that she was morally equivalent to the evil Egyptian pharaoh who beat the Israelites into submission and killed a generation of baby boys.

Perhaps she was. She felt drained, confused, and lifeless, adrift on a sea of grief and uncertainty.

"You win, Captain," she murmured, pushing the bowl of soup away. "And I have much to think about. I have lost my mother, my grandfather, my home, and now my maidservant, for I can never look at Fala in the same light again."

"Mademoiselle Rachelle——," Fala began, her voice husky.

"No." Rachelle held up a quieting hand and struggled to swallow the lump that lingered in her throat. "Fala, forgive me if I have wronged you. I never knew how you felt. I thought—you *wanted* to serve me."

"Mademoiselle, I do, for—"

Rachelle shook her head, cutting her off. "No, say nothing more. From this moment you are free to go wherever you want to go. You are a slave no longer. I shall not hold you."

"But, Mademoiselle Rachelle!" Fala's wide eyes flickered toward the captain, then settled back upon Rachelle's face. She stared out at Rachelle from deep inside herself, like a frightened animal looking out from under a sheltering bush. "Mademoiselle, I have nowhere else to go."

In spite of her sorrow, Rachelle smiled. "That makes two of us."

"Ladies, if I might make a suggestion." Captain Bettencourt's gaze shifted and thawed slightly as it rested upon Rachelle. "Mademoiselle, your maid has cared for you many years, no?"

"All my life," Rachelle answered, feeling an instant's squeezing hurt at the thought.

The captain nodded, his eyes alight with mischief and inspiration. "And Mademoiselle Fala, you have no place in the English colony apart from your mistress, correct?"

"*Oui*, monsieur." Fala had pressed her hands together and now rocked back and forth slightly, her eyes narrow with worry.

"Then I suggest that you continue as you are," the captain finished, leaning his elbows on the table. "You, mademoiselle—" he pointed to Rachelle—"will still need a maid, and Fala is obviously suitable. But you, Fala—" he pointed with his other hand— "will not be a slave, only a servant by choice. Your life is yours to control, and if you wish to leave your mistress's employ at any time, you may do so."

"Employ?" Strange thoughts careened through Rachelle's head, but she couldn't rally quick enough to protest. She had never *employed* anyone. Employment meant wages for work, something she would have to pay . . . if she ever had two shillings to her name.

"Indeed, yes," Bettencourt finished, clapping his hands together. "Mistress Fala will continue to work for you, and you will pay her living expenses and a fair wage. And if at any time she chooses to go, you will allow her to leave you and wish her Godspeed." The captain leaned back in his chair, glorying in his solution.

Rachelle looked at Fala, then lifted an eyebrow. The Indian woman stared at her for a moment, then shrugged as a slow smile crossed her face. "I would be happy to work for you, mademoiselle," she murmured. Her eyes were soft and dreamy, cloudy as a trout pool in the rain. "And I long to be free."

Rachelle sighed heavily, then looked at the captain again. "I must thank you, sir," she answered, her voice dry, "for illuminating my mind this evening. You have shaken my presumptions to their foundations, but you have also taken a load of worry from my mind."

"Indeed?" Bettencourt lifted his glass and held it just below his lips, smiling at her over the rim. "How so?"

Rachelle looked across at Fala, then reached out and squeezed the older woman's hand. "I have reason to believe I am the daughter of an Indian man. And if I am, I could be enslaved as easily as Fala, so it is a comfort to know about the Year of Jubilee."

She felt a vague satisfaction when all three of her companions stared at her in incredulity.

"An Indian?" The captain's face went absolutely blank with shock. "Why would you think—"

"My mother was captured by Indians and returned to her father carrying a child—me," Rachelle said simply, her eyes moving from the captain to Fala. "I read in her journal that my father was descended from the English and from the Indians. My grandfather had reason to doubt my mother's truthfulness, and so I am driven to find my father on my own."

"Do I understand," the captain spoke slowly, a glint of wonder in his eyes, "that you want to find your father only to discover if you are . . . Indian?"

"No." Rachelle's dark eyes locked into his, seeing nothing else. "I want to find him because my mother asked me to return the love she stole from him. But more than that, I am part of him, and I cannot be complete without knowing him. Whether he is Indian or English or French, I'll accept him as he is. But I must know who he is—or who he was."

"Are you thinking he's in Boston?" Duncan asked, lifting a bushy brow.

Rachelle shrugged. "I know he worked for a minister in Roxbury, a small settlement outside Boston. I intend to find this minister and pray that my father can be traced from there."

"Mademoiselle—" when the captain spoke again, his voice was tender, almost a murmur—"your attitude is unusual and deserves to be honored. I will take you to find this minister. I give you my solemn promise—I will see you safely to Roxbury or die trying."

▾▲▾▲▾ An hour later, Trace stood at the window, his back to the bustle of activity in his cabin as the cook and a pair of midshipmen cleaned away the remains of his dinner. He had dined with women before, in some of the most noble houses in France, but never had he been as stirred by the sight of a woman's face as he had been tonight. Rachelle Fortier Bailie was like clear spring water, transparent and unsullied. Due to her upbringing she held conventional ideas about slavery, but, to her credit, she had not been slow to admit her maid's humanity when Fala spoke openly of her desire for freedom.

The dark ocean lay empty under the moon, and Trace clenched his fist, resisting a shiver that threatened to creep up his back. *He* was free only as long as he remained on this watery terrain, for few towns offered the hospitality of their hearths to pirates. During the war, privateers like men of the *Jacques* had been heroes in small French ports, but now he dared not show his face in either the Mediterranean or the Bay of Biscay. The crew of the *Jacques* were wanted men, and he would never be truly free again as long as he lived.

But Rachelle Bailie still had a chance. She was young, idealistic, and strong enough to outwit the evilly persistent Lanston Wragg. Away from the regimented society of Charles Towne she might find a place to be accepted, even if she did prove to be half Indian. Fala had fairly gaped at *that* news, as had he and MacKinnon, and in a fit of exuberant support Trace had promised to deliver Rachelle safely to Boston Harbor and Roxbury. Now that promise hung heavily upon him, for Boston Bay was perhaps the busiest seaport of the colonies, thick with British and French vessels, most of whom would be on alert for a three-masted frigate rimmed in blue and gold.

The cook left, the door closed behind the midshipmen, and silence filled the cabin. Trace turned, momentarily regarding his Spartan surroundings, and fought the loneliness that welled in him, black and cold.

If he could start his life over again, would he want to be in bondage or free?

Free. What man wouldn't?

For a week they sailed north without incident. The slaves Trace
had taken from the *Fitz James* flowered under the gentle rays of
liberty, and four of the men showed real promise as sailors.
Three of the other slaves spent the first two days lying flat on
their backs, tossing their dinner back to the sea, but even the
weakest of them seemed to gain sea legs by the third day.

And, Trace noticed with interest, Rachelle Bailie and Fala
walked about the deck arm in arm, looking more like devoted
sisters than a fine lady and her maid. Both had seemed a little
stiff at first, but as Rachelle encouraged Fala to talk, the two
seemed to find a great deal in common. Nearly every time Trace
saw them now their dark heads were bent together, whispering
some secret or sharing some private thought.

More telling were the occasions when Fala stepped away and
explored the ship on her own. The Indian woman was lovely,
with raven hair that flowed over her shoulders in a soft dark tide
that shone in the sunlight as though with an inner fire. She possessed a slim, wild beauty that Trace had not noticed when she
walked stiffly behind Rachelle in the pose of a slave. Aboard the
ship, however, standing on a block and grasping the rigging as
she leaned out over the expanse of the sea, she looked like a
water nymph flung up from the deep. Once, during his turn
about the deck, Trace caught Duncan MacKinnon watching the
Indian woman, masculine interest radiating from the dark
depths of his eyes. Trace cleared his throat and lifted a brow,
insinuating the unspoken question, and MacKinnon quickly
looked away, crimson with embarrassment.

Trace smothered a smile and turned his own gaze to the sea.

Neither he nor MacKinnon would know the luxury of love, save
that which could be fostered in a single night of merrymaking at
a local tavern. Their lives belonged to the sea now; the vengeful
mistress Ocean required their fidelity as payment for the sin committed on her breast. No woman in her right mind would accept
a life at sea with a ribald crew, and the officers of the *Jacques*
would never find peace ashore. They would travel the ocean
until she claimed their lives, unless they were able to retire in
quiet obscurity in some unnamed settlement. It was more likely
they would fade away like one of the fabled ghost ships that supposedly piloted these waters when the moon was full and balls
of St. Elmo's fire flickered among the sails.

"Sail ho!" The sudden cry from the crow's nest interrupted his
musings. Trace scanned the horizon until he saw the white sail
that nicked the skyline; then he pulled his spyglass from his
pocket and struggled to identify the ship.

"What do you think, Monsieur MacKinnon?" he asked, knowing without looking that his first mate had appeared at his elbow.

"A frigate, sir, is how I make her out," MacKinnon replied.
"And coming straight at us in a wee bit of a hurry."

Trace lowered his glass, thinking. According to his calcula-
tions they were five miles south of Boston Bay, close enough to
raise suspicion and excite an alarm. If this ship got a good look
at the *Jacques* and then escaped, they'd have no chance of entering the harbor unnoticed.

"Shall we pull away and slip in tonight under cover of darkness?" MacKinnon asked, guessing Trace's thoughts.

Trace smiled slightly, acknowledging the success of Duncan's
mind reading, then shook his head. "She's seen us. If we pull
away, she'll come after us for a look."

Against his will, Trace's eyes sought out Rachelle Bailie's slender form. She stood alone at the rail now, her arms folded, her
thoughts apparently a thousand miles away. Why in the world
had he brazenly promised to deliver her safely to Roxbury? He'd
been distracted by those dark eyes, entranced by her plaintive

need to reach her father. And if he was not careful, he'd pay for those tender feelings with the lives of his crew.

"Monsieur Webber," he called over his shoulder to the midshipman. "Run up the British flag. We'll see if that satisfies her curiosity."

That remark caught Rachelle's attention. "The British flag?" she called, her voice rising above the splash of the sea and the drumming of Webber's feet on the deck. "But this isn't a British ship."

"Every ship I know carries at least five different flags, mademoiselle," Trace answered, tucking his glass securely back inside his coat pocket. "It is a measure of first resort. If this captain has more pressing matters on his mind, he'll be satisfied with our standard and we will be rid of this curious little frigate."

In answer to the *Jacques*'s flag, a tiny speck of red, white, and blue appeared atop the mystery ship—another British flag. Trace felt his throat tighten in annoyance when the frigate kept coming toward them. "Does she intend for us to have tea with her?" Trace muttered, turning his back to the sea. Thrusting his hands behind him, he barked a series of orders that were picked up by his officers and spread throughout the ship like a wildly careening echo: "Away aloft. Trice up. Lay out, lay out! Let fall the sheets, sheet home. Hoist away there, hoist away. Cheerly there, in the foretop, look alive. Hands to the braces; work with a will. We'll outrun her if we can."

Instantly the ship's shrouds went dark with passing men, racing up the ropes as easily as they climbed their mama's stairs at home. Trace watched with approval as the *Jacques*'s sails filled with wind and pressed on toward the north. The British frigate was approaching from the northeast; with a stiff wind they might run before her into the harbor.

Moving toward the stern, Trace looked over the taffrail and surveyed the rippling wake behind the *Jacques*. With the extra sails, she had increased her speed by at least two knots. She drove through the water, rhythmically plunging her head and raising her stern as though she were surprised to be ridden so hard on such a lazy afternoon.

"All hands to their stations, Monsieur MacKinnon," Trace ordered, seeing that the other ship persisted in her approach. "Cut the evening watch down from their hammocks; time to rise and shake a leg."

"She's signaling, Captain," the lookout cried in a voice calculated to reach down to the deck even in an Atlantic gale.

Trace drew in a deep breath. He had been in tricky situations before but never so close to a harbor filled with so many British ships.

"What is her signal, Monsieur LaSalle?"

"A white flag with a pendant over the flag at the main, sir."

Trace turned to MacKinnon. The British navy was keen on signals and other identifying tactics while at sea since no captain in his right mind would trust the flag of an unknown ship. "What is your guess, Monsieur MacKinnon?" he asked, smiling slightly. "Shall we answer with a blue flag?"

MacKinnon's wide brow wrinkled with uneasy thoughts. "I'd be trying a white flag with a pendant over the flag at the main-topmast head and a blue flag at the fore-topmast head. I seem to recall them using this signal the last time we were near Bermuda."

"Make it so, then." Trace nodded confidently and stepped away, not wanting MacKinnon to read the wariness in his eyes. If this was not the correct response, they'd be hearing cannons next, for the frigate would waste no time before firing upon them.

"Gun crews, to your ports," he called calmly. He nodded toward the frightened midshipman. "Mr. Webber, find the fireman and make sure his bucket is filled with water and ready to douse any flames."

A sudden soft voice caught his ear. "Captain Bettencourt?"

He turned. Rachelle Bailie stood before him, her face locked with anxiety. "Captain, why don't you just sail away?"

"Sail away?" His voice went hoarse with irritation. "Mademoiselle, I must ask you to go below. We may soon be enjoined in a battle."

"Captain, if you're doing this for me—" Her mouth puckered into a tiny rosette, then unpuckered enough for her to continue advising him. "Well, it's not worth it. Sail away and come back on the morrow. I don't have to be in Boston tonight."

Why did women always think the world revolved around *them?* "I made you a promise," he ordered in his most authoritative voice. "And I intend to keep it. Go below." She did not move, so he reached out and took her arms, then gave her a little shake. "Find your maid," he whispered between clenched teeth, suddenly conscious of her warm flesh beneath his hands, "and get to safety. If you do not, mademoiselle, we may never see the morrow."

She flinched at the tone of his voice, then took a hasty back step out of his grasp. "I'll go," she murmured, turning away. "But you don't have to do this."

He inhaled deeply, ready to invoke some of the more colorful curses he had heard in his naval career, but before he could utter another word, she had disappeared down the companionway.

▼▲▼▲▼ Rachelle balled her hands into fists, fighting back the tears that swelled hot and heavy in her chest. That man! Couldn't he see that she didn't want anyone to be hurt? How like a man he was, how in love with his guns and boats and derring-do!

The dimly lit hold was crowded with slaves and the scents of wet wood, bilgewater, and tarred hemp. No benches or berths here, just an assortment of casks, cargo boxes, and human bodies—far too many for comfort. The few slaves who thought they might have an aptitude for sailing were already aloft in the rigging, but many of the others were terrified by the sea. These crouched in the hold, half hidden by shadows.

Fala sat with a group of women whose laps were covered with white canvas. In appreciation of the captain who had liberated them, they spent their days mending or hemming the

Jacques's assorted sails. "Mademoiselle Rachelle," Fala asked, her eyes clear in the light of the single lantern that lit the hold, "what is happening above?"

"The captain is trying to get us all killed," Rachelle snapped, then instantly regretted her words when several of the women went slack jawed in terror. "I'm sorry," she said, her blood running thick with guilt as she sank to the floor near their circle. "But this is all my fault. The captain promised to take me to Boston. I told him to turn around and come back another day, but he will not change his plan."

"Mademoiselle Rachelle, will you be remembering the story of Jonah?" Surprised, Rachelle looked up. Friday stood before her, his benevolent eyes examining her with considerable absorption. "Will you be wanting us to throw you overboard?"

For half an instant she feared he would incite the others to obey his suggestion, then she saw the amusement in his eyes. But reckless though his statement was, what choice did she have? The captain had made her a promise he would not break. Perhaps he had made it in haste, but it certainly wasn't worth risking the ship. Sighing heavily, she bent her knees and pillowed her head on her arms. Perhaps the captain *should* toss her overboard.

"Wait a minute." She lifted her head and grasped Fala's arm. "What about those little boats that usually lie upside down upon the deck?"

"Overboard already." Nodding sagely, Friday answered for Fala. "That's one of the first things they do when they spy trouble. The biggest boat—they call it a barge—is floating behind us right now, tied to the taffrail with a cable."

"He could put us in that boat and flee with the ship." Rachelle's eyes caught and held Fala's as her hand tightened on the woman's arm. A strange, cold excitement filled Rachelle's heart as the idea took shape in her mind. "We could go ashore in the barge while the ship runs away. And then the captain will have kept his promise, and he won't have to worry about us anymore."

"Mademoiselle, you'd better hurry if you want to say something to the captain," Friday said, glancing toward the porthole in the hold. Rachelle followed his gaze, and her breath caught in her lungs when she saw the frigate framed within the opening, a huge ship with cannons bristling from her side like stubby porcupine quills.

"Fala, come with me!" she commanded. She turned, intending to run for the ladder, then one sudden, lucid thought struck her— she no longer had the right to order Fala to do anything.

She turned back to face her maid. Fala wore the inscrutable look she'd always worn when a slave, but her usual expression of good humor was missing from the curve of her mouth, the depths of her eyes.

"Fala," Rachelle whispered, frankly pleading, "*will* you come with me? I'd love to have your company. I—I need you."

Not a muscle moved in the woman's face, but Rachelle saw something flicker in those deep eyes—a tinge of gratitude, perhaps even affection.

Fala lifted her chin in decision. "I'll come," she answered, standing. Then she lifted Rachelle's valise and carried it toward the companionway.

"I'll take that." At the ladder, Rachelle took the valise, then slid the leather strap over her arm and grabbed the ladder railing. As Fala followed obediently behind, Rachelle struggled with her cumbersome gown and cloak and prayed that Trace Bettencourt would listen to advice just this once.

He was standing near the mainmast, the spyglass pressed to one eye, the other squinted shut as he peered toward the ship in the distance. Now that the frigate sailed closer, Rachelle could see that the ship was far larger than the *Jacques,* with many more cannons jutting out from her portholes. She straightened her shoulders and moved toward the captain, determined to settle this havoc alone.

"Captain Bettencourt—"

He did not lower the glass, but his face flooded with color. "Not now, woman! Get below!"

"No, Captain, I won't." She stood her ground until he lowered the glass, then lifted her chin and met his icy gaze straight on. "I've a plan, Captain, that will save your ship. Put me and Fala in the barge and let us row ashore. Your ship can turn around and retreat, thus sparing yourself this encounter."

His countenance was immobile, his eyes hot with resentment, but at least he hadn't sent her away.

"Please," she urged, taking a small step forward and daring to place her hand on his arm. "You made me a promise, and I'm grateful that you intend to keep it, but I cannot allow you to risk your crew and these slaves—former slaves—for my sake. Fala has agreed to come with me, and we are ready to go."

The angry color was fading from his face, but his blue eyes were still narrow and bright with fury. "You cannot go alone," he snapped, his hand tapping against his thigh. "Two women could not handle the barge against the swells."

Rachelle smiled faintly. He was listening, at least.

"Send one of your men with us, then. Can they not rendez-vous with you later?"

"*Oui*. They could." His eyes shifted toward the horizon again. The enemy ship had turned from her direct tack and moved onto a course that would bring her parallel to the bucking *Jacques* in a few more moments. Rachelle had seen a sea battle; she knew what this maneuver signified. The other ship was moving her side-mounted cannons into position for firing.

The captain moved away, his jaw tightening. "Monsieur MacKinnon! See the two women into the barge at once. Monsieur LaSalle! You have the conn and command of the ship. Turn about, take her south, outrun this cursed frigate, and skirt the Cape. If she follows far, lead her over the shoals at the barrier islands. Her draft is too deep; she'll not follow you there."

"Aye, Captain!"

Rachelle could scarcely follow the action, so quickly did the men spring to obey. MacKinnon grabbed Rachelle's arm and Fala's, then led them to the taffrail, where a midshipman promptly threw a web of netting over the side, linking the ship and its trailing barge. As Rachelle eyed the heaving sea—it

looked more menacing, somehow, at this distance—MacKinnon
took her valise and dropped it onto the deck.

"Wait! I'll need that!" Rachelle cried, reaching out for the bag.

"No, you wilna." An easy smile played at the corners of
MacKinnon's mouth as he looked down at Rachelle and Fala.
"I'm verra sorry to have to ask this of you, lassies," he said, "but
you'll have to climb down over this wee bit of netting and hop
into yon boat as quick as you can."

Fala did not hesitate but swung her leg over the rail and into
the gaping net, scrambling downward with the sure grace of a
forest creature. Rachelle hesitated, feeling awkward and foolish
in her farthingale and gown.

"What if I fall?" she asked, her eyes seeking MacKinnon's. "I—
I can't swim."

"You wilna fall if you hold verra tight," MacKinnon
answered, a no-nonsense tone in his voice. "Now go, there's nae
time to waste."

Rachelle timidly thrust one leg over the railing and looked up,
hoping to grasp MacKinnon's hand, but the seaman climbed
upon the taffrail and balanced himself there, swinging his arms.
Before she could call his name, he placed his hands over his head
and leaped out into space, landing far below her with a terrific
splash.

She had to go down alone. Taking a deep, unsteady breath,
Rachelle linked her fingers through the coarse rope webbing and
pulled the other leg over, letting her weight fall onto the net. She
glanced down. The sea rushed below, churning white and eddying in little green pools, a boundless foaming ocean that could
swallow her without qualm.

"Come, mademoiselle." Fala's voice brought her back to reality. Rachelle heard the sounds of splashing and knew MacKinnon
was pulling himself into the barge. The deck pounded with activity as the *Jacques* shifted her sails to change course; in a moment
she would be huffing southward, leaving the barge exposed to
the enemy frigate approaching from the east.

If they were captured, Rachelle wondered, slowly moving

over the web of ropes, would anyone believe that a pirate had willingly released her? Perhaps they would find her story credible, but no Englishman would ever believe that a pirate had willingly freed a valuable slave like Fala. Indeed, no Englishman would believe that any pirate would free slaves, and they'd say Rachelle was a fool for believing him.

Hand under hand, foot under foot.

The slightly sour smell of the wet towrope assaulted Rachelle's nose; she made a face and kept going, her eyes fastened to the webbing and the brightly painted colors of the *Jacques*'s hull. *Don't look down. Don't even think about the water . . . and sharks.* Farther and farther down she moved until she shivered at the familiar touch of Fala's hand upon her back. The webbing ended, thank goodness, well within the barge. Rachelle untangled her trembling fingers from the rope net, then turned and enveloped Fala in a spontaneous embrace.

Moving easily but impatiently, the dripping first mate cast the net out of the boat, then yelled up for a hand on the deck to release the towrope. As the barge began to drift away from the *Jacques*, Rachelle sank to a seat beside Fala and turned around to address MacKinnon.

"Just you?" All her nervousness slipped back to grip her. "Can you handle this barge alone? Those waves are very big, Monsieur MacKinnon."

"Not alone," he answered, grinning through clenched teeth as he leaned back on the oars and strained to move the barge out of the *Jacques*'s wake. "Didn't you hear the captain?"

The captain? Rachelle looked up at the retreating ship. She saw him then, the flash of his blue coat bright against the dark rigging. Trace Bettencourt stood at the railing, then bent to pick up the valise she had dropped on the deck.

Safely free of the churning wake, the barge began to move alongside the turning ship, close enough for Rachelle to see the captain open her valise. Moving with the hard grace of one who has his body under complete control, he shucked off his coat, folded it, and thrust it into her bag, then tossed his hat to a seaman. Another man wordlessly handed him a small pouch, which also disappeared into the bag. Then the sailor produced a pistol and a dagger, its blade winking bright in the sunlight before both weapons vanished into her valise.

Rachelle frowned, confused by the sight of the weapons. "He's not going to—" The rest of the words clotted in her throat.

"Aye." MacKinnon lowered the oars and opened his arms; a moment later the valise flew through the air and landed with a resounding thump on the bottom of the barge.

Rachelle lifted her brows, wryly considering that at least she might have an unbroken *sliver* of a looking glass, but her thoughts halted abruptly when Captain Bettencourt strode to the starboard railing. Without a moment's hesitation, he mounted the railing, glanced up to check the barge's position, and dove headlong into the sea.

"*Non de nom!*" Rachelle shuddered faintly and fought down the momentary doubt that wrenched her stomach. "The captain can swim, no?"

Replacing his hands on the oars, MacKinnon looked at her with an expression of complete unconcern. "Aye, the captain's a verra good swimmer. Lots of the men aren't, for there are as many disadvantages to swimming as advantages."

"Disadvantages?" Fala echoed, holding tight to the edge of the bench where she sat. Rachelle could see an artery throbbing in her slender neck.

"Aye," MacKinnon answered, holding the oars still as he watched the captain's choppy progress through the water. "If a ship goes down or you quietly fall overboard, swimming will do naught but prolong your death, aye? And there's them that say swimming flies in the face of nature—if God had meant man to swim, he'd have given him fins." His meaty face broke into a wide smile. "Ah, here he comes. And again I am verra glad the captain learned to swim."

A cry of relief broke from Rachelle's lips when a pair of wet hands clutched the edge of the barge, followed an instant later by Trace Bettencourt's slick wet head. His blue eyes shone with eagerness and determination as he hoisted himself into the barge, and as he settled onto the seat in front of MacKinnon he gave Rachelle a smile as wide as the sea.

"That'll take them by surprise, eh, MacKinnon?" he asked over his shoulder, ungallantly dripping water all over Rachelle and Fala.

"Aye," MacKinnon agreed, rowing with a will toward shore. "But what did you tell our laddies? Where are we to meet them?"

The captain reached for another pair of oars, slipped them through openings in the gunwales, and set to rowing. "At sunset in two weeks, off the southern tip of Ocracoke Island. The shoals there are very shallow; no English frigate would dare navigate those waters by darkness."

"Ocracoke Island?" Rachelle frowned, trying to remember what her tutors had taught her about the coast's geography. Ocracoke was one of the barrier islands off the northern coast of Carolina, quite a distance from Boston Bay. Did he plan to *row* his way back to Carolina? And why on earth had he deserted his ship?

"Captain Bettencourt," she said firmly, folding her arms as she wrapped herself in the rags of her dignity, "I did not expect you to join us. I am certain you did not want to leave your ship, and you need not feel obligated to help me."

"My men are fine and loyal sailors. They can handle things without me." He bent forward with the oars, digging into the surf, adding his strength to MacKinnon's. A spark of some indefinable emotion flashed in his eyes as he looked at her and smiled. "And I do not break promises easily. I vowed to see you safely to Roxbury, and I shall."

"But Carolina is a long way from Roxbury," Rachelle pointed out, lifting her voice to be heard above the sound of waves breaking against the shore. "What if you do not make it to Ocracoke in two weeks?"

He smiled, thinking about it. "I suppose they will sail to Libertalia without me, eh, MacKinnon?"

MacKinnon threw back his head and let out a great peal of laughter. Rachelle gripped her arms and frowned, looking away from them toward the distant shoreline. They were passing a clump of small windswept islands, uninhabited, for all she could tell.

"Have you any idea where we are?" she asked, beginning to feel that she had stepped off the edge of a populated world into one completely alien.

Bettencourt grinned and nodded at the islands gliding by. "Those are the Brewster Islands, and we're only about two nautical miles from a landing at Point Allerton. 'Tis the closest land, though not the most direct to Boston, but I expect we can hire a carriage and take it wherever you need to go."

Rachelle looked away, slowly digesting this information. She had never in her life hired a carriage, but she supposed other people did it all the time. After all, she had heard that many people in New England lived without slaves at all, so it was perfectly possible and even *permissible* for persons of quality to mix with tradesmen.

Her thoughts came to a sudden standstill. "But I have no money!" she cried, looking first at the captain, then at Fala. "My grandfather—he always took care of everything and carried our purse. And I didn't check—I mean, his things were still on the *Fitz James*—"

"Och, well, you can be sure his gold wasna tossed into the sea," MacKinnon muttered, the muscles in his arms alternately cording and relaxing as he rowed in an easy rhythm. "Someone took it, to be sure."

Rachelle opened her hand, rubbing her palm as if she could somehow cause golden coins to appear there by the force of her will. Her grandfather had been wealthy, but he disliked her so intensely that he'd undoubtedly left his remaining property to the church or to some long-lost relative in France. But she would be wealthy again as soon as she and Lanston were married. So any debts incurred could be repaid . . . eventually.

"I suppose I could send a letter to my grandfather's overseer at Shadow Grove," she murmured, not wanting to explain the circumstances of her poverty. "Yes, there has to be a way. Someone will advance me the money until I can repay them."

She heard Captain Bettencourt sigh, then looked up to see him watching her, his blue eyes soft and gentle. "I'll advance you the money, mademoiselle," he replied, casting MacKinnon a quick glance over his shoulder. "I cannot have you and the maid starving in Boston. Your father, when you find him, would think me less than a gentleman if I presented you in anything less than your present healthy condition."

"Will you then have enough to hire a carriage to take you to Carolina?" Rachelle asked, her thoughts turning to practical matters. She had seen him place a bag into her valise, but even the most generous purse would not be without limits. "I cannot take your gold if you need it in order to return to your ship."

"You are very funny, mademoiselle," he answered, his glance amused and opaque. "I would have thought you would refuse my money on principle. After all, it is pirate's gold."

"Well—" She hesitated, caught between her convictions and her need. "In such a time as this—"

"Rules are made to be broken, *oui?*" He grinned at her as they moved steadily toward the shore, and Rachelle fell silent, her eyes searching the horizon. The *Jacques* had wasted no time in turning and moved now steadily toward the south. Surprised by the abrupt maneuver, the pursuing ship had wasted precious moments in adjusting her course. She now seemed very far away, a mere dot on the eastern horizon.

Rachelle shivered, thinking of how close they had come to another armed engagement. She had been too preoccupied with her grandfather to feel the full terror of the attack upon the *Fitz James*, but she had heard and seen enough to know that battle at sea was deadly serious.

The fierce, steady wind tugged at her hair, lifted her cloak, and pushed the *Jacques* resolutely to safety. After a moment of reflection, she realized that the same bitterly cold wind had to be stinging both the captain and his first mate, since both of them were soaked to the skin and clothed in naught but shirts and trousers.

"Non de nom!" she hissed, her fingers rising to undo the fastening at her throat. "Captain, you must be freezing! Let me give you my cloak!"

His fingers were blue with cold, but he did not lift his hands from the oars. "No, mademoiselle," he answered, not breaking the rhythm of his stroke. "For your sake, I would not have your cloak get wet. Stay warm."

"But—" She slipped the heavy woolen cloak from her shoulders, instinctively shrinking as the breeze knifed her lungs and tingled the bare skin at her neck.

"Mademoiselle—" he spoke with cool authority, and Rachelle could see no gleam of amusement in those blue eyes—"twice today I have been tempted to flog you, and I am not the sort to exact corporal punishment on a whim. Keep your cloak, and be quiet—or I will have to treat you like an errant sailor." He stared at her, his features suffused with determination. "Mademoiselle, I swear to you that I will keep you safe. Now obey me and remain silent."

Stunned into submission, Rachelle retied her cloak strings about her neck and kept quiet.

Rachelle Fortier Bailie

Slavery can only be abolished
by raising the character of the people who
compose the nation;
And that can be done only by showing them
a higher one.

—*Maria Weston Chapman, 1855*

His fingers tight around a rope that stretched from the mainmast to the starboard rail, Lanston Wragg stood on the deck of the wounded *Fitz James* as the wind carried her gently into port. Bracing himself against the slow roll of the ship, Lanston took somber satisfaction in the expressions of consternation upon the loaders' faces as the bedraggled ship limped into her berth at the docks.

The pirate Bettencourt had estimated that the *Fitz James* could return to Charles Towne in two or three days, but he hadn't counted on the failings of Captain Lodge. For ten days Lodge and his idiot seamen had stumbled over themselves in an effort to make repairs, but while they bailed and patched and cursed each other, the torn sheets hung limp, shuddering now and then with useless air as the current pulled them farther out to sea.

Though Lanston held no admiration for the pirate's opinion, he had the distinct impression that the brawling Captain Lodge couldn't pour water out of a boot if it had a hole in the toe and directions printed on the heel. Immediately after the pirates' attack, Lodge and his crew made a bad situation worse by jettisoning badly needed water casks in a foolish effort to lighten the ship. By the third day the remaining food and water had to be rationed among the passengers and crew. For the first time in the winding length of his memory, Lanston actually felt his belly growl with hunger.

But inconvenience and frustration gnawed at him far worse. He had counted on Fortier's valet to attend his personal needs, and that slave had jumped ship with the pirates, along with nearly every other African aboard. Treacherous, conniving, ungrateful race! Thanks to them and that thoroughly disreputable pirate, Lanston now stood at the mainmast disheveled, hungry, and malodorous, smelling nearly as bad as the stinking slaves that arrived regularly from Barbados and the Indies.

"Wot 'appened to you?" one of the loaders called, his face a study in horrified delight. "Meet up with the dread pirate Captain Tew, did you?"

"Worse," Lanston called, clenching his fist, "the infernal pirate Bettencourt." He let out a long exhalation of relief as the dockers caught the hawsers and fastened them to the pilings. A moment later the gangway clattered over the yawning space between the deck and the dock.

Without bothering to take his leave of Captain Lodge—the man had been a fool, after all, to allow himself to be boarded by a pirate in the first place—Lanston charged off the ship and thundered over the docks. Ashton Wragg & Son had an office at this wharf, and his father ought to be there, for the hour was not yet late.

His path carried him through a tight crowd of men, through the low buzz of conversation, whispers, and an occasional silence.

"Isn't that Lanston Wragg?"

"Look at him! Why, 'e's a mess! What do you suppose 'appened?"

"Pirates, did ye hear?"

Lanston pushed on, pursing his lips, inwardly savoring the gasps and expressions of shock that greeted his disordered appearance. A frightful bluish green bruise—obtained when he slipped and fell in an unwary moment—decorated his cheek above his rough beard, but it added a bit of color to his aspect and might prove his valor in the tale he was eager to relate.

The wooden building housing his father's office stood at the northern end of the wharf. Lanston slammed through the doorway and collapsed into the nearest chair. Mr. Glazier, the clerk, leaped to his feet, his plump hand fluttering to his throat in an expression of horror. "Lanston! But you're in Boston!"

"Obviously you are mistaken," Lanston drawled, wishing the little man would get out of the way and summon his father. "We met with pirates."

"'Pon my soul, how terrifying!"

Lanston lowered his chin, shaking his head as if he was at a loss for words. Taking his cue, the clerk hastily rapped on Ashton's door. From within, a curt voice snapped a warning.

"Sir, it's your son." Hesitantly, the clerk opened the door, then nervously pointed toward Lanston. "Back from Boston—er—from the sea."

"Lanston!" Ashton Wragg rose from his chair with explosive force and hurried to his son's side with long, purposeful strides. "What happened?" He crouched on the floor, his hand resting on Lanston's knee. "Tell me immediately! Speak!"

Lanston lifted his eyes and met his father's gaze. "Pirates," he said simply, pleased to see that his hand trembled with intensity. "Captain Trace Bettencourt, a rabid Frenchman. He fired upon our ship, disabling her; then he and his ruffians came aboard. Slave stealers, they are. They lured nearly every slave from our ship with the promise of freedom." He took a deep breath and gave his father a grim smile. "He promised them sanctuary in some mythical place called Libertalia. Simpletons that they are, the black fools took his bait."

"Are you hurt, Son?" His father's eye flickered toward the bruise upon his cheek, then traveled quickly up and down his frame. "Stabbed? Shot?"

"God preserved me," Lanston answered, his mouth tight and grim. "I fought as a man should and managed to keep the pirates off my person." The line of his mouth tightened a fraction as he deliberately exaggerated the pain in his face. "But Rachelle, Father—the malicious scoundrel took her. She is kidnapped, and her grandfather is dead and buried at sea."

"Bertrand Fortier is *dead?*" Ashton's face twisted in a look of disbelief, rage, and frustration. "And the granddaughter is gone? How? How could such a thing be possible?"

"The old man's blood is on the pirate's hands." Rancor sharpened Lanston's voice. "And if he has defiled Rachelle in any way—"

"Hush, now, let me think." Ashton rose from his crouched position and settled into a chair across from Lanston, pressing his hand to his chin. "She will be returned—he is probably holding her for ransom." He quirked his eyebrow in a question. "Does this Bettencourt know Rachelle is the old man's only heir?"

"By now he probably does," Lanston answered crossly. "The old man's valet was among the first to run to the pirate's ship. Rachelle's maid went, too, though I suppose I should be glad she is with her mistress. The slaves are like parrots—they talk altogether too much. And those two—Fala and Friday—knew everything that went on in Fortier's house."

"We must get her back, Son." Ashton's fist fell upon the armrest of his chair. He leaned over and squeezed Lanston's hand. "We'll call the authorities immediately. We will post pictures of this pirate in all the ports along the Atlantic seaboard. Once 'tis known that he's kidnapping young women and stealing slaves, he'll not be welcomed at any dock in the colonies."

"I want Rachelle." Lanston managed a bleak, tight-lipped smile. "She is my betrothed, and I want her back."

"Don't worry, Son, you shall have her," Ashton murmured absently. "Go home, let your mother have a look at your bruises, bathe, and put on some decent clothes. I'll send someone from the governor's office to the house to take your statement about the attack. We'll talk more of this at home."

Ashton's gray eyes had already taken on a distant look, and Lanston knew his father would waste no time implementing his plans.

▼▲▼▲▼ Two hours later, bathed and freshly shaven, Lanston ventured downstairs to the drawing room. His mother reclined upon the upholstered sofa, her spindly legs outlined by yards of soft-spun silk, the tips of her slippers peeking modestly out beneath the hem of her gown. Behind her, a slender black maid waved an ostrich-feather fan, her eyes as blank as a slab of cold, dark marble.

"Lanston, my love." Cambria extended both hands in greeting.

Hurrying forward, he bowed, taking her hands and briefly planting his lips upon each palm.

Closing her eyes, Cambria sighed. "How relieved I am to see you, safe and sound, back in the bosom of your family! Your father and I were concerned about your trip, of course, but had we known you would face such terrors—"

"I am a man, Mama. I can handle myself." Lanston released her and sank into the chair facing the sofa. He crossed his hands at his waist and lifted his eyes to the ornate wainscoted walls, rich with carved details and plasterwork. This room was intended to impress, but it was nothing compared to the drawing room he planned for the house he would share with Rachelle.

"Your father," his mother spoke in a hushed, bedside voice, "will be along shortly. He has already been here and left, all in a rage about your trials at sea." She paused, pressing her hand to her thin bosom dramatically as she drew in a deep breath. "He found a tavern girl at the wharf who knows this dreadful pirate Bettencourt. She has given him a description. A likeness of his face will be placarded throughout the town by nightfall tomorrow."

"Good," Lanston murmured, his mind still burning with memories of his humiliation at Bettencourt's hands. If God was just, the authorities would find the man and hang him down at Oyster Point, the proper place for the scum of the earth. After his rotting corpse had hung on a gibbet for a week or so to warn others who would pirate merchant ships, they would bury Bettencourt's body in the salt marshes. The crabs and scavengers that rode in on the tide would soon obliterate any trace of Bettencourt's remains from the face of the earth.

Sounds from the foyer interrupted his musings, and Lanston stood as his father marched into the room. Ashton Wragg tossed his hat in the slave girl's direction, then fervently embraced his son, slapping him on the back. "It's done, Lanston," he said, satisfaction pursing his mouth. "If Captain Bettencourt dares sail within a hundred miles of this coast, we'll have him and hang him. And we'll find your Rachelle and bring her back to you."

He sank into the new wing chair near the couch. "Sit, Lanston," he commanded, patting the upholstered arm of the chair for emphasis. "There are a few other things we need to discuss about Rachelle's abduction." He tilted his head, lifting his brows. "What will you do if the girl comes back to you—and she is not the, er, chaste maiden she was when she left?"

Lanston waved the matter away with his hand. "It matters not, Father. I will put the episode behind me."

"Are you certain?" His father's brows drew together in an agonized expression. "A virtuous woman, according to the Scriptures, is worth far more than rubies. And if she no longer has her virtue—"

"I care nothing for rubies, Father." Lanston smiled comfortably to himself. "I've thought about this for the last several days aboard the *Fitz James*. And as valuable as chastity is, 'tis not priceless. Bertrand Fortier's fortune is worth far more than many rubies."

"Ah." Ashton tilted his head in acknowledgment of Lanston's reasoning, then leaned forward in his chair and spoke in a more controlled voice. "There is one other thing." His eyes darkened and shone with an unpleasant light. "We know why Rachelle wanted to go to Boston. And her reason had nothing to do with buying clothes."

"I know. She wanted to find her father," Lanston answered, sighing. He had wanted to keep this bit of information from his parents, but apparently they'd learned his secret. The closely knit social structure of Charles Towne matrons was a veritable fount of knowledge—and gossip.

His father nodded soberly, his eyes sending a private message that Lanston did not understand. He glanced at his mother—she knew the secret, too, for wary blue shadows flickered in her eyes. Even the slave girl seemed to be holding her breath, waiting for Lanston to understand—what? That Rachelle had a lover? a brother? That they had discovered another heir to the Fortier fortune?

"What else did you find out?" Lanston demanded, feeling suddenly restless and irritable.

"You may recall, Son," his father began, a hint of censure in his tone, "that the Fortiers left their slave, Virtue, here in the house with us."

"So?" The corner of Lanston's mouth twisted with exasperation.

"So this Virtue," his father continued, his eyes cold and proud, "used to be Mistress Bailie's maid. And Babette was apparently fond of the woman, and fond of reading. So fond, in fact, that she taught her maid how to read."

"Really? An unusual trick, surely." Lanston pressed his hand over his mouth, smothering his impatience. If only his father would get to the point!

"In any case, one morning Virtue happened to walk past her dead mistress's room and saw Rachelle reading from a special book—Mistress Bailie's journal. Rachelle was weeping as she read, and the maid grew curious. She lingered in the hall until Rachelle put the book away, then retrieved the journal from its hiding place and read Mistress Bailie's words." Ashton's features hardened, shifting into an expression of remarkable malignity. "According to the maid, your Rachelle's father had *Indian* ancestors."

Lanston tried to reply, to say it wasn't true, but shock caused the words to wedge in his throat. He could only gape at his father, his mouth open, his eyes wide.

"Apparently this Mr. Bailie lived with the Indians," Ashton went on, narrowing his eyes. "He hunted with them, ate with them, lived with them. Through some misguided quirk of conscience, he probably felt responsible for them."

"Rachelle said he was a clergyman." Lanston finally found his voice. "Many of the clergymen visit the savages and live with them for a time."

"According to Virtue, this man lived with them always," Ashton continued. "And our Mr. Bailie's given name was Mojag. What sort of Englishman gives his son a heathen name like that?" The smile Ashton gave Lanston was utterly without humor. "Of course, the Indian influence is not strong; Mistress Bailie wrote that the man was educated, cultured, and a noble gentleman. And I am certain she wrote the truth in her journal, for what woman would lie to herself?"

Lanston let his head fall to the back of his chair, his thoughts and feelings whirling in a cyclonic rush. If Rachelle had read this journal, then she knew about her father and had kept the truth from him. As if she had any right! He could trace *his* bloodline to half a dozen noble lords and dukes of England, while she who spoke French and played the harpsichord and flaunted herself like European nobility was little better than a savage mongrel. Even if she was only one-eighth or one-sixteenth Indian, she was not far removed from the mulattos and quadroons that were appearing with increasing frequency in the local slave markets.

But how many mongrels stand to inherit the richest fortune in Charles Towne?

He flushed miserably, helpless to halt his embarrassment. What could he do? He could cast Rachelle off and count himself fortunate to be rid of her, but already half the town knew that he'd staggered in this afternoon black and blue, supposedly beaten to a pulp to defend his betrothed's honor. And even now they were looking for Rachelle, racing to protect and preserve a blushing bride for her ardent bridegroom.

"What shall I do?" Completely at a loss, Lanston looked up at his father. Ashton Wragg would have an answer; he always did.

"You shall do nothing." Ashton sat back in his chair and pulled a pipe from his coat pocket. "Bertrand Fortier was no fool; he kept his daughter's disgrace from everyone. And Babette's maid will talk no more; I've seen to it."

Despite his desperation, Lanston felt a shiver of apprehension. Rachelle often spoke fondly of Virtue; she would not be pleased to find her mother's maid missing.

"You didn't sell her?"

"Of course not. She doesn't belong to me," his father answered, absently filling the bowl of his pipe. The sweet-spicy fragrance of tobacco wafted across the room, comforting Lanston as he breathed it in. "But Rachelle's history is secure. The slave no longer has a tongue."

Surprised, Lanston looked up. The excision of a tongue was not such an unusual punishment; a few years before, the Wraggs' butler had been subjected to the same treatment after he unwisely disagreed with Lanston's mother about the proper way to welcome an unwelcome guest. But Rachelle was softhearted and altogether too lenient with her slaves, and she might not understand why Virtue had been . . . disciplined.

With an effort, Lanston forced himself to block thoughts of the slave and concentrate upon Rachelle. "Even if no one else knows, Father," he said with a cautionary lift of his hand, "nothing can change her heritage. She will always be tainted with Indian blood."

"Listen to me, Lanston." Ashton tasted his pipe, but only the barest nip; he was anxious to make his point. "We'll find the girl, and you will marry her. Her estate will become yours, and you can live with her or not, it doesn't matter. But after a month or two, as soon as we have had a chance to thoroughly invest the Fortier estate, you will discover that she has deceived you—that she is, in fact, somehow descended from a savage. And then you shall have the marriage annulled, and you shall give her to me."

"To you?" A dark premonition held Lanston still.

A satisfied glow rose in his father's face, as though a lantern had just been lit within him. "Of course. A comely young thing like that will fetch a pretty price at the slave market, though I'll have to send her elsewhere—'twould not do to sell her around here. But you will be free to marry whatever young lady catches your eye." Leaning back in his chair, he waved a careless hand toward Lanston. "Take a wife and sire a dozen children—you'll be able to afford them."

"Ashton!" Cambria's tone was coolly disapproving, but

Lanston's father shrugged off her objection and cast his son a sly grin.

"Woman, be still," he said, glancing for an instant at his wife. "My son and I are talking man to man, and I would be less than honest if I gave him imperfect advice."

Lanston sat in silence for a moment as his father smoked his pipe. Rachelle behaved as a genteel lady, no matter what her parentage, but he couldn't allow his family, his children, to be sullied by any trace of savage blood.

How the people of Charles Towne would mock him if they knew! The leaders in society were descended from English nobles and French lords; they were wealthy, prosperous people who had come to the New World to *increase* their fortunes, not to make them.

And he was a slave trader. He sold Indian females like cattle, scarcely noting whether one was tall or short or thin or strong, only that they were healthy and of childbearing age. Yet he might very well be selling men and women distantly related to his own future wife. . . .

Rachelle's image focused in his mind. Dressed in buckskin, with her glossy sable hair down about her shoulders, Rachelle could easily be mistaken for an Indian, except that—

She wasn't. She was his betrothed, and his heart stirred when he thought about taking her into his arms. His father's plan seemed heartless and difficult, but the alternative was impossible. And perhaps Bettencourt had simplified things. If Rachelle returned to Charles Towne no longer a virgin bride, he'd marry her—to keep his word—and would then be justified in casting her aside. Though it would be difficult to walk away from her delicious beauty, the world abounded with stunning women—of proper European descent.

In a surge of memory, he saw her standing on the deck of the pirate ship. Beautiful or not, a savage streak did run through her temperament. She had practically rebuffed him back upon the *Fitz James.*

Lanston lifted his gaze to meet his father's steely eyes.

"There's something I didn't want to tell you," he said, nervously tapping his fingertips together. "On the ship—the pirate didn't take Rachelle by force. She *chose* to go with him. I tried to stop her, but she wouldn't listen. She was determined to reach Boston as soon as possible."

Ashton snorted around the pipe stem in his mouth. "Headstrong girl, that one." Settling back in his chair, he removed his pipe and stared at it thoughtfully. "I can understand her reasoning, actually. Mistress Bailie's slave told me something else—this Mojag fellow was allied with a preacher in Boston by the name of John Eliot. The clergyman's dead now, been in his grave many years—the minister at St. Michael's knew him." His eyes narrowed in thought. "But your Rachelle wouldn't know old Eliot is dead—that's why she's so bent on reaching Boston."

He pointed his pipe at Lanston like a pistol. "If—and when—the pirate takes her there, she'll be asking for Eliot, and a pretty girl like our Rachelle will leave a trail."

Lanston forced his lips to part in a curved, still smile. "So you know men who can handle this sort of thing?"

"Son—" Ashton propped his pipe in his mouth again— "the colony of Carolina teems with hunters."

Trace threw another bough on the fire and watched its impact send a volcano of sparks into the night sky. The gentle slope of the overturned barge gleamed in the fire-tinted darkness, and beneath it he caught sight of two dark heads nestled close to one another. The women were sleeping under the boat, out of sight and sheltered from the wind, while Duncan lay propped against the stern, his leonine head thrown back, his mouth gaping in sleep. This was Trace's watch, his time to keep the shadows of the night at bay. His time to think.

Beyond him, the dull thunder of the incoming sea provided a comforting reminder that he wouldn't wrestle with these thoughts for long. Within a day or two he'd see these women safely to the man they sought. Then he and Duncan would steal a canoe or a scull and ride the currents down to Ocracoke.

In time, perhaps, he'd forget he'd ever met Rachelle Bailie.

He looked up at the sky, where a million sparks of diamond light brightened the dark canopy of night. The girl was terribly bourgeois, the product of a pampered environment where the less fortunate served the wealthy, where a slave mattered less than a dog or pampered house cat. Her mind ran in channels that were loathsome to him, and yet she'd proved remarkably resilient when her world came crashing down around her. She had loved the old man—he saw tears in her eyes every time she spoke of him—and yet she had managed to shelve her grief in a time of crisis. She hadn't shrieked or fainted or stormed when the British frigate moved in for an attack, and she'd been right clever in suggesting that he put her ashore in the barge.

"Quite admirable, really," he murmured, shivering from cold

as he pushed his bare feet into the sand until it mounded and spilled over his ankles. With the women safely asleep, he had removed his wet shirt and hung it from a stick near the fire, where it now danced in the wind like a ghostly scarecrow. His boots, still wet from his swim, stood by the fire, stiffening in the flickering heat.

On the morrow, after they'd found this man she sought, he'd bid Rachelle farewell and close the door on all the memories he had made today. After all, she was not a woman he could dream about. She was engaged to Lanston Wragg—an unexpected failing in her otherwise interesting personality—and when she returned to Charles Towne, she would undoubtedly resume her place as mistress of a vast slave estate. She had been born to it, after all, and the experiences of one week were not likely to affect her in any great way.

At least, he thought, looking out across the beach as if he could glimpse a picture of the future in the darkness, *Fala's life will be different.* Rachelle had granted the Indian's freedom, and he didn't believe she would renege on her agreement. So for one slave, at least, the morrow would bring the promise of more freedom than yesterday.

Somewhere out at sea, a gunboat fired: a deep, booming note that echoed from another ship a moment later. Trace held his breath, listening for sounds of active engagement, then exhaled in relief. The guns were no more than a signal from one ship to another, the mariner's way of indicating that all was well.

He glanced over at his charges and saw that Rachelle had turned. Her hair swirled over the sand like the eddying tide of a dark river; a few loose tendrils softened her sleeping face and lifted gently in the sea breeze. One hand lay near her face, the palm turned upward in a gesture of supplication. *For what?* he wondered. Probably the father she'd already risked much to find. Tomorrow he would see her safely to this minister who would know where her father worked, and then he would trust her welfare to God above.

"Bon voyage," he whispered softly, studying the fringe of

dark lashes that crowned her cheek. *Good voyage. Go with God. But for tonight, stay safe with me.*

He wouldn't think about the morrow.

▼▲▼▲▼ Rachelle clung to the soft darkness as hard as she could, pillowing her face on her hand, tasting sand and salt. The sound of lapping wavelets filled her ears; then her body awakened to the realization that someone was pawing at her petticoat.

Panting in terror, she looked up, then melted in relief as she saw Fala crouching at her feet, busily knocking the encrusted layer of sand from Rachelle's gown. Last night they had had to jump from the barge into the surf, and though Rachelle had tried to lift her gown, the waves had drenched her from the knees down.

"Mmm," she murmured, letting her head fall back onto her hand. Then realization struck, and she lifted her head again. "Fala, you don't have to do that. You're a free woman now, remember?"

The Indian woman straightened, then glanced down at her dirt-encrusted hands. "But I thought—I thought I was still your maid, mademoiselle. And old habits—" She lifted one slender shoulder in a shrug.

"They die slowly, I know." Rachelle pushed herself into a sitting position, hitting her head on the boat above. "Ouch!" Grimacing, she rubbed her head and looked across the narrow space toward Fala. "Have you been out?" She lowered her voice, not certain exactly who stirred outside the shelter of the overturned boat. "Is the captain—"

"He and Mr. MacKinnon," Fala's mouth curved in an unconscious smile, "are at the water's edge. They are trying to catch a fish for breakfast."

Rachelle's stomach tightened at the thought of food. They had not eaten since their dinner of sea biscuit and dried beef yesterday at noon, and suddenly she felt as hungry as a winter wolf.

She ducked down on the damp sand and peered out the opening between the edge of the boat and the ground. Captain Bettencourt and his first mate were about fifty feet away with their backs to her. Both men had discarded their boots and stockings and were walking through the shallow surf with bare legs, an odd contrast to their frilled shirts and billowing sleeves.

"How do they fish without a pole?" Rachelle murmured, folding her hands beneath her chin.

"A string and a hook," Fala answered in a matter-of-fact tone. Rachelle glanced over at her maid, then paused, caught by a sudden change in Fala's appearance. The blank, bland look had vanished, replaced by a lovely expression that displayed a canny awareness. Intelligence and independence of spirit shone from Fala's eyes. Had Rachelle been too self-absorbed to see it before now?

"Fala," she said, reaching out to touch the woman's arm, "I need to get dressed. Will you bind my hair for me?"

The light in Fala's eyes dimmed as suddenly as if Rachelle had turned the wick in an oil lamp. "Yes, Mademoiselle Rachelle."

She spoke with a light bitterness, and Rachelle increased her pressure upon her maid's arm. "If you'll bind my hair," she said, speaking slowly, "I'll bind yours." She smiled as Fala's eyes brightened with pleasure. "Though my hair will certainly look more presentable than yours, for I've not the knack for arrangement you have."

"I'll teach you," Fala said, crawling through the sand to sit behind Rachelle. Rachelle tried to sit up and hold her head erect, but soon both women were laughing as they realized they could not accomplish their ministrations in the tight quarters beneath the overturned boat.

"Out in the wind, then," Rachelle said, crawling as she led the way. Outside the boat, dawn had spread a gray light over the beach. She settled atop a small patch of sea grass, resting her hands upon her knees, rejoicing in the familiar touch of Fala's hands in her hair. Before her in the waves, the two men worked together, the wind billowing their shirts and blowing their hair free from the ribbons they used to tie it back.

Rachelle breathed deep and felt a stab of memory, a broken remnant from a dream, a shard sharp as glass. Last night, in sleep, she had opened her eyes to see the captain's shirt suspended by the fire, fluttering in the fire heat. Trace Bettencourt stood beside the fire, his bare back exposed to the chilly wind, his brown hair ruffled by the sea breeze. In his bare arms he carried a load of driftwood, but Rachelle's eyes froze on his back.

He looked very powerful, his back broad and muscular, but the bronzed skin was marked with red and white lines, some smooth, some ridged. Rachelle felt a sudden chill, realizing what she saw. These lines were like the ones she'd seen marking the legs of the little black boys at the Wraggs' house—the same lines that now scarred Fala's back, and Dustu's.

The marks of a whip. By the sheer number of them, Trace Bettencourt had endured more than a few beatings, but from whom? A naval captain? Another pirate?

She turned her gaze toward the sea, her eyes still blurry with the afterimage of those angry scars. No wonder he felt such sympathy for oppressed slaves. His methods did reek of anarchy and lawlessness, but she was beginning to understand why he pursued such an unusual course.

Her eyes followed the captain, and a tiny glow cheered her when, at one point, he turned, searched the beach, and smiled at her in greeting. She managed a shy wave in return, then lowered her eyes as a blush burned her cheek.

He was probably just checking to be sure they had awakened. But happiness filled her heart at the thought that he had taken the time to look for her.

▼▲▼▲▼ They breakfasted on a strange-looking fish Fala had never tasted before, covered their fire pit with sand, and gathered armloads of shrubs in an effort to disguise the boat. "It's not likely that we'll be needing it, but one never knows,"

Fala heard Captain Bettencourt tell Duncan MacKinnon. "And it might come in handy before the day is through."

After making themselves as presentable as possible, the foursome walked over the sand dunes and made their way to a small house not far from the beach. While Trace stood back with Fala and Rachelle, Duncan went to the house, knocked, and offered the bewhiskered man who answered the door a finely made boat in exchange for a horse and wagon. The man flatly refused, probably owning a fleet of fishing boats and not many horses, but when Duncan promised to leave the wagon at Roxbury so the man could retrieve it, the deal was made.

"You don't have to go with us to Roxbury," Rachelle told Captain Bettencourt as they made their way to the barn. "You have a ship and men who need you. I don't expect you to fulfill your promise to the letter."

The captain's mouth twisted in a wry smile. "I cannot leave you on the beach, mademoiselle," he said, taking her arm as they walked around a malodorous pile outside the barn door. "You are quite out of your element."

Fala smothered a smile at that remark. The captain was right. Rachelle thought of herself as an independent woman, but she had been dependent upon Captain Bettencourt ever since she crawled aboard his ship. *And what does he expect in return for his generosity?* Fala wondered, noting the power that coiled within him as he walked. Thus far he had behaved as a model gentleman, but he was a pirate, after all.

The barn doors yawned wide, and the bearded man led out a swaybacked mare lashed to a rough buckboard. "Here's my wagon," he said, his hand firmly clenched around the mare's reins. "Now, where's my boat?"

"Down on yonder beach," Duncan said, pointing back the way they had come. "Covered by brush. You canna miss it if you walk straight toward the sea."

The old man regarded Duncan with a speculative gaze. "How do I know you're speaking the truth? You coulda walked up here from the town."

"My good man, look at us," the captain sputtered, spreading his hands to indicate his sand-encrusted shirt and breeches. "We came in from the sea, and I have left you a boat. Follow our footsteps; our trail is as evident as the light of day."

"You didn't say," the old man drawled, his eyes passing warily from Fala to Rachelle to Duncan and back to the captain, "what business you had out on the sea."

"I beg your pardon, monsieur, but that is none of your concern." A warning cloud settled on the captain's sharp features, and the old man grew still at the sight of it. "Either you take our word—which I guarantee is good—and gain a boat as well as the return of your horse and wagon, or you shall bid us adieu and think no more of it. What shall your decision be?"

A suspicious line darkened the corners of the old man's mouth, but he nodded and released his grip on the horse's reins. "Leave the wagon at Roxbury Church, then," he said, handing the leather straps to Duncan. "And have someone tend the mare. I'll be along to fetch her back before the week is out."

"Merci beaucoup." The captain moved to the wagon and put out his hand to assist Rachelle; Fala moved automatically to the rear, prepared to hop onto the back. She paused, though, when she heard the captain call her name. A new and unexpected warmth flowed through her as she looked up and saw him standing at the front, his hand extended . . . for her.

She would ride up front. This wasn't exactly a luxurious carriage, but she would ride with her head level with—perhaps even higher than—Rachelle Fortier Bailie's.

Slowly, as if moving in a dream, Fala lifted her petticoat and walked to the captain, meeting his smile with one of her own. His strong hand lifted her up to the bench beside Duncan; then he moved toward the bearded man. After consulting with the man for a moment, the captain walked round to the rear of the wagon and leaped aboard, sliding forward until he sat beside Rachelle.

Fala folded her hands in her lap, enjoying the solid feel of the kind seaman who sat next to her. Freedom! Perhaps she would come to like it, after all.

▼▲▼▲▼ Though Captain Bettencourt knew the sea, he did not know the land of this area, and he shared what he'd learned from the old man in the house. They had landed on a narrow peninsula called Point Allerton, and Roxbury lay at least seventeen miles to the northwest.

Rachelle didn't think seventeen miles a very great distance until she saw the wagon-rutted path that scored the earth in this desolate stretch. With a heart grown sore with impatience, she leaned against the back of the driver's seat and settled in for a long ride. A journey of seventeen miles would take at least a full day on a road as rough as this one.

The old fisherman had directed them to keep the sea at their right hand, and so they followed the twisting curves of lanes that passed through settlements at Nantasket, Hingham, Weymouth, and Neponset—unfamiliar names that twisted Rachelle's tongue as she tried to repeat them. The mare's gait was more sure than swift, and the miles crawled by with a deliberate and stubborn persistence.

Duncan and Fala carried on a low and intense conversation on the driver's bench, and Rachelle shifted uneasily, wondering if Captain Bettencourt expected her to entertain him with conversation. He had said nothing since informing her of the distance and the fisherman's directions but sat quite still, his long legs casually stretched out over the wagon and crossed at the ankle, the warmth of his shoulder occasionally touching hers when the wagon jostled in the road. Even though he had swum, fished, and slept in his clothes, he looked remarkably dapper in his dark blue canvas trousers and full-sleeved shirt.

"Captain Bettencourt," she began, hoping she could find some topic that might interest him. She glanced up in time to see his eyes fly open.

"Hmm?"

Rachelle stammered in embarrassment. This man had kept watch over her all night, and she had just interrupted his sorely needed sleep.

"I'm so sorry," she murmured, heat stealing into her face. "I didn't know you were resting. Please, don't let me disturb you."

"Is something troubling you, mademoiselle?" he asked. His face was serious, but one corner of his mouth turned up as if he found her discomfiture somehow amusing.

"Nothing, nothing at all." She folded her arms around her waist. "Sleep, I beg you. Think nothing of me."

He rubbed a hand across his face, and she heard the faint rasp of his morning stubble. "If it's conversation you need," he murmured, his voice low and confidential, "you'd best talk to me because I don't think you'll be finding it from the two driving this wagon. They seem quite taken with each other."

Rachelle smiled, grateful that he had so skillfully turned the conversation from her embarrassing blunder. "I noticed," she said, her fingers drumming distractedly on her wrist. "I do not believe Fala has ever spoken so many words in her entire life . . . at least not to anyone but me."

"She has probably never felt free to speak so much," he answered, but when Rachelle lifted her gaze to his she could find no accusation or blame in his eyes. She looked away quickly, feeling her blush deepen, but he kindly took no notice of her heightening color. "You have done very well, Mademoiselle Rachelle, and I must commend you."

"Oh?" A thrill of pleasure shivered through her senses at the thought that he approved of her. Then a skeptical inner voice clamped down on her happiness. Why was she accepting flattery from a pirate? He approved of *stealing*, after all.

"Captain Bettencourt," she said, impatiently pulling her drifting thoughts together, "I have to thank you for all you've done."

"You are not yet to your destination, are you?" He turned sideways to look directly at her. "Since I took you away from your escort, Mr. Wragg, and your means of transport, it is my responsibility to see you safely to Roxbury."

"Even so," she answered, vowing to show him how independent she could be, "you need not linger with us on my account. You have a shipload of responsibilities and work to finish." She felt her throat close at the thought of what his work actually was.

"My work is keeping my word." He gave her a bright-eyed glance, full of shrewdness. "And I have not yet kept my word. My work is here, until you are safely delivered to someone who will take charge of you."

"Hmm." She looked away before their eyes could lock in open warfare. He was just like Lanston and her grandfather, another man who felt she needed protection. She didn't, but she couldn't deny that having a man along made her way easier. She and Fala would never have been able to handle the barge alone, nor could they have kept a fire going throughout the night. And never, not even using her most brazen flirtation, could she have convinced the obstinate fisherman at Point Allerton to surrender his only horse.

She let her gaze drift outside the wagon. An emerald ribbon of fields and foliage bordered the road, and yet behind the greenery she could still hear the call of the sea. Surely the captain heard it, too.

"I know you must rejoin your men." She paused, listening to the squeak of the horse's harness. "But I don't see how you can reach them in thirteen days. Seeing me to Roxbury will take precious time. You won't be able to take a carriage to Carolina—"

His mouth quirked with humor. "My dear girl, I could scarcely reach Carolina by carriage in a month. No, Duncan and I will go to the port and find a boat. With a faint wind and a fair amount of luck, we'll have no trouble reaching the *Jacques.*"

She shrugged to hide her confusion. "You'll rent a boat?"

His eyes filled with remoteness, though his smile did not change. "I said we'd *find* a boat. We will find our way, mademoiselle, and you need not take thought for us."

Rachelle looked away, as embarrassed as if he'd slapped her. Why was she determined to envision him as some sort of knight in shining armor? He was a *pirate,* a thief on the seas, and he clearly meant to steal a boat in order to rejoin his men. Perhaps he'd even commandeer a crew. After all, he was armed and dangerous—she carried his pistol in her own valise.

She settled back, disappointed that her energies were wasted against his granite personality. But why couldn't he change?

After a long pause, during which she fought for courage and self-control, she tilted her face toward him. "Captain Bettencourt, you cannot do this." She spoke with quiet, heartfelt firmness. "Give up this life and your evil ways. Find some other occupation. If you could convince me to give Fala her freedom, I must try to convince you to beg God's forgiveness and resume your place in a world of virtuous men—"

"You did not give her freedom." His voice rang with defiance as well as a subtle challenge. "You restored it. She was born free. You only set things right. My life, mademoiselle, cannot be set right. I have no choice in the matter, and I hope you will not broach this subject again."

He reached upward, a gesture surely meant to pull his tricorne over his eyes and shut her out, but he had left his hat on the ship. After halfheartedly tugging on a tuft of dark hair on his forehead, he straightened in the wagon and crossed his arms, ready for sleep again.

Rachelle shifted her weight, turning away from him, and let her gaze fill with the vista of silver water, shimmering skyline, and endless cobalt sky. Trace Bettencourt, a monumentally self-confident pirate, had taken her under his wing for reasons she might never understand. But his words had just proved that their relationship would be a temporary and one-sided affair. She would need, he would provide; she would change, he would remain as inflexible as an iron bar.

▾▴▾▴▾ Too agitated to doze, Trace closed his eyes against the sun and seethed with anger and humiliation. Why did she insist upon painting him as some sort of gentleman? He was an outlaw, banished like Cain from Eden, forever exiled from the drawing rooms and fellowship of respectable men and women. He still retained a measure of feeling and honor, but his rules were his own, his ethics born out of scorn for a society that enslaved the weak and defiled the innocent.

She could not expect him to behave like a saint. He had committed too many sins, burned too many bridges—and ships. He was what he was, a fugitive pirate, and if she couldn't bear the fact that a less-than-righteous man had rescued her from a precarious situation, then she would have to embellish the story on her own terms.

He snorted softly, imagining her retelling this adventure over a quiet ladies' tea table in some Charles Towne mansion. She would recount this venture again and again, and with each telling the image of the frightful pirate Bettencourt would grow more vigorous, more valiant, more vulgarly heroic. And when all the ladies were atwitter with alarm and delight, Lanston Wragg would slide open the double doors leading to the room where he held court with a circle of men. "Hello, my darling," he'd say, coming forward to place his hands upon Rachelle's cream-colored shoulders—

Alarm and anger rippled along Trace's spine, and he twisted in the wagon, turning away from the woman at his side and the vision that ripped at his heart. "*Dépêchez-vous!* Move along, horse!" he muttered under his breath. "Spare me from women!"

▼▲▼▲▼ Fala had half listened to the brief conversation between her mistress and the captain, and after two hours of stony silence from the wagon bed, she knew all was not well between them. When they halted to water the horse, Fala took Rachelle's hand and helped her from the wagon, walking beside her mistress as they went into the woods to relieve themselves.

As Rachelle stomped over the ground, confused and crazily furious, Fala sank onto a rock and looked her mistress in the eye.

"Mademoiselle Rachelle," she murmured, thinking that she

had spoken that phrase at least ten thousand times in her life-time, "won't you tell me what is wrong?"

Rachelle flushed to the roots of her hair. "The captain, of course!"

Fala clasped her hands, bracing herself for the explosion to come.

Rachelle's eyes were black and dazzling with fury. "How can a man be so honorable and yet so . . . base? After he leaves us, Fala, he and Duncan will go to the coast and steal a boat or some-thing." Defiance poured hotly from her eyes. "I thought he was an honorable man! I thought so even aboard the *Fitz James,* else I would not have boarded his ship. And yet he says he must con-tinue to steal! He says he cannot change, that he is set on remain-ing as he is."

"Not every man can change," Fala said, thinking of Dustu. Despite his promise to her, he would run again, Fala knew. His wife and child tugged at his heart, and he would never accept the fate life had dealt him.

Rachelle's head snapped around. "What do you mean?"

"Some men," Fala said, slowly lifting her eyes to meet her mis-tress's hot gaze, "are bound by one thing or another to situations they cannot accept. And yet they are driven to do what they must, knowing that by their actions they will destroy them-selves."

Rachelle made a gesture of dismissal. "Trace Bettencourt can change, Fala, I know he can! Don't you see? We are going to find my father, a minister. And surely a minister can make the captain change. That's what preachers do—they change lives."

"Some ministers," Fala inserted, recalling the severe clergy-man who regularly visited the slave quarters. He intoned a monthly service so dry and dull that, apart from Fala, not a sin-gle slave in the Fortier household had ever wished to convert to Christianity.

"My father," Rachelle answered in a tense, clipped voice that forbade any dispute, "is a *wonderful* clergyman. My mother wouldn't have loved him if he weren't . . . exceptional. Mojag

Bailie works among the Indians, *your* people, Fala, and he has managed to convince many of them to convert. If he can reach a savage, surely he can reach a French captain!"

Fala did not answer, stunned by Rachelle's unthinking bluntness.

"But—" Rachelle ran a hand through her tangled hair in a distracted motion—"there is, of course, the introduction to be made first. My father does not know me, or know of me, and I'm afraid he will not—" Unconsciously her brow furrowed.

"You're afraid?"

"Yes." Rachelle's dark eyes brimmed with sudden tears. "Oh yes, Fala, I'm afraid. What if he doesn't believe my story? Or what if he does, but he doesn't like me? What if he doesn't want to be reminded of my mother? What if he holds bitterness toward her? What if I am the last person on earth he would want to see?" Tears flew down her cheeks like rain. "What if he has married again and has other children? Oh, Fala, I don't know what I shall do if he doesn't want me!"

Fala opened her arms, and Rachelle ran to her, kneeling on the wet leaves as she enfolded Fala's waist in a childish embrace. "Fala," she wept, burying her face in the folds of Fala's gown, "what if this is all a mistake? Perhaps I was meant to die in the earthquake or of the pox like my mother. What if God never meant me to do this?"

"Mademoiselle Rachelle, the great God who watches the eagle in the air and the ant upon a leaf will surely watch you, too. How do you know he did not protect you through the pox and the earthquake and the fire?"

Rachelle lifted her head, swallowing hard and biting back tears. "Perhaps you're right." She thumbed a tear from her cheek and smiled at the gleam of gold upon her right hand. "At least I have this," she said, looking down at the ring. "And by this, he will know me. My father will have no doubts."

"Through the goodness of Captain Bettencourt, you still have that," Fala pointed out, nodding toward the ring. "There is goodness in the man, mademoiselle. Believe it."

"Yes." Rachelle stood, smoothed her dress, and wiped the last wetness of tears from her face. "There is goodness in him." She tried to smile, but the corners of her mouth wobbled precariously. "How do you suppose I can help him see it?"

▼▲▼▲ The western sky had begun to blaze with violent shades of copper and amethyst by the time they entered the quiet village of Roxbury. Though Rachelle ached from her shoulders to her toes after jostling all day in the wagon, her heart stirred with anticipation. Rising to her knees in the wagon, she turned and scanned each farmhouse and merchant's shop with eager eyes. In one of them her father might be sitting down to dinner or lighting his hearth fire.

As Duncan slowed the wagon, the mare whickered and shook her head. The bit jangled in her mouth, the only sound Rachelle could hear above the pounding of her heart. "Where shall we go first, Mistress Bailie?" Duncan asked, turning in the seat to look at her.

Duncan's sudden question did nothing to calm the fear that spurred the uneven pulse of her blood. Where, indeed? Rachelle almost laughed. She had come so far and was now so close, but still there was another layer of mystery to strip away.

"We're looking for the Reverend John Eliot," she said, clutching the side of the wagon as she thought. "I suppose the village church would be the most likely place to look. The minister's house is likely close by."

"Aye," Duncan answered, slapping the mare's reins. The mare walked on, her head nodding up and down to the slow rhythm of her feet. Rachelle clung to the side of the wagon, watching the village slide by. Roxbury's narrow cobblestone streets were nearly deserted of traffic and pedestrians, for the hour was late. Two women near the road stopped their conversation long enough to cast curious glances at the foursome as the wagon pushed through town.

Suddenly the point of a thatched roof leaped up from the

other structures. The small building of squared logs sat apart upon a hill and was encircled by a winter gray lawn dotted with granite tombstones. "There." Rachelle pointed to the building, then gathered the bulk of her gown in her hands. "That has to be the church."

She leaped from the wagon scarcely before Duncan brought the mare to a stop. She thought she heard Trace mutter an oath under his breath, but she was too anxious to wait for him to see her properly out of the wagon. She was grateful for his help, but this errand had nothing to do with him.

A faded picket fence, once white, surrounded the churchyard and cemetery. The sprained gate hung open, allowing her to walk directly up the stone steps leading into the building. She opened the protesting door and peered into the silence. No one moved in the dim space beyond.

"Hello?" she called. There was no answering sound, but the air inside had the peculiar muffled quality that Rachelle always associated with churches.

She moved into the tiny sanctuary and marveled that such a revered minister pastored such a small church. The meeting-house was barely twenty feet wide from window to opposite window and thirty feet from the front door to the back wall. No spire adorned the outside. Those who worshiped here sat not on carved pews but on dust-covered benches. A somber pulpit of dark mahogany stood at the front of the room; an altar table draped in white satin rose out of the gloom like a shimmering shadow.

"Hello?" she called again, her footsteps puffing softly over the earthen floor.

From beyond the door she heard the captain's and Fala's voices. They had not followed her in but waited outside, proba- bly stretching and tending to the horse. They would wait for her, she knew, for as long as it took to find someone to give her the answers she needed.

She sank onto a bench and lowered her head, absently pinch- ing the bridge of her nose as she began to pray. "Our Father which art in heaven," she whispered, the desperate words flowing from habit, "hallowed be thy name. Thy kingdom come. Thy will be done—but, God, please, let me find him!"

"May I help you?" A voice as dry as a desert broke the stillness.

Rachelle looked up, startled. A tall, dark figure had stepped from the shadows behind the pulpit. Her eyes, adjusted now to the dim light, saw a small door in the wall there, probably the pastor's entrance. Was this John Eliot?

The stranger, a tall, distinguished-looking man in his late forties or so, stood before her, his hands wrapped around a green plant festooned with small orange fruit. His hands were sprinkled with black dirt, the knees of his breeches stained with grime. Obviously she had interrupted his gardening, but there was no sign of annoyance on his pale, sensitive face. He gazed at her, his gaze respectful and curious.

"Excuse me, Mistress—?"

"Rachelle Bailie." She blushed, realizing that she had been staring at him, then stood and managed a swift curtsey. "And yes, you can help me. I have come a long way in order to find Reverend John Eliot." She lifted her eyes in a ringing impulse of hope. "Are you—"

"No." An infinitely compassionate tone filled his voice, but his smile was strained. "Came far, did you?"

"From Carolina." She lifted her hand and pointed toward the south, feeling suddenly limp with weariness. "Charles Towne."

"The seaport?" He pushed his bottom lip forward in thought. "My father did not have any associations so far south."

"You're John Eliot's son?" She straightened, instantly wide awake. "Can you take me to your father?"

Slowly he nodded, uncertainly studying her beneath a tilted brow. "I am Joseph Eliot," he said, extending his arm toward the small door through which he had appeared. "And yes, I'll take you to my father. Come with me."

He turned on his heel and strode to the door, then held it open for Rachelle to precede him through the low doorway. She gasped in surprise to see that she had entered a small conservatory. Wide panes of glass had been set into the roof of the structure, amplifying what little sunlight was available, and a blazing oven in the center of the room comforted the collection of plants not yet ready to withstand the cold outdoors.

"My avocation," Joseph Eliot said, waving his hand at the plants as he led Rachelle to another door on the far side of the conservatory. "I've always thought that men should have hobbies, and the Sabbath is the only day I'm free to fuss with my wee plants." With one smooth gesture he dumped the rootbound plant he carried into a pot, then wiped his hands on his breeches. With a gallant bow, he opened the final door and waited for Rachelle to exit.

She stepped out into the graveyard she had noticed from the road. Compared to the scorching heat of the conservatory, the cemetery seemed bitterly cold. A chill pearl-colored mist hung in the air and entwined around the gravestones, and Rachelle felt a thin, cold blade of foreboding slice into her heart.

She smiled at Joseph Eliot in pity. Poor man, to find it necessary to walk through the land of the dead in order to reach his house.

"This way," Joseph said, leading her over a path that pointed a curving finger through the burial monuments. Through the trees she caught a glimpse of a small white house, tidy and welcoming. The parsonage, Rachelle assumed. Perhaps the elder Reverend Eliot had retired and left his ministry in his son's hands.

The engraved tombstones shone in the tangerine tints of the setting sun, but Rachelle only glanced at them, so intent was she upon reaching John Eliot. How could she begin to explain her presence? Would he believe her story? He would when he saw the ring. Babette had written that the ring had been a part of Mojag Bailie's family for years; perhaps Reverend Eliot had seen it often.

Joseph Eliot stopped abruptly underneath a sprawling tree,

and Rachelle glanced up, wondering if he had forgotten something.

"There," he said, his voice like an echo from an empty tomb. "Beneath the *Quercus alba.*" His eyes had fastened onto a large, simply carved gravestone at the base of a sprawling white oak. Rachelle closed her eyes, her heart aching, then stepped forward to read the inscription.

> Reverend John Eliot
> Pastor of Roxbury Church 58 years
> "Prayer and pains, through faith in Christ Jesus, will do anything."

A sense of anticlimax washed over her. "Dead?" she asked woodenly, her eyes locked to the gravestone, refusing to believe its message. How could John Eliot be lying here in the black-velvet shadow of an oak tree when she needed him so much?

"My father died seven years ago," Eliot replied, shaking his head regretfully. "But he lived to a good old age." He folded his hands and regarded her, squinting slightly as his jaw shifted to one side. "I can't imagine how you heard of my father. As I said, he had no dealings with anyone in Carolina."

"Mojag Bailie," she whispered, feeling empty and drained. She turned, gazing at Joseph in despair. "I don't suppose you have heard of him."

"But of course I have." His broad face broke into a leisurely smile. "And I'm sorry, I should have put the pieces together."

"You—know me?" Rachelle asked, all her loneliness and confusion melding together in one upsurge of devouring yearning.

"No, mistress, I do not." He shook his head and gazed at her speculatively. "But I know that Mojag Bailie has gone to Carolina."

Rachelle merely stared, tongue-tied and unable to speak, but suddenly she felt a hand under her elbow and heard Trace Bettencourt's voice, deep timbred and strong. "Perhaps, my good reverend, you will offer us a cup of tea while we explain our purpose in seeking Mr. Bailie? If you'd be so kind as to offer us shelter, we could protect the women from the weather."

"Excuse me, of course." Reverend Eliot lifted his hand and gestured toward the small house. "Come with me, all of you. My wife will have a pot of tea on the stove, and we would be delighted to welcome you to our home."

The hand beneath Rachelle's elbow moved up to clasp her own. She clung to it, closing her eyes and taking deep breaths until she felt strong enough to raise her head and follow the minister. John Eliot was dead and gone, but his son knew Mojag Bailie. And though Rachelle was farther from her father than when she had set out to find him, at least she knew he was alive.

She looked over at the captain and gave him a look of relief and thanks, which he acknowledged with just the smallest softening of his eyes. Then together they walked along the path to the minister's house.

Feeling more uncomfortable in a minister's house than he
wanted to admit, Trace squirmed in his chair, accepting a scone
from the tea tray Madame Eliot offered. He had explained his
presence by saying that he and Duncan had stepped in to accompany Mademoiselle Bailie and her maid when her former escort
was unable to fulfill his obligation, and Madame Eliot had been
profuse in her praise.

"Oh, so good and gentlemanly of you to look after a helpless
girl," Madame Eliot crowed, her faintly rosy mouth wide with
pleasure. "To be sure, the Lord will bless you, Monsieur
Bettencourt. He will shower you with blessings in this life and
the next and crown you with honor and loving-kindness—"

"Thank you, madame," Trace interrupted, a wry smile curling
on his lips. "But I would be content with a safe return to my
home."

"And where would home be?" the lady asked. Her round face
showed no more than mild interest, but her blue eyes were alert
in their pockets of flesh.

Trace brought his teacup to his lips, hesitating. He hadn't mentioned that he was a sea captain, though if the woman had half a
nose she would have smelled the scent of salt upon him.

"Madame," he answered gravely, his cup chinking softly as it
came to rest in its dainty saucer. "Home is where the heart is, no?
And at the moment I fear my heart is wandering in search of a
safe place to rest."

"Oh, Monsieur Bettencourt." The woman giggled and pressed
her hand to her ample bosom. "How poetic! I've always heard

that the French were more romantic than the English, and now I know 'tis true."

They had gathered in the minister's keeping room for introductions and explanations, and now that the introductions were out of the way, Reverend Joseph Eliot began to explain the particulars of Mojag's ministry to the Indians. "After King Philip's War," he said, his soil-grimed hands fanning the air as he waxed eloquent, "Mojag Bailie appeared from among the ranks of that dread savage's own people. He lived for a time with his sister, Aiyana Glazier, then announced that life in a praying village was not God's will for him."

"A praying village?" Duncan asked.

"Yea." Joseph smiled briefly. "A bold experiment doomed to fail, I'm afraid. My father hoped that the converted Indians would adapt to our lifestyles and learn how to live and work as we do. But though many were happy for a time, we are fighting a losing battle. Mojag always suspected that the natives might have a difficult time adapting to our Puritan ethics, and I'm afraid he was right. The number of Indians in the praying villages has dwindled considerably."

Joseph turned to Rachelle and studied her thoughtfully for a moment. "After Mojag Bailie left the praying village, we lost sight of him for a long while. Then my father heard that he had gone to live with the Oneida, one of the tribes affiliated with the Iroquois confederacy."

"Yes, that is the one," Rachelle whispered, featherlike laugh lines crinkling around her dark eyes. "That is the tribe—I mean, that's the last tribe I knew about. Where he went from there, I have no way of knowing."

For a long moment the minister said nothing, then he looked back at Rachelle. "Why?" he asked simply, his eyes narrowing with concern and a trace of suspicion. "Why would a lovely French girl cross the threshold of my church searching for Mojag Bailie? He was not well liked among our people—the Puritans, I mean. He said what he thought far too many times, and his thoughts were . . . unconventional, to say the least."

Trace felt his heart constrict as Rachelle slipped the gold ring from her finger and quietly placed it in the minister's hand. Joseph frowned, studying the simple band, then fished his spectacles from his waistcoat pocket. After hooking the frames around his ears, he held the ring up and read the inscription.

A tense silence enveloped the room; then Trace smiled as understanding dawned upon the minister's square face. Eliot sat back and stared at Rachelle, his expression shifting into a look of gratification. "So something good did come out of Mojag's marriage to the Frenchwoman," he whispered, his voice choked with sincerity.

Trace lowered his head to hide his expression of chagrin; apparently the topic of Mojag's marriage had been a matter of debate and discussion among the Eliots for years.

"Is my father well?" Rachelle asked, her face pale and pinched. "I can journey back to Carolina to find him, but I must know if he is alive and . . . able to bear the news I want to bring him."

The minister slipped his smooth hand over hers. "Mojag Bailie is alive, as strong and determined as ever," he said, patting her hand. "We are about the same age, but I wish I had half his endurance. Though his methods have always been unique, he has been a bright light for our Lord in the wilderness." He sighed with exasperation. "When the trouble with the French and Indians erupted around the time of King William's War, I wanted Mojag to come work with us in Roxbury. But he remained with the Iroquois until recently. Apparently he heard something of a Carolina tribe in need—through rumors on the Indian trails, I suppose—and we heard he was off to help them. He has been gone about a month."

Rachelle's face lit in a relieved smile, and the beauty of her expression forced Trace to catch his breath. He had better be careful—he was in the company of a minister and a beautiful woman, the only two forces in the world likely to endanger his soul . . . and weaken his resolution.

Reverend Eliot suddenly snapped his fingers. "Bless my soul,

I should have thought of it sooner. My dear, would you like to learn more about your father? I have letters—an entire stack of them—detailing Mojag's experiences in the wilderness. They begin some years ago, when he corresponded with my father, and the latest are quite current."

"Could I read them?" Rachelle leaned forward, a look of mad happiness upon her face.

Trace felt his own brows knit into a frown. During the week they traveled northward on the *Jacques*, she had confided the story of her mother and father, but Trace suspected there were aspects to the tale Rachelle herself might not know. *Careful, cherie, some things are best left undiscovered. . . .*

"Wouldn't you like to take a bath before dinner?" asked Madame Eliot, who looked askance at the women's dirty, wrinkled gowns. "I could wash out your petticoat and bodice, and your maid's, too."

Apparently the dowager cared little for the filthy, stiff condition of the men's clothing.

"That is very kind of you, Madame Eliot," Trace interrupted, looking over at Duncan. "Why don't we let the good lady of the house tend to the mademoiselles while we see to the horse?" He lowered his voice to a confidential tone and leaned toward the minister. "The beast belongs to a good fisherman who will come to claim it by week's end. If that mare is not fit when he returns, he'll be demanding my head."

"A most suitable suggestion." Madame Eliot stood to her feet and spread her hands over her hips, fixing Rachelle in a steely gaze. "Upstairs, both of you girls, and we'll get you out of those soiled garments."

"But we have nothing else to wear," Rachelle protested, alarm crossing her face.

"Nonsense. I have two day gowns that will suit you nicely. You will wear them to supper while your own clothes are drying, and on the morrow you'll be fit for church."

"Church?" Trace lifted an eyebrow.

"Of course. You'll stay the night and worship with us on the morrow," Joseph Eliot answered, smiling broadly. "You'll need a fresh start in body and spirit if you must return to Carolina. And, my dear Mademoiselle Bailie, you can read those letters tonight."

Trace felt his belly tighten. He hadn't set foot inside a church in years. And to do so now, after the events of the last few months—

Anxiety swelled like a tumor in his chest. He opened his mouth, searching for words of protest, but Rachelle was quicker to speak than he.

"We could never begin to repay you for your kindness," she said, standing. She extended her hand to the minister, then gave Madame Eliot a gracious smile. "I would like nothing better than to accept your offer."

▼▲▼▲▼ An hour later, bathed and dressed in one of Mistress Eliot's gowns (a garment that had obviously fitted that lady in younger, slimmer days), Fala followed her mistress downstairs to supper. A flicker of apprehension coursed through her veins as Duncan graciously pulled out a chair for her at the minister's board table. Though she had eaten with the captain and his first mate on board the *Jacques*, that was an isolated incident, for a ship was a country within itself. This was the *real* world, these were *white* people, and they were expecting her to behave as one of them.

She sank onto the chair, thinking that at any moment Mistress Eliot would realize her mistake and send Fala out to eat in the kitchen, but the minister and his wife took their places, as did Rachelle and Captain Bettencourt. Fala slowly exhaled, letting her gaze gently caress the shining china, the gleaming silver candlesticks, the luscious venison roast swimming in gravy. The drinks were poured into handsome pewter mugs, and she trembled at the thought of lifting one, afraid it might slip through her fingers.

Reverend Joseph Eliot bowed his head for a prayer of thanksgiving, then lifted his napkin and smiled in gratitude at his wife.

As the bowls began to move around the table, the conversation began in earnest.

"The plant you saw me carrying today," Joseph Eliot said, his brown eyes warming with interest in his topic, "is a most unusual specimen. *Lycopersicon esculentum,* of the deadly nightshade family. I've heard that it originally came from the land of the Aztecs, and the Catholic Spaniards brought the fruit to us. They call it a tomato. 'Tis a pity those charming bright fruit are decidedly poisonous."

"Poisonous?" Duncan stared at the minister, then burst out laughing. "That tomato isna at all poisonous. I've had a wee tomato plant since we left Barbados last year, and I eat the little fruit just like candy. Verra delicious, they are, and rather bonny in a stew."

Annoyance struggled with humor on the minister's square face as he stared at Duncan. "Indeed, sir, perhaps you have not a genuine *Lycopersicon esculentum.* 'Tis a rare plant, impossible to grow in these parts unless you protect the young stalks in a conservatory."

Fala saw Duncan open his mouth to protest, then suddenly clamp his jaw shut. She looked down and stifled a giggle, almost certain that the captain had kicked his first mate under the table. The captain had valid reasons for not wishing to advertise his occupation or his various travels, and if Duncan wasn't careful he'd soon be telling the world that Joseph Eliot dined with the dread pirate Bettencourt.

Taking Duncan's silence for defeat, the minister continued to expound upon the dangers of the tomato as the others passed dishes and bowls, eager to eat. Fala glanced toward her mistress, hoping for some sign of encouragement or instruction about how to properly handle the utensils before her, but deep thoughts clouded Rachelle's gaze. Captain Bettencourt wore an expression of pained tolerance, obviously wishing to be elsewhere, and Mistress Eliot was so busy checking silver and napkins and biscuits that she had no time for an anxious guest.

Fala took a biscuit and gently lifted it to her lips. As long as she didn't spill anything or upset the board, she would manage tolerably well.

Soon the minister was deep in a story about Mojag Bailie's father—a man who called himself Daniel Bailie but who was actually the brother named Taregan—and Fala shook her head, too confused to follow the tale. She lowered her eyes, bewildered by the choices of food and dinnerware, then raised her eyes to find Duncan watching her. His gentle eyes searched her face, reaching into her thoughts. He gave her a conspiratorial wink.

She looked down at her plate, feeling a smile nudge itself into a corner of her mouth and push across her lips. She had no business befriending a man who would sail away on the morrow, but Duncan MacKinnon did make her laugh.

"I must find my father." Rachelle interrupted the minister's story, her voice breaking with huskiness. "Do you know *where* he has gone in Carolina? To which tribe?"

"I'm sure I made a note of it," Joseph answered, picking up a pointed knife and spoon. He used the spoon, with the curved end held down, to anchor his slice of venison while cutting it with the knife, then used the spoon to carry the food from plate to mouth. Fala watched carefully and imitated his gestures as well as she could.

"In the morning," Joseph answered after swallowing, "I'll look among my records and see what I can find." He shrugged as he set about cutting the venison again.

"You know," Captain Bettencourt offered, his eyes artless and serene as he watched his host, "they have introduced a new implement in England for use at the board—a fork. With the fork, one does not need to scoop the food into the spoon in order to get it into one's mouth."

"I know about forks." The preacher's brow lifted in amused contempt. "Diabolical luxuries, they are. God would not have given us fingers if he wished us to use such an instrument."

Fala noted the captain's sour grin, then covered her mouth with her hand to suppress her own smile. The preacher furiously shoveled food with his spoon, not using his fingers at all. He seemed to have missed the point.

Suddenly Reverend Eliot dropped his knife and lifted his eyes in a knowing look. "The Seebees!" he cried, giving the captain a look of jaunty superiority. "Mojag Bailie went to the Carolina tribe called the Seebees."

Captain Bettencourt turned to Fala. "My dear lady," he said, his eyes dark blue and soft with kindness. "Know you of this tribe?"

Fala shut her eyes and studied the scattered memories of her past. Her family had been of the Yamassee people, and that confederation included the Santees, the Sampits, the Winyahs . . . the Pee Dees, Cheraws, Catawbas—and the Seewees.

"The Seewees," she whispered, afraid to contradict their host.

"'Tis what I meant, of course." Eliot waved his spoon toward Rachelle. "The Seewees. I know them well. They are famous for their beaver skins."

"Deer pelts," Fala whispered, glancing up at her mistress. "They are great hunters, and deer are plentiful in that area."

"I know of them," Captain Bettencourt said. He grinned at the minister, but the smile didn't quite reach his eyes. "They trade to the English merchants, though they are paid only one-twentieth of what deerskins fetch in England. I'm afraid they are being sorely cheated."

The minister gave Rachelle an exaggerated wink. "That sounds like the sort of cause Mojag Bailie would pursue," he said, reaching over the table for a second helping of succotash. "Well, that's it, then. You find those Seebees, and you'll find Mojag Bailie."

▼▲▼▲ After dinner, Duncan expressed a desire to see the conservatory, and so the garrulous minister lit a candle and led him outside for a moonlight tour of Mistress Eliot's winter-bare garden and his own little hothouse. For want of anything better to do, Trace was about to follow Duncan, but the touch of Rachelle's hand on his arm pulled him back.

"Come aside, *s'il vous plaît*," she said, gesturing toward the shadows of the front yard. Prepared for the brisk night wind, she had pulled her own cloak over Mistress Eliot's gown.

Curious, he followed her, noticing that she had already sent Fala out to stand beneath the dark shadows of a spreading tree.

Direct as always, Rachelle wasted no time coming to her point. "It appears Fala and I need to go back to Charles Towne." Rachelle glanced at Fala, seeking confirmation, then turned her eyes again to Trace. "And you need to go south as well—and quickly, too."

Trace gave her a wry, indulgent smile. "Are you suggesting, mademoiselle, that Duncan and I escort you farther? I believe I promised to deliver you to Reverend Eliot. And that—" he inclined his head toward the garden where the minister's voice echoed— "is exactly what I have done."

Rachelle swallowed hard, lifted her chin, and boldly met his gaze. "All right, then. Fala and I will go alone." She glared up at him angrily. "I'll go to Boston Harbor in the morning and find a ship sailing for Charles Towne."

Fala lifted her hand, daring to interrupt. "The Seewees live at Winyah Bay, mademoiselle." She lowered her head. "Far from Charles Towne."

"Where?" Rachelle's face went blank.

"Winyah Bay," Trace answered, with easy defiance. "I know the place—'tis fifty-and-five miles north of Charles Towne." He felt a thin smile snake across his lips. "Will you walk the distance, then? On foot, through unfamiliar territory, you might reach Winyah Bay in four or five days—if you arrive at all."

She stiffened at the challenge in his voice. "I'm not afraid."

"Neither are you wise, *cherie.*"

She opened her mouth, about to protest again, but he lifted his hand and rested his fingers upon her lips, noting with no small sense of satisfaction that his touch silenced her completely.

"You have no money. How do you intend to book passage?"

He moved closer, his skin tingling where he touched her. "You will end up selling your virtue if you board a ship with nothing to offer but your lovely self."

She took a half step away from him, sputtering protests. "I would never! I am a wealthy woman, monsieur—my grandfather was Bertrand Fortier of Charles Towne. Any ship's captain would be honored to have me aboard. I will pay for our passage once we arrive home."

"Fala." He turned his gaze from Rachelle and gave the maid a gentle smile. "Would you please leave us? You may either join the minister and Duncan in the conservatory or go up to bed. But your mistress and I have a few things to discuss."

"Fala!" Rachelle's voice was like steel wrapped in silk. "I am your mistress, so don't you dare go anywhere!"

Fala hesitated, an odd mingling of wariness and amusement in her eyes, then turned and walked away, her footsteps muffled by the wet leaves and soft earth.

A dark flame of defiance lit Rachelle's eyes. "Well, see what you've done? She used to be an obedient slave!"

"And now she is a free woman." He paused, resisting the urge to smooth Rachelle's riotous hair. "Free will, my dear girl, includes the choice to disobey."

A swift shadow of anger swept across her pale face. She looked away, choosing another tack. "Really, Captain Bettencourt, this is solving none of our problems. Surely you exaggerate the dangers of our travel. Fala and I can go anywhere without fear. I am a lady, well known and respected in Charles Towne, and no one would dare—"

"Your mother was a lady, too, and yet she was not safe in the wilderness." Trace folded his arms tightly. "You may have been a pampered princess in your grandfather's house, but no one knows you here. No one knows you in the woods. And I would bet my last piece of eight that not too many people actually know you in Charles Towne. They may have known your mama or your grandfather, but who would come for you if you were in trouble? Is there a single soul who would risk his life to rescue you if you were taken like your mother? Your precious Lanston is naught but a greedy coward—"

"Stop!" She lifted her hands to her ears and turned away, but not before he saw tears run over her cheek through the dark arch made by her falling hair. He drew in a quick breath as guilt avalanched over him, compressing his lungs with its weight.

Why did he have to spoil everything he touched? This was a young woman, untried and yet strong. Sheer, spiteful jealousy had wrung the comment about Lanston Wragg from him, and if she loved the scoundrel Wragg, he ought to let her follow her heart.

Despite his honorable intentions, he had probably done her more harm than good. He should never have allowed her to board the *Jacques*. But he had, and he could not abandon her now. He would have to see her safely home or to her father, and he could also at least try to make her lift her eyes above the small circle of her egocentric world.

He stepped back, suppressing a sigh of frustration, then spread his hands regretfully and shrugged. "Mademoiselle, listen to reason. It is not safe for you to travel alone and with no money. A sea captain might take you aboard his ship, but you'd be at risk the entire journey." He paused, letting the significance of his words register in her consciousness. "Seamen are not noted for their virtue and self-control, Rachelle. After a double ration of rum—well, anything can happen. And usually it does."

"Then what am I supposed to do?" She threw the words at him like stones. "*You* won't take me home!"

"I never said that." Trace hesitated, grateful that the dim moonlight hid the full extent of his humiliation. He would take her to safety, but he'd do it on his own terms.

"Mademoiselle," he said, furious at his vulnerability to her, "have you stopped to consider what you are asking me to do? If Duncan and I take you to Charles Towne, we will have to sail from Boston. We are not exactly unknown in the port cities; unfortunately my name and face are too well remembered by many a sea captain. You are asking me to risk capture and hanging."

Her face twisted in a grimace of pain, as though someone had suddenly punched her in the gut. Awareness flickered in her eyes, then resignation.

"I'm not asking you for anything, Captain." Her voice was low, final. "You're right. I keep forgetting that you're a dangerous criminal. I wouldn't want you to hang on my account."

She backed away and tried on a smile that seemed a size too small. "I thank you, Captain Bettencourt, for all you have done for me thus far. On the morrow I shall talk with Reverend Eliot. Perhaps he knows someone who will take us southward, or perhaps there is some way he can loan me the money we need to book a safe passage." She lifted her hand, her dark eyes falling upon the golden band around her finger. "There is always this. I could sell it." Her smile slipped slightly. "This ring charges me to live boldly, faithfully, successfully, but I haven't been able to fulfill even a single—"

"Don't." Alarmed, he reached out and clasped her hand, his heart swelling with a feeling he had thought long dead. By all that was holy, why was he doing this? Why was he standing here, fighting his own battle of personal restraint, when he could be on his way to the sea, rowing his way back to his men and a saner, infinitely more sensible way of life?

A slow smile trembled over her face, and in it he found his answer—he was doing this because a delicate slender thread had begun to form between them . . . and he was entranced by the silent courage in her face.

"Let me talk to Duncan." His gaze lingered on the pulse that beat at the base of her throat as though her heart had risen from its usual place. His fingers curled around her hand, relishing the soft warmth of the flesh in his grasp. "There may be a way to resolve your difficulty. If so, we will take you to Boston tomorrow . . . if the good reverend will let you travel on the Lord's Day."

The glint of humor returned to her eyes. "After church, of course," she answered, her smile deepening into laughter as she looked toward the conservatory. "I'm certain he wants us to hear about the evils of that poisonous tomato."

Her gaze turned toward him then, her eyes luminous in the moonlight. "Thank you," she whispered, her voice like a gracious embrace in the chill air. "Thank you very much, Captain Bettencourt."

Her fingers squeezed his, and then she stepped toward him, her breath warm and moist against his face, her lips like rose petals brushing his cheek.

By the time he had collected his senses, she was gone.

▼▲▼▲▼ Though draughts whistled through the eaves in the attic room, Rachelle curled into the long muslin gown Mistress Eliot had furnished while Rachelle's petticoat, sleeves, and bodice hung drying with Fala's clothing near the downstairs hearth. Rachelle splashed warm water from a basin over her face and hands, recalling the poor sponge bath she'd had before dinner. Wistfully, she recalled the staff of servants at her grandfather's house—back in Charles Towne she could have bathed in a full-sized tub. Fala or Virtue would have lathered her curls with perfumed soap, then sluiced her hair clean with buckets and buckets of perfectly heated water.

But some things were more important than baths. Beckoning to Fala so she could use the basin and linen towel next, Rachelle curled up on the stuffed mattress and wrapped a quilt around her shoulders. Before taking their soiled clothes away, Mistress Eliot had brought up several neat bundles of letters, each tied with ribbon and sorted with painstaking accuracy. There were more recent letters, the lady said, a small frown puckering the skin between her thick brows, but Joseph was not as meticulous as his father, and he'd have to search for them.

Rachelle had thanked her for her trouble, and now she brought her knees to her chest, warming herself beneath the expansive gown as she opened the first sheet of parchment. The writing was slanted in a masculine hand, free flowing, proud,

and distinct, the lettering of a learned man. With a flush of pleasure, Rachelle noted the signature: *In the Lord's Service Always,
Mojag Bailie.*

Her father.

The first letters concerned Mojag's work in a tribe allied with
King Philip, whom Mojag called Metacomet. Philip's tribe, the
Wampanoag, had been utterly destroyed in the war that raged
throughout New England in 1675 and 1676, and Metacomet's
death and defeat affected Mojag in a profound way. "Now I understand what feelings inspired the psalmist," Mojag had written John Eliot in the autumn of 1676. "'Thou hast made the earth
to tremble; thou hast broken it: heal the breaches thereof; for it
shaketh. Thou hast shewed thy people hard things: thou hast
made us to drink the wine of astonishment.'"

In a series of subsequent letters, Mojag mentioned Natick, a
village of converted or praying Indians, and told John Eliot that
the Spirit of God had called him to leave that place. "I cannot
remain here while so many of my people are perishing," he had
written, the ink dark around the words *my people,* where he had
pressed on the quill.

A confusing rush of anticipation and dread whirled inside
Rachelle. His people? Obviously, he meant the Indians. Were
they the people of his heart or of his blood? She had thought
about asking the Eliots about Mojag's Indian blood but couldn't
muster the courage.

She lowered the parchment in her hand, glancing over to the
pallet where Fala lay, already asleep. Thick braids hung softly
against her thin shoulders; she looked ethereal, beautiful and
unreal in the dim lamplight. Could they be sisters, if not by
blood, then by a common heritage? The Eliots had not expressed
any surprise that Rachelle traveled with an Indian woman, nor
had they hesitated to offer Fala a place at their table. *Either they
consider me as lowborn as Fala,* Rachelle mused, a cynical inner
voice cutting through her thoughts, *or they consider Fala as
esteemed as Rachelle Fortier Bailie.*

She returned her attention to the letters, skipping to a bundle

dated 1679. Mojag was living among the Oneida then, and she
shivered in anticipation when he wrote that the tribe had "given
shelter to a Frenchwoman and her brother, who were attacked by
a band of young hotbloods from our tribe. They are Christians,
very gentle and refined, but the brother is not well."

In the next letter, dated February 1680, Mojag reported on the
health of the children in the tribe and a stubborn sachem who
would not accept the truth of the gospel. He finished the letter
with this note:

> Reverend John, I had almost forgotten to hope that God
> might have mercy upon my wounded heart. I had
> thought that his calling upon my life would demand
> everything—my heart, soul, spirit, and every energy I
> possessed. But in his great mercy, God sent me a wife at
> whose love and kind regard I shall never cease to mar-
> vel. She is called Babette Fortier, and is the Frenchwom-
> an I wrote of earlier. We have wed in the Oneida way
> and plan to be married in a church as soon as spring
> allows us to travel east. It is my prayer and fondest hope
> that you will do us the honor of blessing our marriage.

Rachelle eagerly opened the next letter, dated April 1680, but
Mojag dully recorded only the most commonplace tribal events:
the birth of twin boys to the sachem's second wife, the ritual killing of a bear, the tribe's journey to trade with the Iroquois. There
was no news of Babette, no word of joy or grief or loss.

Two other letters remained in that bundle—one dated July,
and one October. Rachelle skimmed the missive Mojag had sent
that summer and found more of the same dull rambling as his
spring report, but in October his mood was quite different:

> "Hear my prayer, O Lord, give ear to my supplications:
> in thy faithfulness answer me, and in thy righteous-
> ness. . . . For the enemy hath persecuted my soul; he
> hath smitten my life down to the ground; he hath made

me to dwell in darkness, as those that have been long
dead. Therefore is my spirit overwhelmed within me;
my heart within me is desolate. . . . Hear me speedily,
O Lord: my spirit faileth: hide not thy face from me, lest
I be like unto them that go down into the pit.

"Teach me to do thy will; for thou art my God."

Reverend Eliot, dearest and most esteemed friend, I
know you have heard by now that my wife has left the
tribe. She begged me not to follow or search for her. She
left a letter filled with very hard words. And yet I cannot
believe she did not love me. Perhaps it is only the life
here that she could not love.

But because I love her, I will respect her wishes. I
wish her well, but you should know that I am a married
man and will remain so until I die. It has taken me some
time to be able to write unto you, but I know now that
your son has brought you word of my distressing situation. As you think of me, pray for my wife, wherever she
has gone. Her name is Babette Fortier Bailie.

Rachelle held the parchment under the lamplight for a long
time, rereading the words, hearing the agony in her father's voice.
Finally she lowered the letter to her lap, her sense of loss beyond
tears. How he had suffered! Her mother had suffered, too, for her
faithlessness and lack of courage, but who could say who had suffered more? At least Babette had had a daughter and creature
comforts to fill her days and ease her pain; Mojag Bailie had only
the forest and the Indians to whom he had given his life.

Male voices floated up from outside the tiny shuttered window,
and she listened as Trace and Duncan called their good-nights to
Reverend Eliot. They were walking to the barn, where they would
sleep amid the straw, two well-fed, hearty men who would soon
be on their way back to a life of pirating on the high seas.

Her pensive mood veered sharply to anger. How could God
call himself just when Trace Bettencourt, a thief and a pirate,
slept in a warm barn and lined his pockets with gold while a

godly servant like Mojag Bailie slept in dirt and starved for the cause of Christ? And how could she tingle when a pirate called her name? Why did a trembling thrill race through her each time Trace Bettencourt moved across her field of vision?

She was as unwise as her mother—like Babette, she was becoming emotionally attached to a man who could never make her happy.

"Where is your justice, God?" she asked, lifting her eyes to the wooden ribs of the attic.

No answer came. She heard only the soft and regular sound of Fala's breathing.

Sunday morning dawned warm and blue, the delightful weather lifting Rachelle's troubled spirits as much as the comforting touch of clean clothes and the pleasure of a good night's sleep. A warming zephyr rushed up the hill to the meetinghouse, and she thanked God for it, knowing that the tiny building was unheated.

She stepped inside and noticed with surprise that worshipers crowded the church. With one glance she could tell they were not Huguenots. The Puritan men and women separated themselves, men sitting on one side of the room and women on the other. Rachelle and Fala quietly left Trace and Duncan with the men and found seats among the women.

Reverend Eliot's sermon for the day was based upon Romans chapter eight, verse two: "For the law of the Spirit of life in Christ Jesus hath made me free from the law of sin and death."

Eliot lowered his Bible to the lectern and gazed out across his congregation, his eyes smoldering with the fire of sincerity. "What do we mean by setting a man free?" he asked. His striking brown eyes grew somewhat smaller and brighter, the dark pupils of them training on Rachelle like musket barrels.

How does he know? Rachelle shifted uneasily on the hard bench. She hadn't told him that Fala had been her slave or that her grandfather had owned nearly a hundred slaves on his plantation. But while she hadn't seen any slaves in the Eliot household, Mistress Eliot certainly had to have *some* help. Indentured servants were virtual slaves, though only for a few years.

"You cannot free an unfeeling brute who dwells in a desert," the reverend went on, his gaze moving away from her. Rachelle closed her eyes in relief, and only as the tension went out of her shoulders did she notice it had been there.

"You cannot free a rock, an unfeeling lump that does nothing but sit on the ground, but you can free a river that yearns to rush toward the sea." Joseph Eliot churned the souls of his congregation with a voice like measured thunder, drawing amens and shouts of agreement from the upturned faces. "There is no liberty except the liberty of someone making his way toward something. A man can be set free if you will teach him the meaning of thirst and how to trace a path to a well. Only then will he embark upon a meaningful course of action."

The minister's voice dropped to a coaxing timbre, and his eyes settled on an area of the men's section. "To be free, my friends, you must make your way toward God. We love the master we obey, and we obey the master we love. If you would be free, obey our Lord Jesus Christ. God prefers an honest sinner to a righteous hypocrite, so if you would approach him, do it honestly, and with fear."

Rachelle shifted slightly on the bench and turned her head, trying to discover which hapless worshiper now felt the full impact of the reverend's eyes. She felt a little jolt of alarm when she realized that Eliot now stared at Trace . . . or perhaps Duncan. Divine inspiration may have led him to suspect that they were outlaws of a serious criminal nature.

Straightening her posture, she forced her own expression into lines of devout concentration. Trace hadn't wanted to go to church—in his own soft and mocking way he'd made that clear last night. She had hoped that a minister might make a difference in his outlook, but what good could a sermon about rocks and rivers do a pirate? Trace needed to hear about the evils of treachery and theft, as well as the sin of invoking terror on the high seas.

Vaguely dissatisfied, she folded her arms about her waist, blinking and making her eyes huge just to stay awake.

▼▲▼▲▼ The sun had begun to dip toward the western horizon by the time Reverend and Mistress Eliot drove Rachelle and her companions to the Boston seaport. While the minister and his wife promised to pray for Rachelle's safe journey and happy reunion with Mojag, Rachelle, in turn, promised to write when her journey was complete. She and Fala embraced Mistress Eliot, curtseyed to the minister, and waved farewell as the horse and buggy churned up the dust along the road back to Roxbury.

They had disembarked near the wharf, and Rachelle turned toward the sea and shivered slightly, uncertain what shape the day would take. Captain Bettencourt had not said a word during the long carriage ride from Roxbury, and Rachelle knew he would not share his plan before the minister and his wife.

For all the Eliots know, Rachelle thought, *Fala and I will be escorted by these two fine gentlemen right up to Mojag's hut, wherever that may be.* A wry smile twisted her mouth as she tucked her cold hands into her cloak. Those two good Christians would be horrified to learn that one of the most notorious pirates on the Atlantic coast had eaten at their table and slept in their barn.

Trace prowled the bustling wharf now, his arms behind his back, while Duncan stood between Fala and Rachelle with the watchful eye of a guard dog. Rachelle clutched her valise and watched Trace, noting the way his blue eyes flickered with interest as he inspected each vessel. Once or twice he stopped sailors going aboard or disembarking from various ships; then he nodded and moved on, as aloof and indifferent as thunder.

Finally he stopped in front of one ship that seemed busier than the others. After making a couple of inquiries from passing seamen, he nodded in what looked like relief and resolutely walked back to his companions.

"That is the *Gordon Hawke,* sailing shortly for Charles Towne," he said, coming to an abrupt halt before Duncan. His eyes, as indecipherable as water, moved from Duncan to Fala to Rachelle. "We will go aboard as two married couples. You, Duncan—" he inclined his head toward his first mate— "will speak only when spoken to, and try to disguise that Scottish burr, eh? Forget all you know of sailing. Don't stop to tighten a knot, correct a sheet, or comment upon the weather. You know nothing. You have never been upon the water."

"Aye, Captain." Duncan's eyes filled with a lethal calmness.

"You, Fala—" the captain gave her a grudging smile—"will play the part of Duncan's wife. Stay close to him. Do not speak unless you are spoken to—and then guard your tongue. Do not refer to your mistress as 'mademoiselle' or use her name. Any remark passed on a deck of a vessel seventy-six feet and several inches long is in the nature of a public statement, understand? We cannot drop our ruse for an instant."

Fala nodded, her face closing to guard their secret.

"And you, Rachelle," the captain spoke in a rush of words, apparently not noticing that he had used her familiar name, "you will be my wife. We shall sign on as Mr. and Mrs. Evan Cooper, from Boston. You will speak no French. You will throw no temper tantrums. And no matter what I do, you will trust me implicitly. *Comprends-tu?*"

A dozen questions sprang to Rachelle's lips, but she bit them back, a little unnerved by the hot, bright light that gleamed in his eyes. This was his world, and his life at risk in it. He had proven himself trustworthy thus far; surely he would do so again.

Keenly aware of his scrutiny, she nodded. *"Oui*, I understand."

"I'll need the valise."

Wordlessly, she handed it over and watched as he opened it and fumbled for the money purse he had deposited in it before leaving the *Jacques*. He hefted it into his palm, tossed it up once as if to test its weight, then closed the valise and handed it back to Rachelle. "Wait here while I speak to the captain," he said smoothly, with no expression on his face. "If all goes well, we should be at sea soon."

He turned and moved with fluid strides down the dock toward the ship's gangplank. Rachelle watched him go, her heart in her throat. He said many sea captains knew him—was that by sight or by reputation? Either way, it wouldn't do for him to be discovered.

She closed her eyes, resisting the fear that had dropped like a rock into her heart, sending ripples of apprehension in all directions. Once he left her in Charles Towne, she'd be all right. Once she was among her own people, she could hire a guide to take her to the Seewees. And, in time, she'd forget all about this adventure . . . unless they caught Trace Bettencourt and hanged him down at Oyster Point.

Then she'd remember everything.

▼▲▼▲▼ The captain was busy, Trace reported half an hour later, but was pleased to take on four passengers if they hurried themselves aboard. Without giving her time to think, Trace caught Rachelle by the elbow and firmly escorted her past a sweating crew of slaves and sailors. The seamen, whom Rachelle modestly tried to ignore, tossed her grudging looks of admiration as she picked her way through coils of rope and tumbled piles of canvas that lay like dirty snowdrifts on the deck, their upper layers billowing in the wind.

The *Gordon Hawke* was a cargo ship, she soon realized, for there were no passengers in the dimly lit hold into which Trace led her. A line of water casks lined the back wall, tier upon tier of wooden hogsheads squatting in the shadowy gloom. There were no chairs, no benches, not even a blanket on which to sit. Two small portholes, one on each side of the wide hold, let in light and only the barest breath of air.

"For this—" she spread her hands to indicate the cramped quarters—"you paid good gold?"

"When one is in a hurry," Trace said, lowering himself to the deck beneath one of the portholes, "one cannot be too particular. I'm sorry, but I must meet my crew in twelve days. With a good wind at his back, this captain will have you home in eight. Would you have preferred to wait here a week for more comfortable accommodations?"

"No." She heard the anger in his voice and bit her lip in dismay. "Well," she murmured, casting about for something to sit on, "I suppose I shall make the best of it."

"I suppose you shall have to discommode yourself," Captain Bettencourt answered, grinning as Duncan dropped to the floor like a spent horse, obviously at ease in any situation. "And you may even grow to appreciate it. Though a hold isn't the cheeriest of places, this one is warm, dry, and this high in the ship there usually aren't too many vermin afoot."

Vermin? Rachelle shivered, then slowly sank to the floor next to Fala. Grinning at her, Trace touched his forehead lightly in a mock salute, then leisurely stretched out his long legs. Rachelle spread her legs out straight, too, fussing with the hem of her gown so her ankles were modestly covered, then leaned back against the row of casks and tried to think positive thoughts. *This will all be worth it when I see my father. And God has been good to send us a man like Captain Bettencourt, a seaman who knows the sea and is strong enough to protect us—even if he is a pirate.*

Odd how close she felt to him after only a few days' acquaintance. In a strange way she thought she knew him better than she knew Lanston, to whom she would soon be married. Of course she didn't know the particulars of Trace Bettencourt's past like she knew Lanston's, but she knew what sort of man he was inside . . . and admired him tremendously, despite his obvious flaws.

Perhaps the forced intimacy of the journey to Roxbury had brought them close. Certainly they had spent more time together in the last three days than most husbands and wives did in a week. They had eaten together, washed together, argued, laughed, and reconciled. He had diplomatically asked Duncan to stop the wagon when he thought she and Fala might need a private moment to relieve themselves, and in the silence of that journey she had heard his stomach growling with hunger. Such intimacies were unknown among people in refined society; she could no more imagine hearing her grandfather's stomach growl than she could imagine his belching at the table. And yet she'd heard Duncan belch, and she'd laughed, delighting in the artless way he had complimented Mistress Eliot's dinner.

There was a sharp sound from the deck above; then the hatch over the companionway ladder suddenly lifted, sending a stream of bright sunlight down into the hold. A blizzard of sound spiraled down from the deck: the soughing of the wind, the scrape of lumber upon lumber, a volley of orders through the bosun's speaking trumpet—"Halliards let fly—clap on to that brace—touch up those hands at the brace."

Then Rachelle heard a voice that rang with command: "Mr. Cooper—Captain Pinckert wants to know if you and your party are settled. We'll be casting off now."

Rachelle glanced at Trace, who had risen to his feet and moved forward. He stood half-hunched beside the companionway ladder, his body taut with energy, his face impassive and smooth. "Yes, sir," he called in an odd flat voice stripped of the musical traces of his French heritage. "Tell the captain that we are fine, thank you."

Apparently not trusting Trace completely, the sailor came down the ladder and paused, his eyes sweeping the hold. He smiled at Fala, nodded at Duncan, and let his gaze linger upon Rachelle for a moment. The touch of his eyes made her shiver.

"I said, sir, that we are fine," Trace spoke again, a subtle challenge in his voice. "If we need you, we will call."

"Aye, then." The seaman's eyes roamed over Rachelle one final time; then he winked at her broadly and climbed up the ladder, letting the hatch fall with a resounding boom.

Trace stood at the ladder for a long moment, looking at Rachelle and radiating disapproval as only he could. His unspoken rebuke felt like a chilly breeze on the back of Rachelle's neck, and she looked away, shivering again.

"Not five minutes," he finally said, bouncing slightly on his toes as he thrust his arms behind his back and glared across the hold. "Alone, you wouldn't have lasted five minutes aboard this ship. Not you, nor your maid."

He waited, doubtless expecting her to argue the point, but she bit her lip and looked toward Duncan, feeling suddenly weak and vulnerable in the face of Trace's anger. "You're right," she whispered, her voice lost in the noise of the seamen overhead.

"What?"

"I said—" she returned her gaze to him, acknowledging the undeniable and dreadful fact— "that you were right. You know best, Captain. I was a fool to think I could go home on my own." Despite her iron will, her voice broke miserably and her eyes welled with tears. "Perhaps I was a fool to think I could do anything."

Stunned by the sound of tears in her voice, Trace crossed his arms and pointedly looked away.

Tears rolled heedlessly down Rachelle's face, hot spurts of loss and frustration. She sniffled noisily, not caring what sort of miserable picture she made. Rachelle Fortier Bailie the social butterfly had disappeared forever; there remained only Rachelle Bailie the lost, confused, impoverished girl who consorted with ex-slaves and pirates.

She scarcely knew when Trace moved, but suddenly he knelt beside her, whispering soft, nonsensical sounds. Sinking to the deck, he offered the voluminous drape of his sleeve as a handkerchief.

"I couldn't—," she began, then laughed through her tears as she imagined the delicate, genteel Rachelle Fortier Bailie blowing her nose on a sailor's bedraggled sleeve.

"There, there, *cherie*," Trace murmured, genuine alarm in his voice.

Cherie—darling? He was as confused as she.

"No—I'm all right. I'll be all right. I just need time." Rachelle shook her head, about to explain that her sobs were born of frustration and laughter, not sorrow, but one of his arms slipped around her while the other gently pulled her head to his chest.

Rachelle tensed, at once attracted and repulsed by his tender embrace. Never had a man held her like this, not even Lanston. She had never gone to her grandfather for comfort; Babette had always been the one to hold her and stroke her hair, assuring her that everything would be all right.

She held her own hands close to her heart, uncertain of where she should—or could—place them, and then she heard the captain's voice in her ear. "I do not mean to be familiar, Rachelle," he murmured, his touch sending fire through every nerve in her body. "But we do have parts to play, no?" She heard hesitation in his voice. "And since you have already forgotten and called me Captain and I have called you by name, perhaps we should practice being Mr. and Mistress Cooper." The hand that had begun to stroke her hair pulled away. "Or should I let you go?"

Too shy for words, she answered by turning so that her hands fell upon his chest, a safe haven. She burrowed her cheek into the linen of his shirt, breathing in the scents of salt and sea and wind and . . . him.

He did not speak either, but amusement flickered in his eyes as she lifted her gaze. She smiled and lowered her eyes, content to rest in his arms while her senses roiled in turmoil and new sensations.

Did this mean nothing more to him than a necessary part of their masquerade? *Even so,* she told herself, luxuriating in the solidity of his arms about her, *so be it.*

She gradually relaxed in his embrace, relishing the firmness of his strength beneath her cheek, hearing the steady, reassuring beat of his heart. Here upon the rolling ship, he seemed the only solid reality in a shifting, troubled world. His hand continued to caress her hair, and for an instant his head lowered so that his cheek rested atop her head. Rachelle wondered at the meaning behind this gentle touch, but she didn't dare ask.

Finally he grew still, but she didn't pull away. The loud clumping noises from above ceased, and a slight breeze flowed from one porthole to the other, freshening the hold. She knew without looking that the *Gordon Hawke* had put out to sea; perhaps the gentle motion of the ship breasting each swell had calmed and quieted him. That was the motion of his home, his life.

Tilting her head back, her eyes sought his. "Once again," she whispered, feeling no desire to escape the embrace that held her, "I must thank you."

"Que voulez-vous dire?"

"What do you mean, 'what do you mean?'" she teased, lightly laying a fingertip across his mouth. "And you are to speak no French. You are Mr. Cooper, remember?"

A smile found its way through the mask of uncertainty upon his face. "Mr. and Mistress Cooper," he answered, casually crossing his legs and squeezing her shoulder. "Who have been married three years and live in Charles Towne."

"With their two children," Rachelle answered, pleased at how nonchalant she sounded. "In a big white house on Meeting Street."

"But no slaves."

"No slaves?" Rachelle pretended to pout. "How does Mistress Cooper run her household without help?"

"She has servants, of course," Trace answered, tilting his head back in order to look her full in the face. "Whom she pays very well. And they are devoted to her."

"Are they?" Rachelle smiled in pleased surprise. "That is good, but I would much rather know about Mr. Cooper."

"What about Mr. Cooper?"

"Whether *he* is devoted to Mistress Cooper."

He did not answer for a moment but measured her with a cool, appraising look. "He is as devoted to her—" his hand reached up to smooth a wayward strand of her hair—"as the stars are to the sky."

"The stars?" She sighed heavily, her gaze lowering from his face. "The stars, I fear, are too unsettled. On cloudy nights I go outside and can find nary a star to light my way."

"Just because you do not see them," he answered, his fingers curving under her chin and lifting her gaze to meet his, "does not mean they are not there."

Swimming through a haze of feelings and desires, Rachelle modestly lowered her eyes. Her feelings for him were intensifying—not a good situation for a woman betrothed to someone else. But Lanston was far away . . . and this was only a temporary charade, wrought out of necessity to save Trace's life and bring her safely home.

She smiled, burying her head in his shoulder's warmth as she drank in the comfort of his nearness. Content to rest at his side, she allowed her deep satisfaction to push away her worries until she fell into a dreamless sleep.

▼▲▼▲ Outside the ship, the sunset spread itself like a peacock's tail, luminous and brilliant across the watery horizon. Trace sat still, barely daring to move until Rachelle's breathing deepened and slowed; then he shifted his weight slightly, allowing her head to fall into the hollow between his shoulder and neck. He was not surprised that the events of the last several days had exhausted her; his own eyes felt sandy, and his bones ached with weariness.

He glanced across the hold where Fala and Duncan sat next to each other, their heads bent close in a whispered conversation. The two of them seemed well suited for one another, and he found himself smiling, happy for his friend. Perhaps after he'd delivered Rachelle safely to her home, he would bargain for an Indian wife from the trappers who gathered at the mouths of rivers, always searching for a white sail with goods to trade. An Indian wife might be agreeable to the sea. She wouldn't be accustomed to all the fine things Rachelle would expect, and she wouldn't have Rachelle's sharp tongue or her rapier wit.

He bent one knee and rested his free hand upon it. *Oui*, a wife might be a comfort. Lately he had begun to develop a new appreciation for feminine charms.

He felt Rachelle stir against him; then she pulled away, her eyes wide with sudden shock. "I'm sorry," she murmured, smudges of fatigue under her dark eyes. "I never intended to use you as a pillow, Captain."

"'Tis all right," Trace answered, feeling a sudden chill where the warmth of her body had vanished. She slid away from his contact, looking toward Fala as she nervously smoothed her hair.

He rested his hand on his knee, feigning an indifference he didn't feel. Fala and Duncan were still talking; the maid had scarcely even glanced up at her mistress. Trace lifted his eyes to the wooden beams above, trying to lift his thoughts to things nautical, but for once he couldn't think about the sea. First, he'd told himself not to think like a captain on this voyage; the risk of discovery was too great. And second, he could think of nothing but Rachelle when she sat so close.

"Rachelle," he said, keeping his voice low, "may I ask you a personal question?"

Her mouth opened slightly in surprise, but then she smiled. "Of course, Captain. After all we have been through, I scarcely think I could withhold any secret from you."

Despite her pleasant expression, he sensed her vulnerability, so he lifted his hand and gentled his voice. "Can you explain to me why you are betrothed to Lanston Wragg? I know him, and I know you, and a more desperate *mésalliance* I could not imagine."

Her smile vanished as suddenly as if he had run a cloth over her face to erase it. "Why need we be alike?" She lowered her thick, black lashes for an instant. "Some say that opposites make the best pairs."

"Opposites in interests, perhaps." Trace frowned, seeing that a glaze had come down over her swimming eyes. "But you are opposites in nature. How can fire live with ice? Either the flame will melt the ice or the ice will put out the fire."

"Are you saying I'm cold?" She shot him a withering glance. "Or am I the fire, perhaps with a burning temper?"

"I'm not saying you are either." Trace lifted his eyes to the deck above, wishing he'd kept his mouth shut. "I only meant that you and Lanston Wragg are opposites. You are tender-hearted; he is hard. You are gracious; he is grasping. You seem to have a measure of intelligence and mercy; he has neither—"

"I'll thank you to keep your further opinions to yourself." She wore an arrested expression, and a moment later he saw a change come over her features, a sudden shock of sick realization.

"Lanston's father has known my grandfather for years," she whispered, her brows a brooding knot over her eyes. "And my grandfather arranged the marriage with Lanston's parents. I have always heard that Lanston was the most handsome, most charming boy in Charles Towne, and when we were introduced—well, he said he loved me. Why shouldn't I marry him?"

Her expression softened into one of fond reminiscence, and Trace spoke before she could dissolve into sentimental tears. "The Wraggs are slave traders, Rachelle. I have heard of things Lanston has done—well, modesty prevents me from mentioning particulars, but they are deeds that would make your blood run cold."

"Lies and exaggerations," she answered hotly, but with little conviction in her voice. "Lanston and his father run a business. And they only enslave people *legitimately.* Individuals captured in a just war forfeit their lives to their captors."

"Rachelle, think." He leaned closer, irked by her aloof manner. "Fala was a child when she was taken into slavery—what child willingly participates in a just war? She was no warrior—she was merely in the wrong place at the wrong time."

"Fala is different." Rachelle's eyes drifted over to her maid's slender form. "She loves me. I gave her freedom, didn't I? And you see that she is still with me! She *wants* to be with me!"

"Don't be a fool, Mistress Cooper," he drawled with distinct mockery. "Will she want to remain with you when a better life presents itself? As long as she remains in your shadow, she is still a slave; she has not yet learned the full meaning of freedom."

Rachelle's lower lip trembled as she returned his glare, and Trace realized that his words had truly shaken her. Without giving her time to respond, he went on: "Why would you marry a slave trader, a man you cannot respect?"

Her countenance shifted; the confusion in her eyes evaporated, replaced by a look of pure disdain. "Who are you to speak to me?" Her face paled with anger. "Why would you persist in piracy, knowing you cannot respect yourself?"

He felt himself shrivel before her thunderous expression, but he had no answer to give. He had committed his mortal sin long before he met her; she could not know or understand it. Her sin—the offense of marrying Lanston Wragg—still lay before her, but she would not listen to him.

As long as he remained who he was, he could never earn her respect.

He rose slowly to his feet, then turned in the gathering darkness to face her. "Why, indeed," he murmured. "When you can give me a new name, a new face, and a new soul, mademoiselle, perhaps then I shall be good enough to please you. Until then, I give you good night."

He retreated, leaving her alone in the gloom.

Fala

In giving freedom to the slave, we assure
freedom to the free—
Honorable alike in what we give and
what we preserve.

—Abraham Lincoln, 1862

"So you have no news to report."

Sitting behind the desk in his office, Lanston Wragg studied the man before him intently. The sailor, a short, muscular-looking fellow with a fleshy, pockmarked face, had been recommended as one who might have a vested interest in chaos. He'd gathered quite a reputation among the wharf rats as a rabble-rouser, and Lanston had hoped to rouse the particular rabble that might betray one Captain Trace Bettencourt for the sum of one hundred pounds. But apparently the pirate had vanished from the sea.

"No, I do 'ave news," the informer croaked, filling Lanston's office with his stench. "One seaman on a British frigate says 'e saw the *Jacques* a few days ago near Boston, but then she turned tail and 'eaded out to the open sea as they prepared to fire on 'er."

Lanston leaned back in his chair and lifted his pipe slowly to his lips. His father had sent Devin Garr, the slave overseer, to find Rachelle, but Garr had been at sea for only five days and would not reach Boston for at least another five. If he did find her in Boston, there'd be another ten days for the return journey—and this with a wedding only sixteen days away!

He drew heavily on his pipe, then lowered it to the desktop and let a thin plume of smoke drift from his pursed lips. He would bet a matched pair of Africans that Bettencourt hadn't taken Rachelle to Boston. He may have *attempted* to take her there in order to convince Rachelle that he intended to fulfill her request and then turned for the open sea when a British ship fired upon him. In a few days, once Rachelle was convinced that

Bettencourt couldn't safely see her to Boston, the pirate would bring her back to Charles Towne, where her fortune lay.

Lanston closed his eyes, imagining the scene. Bettencourt would dock outside Charles Towne, stalling Rachelle with some feeble excuse while he sent word that he held Bertrand Fortier's granddaughter hostage.

Lanston felt a grudging smile lift the corner of his mouth. This pirate was more clever than he'd imagined.

"Thank you," he said suddenly to the informer. From a desk drawer he withdrew a small sack of coins and thumped it toward the edge of the desk. "Take it, and know there is more if you are the first to tell me when Trace Bettencourt is sighted near Charles Towne Harbor. For he will come here. I am certain of it."

The man snatched up the bag in a possessive gesture, then gripped the edges of his hat and bobbed in an earnest imitation of a bow. "Thank you, sir. Thank you very much. I'll keep my nose to the ground, as it were, and an eye to the sea."

"See that you do," Lanston answered, waving the man away. "And I'll see that you're properly rewarded."

The informer gimped his way out the door, and Lanston lifted his pipe again, idly scratching his stubbled chin with the mouthpiece. Trace Bettencourt was a cobra—deadly, charming, and ruthless. Rachelle had fallen prey to his charms, that much was plain to see, but he was only a man—and a pirate. One who might be arrested on sight and hanged after a speedy trial.

So when someone spotted him near Charles Towne, it would be no trouble to persuade the authorities to do the right thing. *Pirates*, Lanston thought, smiling to himself, *have no place in Charles Towne*.

"Do you think, sir," Duncan asked, looking up from the unappetizing meal of sea biscuit and dried beef that the passengers of the *Gordon Hawke* were given twice a day, "that the men are remembering to care for my wee plant? Webber had an eye for it, but I'm afraid they're forgetting to take it down into the hold on cold nights. It's been verra cold of late, and the little tomato can't bear freezing."

Rachelle cut a quick glance at Fala, and the two women shared a smile. The muscular sailor's concern for his "wee plant" was touching, and after five days at sea Rachelle could understand why he loved it. Surrounded by blue water, with nary a shore in sight, the presence of a living, growing green plant would be comforting indeed.

"I shouldn't worry about it much," the captain answered, a trace of unguarded affection lingering in his eyes as he looked across at his first mate. "If the plant dies, Mistress Cooper here will buy you a new one."

"Me?" Rachelle laughed, sincerely amused. "With what shall I buy it? My grandfather always held the purse strings in my family, and he was never inclined to be overly generous on my account."

She smiled and bit off another hunk of the tough, salty jerky, then suddenly stopped chewing when she saw that all three of her companions were staring at her with wide eyes. "What?" She swallowed hard, then glanced down to make certain that some hairy spider or rat wasn't crawling over her petticoat. They were all sitting in a small circle on the floor, their dishes and mugs spread between them.

"Rachelle," Trace murmured, watching her in a way that made her feel like a child of ten, "have you truly no idea?"

"No idea of what?" She felt a disturbing quake in her serenity.

Trace rolled his pewter mug slowly between his hands, then glanced up at Duncan. "An innocent," he murmured softly.

Rachelle's cheeks flushed hotly in the cool air. "What do you mean? What should I know that you're not telling me?"

"Your grandfather." He looked at her with an enigmatic expression. "Rachelle, he was one of the wealthiest men in Charles Towne, no?"

"Of course. I told you so." Her mouth twisted in annoyance.

"Yes. So—who inherited all his property?"

She bit down on her lip. "Why, my mother, of course. But— she's dead, too."

Trace nodded silently. "You see? You have inherited one of the richest fortunes in Charles Towne."

She snapped her mouth shut, stunned by his bluntness. It was only natural he should suppose her rich, but he didn't know that her grandfather had disliked her intensely until the moment of his death. Even then, fear and guilt had prompted his change of heart, not any real concern for her well-being.

"I'm sure I'm not rich," she murmured, looking down at her hands. "The earthquake destroyed the house, and the fire swept away all our belongings. When I left Charles Towne we had nothing. The Wraggs loaned us even the clothes we wore." Her hand fell upon the fabric of her silk petticoat, soiled now by hard travel. "This gown isn't even mine."

"Your grandfather was a canny man, Mademoiselle Rachelle," Fala whispered, her eyes almost black in the dim light of the hold. "I'm sure he provided for you."

"I don't think so." Her face burned as she remembered his diffidence, his disapproving stare. "I believe he left whatever might have remained to his church—he was a devoted member of the French Huguenot congregation in Charles Towne."

"Whether he left anything to the church or not, your grandfather left you a great deal." Trace picked up his sea biscuit and knocked it against his palm, jolting a few weevils from their hiding place. He held the biscuit aloft, studied the edge, then turned his eyes back to Rachelle. "I am as certain of that as I am of the tide."

"How can you be so sure?" Rachelle watched in horror as he bit into the biscuit. She had painstakingly broken hers into tiny pieces, preferring to go hungry rather than eat anything the least bit questionable.

Trace chewed a moment, then swallowed and gave her a twisted little smile. "Easy," he said, his blue eyes studying her. "Lanston Wragg. I do not know the man well, but I know his type." A sudden thin chill hung on the edge of his words. "If you weren't an heiress, my dear, and a bountifully wealthy one, his offer of marriage would have vanished in the flames that consumed your grandfather's house."

"How dare you!" Her words were sudden and raw and spiked with anger. She shook her head and trembled, anger singeing the limits of her self-control. "You think Lanston wants to marry me for money only?" The thought ricocheted against others in her head, sparking her anger with each new impact. "That's the sort of comment I'd expect from a pirate. All you think about is gold, profit, money. Why—" she deliberately exaggerated the contempt in her expression—"I'm surprised you haven't proposed to me yourself, Captain Bettencourt! If I'm an heiress and all you think about is gold, why haven't you?"

"Hush, you little fool!" In one gesture he reached out and clapped his hand over her mouth, then lifted his eyes to the deck above as if he expected Captain Pinckert to appear at any moment. Rachelle struggled for only an instant, then realized what she'd done. In one outburst, she had nearly exposed them all.

Keeping his hand over her mouth, Trace nodded to Duncan, who silently pulled a dagger from his belt and moved to the companionway ladder. The blade in his hand gleamed like an angry lion's eye, and Rachelle felt a cold panic rise from between her shoulder blades and prickle down her spine.

A chill black silence surrounded them, and even Fala, Rachelle noticed, had gone pale with fear. Rachelle held her breath, straining to hear any unusual sound from the deck above, then realized that the *absence* of sound would be far more significant. If the seamen above were planning to charge into the hold to capture the fierce pirate Bettencourt, they certainly wouldn't announce their intention.

"Fall not off, wear no more!" Slightly muffled by the deck, the bosun's call reached Rachelle's ears. "Keep her to, touch the wind, but have a care of the lee latch there!"

The following uneventful moments were the longest in Rachelle's life, but finally Trace pulled his hand from her mouth and looked her directly in the eye.

"You can be quiet now, no?"

"Yes." She lowered her head, relief and humiliation mingling in her voice.

"Very good." Trace gestured to Duncan, who came away from the companionway ladder and sheathed his dagger.

Closing her eyes, Fala lowered her forehead to her fingertips.

Trace still hovered near Rachelle, and his breath was warm on her cheek as he bent down to whisper in her ear. "I am very sorry, mademoiselle, if my reluctance to propose has brought you distress," he murmured.

Rachelle swallowed hard, feeling her cheeks blaze as though they'd been seared by a candle flame.

"But I knew you were promised to another," he went on, a faintly mocking note in his voice, "and I am wed to the sea. So you must understand that I meant you no insult."

"I'm sorry," she whispered, and the words hurt her throat, as though she'd swallowed some sharp, jagged object, "for yelling your name. I was angry, but I would not purposefully endanger your life."

His gaze was now as soft as a caress, and he offered her a forgiving smile. "Don't fret yourself, *cherie*," he answered, casually scooting back toward the tin plate that held the remains of his dinner.

▼▲▼▲▼ Later that afternoon, as the swollen orb of the sun hung low in the west, Rachelle walked to the starboard port-hole and sank to the deck, carefully arranging her petticoat around her bent knees. Trace sat there, his gaze fixed to the unbroken round of the sea and the dome of the sky, but she hoped to draw him into conversation. They had each hurt the other earlier in the day, and Rachelle yearned for a bit of casual dialogue to reestablish the easy camaraderie that had existed during the first few days of their voyage.

"Tell me, Mr. Cooper," she said, her voice shakier than she would have liked, "how you came to be on the sea."

"Hmm?" Distracted, he looked at her, then smiled. "I suppose it was escape. I was unhappy at home, so I ran away to the sea. I was only ten—so I suppose I grew up on the water."

"Really? Did you join—a pirate's ship right away?"

He snorted softly and glanced sideways at her in surprise. "Pirates? No, lady. Twenty years ago I joined the navy. His Majesty Louis XIV's ship the *Beltone.* I enlisted as a midshipman—

"As a ten-year-old?"

A gimlet gleam shone from his eyes. "They thought I was fourteen. I was tall for my age." He shrugged and continued with his story. "I worked my way up through the ranks. In time, I was made first mate of the *Adrienne.*"

"So . . . " Rachelle paused, delicately twining a finger in the curls at her neck. Outside, the sun had dropped behind the horizon, to slip sizzling into the ocean. "How did you happen to become captain of the *Jacques*?"

Trace brought his knees up and clasped his arms loosely around them. Frowning, he looked into the sky, where stars were beginning to spring out in the vault of the heavens. "I don't suppose you know much about naval discipline, Rachelle, but the *Adrienne* was a taut ship—too taut, by any man's standard. One afternoon as we were at sea during a heavy swell, the captain commanded me to flog a midshipman—a young lad, not much older than I was when I joined the navy. In any case, I couldn't do it. The captain was about to have me flogged and manacled for insubordination, but Duncan stepped forward and ordered the captain to his cabin."

Rachelle's breath caught in her throat. "Mutiny?"

Slowly, staring out the window as though he watched the scene replaying itself on the deep purple sky, Trace nodded. "We didn't want to hurt the man, but he moved to throttle Duncan and the gun went off."

Rachelle shivered with a cold that was not from the air. Finally, the corner of Trace's mouth twitched, and he gave her a dry, one-sided smile. "What could we do? We had killed the captain, a hanging offense no matter what our reasons. But the crew of the *Adrienne* stood behind us and swore they'd follow no matter what we decided to do."

A chilly breath of wind raked his hair as he turned toward the porthole again. "But the mutiny wasn't the worst of it. I have never spoken of this to anyone. I don't even like to think about it." Raw hurt glittered in his eyes as he looked back at Rachelle. "I had forgotten that Captain Mariveux's daughter—a blind girl—sailed with us in the captain's cabin. After the captain's death everything was madness and confusion. The girl heard the shouting and celebration and came out, probably thinking her father had given us leave to make merry."

His voice scraped terribly, as if he labored to produce it, but the words began to come faster. "She was but thirteen, a sweet and innocent maiden, and she walked slowly among us while we froze with the guilty consciences of Cain. She softly called her father, feeling her way across the deck, then slipped in the pool of blood and felt the warmth upon her small fingers."

A hot tear rolled down Rachelle's cheek, and she hugged her knees, her heart breaking in compassion.

Pressing his lips together, Trace said nothing for a long moment. When he spoke again, he could manage no more than a hoarse whisper. "She knew, God bless her heart. She knew what we had done. I believe she understood what manner of man her father was, but his harshness with us didn't matter, for the captain had never demonstrated anything but kind tenderness to his daughter."

Rachelle blinked as tears blurred her vision.

"And then," Trace went on, speaking between clenched teeth, "she staggered to the rail. Duncan and I both sprang to catch her, but she heard us coming and jumped."

Rachelle tried to make a small comforting noise, but her throat had closed too tightly for any sound to come forth.

Trace lifted one shoulder in a shrug and quickly brought the back of his hand to his eye. "She was gone. Duncan and I both went overboard to save her, but she vanished from our sight. Try as we might, we could see nothing under the water."

Neither Trace nor Rachelle spoke for several minutes. The light was fading fast, color bleeding out of the air. Rachelle sat silently in the gloom, her heart breaking for the captain's daughter and for Trace, who had been helpless to stop the girl's tragic death. In relating that story he had told her more about himself than anything he had said in all their days together.

"I begin to see why you and Duncan are so close."

He looked up, and their eyes met for the first time since he had begun his story. *"Oui—"* his eyes narrowed in pain—"we are bound by affection, duty, and blame. Duncan's pistol killed our captain, but I was responsible for the mutiny and the crew. If we return to Paris, Duncan will be executed immediately." He gave her a bitter smile, his eyes burning with the deep blue that glows in the heart of a flame. "He's a foreigner, you see. I will at least be granted a trial before they hang me."

"But you had good reason to mutiny," Rachelle insisted. "And Duncan shot the captain in self-defense."

"The authorities would never see it that way." His icy blue eyes radiated torment and contempt. "Duncan's a dead man if the French ever get ahold of him. And the pirate Bettencourt is as good as dead with the English. So, together we are quite a popular pair."

Rachelle could not reply. She hugged her knees, her misery so acute that it was like a physical pain in her heart.

"We named the ship the *Jacques*," Trace went on, as casually as if he had been discussing the weather, "in honor of our deceased captain. We served as a French vessel for the remainder of the war with England, legally privateering and preying upon English ships."

"And after the war?" Rachelle asked, surprised that she still had a voice.

Trace sighed, then gave a resigned shrug. "We decided to keep going as we had been. In a tavern on Barbados, Duncan and I had heard about Libertalia, and the idea intrigued us. We wanted to liberate slaves, you see, but where could we send them?"

His blue eyes locked on hers. "Do you remember Reverend Eliot's sermon? He said there is no liberty except the liberty of someone making his way *toward* something. We were willing to liberate slaves, but we had no place where they could be free. We couldn't take them back to Africa—their families were gone, and they'd only be captured again. And we couldn't take them to the Indies, for they'd be captured as runaways. So we decided to take slaves to Libertalia—if we can find it."

Rachelle stared at him, astounded. "You mean you've never seen this place? How do you know it exists?"

She thought she caught a glimpse of laughter in his eyes as he returned her stare. "'Blessed are they that have not seen, and yet have believed,' eh? I'm not so certain I could ever be happy in a place established by pirates . . . but every man yearns to be free."

The shades of night had completely fallen in the hold. Trace closed his eyes and stretched out on the deck to sleep, effectively ending the conversation. Rachelle watched him, quietly reliving the pain of the story he'd shared. At her request he had sliced opened a newly healed wound, and he struggled even now with the pain, his face twisting as he abandoned himself to sleep.

As soundlessly as she could, she rose and moved to the other side of the ship, where she would sleep next to Fala.

The ocean glowed with dull green light as the sun rose from the water and bullied its way into the low-hanging clouds of a new day. Rachelle yawned and stretched, then groaned as numerous aches and bruises announced their presence.

She exhaled softly as she sat up. Yesterday Trace had called her a wealthy woman, but what wealthy woman slept on a damp wooden deck with naught but a soiled cloak for a blanket? At least twice in the night she had felt something squirm over her body, and she had stiffened, preferring to ignore the sensation rather than open her eyes and spy a rat.

She and Fala helped each other with their toilette as best they could with only a bucket of water to share; then Fala went over to the corner where Duncan had wrapped his hands around two small casks. With his face set in determination, he hoisted the casks to his shoulders, then rhythmically bent his knees, squatting and standing, forcing his weight up and down. Fala watched, her eyes wide with fascination, and Duncan kept up a running conversation, obviously enjoying her admiration.

Rachelle drifted toward the starboard porthole where Trace sat, hoping he would continue the earnest and honest conversation they had shared the day before. But the urge to talk had apparently left him, for he answered her questions with short, pointed answers, adding neither observation nor comment. After a few moments, she gave up and surrendered to his need for silence.

His eyes clung to the horizon like seaweed to a rock, and occasionally he thrust his head completely out of the porthole and squinted upward toward the sun. She frowned, wondering if this time of solitude and boredom had driven him to lose his senses; then she realized with a sudden start that he was *navigating*.

Dead reckoning, Duncan had explained to her earlier, helped a captain plot his course if he kept a record of the distance sailed each day and the compass course being steered. While there was no way a mariner could determine his longitude at sea, a captain could pinpoint his north/south location within five or ten miles. Only by noting landmarks on the coast could he pinpoint his east/west position.

He is looking for the Jacques. The thought froze in her brain. Time was passing quickly. In only seven days he had to reunite with his crew. Wherever she was, the *Jacques* would soon be making for Ocracoke Island . . . and Trace wanted to be there to greet his ship.

A cold knot formed in Rachelle's stomach. Would he slip away in the middle of the night, jumping from the deck and swimming to the island as they passed? Today Captain Pinckert had chosen to sail the *Gordon Hawke* within sight of the coastline; perhaps he was wary of pirates and wanted to head into shallower waters if a strange ship approached. But this would only make things easier for Trace and Duncan, who swam as well as fish. When the appropriate moment arrived, they would drop from the boat as silently as tears from Rachelle's cheek, leaving her to her own devices.

Inexorably, her mind returned to the memory of Trace's determined face in the barge off Point Allerton. Shivering, wet, and thoroughly angry with her, he had had far more reason then to desert her . . . and yet he had still given her his promise of protection.

She glanced over at him, wondering if she could read his thoughts on his face. The marks of yesterday's grief were clear, etched in the lines beside his mouth and eyes, thrown into darkness by the shadows of the hold. He was a resolute pirate, devoted to his men and to his cause, but he was nonetheless an honorable man. He had sworn to keep her safe, and he had declared that she wouldn't be safe on this ship without an escort. So he wouldn't slip away and leave her . . . would he?

Something cautioned her not to ask.

Her fears grew with every passing hour, though, for the steady winds carried them southward at an alarming rate. They had been six days at sea, and Trace had predicted they would reach Charles Towne in eight. So surely they were near Ocracoke.

An overcast sky descended during the morning, painting the ocean the same gray color as the sky. A treacherous fog blanketed the coastline, smothering the wind. Trace stood at the porthole and stared out at nothing, his tension like a scent on him. The fog got into the hold as well—clammy gray tendrils touched Rachelle's face and drifted between the looming water casks.

The gloom felt heavy, wet, and threatening. Rachelle sat next to Fala, both of their backs supported by the stem of the mainmast, both of them shivering. Fala shivered from the cold, for her cloak was not as warm as Rachelle's, but Rachelle's teeth chattered from the spasmodic trembling of fear within her.

Doubts congested her mind, preventing her from thinking clearly, but she knew she ought to voice her concerns.

"Mr. Cooper," she finally found the courage to call. When Trace turned to look at her, she injected a light tone into her voice. "Do you see anything of interest out there?" She chose her words carefully. "You've been watching the sea all day today."

He gave her a narrowed glinting glance. "Habit, I suppose," he answered, a pensive shimmer in the shadow of his eyes. "Don't let me concern you, Mistress Cooper. I'm feeling a bit like a fish out of water, I suppose."

The wind freshened as he spoke. The sounds of creaking blocks and flapping sailcloth echoed down from above, emphasizing the unnatural silence that had existed in the calm. Trace's expression lightened considerably, and he turned toward the porthole again, watching. Outside, the breeze was tearing great windows in the fog, and as Rachelle gazed through the porthole she caught a sudden vision of verdant trees, cinnamon sand, and the emerald color of shallow water.

"Duncan!" The captain's cry brought his first mate to his side in an instant, and together they stared out at the land that had been hidden only a moment before. "Is it—?"

"It looks verra much like it," Duncan muttered, running his hand through his long hair. "I'd think so. The time is right, too, e'en with this calm of an hour past."

Rachelle took a wincing little breath when Trace looked at her. "My dear Rachelle," he said, giving her a polite smile. She braced herself, waiting for the inevitable. He was about to tell her farewell. He was going to leave her with only her maid for defense.

He tilted his head and gave her a polite smile. "I must beg leave to rummage through your valise."

"What? Why?" Bewildered, Rachelle reached out and gripped the bag with both hands. He had taken the money purse; nothing of his remained in the valise but the pistol and cutlass.

He rose and moved toward her with graceful economy. "Duncan," he said, ignoring her stricken face as he took the bag and opened it, "lift the hatch and see who moves about on the deck. Ask if you must, but see if you can spy the captain."

Duncan began to climb the ladder; then Rachelle felt her mouth go dry as Trace lifted out the pistol, checked it, and dropped the bag back into her lap.

"You're not going to shoot him!" she cried, her mind spinning with amazement.

"Hush," he hissed vehemently, crouching by her side as if he expected the entire crew to come barreling down the ladder. "Do you want to ruin everything?"

Rachelle clutched the valise to her chest, her heart hammering, her breathing ragged. "I won't let you do this." She reached out and wound her fingers in the lace-edged cravat at his throat, pulling him closer. "How could you do this after what happened aboard the *Adrienne?* You can't hurt the captain. Jump—swim, if you must! There are other ways to get to your ship."

"My ship?" His brows shot up in surprise, and he spoke aloud, momentarily forgetting himself. "What has the *Jacques* to do with this? I'm only intending to ask our captain to make an unscheduled stop." He pointed out the porthole to the small strip of greenish land beyond. "That is Winyah Bay, if I'm not mistaken."

"Winyah Bay?" Her thoughts scampered around vaguely. "But this ship is going to Charles Towne."

"And your Seewees live at Winyah Bay." Trace pulled out of her grasp and stood, resting the heft of the heavy pistol in his left hand as he gripped it with his right. "We have no time, Rachelle, to go to Charles Towne and backtrack."

She clamped her mouth shut, suddenly understanding. He had never intended that they should remain on board until Charles Towne. With a little persuasion from the pistol in his hand, he would force the captain of this ship to set them ashore here.

Gratitude and grief whirled in her brain. He wasn't going to abandon her, but she couldn't let him participate in an act of violence upon her behalf. She blew a hank of straggling hair from her forehead. He might be an honorable man at heart, but he was still a pirate by habit, taking other men's ships by the threat of violence whenever it suited him.

"No guns." She rose to her knees, girding herself with resolve. "You may ask the captain to set us off here, but do not take your pistol. You are not a pirate at the moment, you are Mr. Cooper, a gentleman who would never threaten harm to another soul."

Her reaction seemed to amuse him. "Yea, lady?" He grinned at her briefly. "Well, Mr. Cooper doesn't take orders from his wife, either."

"Not even when he's on his wife's errand?"

"Not even—" he bent toward her, his face set in a devilish smile—"when his wife's rich and bold and brassy."

Rachelle could feel herself flushing, rattled by his arrogance. Fala giggled, then clapped her hand over her mouth as Rachelle flicked a basilisk glance in her direction.

Trace crossed to the companionway ladder in three long strides, looking up expectantly for Duncan's report. "Aye, I see him," Duncan finally replied, looking down from his perch on the ladder. "The captain is standing amidships, looking toward the west. The barge is on board, in good repair, and there are hands aplenty to drop 'er down."

"Good." Trace lowered the gun to his side, then expertly—or so it seemed to Rachelle—hid it among the folds of his frock coat.

"Wait!" Rising from the floor, she hurried toward him. "Don't use your gun," she whispered, knowing that her voice drifted up toward the companionway hatch. "Let me ask the captain for permission."

"*Ask?*" He chuckled with a dry and cynical sound. "Rachelle, do you think this man is your grandfather? He's not someone you can wheedle into doing your will. The captain is the lord and master of his ship, commander upon the high seas. He will no more grant you permission to depart at this godforsaken strip of beach than he would allow you to burn his sailcloth and poison his crew."

"You have no faith, Mr. Cooper," she said, giving him a withering stare. "You have not because you ask not."

"That may be—" Trace waved Duncan aside with a sweep of his hand—"but I know better than to ask a captain to anchor where he has no business anchoring. First he'll laugh, and then he'll cuff me for impertinence."

"He wouldn't cuff me." Rachelle drew herself up to her full height, then threw back her head and placed her hands on her hips. Something in the gesture must have charmed him, for his bold glare assessed her frankly and a thoughtful smile curved his mouth.

"Mistress Cooper, I am your servant," he said simply, stepping away. He bowed gallantly and lifted his hand toward the ladder, inviting her to precede him.

Rachelle stepped forward, her mind whirling with a crazy mixture of hope and fear. What had she done? In an effort to keep Trace Bettencourt from damning himself further, she had just set herself up for possible humiliation and disgrace.

But he was right. They would waste valuable time returning to Charles Towne, and Trace had good reason for not wanting to show himself in that port. The *Fitz James* would have returned by now, and seamen who knew his face would undoubtedly be lounging around the docks, waiting for repairs to that ship to be completed and another cargo to be loaded.

Imposing an iron control on herself, she moved toward the ladder and nodded at Duncan, deliberately ignoring the captain behind her. She'd not had much experience at trying to wheedle a favor out of a man, but perhaps she'd be good at it . . . if the dirt and grime of this journey hadn't completely obliterated her charms.

The hatch door fell back with a slam that reverberated like thunder over the deck, and twenty pairs of eyes turned to stare at Rachelle. Two seamen, sitting on water casks directly in front of her, had been engaged in a bit of personal vanity—the one sitting still, his friend combing through his long hair and plaiting it up for him—but both froze in a paroxysm of astonishment as Rachelle stepped out onto the deck.

She moved forward, then heard the heavy clump of boots behind her. So Trace had followed, then. Probably with the pistol still hidden in his frock coat.

"I beg your pardon, sir." She happily batted her lashes toward the sailor whose fingers were firmly entwined in his shipmate's stiff hair. "But I would like a word with the captain."

The man's brows shot up in surprise, but he managed to extract one hand and point wordlessly over his shoulder. Rachelle saw him then—a massive self-confident presence with an air of isolation about his tall form, the captain of the *Gordon Hawke* did not look capable of any pleasant emotion.

She gathered her petticoat in one hand, lifting it above the cluttered deck, and paused to toss a whispered question over her shoulder. "His name?"

"Pinckert," came Trace's reply, his voice courteous but definitely patronizing.

"Captain Pinckert!" Rachelle lifted her hand, catching his attention, and saw the man stiffen.

"Mistress Cooper," he answered, offering her a distracted nod. His eyes moved past her to Trace. "I thought, Mr. Cooper, that we had an understanding. I do not allow passengers upon my deck—especially women. They distract the men, you see."

Rachelle pressed on, feeling the pressure of Trace's burning eyes upon the back of her neck. "It is my fault, Captain Pinckert. I have been a very disobedient wife. But my husband informs me—" she leaned forward and pointed toward the land sliding by the starboard bow—"that we are approaching Winyah Bay." She sucked her mouth into a deliberate rosette, then gave him her most charming smile. "Winyah Bay, Captain," she said in a silky voice, "is exactly where we want to go. We have business with the Indians there, for they might know a man we are seeking. If you would be so kind as to anchor so we can go ashore in one of your little boats—"

"I'm afraid that is quite impossible, Mistress Cooper," Pinckert interrupted, shrugging dismissively. "And you need to get below at once. We will be at Charles Towne in two days. You can make arrangements to visit Winyah Bay from there."

"But, Captain!" Rachelle stamped her foot, debating whether she should demonstrate a temper tantrum or urge tears of frustration to flow, but a flash of silver in the corner of her eye made her halt in midbreath.

"Move aside, Rachelle."

Fear and anger knotted inside her as Trace's voice cut through the silence. Her little game was over, the wager lost. She swiveled to the rail to face Trace and saw his pistol pointed squarely toward the captain's head, eighteen inches of silver weapon braced upon his forearm, his eye squinting down the shaft.

"Now, Captain," Trace said, his voice hardening to a chilly tone Rachelle had never heard, "I suggest you do as the lady says. Drop anchor now, and set a couple of hands to lowering the barge. And then you and my man will row us to land. We'll leave you in one piece and with oars, so you can return to your ship. You have my word upon it, but you must do exactly as I say."

"And if I don't?"

Trace sighed, then shifted his weight, narrowing the eye that squinted down the pistol's shaft. "Then I'll have to blow a hole in your head and take up the matter with your first mate."

Rachelle backed away, floundering in an agonizing maelstrom of emotion. She was traveling in the company of a murderer—*but he isn't!*—a desperate pirate—*no, a gentleman!*—an enigma that both repulsed and attracted her. She stumbled backward, then felt the railing behind her, slick with sea spray.

"You'll hang for this, you and the woman, too," Pinckert answered, his eyes flicking toward Rachelle, driving her back farther along the rail. "Kidnapping, that's what it is. Attempted murder."

"Duncan! Fala! Come up here!" Trace bellowed, his voice booming like thunder over the deck. One of the seamen, a burly fellow nearly as wide through the shoulders as Duncan and Trace combined, picked up a thick block and hefted it upward, holding it beneath his chin. Rachelle saw the motion, but so did Trace.

"Captain," he called, dark promise ringing in his voice, "tell your men to drop back and clap their hands to their foreheads. I wouldn't want to turn and blast one of them, but I would just as soon use this shot on a sailor as on a captain."

Hesitantly at first, the seamen looked at one another, then dropped whatever they carried—combs, ropes, blocks, sail-cloth—and placed their palms upon their faces, looking rather foolish. Rachelle saw more than one of them flush with anger and humiliation, and she knew their acquiescence would not last long. Trace might be able to get the captain and the four of them into the boat, but there was nothing to stop the men from pulling out their pistols and shooting as the small boat rowed away. If this Captain Pinckert was not well liked, they might even consider it a blessing if an errant shot struck him.

She leaned back, retreating from the desperate situation, and felt the solidity of the ship's railing at her hip. Behind her, the deadly sea surged with a steady rhythm, and just beyond that, the shoreline beckoned.

Jump.

She did not know how the idea got into her head, but she

recoiled from it, swallowing to bring her heart down from her throat. She couldn't jump. She couldn't *swim*. And Trace might not be able to save her, for he couldn't save that other girl, and if she jumped she would open the door on a host of memories he had tried hard to lock away. He'd hate her if she jumped, and if she died he'd never get over it, never forgive her for bringing him to Winyah Bay in the first place. . . .

Jump.

The voice was both within her and outside her, but it was a voice of certainty, finality, and faith. Over the past few days she had prayed for divine help—was this her answer?

"*Mon Dieu*, help me." Gingerly she placed her hands on the railing and swung one leg over. For a moment she thought everyone else on deck so intent upon the confrontation between the captain and Trace that no one noticed her, but as she brought her second leg over she heard Fala's frightened cry: "Mademoiselle! No!"

Taking a deep breath, Rachelle let go of the railing and threw herself off, her petticoat rushing up to her face, cold wind on the back of her legs as she shot toward the churning water below. Then she hit the surface, felt the impact upon the soles of her slippers, heard bubbles rush thundering past her ears. The shocking cold squeezed the air from her lungs in an explosive gasp; the salty taste of seawater filled her mouth. And all the while her heavy gown absorbed the water and pulled her down into the muffled silence of the deep.

In a surge of memory, MacKinnon's voice came back to her: "*If a ship goes down or you quietly fall overboard, swimming will do naught but prolong your death, aye?*"

She didn't know how to swim. Would that she did! Every moment, every second, counted now.

Above her, a muffled watery sound, a flash of light, another body in the sea. Rachelle looked up, catching a glimpse of a man's stockings and shoes, and knew that Trace had leaped in after her. He had not been able to save the captain's daughter, but that day guilt had blinded him.

She curved upward, looking at the rippled silver underside of the surface, and kicked through the fabric of her petticoats, desperately trying to untangle her feet long enough to propel herself upward.

Her faltering efforts could not counteract the pull of the sea. She sank lower, her flailing hands brushing across the bodice of her dress, sending a thousand tiny silver bubbles rushing past her face. She was clawing her way through liquid blackness now, the surface fading like a setting sun. Then an iron hand encircled her arm, a strong body caught and supported her, propelling her upward, toward light and life.

Her lungs were burning by the time her head broke the surface. She gasped, her belly a sea of nausea, then struggled in a sudden flurry of panic.

"Be still, *cherie*," a voice whispered in her ear. "Rest, be calm, and you will rise above the deep."

Though the advice was entirely against her nature, she obeyed, thrusting her head back upon the swell of a wave, allowing her legs to rise. To her surprise, Trace was right—she wasn't exactly floating, but she did not have to struggle to keep her face above water.

The silence was broken by a triumphant cry from the ship and the sound of two other loud splashes.

"What?" Rachelle cried, blinking the water out of her eyes. "What are they doing?"

"Tossing Duncan and Fala in after us," Trace replied, his voice calm and blessedly rational in her ear. "'Tis just as well; they are both swimmers. Your little distraction brought us close enough to shore; I don't suppose we need a boat after all. Though I did hope to keep you from getting wet again."

Confused, Rachelle lifted her head. Ahead of her, scarcely one hundred feet away, lay a beach bordered with tall trees and a faint white edge of lapping wave.

"Lie back, and I'll pull you in," Trace instructed, his strong arm slipping around her waist. Rachelle did as she was told, lowering the back of her head into the water and waving her hands, trying desperately to stay afloat. She forced herself to breathe deeply, inflating her lungs, and stared at the gray dome of the sky above.

"The captain was flying blind," Trace muttered, his steady sidestroke bringing them closer to shore with each breath. "A fool, actually, staying on that tack and beating up against the swell when he couldn't see ten feet before his bow."

Welcoming the conversation, she took a moment to catch her breath. "You—you weren't going to shoot him?"

"How could I? The pistol wasn't loaded."

His steady stroke altered; he released her and bobbed underwater for an instant, then reappeared, shaking his head like a dog. "You can stand here," he said, holding her until her questing feet felt sand beneath her toes. She breathed a quick sigh, then hiccuped as she realized how close she had come to drowning. Behind her, she heard splashing, then saw Fala's and Duncan's heads approaching through the gentle surf.

Trace's arm slipped around her waist and supported her as they climbed through the breakers. "So you weren't going to shoot him?" she repeated, feeling a little like a dull parrot. She turned and stared up into his face, sparkling now with droplets of seawater. "How did you expect to commandeer a boat with an empty pistol?"

"Well, Captain Pinckert didn't know it was empty, did he?" His boyishly affectionate smile made her want to box his ears. "He would have given us the boat, too, until you behaved like a flying monkey and jumped overboard."

"I—" She caught her breath, unable to frame words around the emotions swirling in her chest. "I didn't want you to be guilty of—I didn't want—"

"You are too late, *cherie*," he answered, dropping his arm from her waist. "I am already guilty of too many things. When a man's heart is as black as tar, what's the harm in one more stain?" Turning toward the beach, he kept walking through the ankle-deep surf, leaving her to follow on her own.

▼▲▼▲▼ As Duncan settled the women and began digging a fire pit on the beach, Trace wandered away, ostensibly to search for firewood. The scrubby palmettos gave way almost immediately to tall, thin pines, and Trace wandered among them for ten minutes without pausing, lost in his thoughts.

What in the world had Rachelle intended? Like a foolish, impetuous female she had leaped off that ship and into the water, knowing he would be forced to come after her.

He shook his head, smiling despite himself. In all his days on the sea, he had never met anyone with such blind faith . . . in him.

Why had she done it? Why did she believe in him? He hadn't done anything particularly brave on her behalf. He had promised to see her safely to Roxbury and couldn't very well abandon her now, especially in the bowels of a ship commanded by a scoundrel like Pinckert. That little toad would not have hesitated to hang Rachelle and Fala from the yardarms, if—

Trace stopped on the path, feeling everything go silent within him. If Rachelle hadn't jumped overboard, they'd all be swinging from the yardarms now, their faces purpling above a hanging noose. Trace had hoped Pinckert would submit easily, but in that instant when their eyes met above his pistol, he realized the Englishman wouldn't capitulate.

Cold air brushed across the backs of his legs, and beneath the damp hair on his head his scalp tingled. Trace sank to a fallen log on the ground, then lowered his head and ran his hands through his hair.

"*Mon Dieu.* I nearly killed us all."

He felt himself flush with shame, but the rising emotion was the mere tip of a long seam of guilt that snaked its way back through the years. His guilt was his burden, his cross to bear, and though he had prayed for forgiveness, had *begged* God for understanding, the load had never been lightened.

He had sought God in chapels and lain awake under the stars and poured out his heart to the master of the universe. Though some part of him hoped that Christ's forgiveness included mercy enough to allow holy absolution, Trace had never felt any emotion but despair during his solitary confession.

Did he confess only to himself? Sometimes he felt as though his prayers went no higher than his hat. Prayer brought him no relief from pain; the haunting sorrows and hurts of his past were still festering sores. Though he would never admit it to his crew or even to Duncan, Trace could not forget his sin or put it behind him.

One minister had told him to simply take forgiveness by faith. Not wanting to sin further by calling God a liar, Trace did his best to believe he was forgiven, but he could not escape the misery and bitterness in his life. Forgiven or not, he was still an outcast, still a wanted man.

Perhaps, he thought, clasping his hands as he looked up at the tall trees soaring overhead, God forgave his sin but kept the memory of it alive for a purpose.

But why? Surely God did not intend for him to live the rest of his days as a pariah. Trace would not have minded a life of solitude, but then Rachelle had entered his world, stinging him with thoughts of softness he would never know, blinding him with beauty and sweetness he would never possess.

"There must be something more," he whispered, his eyes falling to the velvet shadows at his feet. Thick snaking roots covered the ground; the interwoven pines shaded his head, sheltering him in a perfect forest cathedral.

But for him, it was wasted beauty. Either forgiveness was some sort of spiritual ticket to heaven, no more and no less, or Trace was not worthy of the forgiving grace of God.

▼▲▼▲▼ As the setting sun stretched its glowing fingers across the sky, Trace and Duncan set about making a fire and shelter on the beach. Rachelle realized that the night she and Fala had slept under the overturned barge would seem positively luxurious compared to the night ahead. Her clothing was soaked and stiff with salt, the skin under her bodice chafed with wet sand. But there was no freshwater nearby, and she did not possess the energy to search for any.

When Duncan returned with an armload of wood, he told Trace that a trading post lay only a mile north on the beach, at the junction of a river and the ocean.

"Yes, I saw it as we sailed by," Trace remarked, tossing another branch onto the fire. The wood was so dry it seemed to thirst for the flames, tonguing high into the air. Rachelle sank onto the damp sand and extended her hands, eager for the fire's warmth. She had lost her shoes and stockings in her swim and now felt chilled to the bone.

For a long time no one said anything. Fala sat beside Rachelle, occasionally sending a quiet smile across the fire to Duncan, and Trace stretched out on the sand, apparently not even feeling the cold. After a few moments, Duncan stood, made a courtly bow to Fala, and asked her if she'd be willing to gather wood with him. Rachelle looked up in surprise as her maidservant and the pirate walked away through the shadows, leaving her alone with Trace Bettencourt.

She ought to have been scandalized, or at least concerned that she'd been left without a chaperon, but the sudden sweetness of certain privacy seemed not to affect the captain. He lay by the fire, stretched out like an old dog, a slender twig between his teeth, his hands folded behind his head. The very picture of a contented pirate, just escaped from certain death.

Watching him, Rachelle sat in practiced repose, her hands in her lap, her ankles crossed. The shadow of his emerging beard gave him an even more manly aura, muting the sharp and confident line of his profile. For a man who professed his heart to be "as black as tar," he held his head high with pride, and touches of humor lined his gentle mouth and eyes.

Was this the face of a criminal? Rachelle didn't know much about men, but she would have wagered her life that Trace Bettencourt possessed the soul of a gentleman—until he'd pulled the pistol from her valise.

"I thought you were watching for Ocracoke Island," she said, eyeing him with a calculating expression. "Time is short, and you must get back to your men."

His lips parted slightly in surprise as he turned his head. "Ocracoke? We passed that island yesterday."

Rachelle felt her flesh color, and she looked down at her hands, hoping the firelight would disguise the blush on her cheeks and neck. "I know. And I thank you for staying with us, because now I see the wisdom in what you've done, but I didn't expect you to do so much."

His expression stilled and grew serious. "Rachelle Bailie," his voice gentled and dropped in volume, "has no one ever loved you enough to do so much?"

Certain that she detected a note of condescension in his attitude, she went crimson with resentment and humiliation. "Of course!" she snapped, jerking her shoulders upright. "My mother adored me, and my grandfather—"

She wanted to say, "*Grand-père* loved me, petted me, pampered me," but the words would not come. Fala knew the truth. Trace knew it, too, she was certain, though she couldn't see how or why he should know so much about her. The truth was that no one but her mother had loved her, not even Lanston, who sought her with the enthusiasm he reserved for gambling and slaving . . . and wealth.

The blood began to pound in her temples, and she looked away into the darkness, humiliatingly conscious of the captain's scrutiny.

"I haven't thanked you properly," she said, drawing a deep breath in hopes of changing the subject, "for saving my life yet again. I thought I could swim, but the task was harder than I thought 'twould be in this heavy petticoat. I wasn't doing a very fair job of it, but—"

"You sank like a stone." He raised himself up on one elbow, grinning at her. "But you did manage to surprise the captain and his crew long enough for me to toss the gun away and dive in after you."

"It's a wonder you weren't killed."

"They tried." Laughter floated up from his throat. "The captain grabbed my pistol as I was diving and fired." He grimaced in good humor. "Good thing it wasn't loaded, *oui?*"

"You are a most illogical man," she murmured, half laughing, half crying as her eyes filled with moisture. "You nearly got us all killed; you have done nothing but bring me trouble since the moment I met you."

An expression of mock hurt flitted across his face. *"Moi?* Mademoiselle, you are mistaken. It is I who have suffered ever since our first meeting. I was forced to leave my ship, take you to Roxbury, and sleep in the sand. I had to use my best barge to bribe a stingy fisherman in exchange for a mangy horse and rough wagon. And I had to endure a minister who insisted upon regaling me with the glories of his conservatory and the evils of tomatoes."

"If you had not attacked our ship," she pressed her lips together, trying not to smile, "I would have gone to Boston with Lanston and found the Reverend Eliot myself. And I wouldn't have had to do it in a filthy, torn gown, and I wouldn't be sitting here, starving, freezing, and drenched to the bone."

"You are cold?" He sat up and extended a hand, clearly inviting her to come closer. "Come, mademoiselle, and let me warm you," he called, a trifle too sweetly.

She frowned, understanding that he meant the invitation only in jest, then looked into his face. His expression had softened, and his steady gaze bore into her in silent expectation. Slowly, his hand fell to his side, but his gaze did not leave her face.

Her heart jolted; her pulse pounded in response. The smoldering flame she saw in his eyes startled her, and the implication sent an unwelcome surge of excitement through her veins.

This attraction would be perilous. It was already dangerous, for she was a woman betrothed, and he was a condemned pirate. And yet there was an air of capable efficiency about him that fascinated her. Something in his manner soothed and comforted her in a way Lanston Wragg probably never would.

"I think," she said slowly, her words sounding strange and

thick in her ears, "that I should get some sleep." She pressed her hand to the sand, wishing suddenly for the luxurious cloak she'd left on board the *Gordon Hawke.*

That's it—think about the cold, the sand, the night, the sounds— anything but the man across the fire.

"Good night, then," he answered. His gaze moved toward the fire, apparently seeing nothing else.

Fala awakened to the liquid duet of mockingbirds from the
fringe of trees beyond the beach. Slowly she adjusted to wakeful-
ness, aware that Rachelle lay nested against her back, like a
puppy seeking warmth from a littermate.

Pressing her hands to the beach, Fala pushed herself up, blinking rapidly as she looked around. Duncan had tossed a load of
dew-damp wood on the smoldering fire, and curls of smoke
streamed from the broken branches like spirits hurrying back to
the woods from which he had dragged them.

She brushed stray tendrils of hair from her cheek, then looked
across the fire to where Duncan squatted in the sand. There was
a flash like light caught in water when her gaze crossed his.

"Good morrow," he croaked in a morning voice.

Mindful of her sleeping mistress, Fala slowly straightened,
then gave him a shy smile. "Good morrow. Thank you—for the
fire. It feels wonderful." To illustrate the depth of her gratitude,
she lifted her hands to the reluctant flames.

"Aw, 'tis not much. I canna find much decent wood here. 'Tis
likely the Indians and traders have burned it all up."

Fala nodded, not knowing what else to say. Slavery had
taught her to keep silent unless spoken to, and then to speak
quickly and directly. She had no gift for trivial conversation, and
the pleasantries Rachelle routinely rattled off would only sound
foolish on Fala's tongue. Though she and Duncan had shared
some lengthy discussions, he was the one who seemed to keep
the conversation flowing.

"Did you sleep well?" Duncan asked, a smile flashing through
his blond beard.

Fala crossed her legs beneath her wet petticoat, then rested her hands on her knees. "Yes." *Always agree, never offer personal opinions—no one wants to hear them.*

"I had a bit o' trouble myself. The sand was warm enough, once I burrowed down into it, but it isn't verra soft . . . is it?"

He looked up at her from beneath craggy brows, seeking an answer, seeking conversation. Fala lowered her gaze in confusion, tormented by perplexing and unfamiliar emotions. Her mistress was sleeping; she ought not to be talking at all until Rachelle awoke. And then she would have to tend to Rachelle's needs. Perhaps after an hour or two she would be able to speak as freely as she had during their walk last night, but not yet.

A sudden thought struck her, and Fala glanced around, then looked back at Duncan. "Captain Bettencourt?" she asked, vowing to at least be useful. When Rachelle awoke and found the captain missing, she'd want to know where he had gone.

Duncan jerked a thumb over his shoulder. "He went up the beach to spy out that trading post. He's in a bit of a hurry, you know, and wants to find that tribe before nightfall."

Fala nodded, gratified. Rachelle would be pleased.

Silence, thick as wool, fell between them again, broken only by the steady rhythm of the sea and the continuous churr of insects from the woods beyond. The empty air between them vibrated, filled with unspoken words and feelings; then a sharp and brittle crack of weathered wood snapped like a whip through the silence.

The sailor sprang to his feet, his knife in his hand, and Fala felt fear rush into her heart. Duncan's eyes had gone wide with the sight of something in the trees. Fala turned slowly, not wanting to and yet compelled to see what frightening apparition the woods had brought forth.

An Indian stood behind her, his face painted with white streaks, his long hair pinioned with eagle feathers and strips of deerskin. He wore moccasins, a frilled shirt of English origin, and a breechclout of soft leather. Tall and straight, muscular and supple, he looked as though he could easily take Duncan in a fight—though Fala hoped it wouldn't come to that.

Intelligence and hard-bitten strength were etched into every feature of the Indian's face; his eyes were as cold and polished as obsidian beads. His gaze moved slowly over the campfire, in one perusal taking in the sight of sleeping Rachelle, the fire, Duncan's size and weapon. Then his sharp and assessing gaze fell upon her, and Fala saw something flicker far back in those eyes—pain and anger, perhaps, or even fear.

"Do you speak his language, Fala?" Duncan asked, spacing his words evenly. "I think we'd best try communicating with him."

"I don't remember much," Fala murmured, her heart thumping against her rib cage. "I don't know if he is from my tribe. I was Yamassee."

The Indian stiffened at the word, then brought his hand to his chest. "Yamassee." Something akin to a smile flashed across his face. "I am Yamassee."

"You have the English?" Duncan asked, opening his palms before the man. The dagger was locked between his thumb and index finger, but it was clear from Duncan's gesture that he could be persuaded not to use it.

"Yes," the Indian answered, his voice rumbling through their little camp like thunder.

Fala felt Rachelle jerk on the ground behind her. "Fala, what—?" she asked. She lifted her eyes and erupted in crazy, full-throated shrieking.

With a calmness she didn't necessarily feel, Fala reached back and clapped her hand over her frightened mistress's mouth. "She was asleep," she told the stranger, glancing up. He was eyeing Rachelle as if she were a bad smell, but Fala could see no signs of threat in his appearance. His knife remained sheathed in his belt, his hands hung open at his side, and he was alone, while they were three.

Apparently realizing how foolish she appeared, Rachelle grew silent under Fala's hand.

"Mademoiselle," Fala whispered, bending low, "he will not harm us. But perhaps he can take us to the Seewees."

Rachelle's eyes teared with relief, and she nodded; then Fala removed her hand and helped Rachelle sit up. After taking a moment to wipe the sand from her face, Rachelle turned to their visitor with the air of a queen granting favors. "Welcome to our fire," she said, regally gesturing toward Duncan's pile of smoking sticks. "I am Rachelle Bailie, and these are my companions, Fala and Duncan MacKinnon. And you are?"

She paused delicately, lifting a questioning brow, and the Indian weighed her with a critical squint. "Ezhno," he answered finally, placing his hand upon his chest in a gesture of grave dignity.

"The solitary one," Fala murmured, surprised that she could remember the meaning of the name. The Indian fixed her in a questioning look, but Fala lowered her gaze, yielding the conversation to her mistress.

"Ezhno, how lovely to meet you." A small smile of enchantment touched Rachelle's lips, then faded as the warrior frowned with a vague hint of disapproval.

"Do not use his name to his face." Fala whispered in order to avoid further embarrassing their visitor. "It is disrespectful. And welcome him to sit; only those with bad manners discuss matters while one is standing."

Rachelle hesitated, blinking with bafflement, then turned her eyes toward the Indian again. "Sir—won't you please sit by our fire?" The warrior hesitated a moment, glancing at Fala as if for some sign of reassurance, then slowly sank to the ground. Duncan stood over him for a moment, his hands on his broad hips; then he sat as well, a momentary look of discomfort crossing his face.

"Welcome," Rachelle said, smiling at the Indian though her eyes were a little wary, a little haunted. "I apologize that we have nothing to offer you, but—" she flapped her hand toward the ocean—"we were just washed ashore last night."

The Indian turned his gaze toward Duncan, who still held his dagger in his hand. Rachelle saw the glance and immediately gestured for Duncan to put the blade away. He did, a trifle reluctantly, Fala thought.

"Friend," Rachelle said, leaning forward in her eagerness, "we have come here to seek a man who has come from the north. He is called—" She glanced at Fala, seeking permission to use the name, and Fala nodded. "He is called Mojag Bailie," Rachelle went on, "and he might have arrived here more than a month ago. We expect to find him with the Seewees."

Ezhno's eyes darkened at the mention of that tribe. The look he gave Rachelle was compassionate, troubled, and still. "The Seewees are gone." His gaze traveled past their fire and moved toward the open sea.

"All of them?" Surprise filled Rachelle's voice. "Surely they are not all gone. If the men are hunting, surely the women remain in camp."

"No one remains," Ezhno answered, and Fala stiffened at something jagged and sharp in his voice, like words torn by the blade of a knife. "They went to sea many days ago in their canoes. None have returned."

"They dinna go to sea in a canoe!" Duncan's eyes went round with surprise and speculation. "Impossible! There's not a canoe built that could withstand e'en a wee squall or some of the waves that kick up out in the currents—"

Rachelle held up a hand, quieting him. "Why did they go, friend?" she asked, her soothing voice probing further. "Why would they leave their lands?"

The glitter in Ezhno's half-closed eyes was both accusing and sorrowful. "The English pay too little. The sachems learned what the English received for deer pelts on their island and decided to take the deerskins across the Great Sea." He paused a moment, then continued in sinking tones. "The tribe lashed their pelts to their canoes, loaded up their women and children, and set out . . . from this place."

Fala listened with rising dismay. She knew little of the sea, but she'd seen enough to know that a canoe could never weather the rough waves and sudden storms that could spring up at a moment's notice. It was only natural that the Seewees had chosen to transport the entire tribe, for they always moved together. They knew the land of the English was far away but had probably thought to reach that far-flung shore in several days, then camp on the land while the tribal leaders conducted business with the English merchants.

"You mean," Rachelle said, speaking slowly, "that they went to England in order to avoid dealing with the traders here?"

Ezhno nodded, his face quiet, withdrawn, and worried. "They have not come back." He turned his eyes toward the horizon again. "I am to marry a woman of the Seewee tribe, and I have waited here every day for a sign of their canoes."

Fala looked away, stricken by the certain knowledge that Ezhno's promised bride would never return. Added to her despair was an inexplicable feeling of guilt. As an Indian who had lived among the English, she could have told them that canoes would not be adequate for the journey . . . if she had only lived among them.

"Fala," Rachelle whispered.

Fala jerked her head up and looked at her mistress, understanding the unspoken question behind Rachelle's dark eyes. *No, I cannot tell him,* she answered silently, shaking her head. *I do not have the courage.*

A group of roosting birds flapped suddenly into the sky, and Fala looked up in time to see Captain Bettencourt approaching, his features twisted in a grim expression of concern, his hand resting upon the hilt of the cutlass dangling from his belt. His dark, gun-barrel-like eyes strafed the gathering, then trained in upon the Indian. He approached slowly, cautiously, and Fala saw the Indian stiffen as the captain circled.

"Greetings," the captain said simply, his blue eyes evaluating the Indian with a critical squint. "We have a visitor?"

"A friend," Rachelle quickly interjected. She gestured toward an empty place on the ground next to her and motioned that he should sit. He did, albeit slowly, then turned his eyes toward Duncan.

"Is all well?"

"Aye, Captain." Duncan swiveled his eyes toward the captain's face. "This is Ezhno, and he has told us that the Seewees are gone."

"*Oui.*" Trace propped one elbow upon his lifted knee. "So you've heard. I heard the story at the trader's house about an hour ago."

Rachelle fixed her penetrating gaze upon him. "They really left in canoes?"

"Loaded canoes, I'm afraid," Trace answered, absently brushing a thick layer of sand from his boots. "They knew they were being cheated and decided to open their own export business. But the canoes were swamped, as you can well imagine, less than a mile offshore."

Fala heard Ezhno's quick intake of breath. "Swamped? What do you mean? There are no swamps on the sea!"

Captain Bettencourt lifted his gaze to the Indian, then pensively bit his lower lip, apparently wondering if he'd said too much. Rachelle, judging his thoughts, reached out and placed her hand on his arm. "Our friend Ezhno has been coming here every day to seek a woman of the Seewee tribe," she said, keeping her features deceptively composed. "He has heard nothing since they left."

For a long moment Captain Bettencourt stared mindlessly at the fire; then Fala sighed heavily as he lifted his gaze to meet their guest's. "I am very sorry to be the one to tell you this." His voice filled with anguish. "But the canoes could not ride the mighty waves of the sea. They were too heavily loaded with pelts, and the water came aboard until the sea swallowed the canoes."

"The women? And the children?" Ezhno's watery eyes followed the captain with absolutely no expression.

"I do not know for certain," Bettencourt answered, his eyes

large and fierce with pain, "but the trader has heard that ships in the area plucked some survivors from the sea."

Ezhno smiled in hope, but Trace shook his head, continuing quickly. "I am sorry, my friend, but the Seewees who survived were taken to Barbados."

"Barbados." Ezhno tried the word on his tongue, pronouncing it stiffly. "Is it far, this Barbados?"

"Across the sea," Trace answered, his voice gone strangely flat. "A canoe cannot make the journey. I do not think they will be coming back."

They were sold as slaves. Though the captain had not dared to say it, Fala knew what fate had befallen the surviving Seewees. Which of them were the most fortunate—those who drowned or those who would spend the rest of their lives subjected to harsh masters in a foreign land?

She heard a muted whimpering sound and looked up, realizing from the stricken look on Rachelle's face that her mistress had realized the truth, too. And Duncan. The Scot's broad face had heated to a fierce red color.

Ezhno bore his grief with grave and solemn dignity. His square jaw had tensed visibly during Trace's recounting of the Seewees' journey, and the aloof strength Fala had first noted now seemed subdued, drained somehow. But still he looked up at them with indomitable pride and offered the hospitality of his village.

Just as gravely, Captain Bettencourt accepted on their group's behalf.

▼▲▼▲▼ The barren soil of the beach gave way to the green of the trees in a line so sharp it appeared to have been drawn by a celestial hand. Trace found himself following Ezhno through a virgin forest filled with mist and gray-blue light. A faint wind breathed through the trees, and the atmosphere was alive with screeches, trills, and whirs from unseen birds far overhead. The coldly pungent scents of pine and cedar overcame his own earthy odors of stale sweat, grimed skin, and the tang of the sea.

Ezhno walked alone at the front of their party, ostensibly to lead the way, though that position afforded him a modicum of privacy in which to gather his thoughts and explore his grief without enduring the curious glances of four strangers. Fala followed the Indian, her eyes wide and curious as they went deeper into the woods, and Duncan followed Fala, eager to offer assistance if she should need it. Trace brought up the rear of their small procession, thoughts of Mojag Bailie occupying his brain as he doggedly followed in Rachelle's steps.

Was Mojag Bailie among those who had died in the sea? Or was he, perhaps, a prisoner in Barbados? From what Rachelle had told him, Trace knew that Mojag probably looked like an Indian. And even though Bailie was skilled and literate, a slave trader was not likely to overlook a pair of tattooed arms and the promise of silver a healthy slave would bring. If Bailie had been with the Seewees, he was either drowned or a slave. And finding one slave among the thousands who were sold and bartered without accurate identification or proper records would be as impossible as counting waves on the seashore.

"You are thinking about my father." Rachelle flung the comment over her shoulder, glancing briefly back as she followed Duncan.

"Yes." He felt the corner of his mouth twist—apparently the girl had learned to read his mind.

"You're thinking that my father would not have allowed the Seewees to attempt such a foolish journey."

"Again, mademoiselle, you are correct," he lied. He thrust his hands behind his back, staring at the ground in order to avoid her piercing eyes.

"That is what I thought—I mean, that is my feeling, too." She stopped suddenly in the trail and turned to face him. "My father is no fool, Captain Bettencourt. And I know he is a compassionate man. He could not have reached the Seewees in time."

She was staring at him, and Trace recoiled from her gaze,

scarcely able to bear the touch of her eyes' question and the look of hope behind the question. She needed comforting, something to hold on to. She wanted him to say that it was quite impossible for a man like Mojag Bailie to cast his lot with the unfortunate Seewees, that she would find him alive and well somewhere in this area, but he knew nothing about Mojag Bailie except that the man had sired an extraordinary daughter.

"I am quite certain you are right, mademoiselle," he finally answered. He looked into her eyes. "Of certain your father did not reach them in time. He would not have gone with them, neither would he have allowed them to go."

A blush of pleasure rose to her face, as if his assurance had caused confidence itself to fill her veins. "You are a man of infinite wisdom, Captain Bettencourt," she answered prettily, turning. She lifted her petticoat and sprinted ahead to catch up with Duncan.

Trace closed his eyes, dreading what might lie ahead. "We will see if you still think so," he murmured under his breath, "when we talk to the Indians here and see what truly became of Mojag Bailie."

▾▲▾▲▾ Ezhno, Rachelle decided, had been a dedicated lover, for the walk back to his village took at least an hour. Though he was of the Yamassee tribe, he explained during the last few minutes of the journey, his village had grown smaller over the last several years. For this reason he had agreed to take a wife from the Seewees, in the hope that his people might be influenced and reborn with the spirit of another tribe whose strength could be added to his own. "But I did not agree to marry Aponi only for my people's sake," he added, with great depth of feeling. "She was a fine woman."

Rachelle felt a shock run through her when they entered the open gate of the wooden palisade surrounding Ezhno's village. The settlement inside, though small, boiled with life. Small children, naked but for the necklaces and bracelets they wore, came running to greet the visitors, their eyes alight with excitement and their tongues jabbering questions she couldn't understand. They took her hands, prodded her voluminous petticoat, giggled at her bare toes beneath the hem, and twirled her curly hair between their fingers as if comparing it to their own.

Fala and Duncan were undergoing a similar examination, she noticed, but the women around Fala were older and seemed generally more respectful. They were holding Fala's arm, tracing their fingers over the long, slender lines of her tattoos, murmuring quiet phrases to one another in tones of repressed excitement.

"Come, there is food by the fire," Ezhno said, leading the way. He uttered a harsh rebuke that sent the children flying away from Duncan and Rachelle but said nothing to the women around Fala. With a shrug of disinterest, he led Trace, Duncan, and Rachelle to a circle where several adults were eating what Rachelle assumed was breakfast.

A copper cauldron bubbled with some sort of stew over a stone-lined fire pit. One of the women hovering near the fire handed each of the guests a wooden bowl and a stone ladle, and with this Rachelle gratefully scooped up a healthy portion of the vegetables and meat. Her stomach, urgently awake and eager, sent an audible growl shivering through her midsection.

She sank onto the ground with the others, vowing not to look too carefully at what might be in the stew. The porridge was delicious—hot, thick, and completely satisfying, a far better repast than anything they had eaten aboard the *Gordon Hawke.* Stale ship's biscuit and dried beef filled the emptiness in her belly, but this—she breathed deeply of the aromatic porridge—this was *food.*

After breakfast, the women of the village descended upon Rachelle and Fala with single-minded concentration. Ignoring Rachelle's protests, the two women were taken to a freshwater stream and convinced—by pantomime—to remove their salt-encrusted garments for washing. Overcome with sudden modesty, Rachelle balked, then realized that the women had taken pains to choose a spot densely sheltered by trees and foliage. No man would see her here, and the water would feel deliciously cool.

Sighing in anticipation, Rachelle jerked the ties of her sleeves, dropping them to the ground as a pair of young girls squealed in glee. Each of them took a sleeve and ran off—to wash it, Rachelle hoped—and within another moment she had divested herself of petticoat, bodice, farthingale, corset, and pettipants. Shivering, she slipped into the cool water and closed her eyes, feeling the sting of salt and sand leave her goose-pimpled skin.

She suspected that her lips had begun to turn blue by the time the women brought out buckskin garments, one for her and one for Fala. Rachelle tried to protest, insisting that she preferred her own clothes, wet though they may be, but Fala laughed and crinkled her nose. "They say," she said, nodding at an elderly Indian woman who was lecturing in a stern, no-nonsense voice, "that your clothes smell of rotten food. They will soak them in a pot, but you cannot wear them yet."

Rachelle rolled her eyes and surrendered to her good-natured handmaids, quietly amused by the sight of Fala enduring their ministrations with the same patient attitude Rachelle had always adopted whenever Babette forced her to change out of a favorite garment.

After dressing, the Indian women set about plaiting Rachelle's and Fala's hair into long, loose braids, carefully twining feathers into several strands. Rachelle felt her mouth drop with wry disappointment when she compared her coiffure with Fala's—she had been given only one feather, whereas Fala wore three.

While two women worked on their hair, a young girl brought forth two pairs of soft leather moccasins. Rachelle slipped into hers thankfully, since she'd lost her shoes and stockings when she leaped from the ship. The shoes were a little large, but they were warm and a comfort to her trail-weary feet.

As the women pampered and cared for them, Rachelle was quietly amazed at the tribe's generosity. Why should they care so much for two pirates, a French colonist, and an ex-slave? The reason became evident later in the afternoon when two old women, white haired and nearly toothless, led Fala away to a small circle. Another woman took Rachelle's arm and led her to a larger circle where the tribal elders had gathered around the common fire. Ezhno, Rachelle noticed, sat next to the place of honor, where a wizened old man, presumably the sachem, smoked on a long pipe and regarded the proceedings with indifferent eyes. Sighing in relief, she sank into her place between Trace and Duncan. Now, finally, they'd be able to ask about Mojag Bailie.

When Rachelle had been seated, the old man dropped his pipe and looked around the circle. He spoke in a clipped, guttural tone that Rachelle could not follow, but Ezhno provided a translation each time the sachem paused for breath.

"Among the Yamassee," he said, his dark eyes shifting from one stranger to the next as Ezhno translated, "there are Suns, Nobles, Honored People, and commoners. I am the Great Sun, descended from the sun above. My wife, my children, are descended from the sun as well."

The sachem paused to draw deeply on his pipe, then turned his attention to Fala, who sat with the old women outside the circle. He studied her face with his enigmatic gaze for a long moment, then spoke again.

"A man's rank is acquired from his mother at birth," Ezhno translated, "though our Honored People are those who have accomplished great deeds."

Rachelle stared in expectant silence, waiting for the old man to make his point. He seemed to have something important on his mind, but he was taking forever to share it, and she was impatient to ask about her father.

The sachem's eyes turned toward her, and a sudden icy contempt flashed in his gaze as he spoke again. His eyes narrowed, and his back became ramrod straight as Ezhno interpreted.

"My sister," Ezhno said, nodding to the sachem to indicate that he spoke for the older man, "was descended from the sun, and her son would be the tribe's next Great King. But many winters ago, a group of English crept up upon them and killed her, her husband, even the babe in her arms."

Rachelle opened her mouth in dismay, feeling suddenly guilty and selfish. This man had known tragedy, as had Ezhno, but what had his sorrows to do with them? A sudden sensation of fear and desolation swept over her. Surely he hadn't fed and clothed and cared for them only so he could later take vengeance upon his murdered sister and her family?

The old man's mouth twitched in a grimace; his eyes were half closed, hooded like a hawk's. "My sister," he continued slowly, as Ezhno translated, "had a daughter, too. A girl who had seen seven summers and was marked with the sign of the tribe and her rank."

Alight with secret knowledge, his dark gaze arched slowly from Rachelle to the place where Fala sat outside the circle with the women, and suddenly the light of understanding dawned in Rachelle's brain.

Fala! The shock of discovery hit her full force. Fala was the sachem's niece; he had recognized her tattoos.

"You must leave her here with us," the old man was saying now, the veins in his throat standing out like ropes as he waited for them to respond to the translation. "She is one of us. She is of my people. She should not be with you. They tell me she is your servant, and this is not right. She is a Sun. You are a commoner."

A tumble of confused thoughts and feelings assailed Rachelle, and she looked at Trace, hoping for some sign of an answer. He caught her questioning glance and shrugged, crossing his arms as if to say, *It's your decision*, then smiled his mercurial smile.

She turned her eyes away and stared at the ground, her thoughts racing. Could she leave Fala here? She had already granted Fala freedom and agreed to pay her wages, must she surrender her completely? In the last few days she had begun to understand the true meaning of friendship, and certainly she had never felt as close to anyone else. Leaving Fala was tantamount to leaving an arm, a leg, a shadow of her heart. She could not do it, but neither could she ignore the challenge in Trace's eye.

She looked up at the sachem and managed a small, tentative smile. "Great King," she said, dipping her head in what she hoped was a suitable sign of respect, "know this. Fala is my friend and my maid. But she is also a free woman. I cannot decide her fate—she must decide her own. If you would have her stay here, you will have to speak to her. The decision must be hers alone."

Ezhno translated her response, and Rachelle sat without moving, impaled by the sachem's steady gaze until Ezhno had finished. Then the sachem nodded, the tense lines of his face relaxing. "It is well said," he told Ezhno, reaching for his pipe.

"There is one other thing." Trace smiled at the sachem and spoke in careful English for Ezhno's benefit. "We have come here to find a man called Mojag Bailie. He lived for a time with the northern tribes and follows the Great God Jesus. Has he visited your people?"

The sachem listened to the translation without moving, a certain tension in his attitude, then shook his head. "No man like that has come among us," he replied, a firmness in his voice that verged on threatening. "We would not welcome him."

As a signal that the interview was complete, the sachem returned his pipe to his mouth, stood, and walked slowly to his small frame house. Ezhno said nothing as his leader departed, then regarded his visitors with an expression of weary dignity. "He will send for Fala before the sun sets," he said, an edge to his voice. "He will invite her to remain here. And you are welcome until she decides what she will do. And then you may go with her or without her, however she decides, but you must go."

"Have the English treated your people so badly?" Rachelle murmured, almost able to see the dark mood that hung above the Indian like a cloud.

He had turned to rise but froze in his position, then gave her a look so harsh and bitter that she bit her tongue. "If you had not had the woman Fala with you," he said, his voice sharp and sudden as a thrown knife, "I would have left you to starve on the beach."

"I'll speak to him now, mind you, or mop the floor with your head, young man!"

Lanston Wragg stiffened as the angry voice filled the small waiting room outside his office, and one hand went automatically to the drawer where he kept a pistol, primed and ready. He wasn't certain if the irate man outside was a disgruntled customer, a council official, or the father of a young lady, but no matter who it was, it was best to be prepared.

The door slammed open and hit the wall, the force of the blow nearly cracking the plaster. A red-faced, bearded man in a tricorne and a blue coat stood in the doorway, his jaw thrust forward and his thin mouth curled as if about to erupt in a string of particularly colorful curses.

"Lanston Wragg." It was a demand, not a question.

"Yes?" Lanston's hand slipped into the drawer and curled around the pistol's handle. He smiled and lifted a brow in polite surprise.

"I've come for the reward." The man marched forward and slammed a placard on the desk, then pinioned it with a bony index finger.

Lanston frowned at the lettering. "This is the offer of a reward for the pirate Trace Bettencourt."

"I know what it is." The man's beard parted in a dazzling display of crooked yellow teeth. "And I know where your pirate is, too."

"You do?" Lanston released the pistol and gave the man a sidelong glance of utter disbelief. "Where is he? And is the girl still with him?"

"Aye." The man tucked his fingers into the waistband of his breeches and rocked on his heels in self-congratulation. "They were aboard my ship, posing as Mr. and Mistress Cooper, but I knew who they were. And not fifty miles from here, the lady comes up on deck and begs to be put off at Winyah Bay. Of course—" he gazed at Lanston with a bland half smile—"I'm not putting them off there by any means, but then the man draws a gun. So I overpower the pirate, and we cast the lot o' them into the sea."

"You fool!" Breathless with rage, Lanston rose from his chair. "You drowned them? What good are they to me dead?"

"They did not drown!" The older man replied sharply, reacting to the challenge in Lanston's voice. "I saw them swim ashore; we weren't but forty yards out. It was foggy, you see, and they cast themselves up on the beach, the pirate and his mate, as well as the two women."

"*Two* women?" Lanston's thoughts raced, trying to put all the pieces together.

"Aye, the woman had a maid—an Indian. And the pirate had a mate, a big brute with blond hair who spoke like a Scotsman."

Lanston sank down in his chair, forcing his temper to cool. So Fala had remained with Rachelle—an interesting, if predictable, turn of events. And the pirate had been separated from all his men but one—which might make things considerably easier. But what was he doing alone with Rachelle?

After glowering at his guest for an instant, Lanston turned away and stared at the wall, forcing his thoughts to clear and settle. He'd been at least partly right—Trace Bettencourt was returning to Charles Towne to claim Rachelle's fortune. And he was being exceedingly clever, coming by land instead of by sea. Lanston had placed spies around the port, watching for any sign of the cunning pirate, but he had not thought to position lookouts on the roads leading in and out of the city.

"So do I get the reward?" The captain's eyes shone with the stimulation of alcohol and the prospect of gold.

Lanston pressed his lips together, then turned to face his

demanding guest. "Answer my questions first," he said, his voice composed and steady. "What is your name?"

The man blanched but did not hesitate. "Captain Horace Pinckert, of the *Gordon Hawke*, arrived in port no more than two hours ago."

"Where did you pick up these passengers?"

"Boston."

"When *exactly* did you cast them overboard?"

The captain furrowed his brow in thought. "The Sabbath, near sunset. Right past the trader's point at Winyah Bay. The woman said they had business with the Indians there, as they were seeking a particular man."

Lanston settled his elbows on the desk and steepled his fingers. So Rachelle still had no idea she had been kidnapped by a desperate fortune hunter. This pirate Bettencourt was pretending to lead her on this search for her mythological father as he brought her back to Charles Towne. But soon, no doubt, he would take a stand and demand a healthy ransom for her life. The Sabbath was two days ago; a runner might be carrying a message to Charles Towne even now.

Lanston frowned as another thought presented itself with fearful clarity. What if this pirate was—heaven forbid—attempting to steal Rachelle's *affections*? Though Lanston believed her to be faithful and devout, a few days in unusual, dire circumstances—all artfully engineered by this ruthless pirate—might induce her to surrender her love to this man. Perhaps Bettencourt intended to return to Charles Towne with Rachelle as his bride and thus claim her entire fortune.

"I'll give you half the reward now." Lanston turned his gaze toward the pompous man before him. "And half when we find the pirate and the girl—alive. Enlist all the men of your ship, and I'll gather additional men here. We'll go into the wilderness and find them."

"But if they are with the savages—" Captain Pinckert's expression suddenly shriveled.

"There is no reason to worry, Captain." Lanston gave him a

bold smile. "The council has passed a law—any Indian who commits a hostile act against a white settler is to be captured and sent into slavery. They will not resist us—and if they do, we shall legally have them at our disposal."

This explanation seemed to satisfy Pinckert, who bowed stiffly. "I'll be back with a hundred men, as soon as I can spare 'em. I'll need to keep fifty aboard my ship for the repairs and stowage."

"One dozen or one hundred, the more the merrier our little hunting party will be," Lanston exclaimed with intense pleasure. "Gather your men within the next hour, and have them meet me here by six o'clock. And withhold their ration of rum, Captain. They will need clear heads for the hunt!"

Feeling suddenly relaxed and invincible, Lanston stood and offered Captain Pinckert a firm handshake. Within a few days, Rachelle would again be in his custody and care, Bettencourt would face the knot of the hangman's noose, and at least a score—possibly even a hundred—of Indians would be awaiting the next slave auction.

"Thank you, Trace Bettencourt," Lanston murmured, watching Captain Pinckert's cocky little figure retreat through the doorway and outer office. "You will make this venture more profitable than I ever dreamed possible."

Though the twilight was dim in the small thatched house, Rachelle saw Fala's luminous eyes widen in astonishment when she asked what her maid intended to do.

"I don't know." Fala's voice broke off in midsentence, and she lowered her gaze, looking at her tattooed arms as if she'd never seen them before. "You must believe me, Mademoiselle Rachelle, I had no idea my mother was the sachem's sister."

"I know you didn't," Rachelle answered, daring for the first time to speak bluntly to her maid. During their time in camp, Fala had spent most of her time with the Indian women, as though desperate to soak up the colors and flavors of her people before she was wrenched away again. Rachelle did not want to rush Fala's decision about where she would spend the rest of her life, but this sunrise would signal the beginning of their fourth day in the Indian camp. Trace had to rejoin his crew at sunset tomorrow, and wherever Mojag Bailie was, they were doing nothing to find him by remaining here with the Yamassee. Ezhno had sent four runners to nearby villages to inquire about Rachelle's father, and three had already returned with no news.

"Mademoiselle Rachelle—" Fala's eyes drifted to the other side of the fire pit, where Trace and Duncan lay sprawled on their backs, apparently deep in sleep—"if I may be honest—"

"Please, Fala, speak your true thoughts," Rachelle urged, understanding some of the pain and indecision in the woman's eyes. "I will agree with your decision, whatever it is."

Fala did a long, slow slide with her eyes until her gaze rested upon the sleeping Scot. "I had never thought to know a man's love," she whispered, her voice soft with drowsy contentment.

"But in these last few days I have known the love of a man, the love of a people—" her eyes turned to Rachelle—"and the love of a friend." She lifted her shoulder, a slow, shy smile blossoming on her face like a night-blooming flower, rare but radiant. "If I leave here, I shall lose the love of my people. If I remain, I lose my friend and my man. If I go to Charles Towne with you, I lose my man and my people. If I go with Duncan, I shall lose my friend and my people."

She looked up, and the expression in her eyes pierced Rachelle's soul. "Can you see why I would like to remain here forever, with you and Duncan by my side?" She shook her head ruefully. "But I know you cannot remain. Your place is in Charles Towne; Duncan's place is with Captain Bettencourt."

Rachelle felt her heart leap uncomfortably into the back of her throat. "Has Duncan asked you to go with him—to sea?"

Fala placed both hands over her eyes as if they burned with weariness. "To go with him—yes. To sea? No. He is bound by duty and honor to Captain Bettencourt. He says he will go wherever his captain goes."

She lowered her hands, and tears glistened on her pale, heart-shaped face. "Which do I choose, mademoiselle? My friend, my people, or my man?"

"I think, Fala," Rachelle whispered, a strange and bitter jealousy stirring inside her, "that I would follow the man who loved me."

Rachelle would—but Trace Bettencourt hadn't asked anything of her.

▼▲▼▲▼ Trace heard the soft murmur of the women's voices and opened one eye, looking across the small hut to the grass mat where they lay on their stomachs, their heads bent together in some deep conversation. He could see Fala's face, bewildered and tearstained. Rachelle had slipped her arm around the woman's shoulders, comforting her.

He relaxed and lowered his lids, not wanting them to know

he was awake. Duncan, he noticed, still snored steadily from his place by the door. Though they had received nothing but hospitality from this group of Yamassee, he had thought it prudent to plant Duncan's imposing bulk near the entrance in case a wandering warrior decided to test their willingness to defend the women.

"So that, in truth, is your decision?" Rachelle's awed, husky whisper reached his side of the house. "Fala, I would understand if you want to remain here. These are your people. They will make you a princess if you stay. And—" she paused, a trace of humor warming her voice—"it's time I learned to stand on my own two feet, don't you think?"

Fala buried her head in Rachelle's shoulder, her laughter a deep, warm, rich sound in the room. Trace closed his eyes, wondering for the fiftieth time if he could persuade Rachelle to consider a life at sea. She had proved herself more adaptable than he had thought possible, sleeping without complaint on sand, flea-bitten animal skins, and the hard, damp planks of a ship at sea. The sheltered princess of Charles Towne had vanished, and in her place a remarkably resilient and determined young woman had arisen. Of course, she still might have her heart set on returning to Charles Towne and marrying Lanston Wragg, but she had not mentioned that man since Trace suggested Wragg was vitally interested in Rachelle's wealth.

He snorted softly, imagining Rachelle's soft form standing by the railing on the deck of the *Jacques*. As much as he'd love to have her in his life and warming his cabin at night, she'd ruin him at sea. He'd never attack another slave ship, knowing she might be injured in the battle. He'd never risk another entry into Charles Towne, knowing she could be condemned as his accomplice and strung up on the gallows beside him if they were caught. He shuddered inwardly at the thought.

No, it was better to turn his thoughts toward Ocracoke, where his steps would have to take him today, for time was short. If he and Duncan left soon, they could make the rendezvous planned for the morrow. They'd have to move quickly, but without the women to slow their pace, he and Duncan could make it.

He turned onto his side, already feeling an acute sense of loss.

The soft silence of early morning shattered in an instant.

Trace sat up, his stomach dropping like a hanged man, as screams, curses, and war whoops rang through the thickened morning air. He took a deep breath, felt bands of tightness in his chest, and saw that Duncan had awakened as well. The Scot crouched in the doorway, one eye peering out from behind the mats that covered the frame of the house, the blond hairs on his forearm erect.

Trace glanced over at the women. They were clinging to one another in earnest now, the light gone from Rachelle's eyes and Fala's face stiff with fear. A sudden rise of panic threatened to choke him, but his throat worked well enough for him to issue a warning: "Stay here."

Wishing desperately for the pistol he'd left on the *Gordon Hawke,* he pulled his cutlass from its sheath and crouched next to Duncan, trying to discern what sort of enemy had descended from the silent forest.

"By heaven above, they're Englishmen!" Duncan muttered, growling with surprise and frustration. "Canna they tell these are peaceable people?"

"I think peace is the last thing on their minds," Trace answered. He waited as a tall man in a dark blue coat dragged an elderly Indian woman from her house, then gripped his cutlass and stepped out to defend her, his blade alive and eager in his hand. Behind him, he heard Duncan take a deep breath, release it, then snap into movement like a sprung bear trap.

Trace struck the woman's assailant in the shoulder, freeing her, then turned to grapple with his enemy. For a few moments they struggled against each other, pirouetting around the camp in a dance of death, upsetting cauldrons in the fire pit, breaking the fragile frame of a house. Blood spattered indiscriminately as they struck each other with fist and blade and boot. Trace could not tell how many had attacked, but the fighting raged all around him, the Indians whooping and screaming, the women rushing forth from their houses as eagerly as the men. Trace finally managed to quiet his opponent; then an unseen assailant struck from behind, slamming something against the side of his head, sending a spray of darkness across the back of his eyes, like shards of exploding black glass.

He staggered through an opening in the burning palisade, his blade carving ineffective, wobbly patterns in the air in front of him, and wondered if he would have the strength to slash effectively against the next man to come against him. Suddenly, from out of a foliage screen, a booted foot kicked his wrist, breaking the bone with a loud snap and propelling his cutlass into the bushes. Trace turned, crying out in dazzled torment as his body sang with pain, then realized that he stood before Lanston Wragg.

Blood from a cut in Wragg's forehead had painted his face into a glistening devil mask; sweat and blood soaked the hair of his chest and stained his linen shirt. He seemed to swell as he grinned at Trace. Then he pulled his pistol from beneath his coat. Aiming the barrel squarely at Trace's head with his right hand, he arrogantly brought his left sleeve across his face, wiping away a fleck of saliva at the corner of his mouth.

"I would love," he panted, his eyes dark and insolent and steady, "to put a hole in your head right now, but I have other matters on my mind at present. Where is Rachelle?"

Trace took a deep breath, struggling to master the pain that sought control of his senses. He could not help Rachelle if he were unconscious. "She is safe." He fastened his gaze to Wragg's. "Call off your hounds, lest she be hurt in this fray."

"Do not worry. We're not out to kill anyone," Lanston answered. A smile crawled to his lips and curved itself there like a snake. "Under the full authority of the law, we are gathering all Indians who have committed hostile acts against our people. I've sent men to every village within twenty miles of Winyah Bay."

"What hostile acts?" Trace clenched his jaw, his eyes blazing. "Which of these people has done anything to you?"

Wragg's smile diminished slightly as he shrugged. "We walked into their houses, and they rose to attack us with axes and clubs. Would you not call that a vicious and aggressive act?"

Trace's breath came raggedly in impotent anger. He would love to smash his fist into Lanston Wragg's jaw and feel the bones give; he would willingly chain Wragg and all slave traders like him to the flogging post and later offer their whipped and ruined lumps of flesh at a slave auction—

Wragg must have read the gist of Trace's thoughts in his eyes, for his face suddenly distorted with anger. "You will not die today either, Captain Bettencourt. Your dead body will hang on a gibbet as an example to all those who would commit piracy on the high seas. I have an order from the council at Charles Towne to arrest you and bring you back to stand trial." He pressed his lips together in a smug expression of conquest. "You will be found guilty, I can assure you, for I myself will testify that you stole my slaves and kidnapped my wife."

"Not your wife," Trace spat between his clenched teeth. "She's not!"

"She will be, and very soon." Wragg smiled, a curve of quick, dry lips. "My darling Rachelle and I will stand at Oyster Point while they carry you to the gallows in a mule-drawn cart. Have you ever seen a public hanging? I have, my friend, and 'tis not a pretty sight. One moment you will be standing beneath the limbs of a sprawling live oak. You will feel the drums beating through the soles of your feet as you stand on the cart, you will smell the scent of the sea. And you will see me smiling at you, and Rachelle upon my arm, her lovely eyes turned away from the sight of one so evil and degenerate—"

Something snapped in Trace's mind; perhaps Wragg had intended to stir his bloodlust to a fever pitch. Trace charged forward, his hands stiff and intent upon wrapping themselves around that arrogant throat, but before he could reach Wragg, the air filled with a thunderous roar and the acrid scent of gunpowder. The ground rose to meet him. Colors exploded in his brain. His flesh erupted in blood and torn bits of flesh and bone.

Blinding white pain streaked to Trace's gut. His nostrils filled with the scents of blood and vomit and dirt. He struggled to rise but fell back to the earth, seeing Lanston Wragg's cruel smile. Then a final sheet of anguish drew a black curtain over his eyes.

▼▲▼▲▼ Three men burst into the small house and pulled Fala and Rachelle out, scarcely bothering to look at them. Other men herded them together with the other women and children into the center of the camp. Then, one by one, wounded warriors were added to their group. By the time the sun had breasted the tallest of the trees surrounding the village, all of the Indian men were either wounded or dead. Every living inhabitant of the camp stood together, surrounded by a circle of English muskets.

Standing silently with one arm around Fala's slender waist and another around a trembling child, Rachelle stood in transfixed horror as Lanston Wragg stepped through the charred remains of the palisade and began to cull his captives. "Take that one away," he said, pointing to a small Indian woman whose white hair was bound at the back of her neck with leather thongs. "Too old. We can't use the old ones, or the tiny babies. But the children who are old enough to walk, yes, keep them." He glanced behind him toward a man carrying a length of rope. "Bind their hands; then slip a noose around each slave's neck. We'll march them behind the horses, and they'll keep up or suffer the consequences."

Rachelle watched in horror, a deep sense of shame overwhelming her. Part of her wanted to hide, to forget that she had ever known the monster before her, but even more stupefying was the realization that she *had* known what he did—she had even supported him. His florid, self-satisfied face epitomized the girl she had been; his appalling lack of compassion was an indictment against every slaveholder in Charles Towne.

She lowered her eyes, hoping that in her buckskin dress and braids Lanston might overlook her. But he was walking slowly now, lifting the chins of the weeping women before him, judging the worth of those he would offer at auction. She looked away, feeling herself tremble, recognizing the heat in her chest and belly as pure rage.

"This one," he called, uncomfortably close now. She lifted her head for a moment, in time to see his fingers dig into the soft flesh of a young girl's arm. "Take her in the wagon; she is a rare flower. Don't let her skin be marked by the lash." One of the men shuffled forward to pull the flower from her place, and Rachelle lowered her gaze, steeling herself for the confrontation.

"Rachelle, my darling." Lanston's greeting contained a strong suggestion of reproach. Numb with increasing shock and anger, she lifted her eyes to his. A smile lit his smug face, and his hand lifted as if to touch her. Reflexively, she pulled away, but his hand persisted, tracing the air, outlining her cheek and jaw.

"My darling, have we frightened you?" he asked, his voice a quiet purr amid the sound of the women's weeping. "Come out from among the prisoners. You have no place here."

He reached out and took her hand, lacing his fingers with her own in an iron grasp, then pulled her away from Fala.

"I won't go with you," she said, boldly meeting his gaze. Triumph flooded through her when he winced at her words, but her feeling of victory lasted only an instant.

"Captain Pinckert," Lanston called, summoning a man who stood behind him. A soft gasp escaped Rachelle when she recognized the captain of the *Gordon Hawke.* A satanic smile spread across that man's thin lips as he looked at her; then he turned his attention to Lanston.

"Captain, I've already shot the pirate Bettencourt, have I not?" Lanston drawled, his eyes attuned to Rachelle's face.

Dear God, no—

"Aye, that you have," Pinckert answered, his brows flickering a little.

"Shoot the first mate, then," Lanston commanded, his grip tightening around Rachelle's fingers as she instinctively jerked away. "Shoot him dead."

"No!" Fala screamed, her wail lancing the silence, piercing Rachelle's heart and soul. "No, no, no!"

"Lanston," Rachelle cried in a choked voice, "how could you? Don't do this, I beg you. If you hold me in any regard—"

"The pirate and his men are outlaws, my dear," he interrupted, unruffled. "It is practically my duty. And now, unless you want me to dispatch others, including your maid, you had best do *your* duty and come home with me."

The shock of defeat held her immobile for a moment; then she reached out to Fala with her free hand. "I want Fala with me," she told Lanston, leaning toward her sobbing friend. "I won't go anywhere without her."

"Of course not, my dear. I know how dependent you are upon your slaves." His words were playful, but his meaning was not, and his hand tightened possessively around hers as he jerked his head toward one of the men. "She'll ride with me," he said, linking his arm around Rachelle's waist as he pulled her to his side. "The tall Indian is Fortier property; bring her, too. Rope the others and drive them to Charles Towne, taking your time. I want them in fit condition to auction as soon as possible."

Rachelle glanced around for any sign of Trace, but her eyes found only carnage and despair. The remaining Englishmen set about confining the captives or firing the houses, and as Rachelle stumbled away she breathed in the horrifying scents of burning wood and charred flesh.

It was a fitting place for tears, and she hung her head and wept.

Rachelle stood on the beach. A lonely ghost ship rode the waves beyond her, its shredded sails fluttering like tattered cobwebs in the rhythmic roiling of the sea. Rachelle shivered, feeling a chilly dew on her skin, then from behind her came the mournful call of a wolf, lonely as the cry of a lost and wandering spirit.

Slowly, she turned, the sight of the ruined Indian village before her eyes. The tidy houses were now smoking embers, the fire pits funeral pyres for the dead.

One structure remained, the spent shell of a house. Crouching in the faint smoke rising from the embers, three old women clutched tiny babies to their wizened breasts. And their eyes— oh, merciful heaven—their knowing and accusatory eyes looked out at her from faces like marble effigies of contempt. *You knew,* the women seemed to say, their voices floating on the wind and echoing in the breath of the tall trees. *You knew what he was, and you led him to us; you did nothing to prevent the destruction of our people.*

Rachelle lifted her hands to her ears, trying to block out the haunting sound. They were wrong, so wrong! She was Mojag Bailie's daughter—she had done nothing but seek her father. In truth, she wanted to be like him, to help the Indians.

A low moaning sound caught her ears, and she followed it, moving behind the women's shelter. A hot gust of wind smote her full in the face with the coppery scent of fresh blood, and then her eyes fell upon a sight more hideous than anything she could imagine. The badly wounded lay here, stretched shoulder to shoulder over the earth, their eyes either screwed tight in agony or open to the sky, blank with unseeing. The moaning sound came from those who lived—it was not a scream for help or even a begging for mercy, but a plea for release at any cost, even death. She felt a tapping in her stomach, the scratching of fear as she moved forward and looked down at the bloodied faces. She recognized Ezhno, Duncan . . . and Trace.

"No," she moaned, twisting in an effort to escape. But something gripped her, as if iron bands constrained her arms, holding her tight.

Awareness hit her like a punch in the stomach, and Rachelle opened her eyes. Virtue stood over her, her strong hands clinging to Rachelle's arms, her eyes brimming with concern and compassion.

"Virtue," Rachelle breathed, sighing in relief. The maid did not answer, but her worried expression relaxed into a broad smile. The soft hands left Rachelle's arms, and the maid sank onto the edge of the bed, her eyes searching Rachelle's face.

Rachelle lifted her head. A faultlessly clean linen sheet covered her, and she was lying on a massive four-poster bed situated in a room with tall windows where light spilled through with glorious abandon. She lifted her hand to push a shock of hair out of her eyes, and she realized that her hair was damp and clean. She sat up and thrust the covers back—her skin was pink and rosy, scrubbed from head to toe, and she wore a frilly gown edged with white lace.

"Did you," Rachelle whispered, looking up at Virtue, "did you bathe me? dress me?"

The slave nodded slowly, water rising in her eyes like a slow fountain coming up.

Rachelle pursed her lips, rigidly holding her tears in check. "Thank you, Virtue." She threw her arms around the woman's neck, exulting in the solid feel of *family* in her arms. Virtue's shoulders shook as if she wept, and Rachelle closed her eyes, grateful that the woman rejoiced in the same feeling. She patted the maid's shoulder, then pulled back and gave Virtue a quavering smile. "Now—where is Fala? Something—something terrible has happened, and Fala may need me."

Virtue's face twisted. Clamping her lips tightly, she lifted her fingers to her mouth and looked toward the window. A stream of fat and sloppy tears ran from the corner of her eye and dripped over her ebony cheek.

"Virtue, what's happened to Fala?" Rachelle cried, lifting her voice in panic. She gripped the woman's shoulder. "Don't keep the truth from me—where is she?"

Pattering footsteps flew down the hall; then one of Mistress Wragg's slaves burst through the door. "Goodness sakes almighty," the young girl shouted, looking at Rachelle with alarm. "Don't yell at Virtue, Mistress Rachelle. She can't answer you."

Rachelle blinked, still struggling through the cobwebs of her nightmare-filled sleep. "Why not?" she asked, squeezing Virtue's shoulder just to be sure she held flesh and blood in her hands.

"She ain't got a tongue, that's why," the maid snipped, one hand on her hip as she approached the bed. She regarded Virtue and Rachelle with a stern expression. "Now let her go, and ask me what you want to know. Virtue ain't supposed to be up here. She's supposed to stay in the kitchen."

Rachelle felt her stomach drop and the empty place fill with a frightening hollowness. "No tongue," she whispered, her eyes moving into Virtue's swimming gaze. "Sweet heaven above, Virtue, who did this to you?" She pressed her hand to her lips as terror stole her breath. "Mr. Ashton?" she whispered, her words intended for Virtue's ears alone.

Virtue looked quickly away, but Rachelle saw her chin dip in a barely discernible nod.

"*Mon Dieu!* Virtue, what about the others from our house?" She paused, mentally running through the list of slaves who had remained behind in Charles Towne. Most of them worked at the rice plantation. But Virtue had remained with the Wraggs, Friday had gone with *Grand-père*, and—

"Dustu—the Indian." Rachelle took Virtue's hand. "Is he well?"

"That Indian is dead," the maid replied flatly, coming around to the side of the bed where Virtue sat. "Shot through the back as he tried to go over the wall. Stubborn as a cross-eyed mule, that one, and he deserved what he got. The master had warned him before."

Rachelle trembled at the maid's words and stared at Virtue in hypnotized horror. Had she known such atrocities would occur in this house, she never would have left her people unprotected. *But you did know,* an inner voice chided her. *You noticed that the Wraggs' butler never spoke. You saw scars on the little boys who raked the garden. But you didn't care.*

The truth crashed into her consciousness like surf hurling against a rock. She had been selfish, immature, blind to the sufferings of others, but the events of the last few days had opened her eyes to the truth. What was it Reverend Eliot had said? God preferred an honest sinner to a righteous hypocrite, yet she had been the most hypocritical of all, supporting the slave industry while scorning Trace Bettencourt. At least he was an honest sinner. At least he cared enough to risk his life.

"Virtue." She covered the woman's hand with both of her own. "Please, search for Fala, and bring her to me. Are there any others of our people here?"

Virtue shook her head, a weight of sadness on her thin face.

"Very well." Rachelle patted her hand. "Find Fala, return with her, and wait while I dress. We are leaving this place, the three of us, and I'm giving you your freedom."

Virtue's eyes went suddenly round.

"And if you wish to spend your freedom living with me, I'll take care of you," Rachelle promised, holding tight to Virtue's hand. "But you will no longer be a slave, Virtue. You took care of my mother, and I would be honored if you'd let me take care of you."

With a choking cry Virtue tore herself away, dabbing at her streaming eyes with her apron as she moved toward the doorway. The other slave crossed her arms and regarded Rachelle with a narrow, speculative gaze. "I don't think you're feeling at all well, Mistress Rachelle. You're not talking sense. I expect you should lay back down and get some sleep while I send for Mistress Cambria—"

"You'll do no such thing." Rachelle flung the quilts off her legs and swung her feet to the floor, then swayed for a moment as she stood up a little too quickly. She wasn't certain how long she'd been asleep, but her mind felt queer and fuzzy.

"It's the laudanum." The maid nodded sagely. "Mr. Lanston directed the physician to give you a draught so you would sleep. He said you were exhausted from your ordeal with the savages."

"Of course he did." Rachelle leaned against the bed, trying to remember all that had happened. She recalled at least two blurry days on horseback when she'd been wild with grief and regret. As darkness fell she had slept on the ground next to Fala, holding her shoulders as she sobbed for Duncan MacKinnon, whose lifeless body they'd seen on the ground as they rode out of the village. Rachelle had seen no sign of Trace, but she'd been afraid to look after seeing the big Scotsman. She never wanted to look death in the face again.

Rachelle could scarcely recall her reactions to the carnage. She thought she had been too stunned to weep, too filled with darkness and shadows of the terrifying sights she'd seen in the Indian village. She remembered creeping into Charles Towne under the cover of darkness. She recalled women fussing around her, male voices arguing, someone offering her something to drink. . . .

"Where is Mr. Lanston now?" Rachelle asked, deliberately wiping her face of all expression as she looked up at the maid.

"Why, at church, of course," the girl answered, moving to the wardrobe. "The Wraggs always attend church on Sunday. After services they're meeting with the minister to discuss the wedding." With a flourish, the maid flung the wardrobe doors open, displaying a snowy white mound of silk and lace. "Look here, Mistress Rachelle." She turned and grinned with no trace of her former animosity. "Your wedding dress. Mistress Cambria had it sewn up while you were away with your grandfather."

Rachelle bit the inside of her lip, steeling herself not to react.

Apparently the Wraggs had carried on in her absence as if nothing had changed. No one in the city knew where she had been, nor did they know the truth about Lanston Wragg . . . and Captain Trace Bettencourt.

A fresh wave of sorrow threatened to sweep her off her feet at the thought of Trace's last moments in Lanston's presence, but she clung to the edge of the mattress and forced a smile across her face. "It's beautiful." She nodded blankly at the extravagant gown. "Er—when is the wedding?"

"Why, tomorrow, of course." The girl's left eyebrow rose a fraction. "That's why the Wraggs are meeting with the minister— they're hurrying all the arrangements. Some folks say it wouldn't be proper for you to live here with Mr. Lanston unless you are rightly wed to him."

"Where's my maid? Where's Fala?" Rachelle moved anxiously toward the door, wondering why Virtue had not yet returned.

The slave made a tiny curtsey. "I'm your maid now, Mistress Rachelle. A wedding gift to you from Mistress Cambria. My name is Mercy, and I know a bit of French. I've been a ladies' maid ever since I came to Charles Towne, and I can sew a straight seam nearly as well as I can plait a lady's braids—"

"Be silent," Rachelle blazed, turning upon the talkative girl with barely restrained fury. "I want Fala. You may be a wedding gift, but I'm not married yet. So find my maid, and send her to me immediately."

Mercy clapped her mouth shut, looking as if Rachelle had slapped her. Lifting her chin, she moved toward the door, her head held high.

With her guard gone, Rachelle ran to the wardrobe, shoving aside the billowing yards of silk wedding dress in search of a plain, everyday petticoat and bodice. Cambria must have intended to furnish Rachelle with an entire trousseau, for the wardrobe held several sets of clothing, all in Rachelle's size.

She pulled the nightgown over her head, then stepped into one of the plainer petticoats, her awkward fingers fumbling at the waist for the hooks. When at last a single hook found its grip, she fought her way into a matching bodice and groaned in frustration. She'd never get these hooks closed.

She blew out her cheeks in relief when Virtue moved through the door, her arms open wide in an empty gesture. "Let me guess—you couldn't find Fala, could you?" Rachelle asked, moving toward Virtue and then turning so the maid could fasten the row of bodice hooks. She glanced back in time to see Virtue shake her head. The woman's swift fingers moved quickly over the fastenings, and Rachelle took a deep breath, guessing Fala's whereabouts.

With pulse-pounding certainty she knew Lanston wouldn't want Fala around. For one thing, she was a free woman now, and Rachelle would certainly attest to that truth. But more important, Fala knew the truth about what had happened on the journey to Boston and in the Indian camp. Rachelle could tell the truth until she was blue in the face, and Lanston would only pat her on the back and say the terrible ordeal had left her a little daft and disturbed. But he wouldn't be able to deny Rachelle's story if Fala confirmed it.

"Find a pair of sleeves—there, the cream ones will do—and get me into them," Rachelle told Virtue, diving into the wardrobe to help the maid. The two women bumped heads in the dark, and as they groaned and rose from the wardrobe, Virtue's eyes crinkled in a soft rebuke.

"I know, I'm in the way," Rachelle said, forcing herself to stand still. "But we must hurry, Virtue. The Wraggs will be back soon, and we must be away by then."

Nodding in silent understanding, Virtue slipped the long sleeves over Rachelle's arms and fastened them with the speed of a striking serpent.

▼▲▼▲▼ They slipped out through one of the servants' doors, and Rachelle glanced up at the sky as they set out, not certain what time of day it was. The sky gave her no clue, for the sun had disappeared, hidden by bands of weeping clouds against a steely gray sky that deepened to black on the eastern horizon. Far to the east, a nasty choppy sea churned up the bay beyond the wharf.

Rachelle stepped out onto the cobbled street and hesitated, feeling oddly like a stranger in the city where she was born. Nothing had changed—the street and the buildings looked the same as when she'd left them—yet something seemed profoundly different. A black slave swept the street in front of the Wraggs' house, and she peered at him, noticing that he had a humorous, kindly mouth beneath brilliant black eyes that remained fixed on the cobblestones. Shaking her head, she reached for Virtue's hand and pulled her down the street.

She consulted the mental map in her head, trying to decide which streets to take. She wanted to avoid Church Street if possible because she couldn't risk running into either the Wraggs or their minister as they left St. Philip's Anglican Church. Unfortunately, the Wraggs' church sat only a block from the barracoon where Ashton Wragg & Son held their stock—slaves to be auctioned at the first available opportunity. At least it was Sunday, and no auctions would be held today. Perhaps the building would be deserted.

Rachelle turned onto Chalmers Street, then quickly ducked behind the pillar of a warehouse on the corner. Ashton and Cambria Wragg were walking at the end of the block, their heads bent low in conversation as they slouched before the gusting wind. They paused in the center of the newly cobbled road, and Rachelle caught her breath as they turned toward their carriage, which now came into view.

Virtue tightened her grip on Rachelle's arm.

Once Ashton and Cambria had been seated, the driver cracked his whip above the horses' heads, and the carriage moved away. "Come," Rachelle said, grabbing Virtue's hand. She hated to take Virtue into a despicable place like the barracoon, but there was no help for it.

She wouldn't abandon Fala and Virtue to the Wraggs.

Together the three of them would leave Charles Towne and make a life somewhere else. Perhaps they could make a home in Boston or Roxbury. The Eliots might know of a governess position where Rachelle could support Fala and Virtue while she continued to search for her father.

"Mistress Bailie? Can that be you?"

Rachelle groaned as a short, plump man in a tricorne and his Sunday best hailed her from the opposite side of the street. She hesitated, squinting to see if she recognized him, then decided she did not. She'd make quick conversation and be rid of him as soon as she could.

The stranger moved across the street with stiff dignity and paused in the road before her. Doffing his hat, he gave her an elaborate bow, the white fringe of his hair blowing in the wind.

"Erik Hawkins, at your service," he said, standing erect. He had the sort of round, cheerful face whose natural expression was a smile, and Rachelle stared blankly at him, trying to determine why he should know her.

"Mademoiselle," he said, making a faint moue of sorrow as he gripped his hat in his hands, "I must say I was very sorry to hear of your troubles." He shook his head in regret. "First your lovely mother, then your grandfather—a tragedy, to be sure. But then we heard about your kidnapping!"

"Er, Mr. Hawkins," Rachelle said, folding her hands at her waist, "obviously, I am not kidnapped. And I would love to talk to you, but my friend and I are on an errand."

"Your friend?" Completely ignoring Virtue, he glanced around as if searching for someone else, then lifted his brows in the slow dawning of comprehension. The fool. He thought her completely mad, out for a walk with an invisible companion.

"Of course, my dear, I heard this morning that you were not well. The Wraggs were in church, of course, offering prayers for your, um, complete recovery."

Rachelle rolled her eyes and nodded, resisting the urge to tap her foot with impatience.

"There is only the matter of your grandfather's account—but

we can discuss that later. After you're married, I'll broach the subject with Lanston."

"My—my grandfather's account?" she whispered, her irritation vanishing.

The little man bobbed his head. "Yes, in the Bank of England. I'm the trustee, but I don't expect you to worry your pretty little head about such things." He gave her a quick smile, then tilted his head as if to be certain no one else hid behind her petticoat. "I give you good day, Mistress Bailie."

"Wait, Mr. Hawkins—," she said, wholly taken aback.

"Yes?" He paused, his hand flying up to hold his tricorne as he turned into a gust of wind.

"Are you saying—am I my grandfather's heir? I inherited his . . ." She paused, not certain how to continue.

"You inherited everything, of course," Mr. Hawkins said, exuding excitement like a scent. "The plantation, the property in Charles Towne, the slaves, the account in the Bank of England. Your grandfather came to visit me right before your mother died, and together we amended his last will and testament."

Rachelle fell silent, too startled by the revelation to speak. Her grandfather had provided for her, and before her mother died. Perhaps his heart had begun to soften even then.

"How much—" She tried to keep the stunned disbelief out of her voice but failed. "How big is this account of my grandfather's?"

"Oh, it's quite sufficient." Hawkins chuckled as with a happy memory. "More than enough to take care of you and young Lanston."

He turned, but Rachelle called him back. "Mr. Hawkins—*how much?*"

His eyes squinted against the wind as he turned this time, but his face went rounder still in the most extraordinary expression of alarm. "Mistress Bailie, ladies ought not fret about such things. 'Tis unwomanly."

"Mr. Hawkins—" Rachelle gave him a glare fit to sear his brows—"how much money is in that account?"

His face fell in an attitude of resignation. "Fifty thousand pounds sterling," he said, his voice flat. "Now if you'll excuse me, Mistress Hawkins will have a nice roast ready for my dinner."

Still clutching his hat, he raced off against the wind, and Rachelle smiled grimly, watching him go.

So Trace had been right all along. Lanston knew about *Grandpère*'s money; he had obviously talked to Mr. Hawkins on at least one other occasion. And he was poised and ready to gather that fortune in order to expand his business selling more human souls.

"Come, Virtue," Rachelle said, gripping the woman's hand. "We're finding Fala and leaving this place."

▼▲▼▲▼ A graceless wooden warehouse on Chalmers Street served as a barracoon and jail, and a more drab and cold structure Rachelle could not imagine. Standing outside the double doors she felt an instinctive rise of fear, then swallowed it down. Trace Bettencourt hadn't been afraid to risk his life to free the unfortunate, and neither had Duncan MacKinnon. She could do no less.

She tugged on the heavy door, pulling it open, and stepped inside the vestibule, blinking as her eyes adjusted to the gloom. There were no windows here; the only light seeped in from beneath the door. Two doors were visible in the dim light—one ahead of her and one to the right, painted with bold lettering that advertised that she'd reached the offices of "Ashton Wragg & Son, Importers and Exporters." A faint stench reached her nostrils—the odors of sweat, urine, and filth—but the room was nearly empty. Two wooden benches along the walls faced each other; a wad of paper, several dead roaches, and a boldly printed placard littered the floor.

A word on the broadside caught Rachelle's eye, and she bent to pick up the sheaf of stiff paper. Though a dirty footprint overlaid the printing, she had no trouble reading the announcement:

WANTED:
THE PIRATE CAPTAIN BETTENCOURT
DEAD OR ALIVE
FOR MALICIOUS KIDNAPPING, THEFT, MURDER,
AND PIRACY ON THE HIGH SEAS

"Murder?" Rachelle swallowed hard, trying to force her confused emotions into order. "Whose murder? Trace killed no one—"

"How could you forget your grandfather?"

She whirled around, ignoring Virtue's frightened squeak. The door at the back of the room stood open, and Lanston's tall frame filled the doorway. Dressed in his Sunday best, he leaned against the doorjamb, his arms crossed, and smiled at her with an attitude of self-command and studied relaxation.

"Trace did not kill *Grand-père!*" She bit her lip, shaking with impotent rage and fear. "What have you been telling people? Trace did not kidnap or kill anyone. In all his dealings with me, he behaved most nobly."

She stopped short in dismay, feeling the nauseating sinking of despair. What did it matter now? Trace Bettencourt was dead, Duncan was dead, and the men of the *Jacques* had already called at Ocracoke. They had probably waited through the night, then pulled up their anchor and sailed away in search of Libertalia and freedom.

"Rachelle, my darling—" Lanston slowly uncrossed his arms—"I'm surprised to find you here, and in such a temper. Why aren't you home in bed? The physician said you needed rest and care. My mother has done her best to provide for you, but if you need anything else, you have only to ask."

"I saw your mother's provisions," Rachelle said, remembering the wedding dress and the overeager slave. "She is—so thoughtful." She knew her voice was cold, but Lanston did not seem to take offense at her tone.

"So, darling," he said, scanning her critically, "why are you here? You should be home. We've moved the wedding up to tomorrow night, you know. The guests have been invited. Everything is arranged." Slowly, his gaze slid downward, raking over her body. "I am rather looking forward to our wedding night."

Rachelle flinched, resenting his familiarity and the bold look in his eyes. "I came for Fala. You said I could have her. And I know she's here."

Lanston smoothed his hair, then laughed. "Why would you want a skinny maid who won't say two words without prodding? Forget the Indians, Rachelle. They do not make good slaves. I understand my mother has given you the best black girl she could find."

"I don't want that girl. I want Fala."

Closing the door behind him, Lanston came forward, loosening the cravat at his neck. "She's not here," he whispered, lifting a brow as he passed by Rachelle. "Perhaps she escaped as we reentered Charles Towne. I didn't see what happened to her, as my attentions were focused entirely on you, my dear."

"You're lying." She spat the words contemptuously and dared to reach out and grasp the edge of his frock coat. "I know you're lying, Lanston Wragg!"

"Oh!" His eyes went round with glee. "I *do* like your newfound temper! Quite a little fire under that blanket of reserve. I never would have guessed you had it in you."

She jerked her hand away as if the touch of his clothing had burned her, but he stepped forward, his hands gripping her elbows, pulling her into his arms. Behind her, Rachelle heard the frantic sound of clapping and knew Virtue was trying to get her attention.

"Virtue," she called over her shoulder, not daring to take her eyes from Lanston's treacherous face, "go outside and wait. I'll call you when we're ready to leave."

"How very clever of you." Lanston brought her closer as Virtue ran from the room and slammed the door. "Sending her away. Now we are quite alone."

"Not quite," she protested, recoiling from the scent of his breath on her face. "There are prisoners in the cells beyond this room. I want to see them."

His fingers were cool and smooth as he ran his hand along her jaw. "They are not a fit sight for a lady," he murmured, a distant stillness in his blue eyes.

"This lady will see them," she answered, "or I'll not marry you. I'll throw a temper tantrum. I won't even put on that cursed wedding dress."

He shrugged, but a vein in his forehead swelled like a thick, black snake. "I don't care if you wear sackcloth."

"I'll stand before the minister and refuse to assent."

He paused, weighing the sincerity of her words. The grip that held her elbow suddenly eased. "Come, then," he said, his smooth skin glowing with pale gold undertones in the dim light. "I suppose you should understand how I'll be earning your living in the days ahead, my dear."

He grasped her hand with a grip like iron and pulled her through the doorway through which he'd come.

The odor she had noticed in the front room was thick here—the smell of prison and the sharp stink of fear. Rachelle coughed softly, finding it difficult to draw a deep breath. At first she could see nothing in the windowless space; then Lanston dropped her hand and lit a rushlight torch on the wall. Three large jail cells leaped up at her from the fire-tinted darkness, each filled with nearly two dozen Indians in various stages of wholeness. Faces turned toward her, blinking in the sudden light. Many of the prisoners' faces, she noticed with horror, glistened black and red with spatters of dried blood and oozing wounds.

"Mon Dieu!" A whisper of terror ran through her; she was actually trembling now. "How can you condone this?" She moved forward on legs that suddenly felt as insubstantial as air, her steps slow and unsteady. She tried to hide her inner misery from the probing stares that lifted to meet her, and her heart squeezed in anguish when she realized that they saw her as just another white woman, one of the invaders who had come to enslave, maim, and kill.

She turned her eyes to the brick wall at her side, the swell of her pain beyond tears. She could not save them all, but she could save one. "Fala!" she cried, a sudden flash of loneliness stabbing at her as she scanned the occupants of the cages.

"Mademoiselle!" It was Fala's voice, hoarse but joyful, and Rachelle turned at the familiar sound and ran toward the last cell, where Fala was shouldering her way through a crowd of browbeaten captives. She moved easily, and though her face and arms were streaked with dirt and grime, Rachelle could see no sign of injury—

"Oh!" she breathed, bringing her fingers to her lips. An unmistakable bloodstain had soaked the soft buckskin of Fala's tunic. "Are you hurt?" Rachelle reached out through the iron bars. "Did someone hurt you, Fala?"

"No." Fala's dark eyes brimmed with tenderness and joy. "I've been tending the captain. He is—" she hesitated, her dark lashes hiding her eyes—"he is not well."

"He's alive?" Rachelle clung to the bars as a wave of shock slapped at her. "Trace is here? And he's alive?"

Fala reached out and slipped her fingers between Rachelle's. "Yes." A gentle smile crinkled the corners of her eyes. "Yes, he is alive but unconscious now. And he has been concerned for you."

One of the Indians snapped a question at Fala in the Indian tongue, and she turned away to answer him. A moment later the crowd of prisoners parted, allowing Rachelle to see the dim outline of a body on the packed earthen floor. Trace's cheeks were sunken beneath his brown beard, his eyes were swollen and shut, but there was no mistaking that stubborn jaw.

Rachelle curled her fingers tighter around the iron bars, a great exultation filling her heart. Thanks be to God, Trace was alive!

The thought made her smile, but then a thrill of fear shot through her. Trace was a prisoner in Charles Towne, a city that meant to hang him, and in the custody of Lanston Wragg, who meant to see him suffer.

Rachelle glanced toward the doorway through which she'd come. Lanston had disappeared, apparently not caring who or what she saw in these cells. He knew she would find Fala and

Trace, and he knew she was powerless to do anything to help them.

Turning back to the cell, she rattled the unyielding door and clenched her jaw to kill the sob in her throat. From the looks of him, Trace was badly wounded, perhaps dying. A dirty strip of fabric bound his wrist, and the fabric of his breeches was black with blood.

Rachelle lifted her gaze to Fala's. The Indian woman looked at her, her eyes open with trust and hope, waiting to see what Rachelle would do. What could she do? Helpless, she turned her eyes back to the captives in the cell. Flinging out her hands in simple despair, she closed her eyes in prayer.

Father God, help me now. You have brought me to this place; now show me the way! What can I do to help these people? I cannot allow Trace to die. I cannot let Fala be sold again. And these others have done nothing amiss—they do not deserve to go into slavery.

Moaning softly, she sank to the earthen floor and brought her knees to her chest, wrapping herself in a cocoon of anguish. Why in the world had God allowed all this to happen? She had opened her eyes. She had learned her lessons. She had lost and abandoned her former life. Was her lesson worth this toll in human suffering? If not for her, Lanston would not have raided the villages. These captives did not deserve to suffer on her account.

A quiet, familiar voice nudged her out of her despair.
Jump.

Rachelle lifted her head, her heart pounding. She dashed the tears from her eyes as a strange numbed comfort coursed through her veins.

She'd jumped before. For Fala's sake and Trace's and Duncan's, she had jumped toward certain death, placing her faith in the one who spoke to her heart. It was time to jump again. If Trace could risk his life in pursuit of Libertalia, a place he had only heard about, she could certainly risk hers to win freedom for these captives.

Love had left her a fortune. And faith would give her the courage to use it.

She was *not* helpless. She was the sole heir to fifty thousand pounds sterling, a plantation, a house, and one hundred slaves—all of whom would be freed as soon as she could draw up manumission papers. For that matter, she could use her grandfather's money to buy every Indian held in Lanston's barracoon—but freedom for a condemned pirate could not be legitimately purchased.

Illegitimately, then.

Until she married, she probably wielded more power than anyone in Charles Towne. Now was the time to use it.

Jump.

"I will."

God had enabled Trace to save her after her first leap of faith. Perhaps this time God would use her to save him.

Rachelle turned, met Fala's eyes, and drew a deep breath, forbidding herself to tremble. If Lanston Wragg wanted her as his wife, he was going to have to complete a bit of negotiation first.

Rachelle found Lanston in the dusty office, his feet propped
firmly upon the desk, a pipe in his hand. A look of malign satisfaction came over his face as she entered the room. Why, he was
practically gloating!

"Well," he said, puffing heartily to start his pipe, "did you
find the woman? Not much to look at anymore, is she? I told you
the black girl would be more suitable."

An empty chair sat before the broad desk, and Rachelle sank
into it, keeping her posture erect. She had no intention of permit-
ting herself to fall under Lanston Wragg's devious influence;
only the safety of those poor prisoners mattered.

"Lanston," she said, her courage and determination like a
rock inside her, "I will marry you tomorrow night—"

"Of course you will," he interrupted, grinning. "Any woman
in town would be happy to take your place."

She ignored the obvious insult and continued. "I will marry
you—on one condition. As a wedding gift to me, you will release
every single prisoner you now hold within those cells. You will
also draw up and sign manumission papers so they will never be
recaptured and forced to endure these indignities again."

"Indignities?" He seemed casually amused. "Well, my
dear—" he set his pipe on his knee as he watched her—"I must
say that's an unexpected and rather charming notion. But I'm
afraid I can't agree. There are over one hundred slaves in that
room, along with the notorious pirate who has terrorized the
coast from Boston to Barbados. I'd be an irresponsible citizen if
I let any of them go."

"Most of the Indians are wounded." She tossed her head in a

defiant gesture. "They won't bring you top dollar at auction. Let them go."

"I can't do it." He slammed his hand on the arm of his chair for emphasis. "They broke the law. I'm entitled to take any Indian that lifts his hand in hostility against a citizen of this colony."

"They did not lift the first hand—you did." She leaned forward, resting one elbow hard on the arm of her chair. "I was there. I'm a witness, and I'll swear to the truth in any court, to any authority."

"A wife cannot bear witness against her husband," he snapped.

"Oh no? Then I'll not be your wife unless you release them," she answered, a heavy dose of sarcasm in her voice. "If you release them, I'll have nothing to report against you."

He smiled for a moment and scratched his cheek, his brows furrowed with thought. Rachelle lifted her chin, a new sense of strength flooding her soul. She saw Lanston Wragg now with abrupt clarity, and he was nothing—a money-hungry worm, a schemer, lower in morals than Trace Bettencourt, Duncan, and the Indians she'd met in the forest. Surely God did prefer honest sinners to righteous hypocrites.

"I would like nothing better than to release the prisoners," he finally told her, taking charge with quiet assurance. "But, Rachelle, my dear, you know nothing of business. Truth be told, I can't afford to release them. They didn't all come from that paltry village where we found you; several other Indian camps were legitimately raided. I spent a fortune on your rescue, and I need to sell these slaves in order to recoup my expenses. If you want to live in the style to which you have become accustomed—"

"Be silent, Lanston." She sat up straighter, her body vibrating with purpose. "I am not the fool you think I am. I know our marriage gives you control of my grandfather's money, and the profit from these slaves is nothing compared to what I will bring you. Look at it as a purchase, if you like. With the money I bring to our marriage, I am buying these slaves . . . and the release of the pirate Bettencourt." A melancholy frown flitted across his features, but she ignored it, pressing her advantage. "So this is what you will do—you will release those slaves today and send them safely back to their homes. There will be no patrols in the woods to capture them again, no searches, no raids of their villages. And before you send them away you will arrange for a physician to tend the ones who are wounded."

He gave her a hard, cold-eyed smile, but he did not protest.

"Then, also today," she went on, gathering her strength, "you will release Trace Bettencourt into Fala's custody so she may look after him. You will say nothing of his presence in this town, or I will leave you standing alone at the altar, and you shall not put your hands upon a single farthing of my money."

His eyes glittered with challenge. "The pirate won't get far. What's to stop me from reporting him once we are married? Or what if someone else sees him in town? That announcement was placarded all over the wharf."

"You'll give Fala a wagon and a horse," Rachelle answered quickly, struggling to maintain her curtness. *And they will ride away to safety—the two dearest people in the world to me—and I will never see them again . . . but it will be worth it.*

Lanston leaned back in his chair, brought his pipe to his lips, and turned his eyes toward the wall, thinking. After a long moment, his eyes moved into hers again. "Anything else, my dear?" he asked in a low, resentful tone.

Rachelle twisted her hands and thought hard, hoping she had remembered everything. Duncan was dead. Fala would go with Trace. Trace would make it safely back to Ocracoke. The Indians would be freed. She would draw up papers for the plantation slaves tomorrow, before the wedding. Lanston need not know about their liberation until later . . . when it would be too late.

"Only Virtue," she said, casually leaning forward to flick an imaginary speck of dirt from her petticoat. "She shall be my personal maid for as long as she wishes to remain with me. Today you will draw up the papers guaranteeing her legal status as a free woman, and when we are married, you will pay her regular wages for as long as she wishes to serve us."

Stroking his chin, he regarded her carefully. "You ask a lot, Rachelle."

"You're getting a lot in return." She forced the words over her choking, beating heart. *My life. My heart. My only hope for happiness. I'm giving all this to you though it rightfully belongs to another.*

"Well, then." Abruptly, he lowered his feet to the floor, then pressed his hands to the desk and gave her a forced smile. "I suppose I'd better get busy. You'll excuse me, of course, while I attend to those matters you specified. You should go home; my mother has a sempstress coming for a final fitting of your wedding gown."

"One more thing." She struggled to discipline her unsteady voice, to maintain complete control. Lanston seemed to respect power, and after their wedding she would no longer have it.

"Yes?"

"I want a private word with Captain Bettencourt." She forced remote dignity into her voice. "I owe him my life; I must thank him."

Lanston's face darkened for a moment; then he nodded slowly and stood. "I'll have to get him cleaned up. I'll bring him out from the others, and you can speak to him in here."

Clutching the armrests of her chair, Rachelle inclined her head. "I'll wait."

"Good." He smiled smoothly, betraying nothing of either annoyance or anger, then left the room, leaving her alone with regrets she dared not utter.

▼▲▼▲▼ Trace stirred on the earthen floor, tasting blood and sand on his lips. He heard a soft voice murmur comforting words, and he forced his eyes open. "Rachelle?"

"No, Captain." His blurred vision sharpened, and he recognized Fala. She was sitting next to him on the floor, an expression of concern in her dark eyes. "Rachelle was here," she whispered, a soft smile on her lips. "Perhaps you heard her voice."

He struggled to lift his head, then groaned as headache pain began digging into the flesh above his right eye. He gulped, forcing down the sudden lurch of his empty stomach as he moved his broken wrist. Blinding pain marched along his nerves like an army of determined fire ants.

The outer door screeched and closed with a solid thunk, and Trace reached for Fala's hand. "Is it Rachelle?" he asked again, struggling to sit up. He didn't want her to see him like this, flat on his back in defeat. The musket ball had shattered his left kneecap and flayed the flesh of his leg, but he thought he had strength enough to lean against the bars and pretend he did not suffer.

The sound of clomping shoes echoed loudly through the corridor in front of the cells. "No," Fala whispered, hearing the sounds. "Not Rachelle." The sound of voices in the prison abruptly ceased, waves of silence spreading from the door and following whoever walked in those heavy boots.

The footsteps halted, as Trace suspected they would, outside the cell he shared with Ezhno and the others from his village.

"Captain Bettencourt." Wragg's voice wasn't much louder than a whisper, but the effect was as great as if he had shouted. The Indians slunk away from the door, their faces pale with fear and loathing.

Trace glared up at the Englishman he had come to despise. "I am here," he said, his voice ragged with suppressed fury. What sort of torment did the slave trader intend for him now?

"A word, if you please," Wragg answered with staid calmness. "Can you come to the bars?"

Arousing himself from the numbness that weighed him down, Trace reached out for Fala's shoulder and allowed her to help pull him up. His chest rose and fell like a human bellows from the effort of standing, and his left leg felt gelatinous, completely unable to support any weight. With each step forward with his good foot he had to lean on Fala and drag his shattered leg over the ground, and for a moment the world went black and he feared he would faint. But Fala slipped her arm about his

waist and supported him until he was able to hobble forward
and rest his weight on the unyielding iron bars.

"Answer one question, and you shall earn your freedom,"
Wragg announced, his expression as implacable as stone.

Trace looked up, disoriented. Freedom? As far as he knew,
Lanston Wragg had never freely offered anything to anyone. He
faltered for a moment in the silence that engulfed them. "What
question would that be?"

"A simple one." Lanston's eyes were a vicious glint in the
rushlight, and his voice rumbled through the silent barracoon.
"In your journey, did you touch Rachelle Bailie?"

Trace curled his fingers around the damp iron, looking past
Wragg into the darkness. What a fool the man was! He knew
nothing of the girl he was betrothed to marry, knew nothing of
her virtue or her honor. This question had sprung from Wragg's
own jealous and greedy male pride.

His suspicions were confirmed a moment later when Lanston
stepped back and shrugged diffidently. "It doesn't matter, I suppose." He fixed Trace in a blue-eyed vise. "We're to be married
tomorrow night." His eyes flicked toward Fala. "As a favor to
my bride, who seems to think you saved her life, I'm sending
you away with this woman." A faint bite laced his deep voice. "I
won't have the pleasure of seeing you hang, but I imagine someone in Virginia will."

Trace smiled, understanding Wragg's predicament all too
clearly. Rachelle had probably ordered him to release her companions, and yet Lanston dared to cloak this act in his own generosity.

At the thought of Rachelle, a suffocating sensation tightened
Trace's throat. She was a smart girl. A foolish girl. And a very,
very brave lady.

From his pocket Lanston withdrew a ring of keys, then fitted
one into the lock and slowly unlocked the iron door. "She's waiting for you in my office. She wants a private word. Then you
and Fala will take the wagon and horse out back and leave
Charles Towne. And if I ever hear of you or your ship near this

harbor again, I'll use Rachelle's own money to hunt you down like a dog."

The door swung open, the hinges screeching in violent protest, and for a fleeting instant Trace considered lunging at Lanston Wragg and wrapping his hands about that arrogant neck. But Lanston had two healthy legs and a full belly, while Trace struggled even to stand upright and hadn't eaten in three days.

With Fala holding him, he staggered clumsily out of the cell, then turned toward the door. He had been right—Lanston Wragg never gave anything freely, and it was all too clear who had paid the price for his freedom.

Trace bade Fala leave him at the door to the small office—he didn't want Rachelle to see him clinging to a woman for support. Fala backed away obediently but pressed her hand over her mouth as if choking back an objection.

The corner of Trace's mouth twisted in a wry smile. With every day of freedom, the Indian woman was becoming more like her outspoken mistress.

He turned the knob, pushed the door open, and saw Rachelle sitting in a chair beside a single small window. Instantly she turned and looked at him, her eyes wet and shining, her hair spilling from beneath her cap in a tumble of black silk. A rush of pink stained her cheek, and she gave him a smile he would willingly accept as his last view on earth.

The smile vanished as her eyes traveled down to what remained of his knee.

"*Mon Dieu!*" she whispered, rising from her chair. "You shouldn't be walking!"

"It is nothing." Closing the door, he dropped heavily to a bench against the wall. He tried to keep his heart cold and still as he smiled at her, but his pulse began to beat erratically at the sight of tender concern in her eyes.

God in heaven, if you have any mercy remaining for me, bestow it now.

Gripping the edge of the bench, he leaned against the wall, steeling himself against the pain in his body in order to deal with the greater agony of this parting. For Rachelle had agreed to marry Lanston Wragg; he could see the resolution in her face and the evidence of that decision in her appearance. Tidy and respectable, she was the picture of wealth and propriety in a pristine cream-colored gown.

"Trace," she began, lifting her hand, but he shook his head.

"Be still." He drew a deep breath. "Just let me look at you."

She sat motionless in the chair, her body straightening in the tension of the moment, her eyes filling with an expression that made him feel as though the room whirled madly around him. What had happened to the young girl who boarded the *Jacques* less than a month ago? She had blossomed like a rose, opening slowly to loveliness despite the harsh winds of adversity and sorrow. Tragedy had etched composure and dignity into her face. Her eyes were now lit with a tenderness he'd never seen in them before.

"Trace, I am so sorry," she whispered, an almost imperceptible note of pleading in her lovely face. "If not for me, you would be on board your ship with your men, helping slaves escape the cruelty of this colony. I have brought you nothing but trouble and pain, and in return you have saved my life more times than I would care to admit."

"*Cherie*—" he tried to smile at her, but his features only flinched uncomfortably—"I couldn't help myself." He paused, trying to inject a brisk tone into his voice. "I have the feeling that I now owe you *my* life. Mr. Wragg tells me you are to be wed tomorrow night."

"*Oui*." She averted her eyes, staring at the wall. "It was—well, no matter. Lanston has agreed to release all the slaves in the barracoon. And he will give you and Fala a wagon so you can be away tonight, under the cover of darkness." She turned back to him, her voice suddenly low and tense. "You must hurry northward, Trace. Tarry not. Fala will help you with your wound, and she is a free woman. You two can take care of each other until you are safe."

He gave her a lopsided smile. "Who will take care of you, Rachelle?"

From lowered lids, she shot a commanding look at him. "That is not your concern. I have made my decision."

"To marry the devil's spawn?" His words hung on the air, verbal flags of battle, and for a moment they stared at each other across a sudden ringing silence.

"Well," she said, primly folding her hands in her lap, "I was almost afraid to ask Lanston to arrange this interview. I was afraid I'd cry and say something we'd both regret. But I did want to thank you for helping me see things as they really are."

Her neat little smile dissolved into a bewildered expression of hurt as she looked away. "On the way back to Charles Towne, I found myself wondering what had happened to Lanston in my absence to make him so cruel and heartless. And this morning, when I awoke in his house—" she looked at him with eyes filled with life, pain, and unquenchable warmth—"I realized that Lanston had not changed at all. He is just like he was, just like all the slaveholders of Charles Towne, just like I used to be."

Her extraordinary eyes blazed and glowed as she looked up at him. "I was the one who changed, Trace. Because of you and the things you taught me. But perhaps . . . we should not speak further."

"Rachelle." He leaned forward, shifting his weight, and felt shooting stars of pain streak from his knee up to his stomach. Sweat beaded on his forehead and under his arms, but he gritted his teeth against the pain. When the worst of the brilliant agony had passed, he looked up, holding her in his gaze. "Rachelle Bailie," he spoke with all the conviction he could muster, "Lanston Wragg will hurt you. He is not a fit husband for any woman. You don't love him, and with good reason, for he cannot be trusted. Don't do this. Don't marry him to save me. If God chooses, he will deliver me from the hangman's noose. Trust in the Almighty, not in Lanston Wragg."

"I do trust God," she whispered, a faint tremor in her voice. Her face had gone pale and still, like the colorless countenance of a corpse. "And I trust Lanston's nature. Until he controls my grandfather's estate, I know he will behave honorably."

Trace fought to control his swirling emotions. "Search your heart, *cherie*, my Rachelle, and tell me who you find there. 'Tis not Lanston Wragg who loves you."

"I know who loves me." Her voice was a husky whisper, and she looked away. "I know who risked his life to save mine. I know who fought for me, lied for me . . . who would have died for me." An almost imperceptible tremor shook her chin as she lifted her eyes to meet his. "I know whose name is written upon my heart. And if I let you die . . . I couldn't bear it."

They exchanged a long, deep look. "I'll come back, then," Trace finally said. "I'll sneak back into town and take you away from him." He laughed bitterly. "I'm already a condemned man. What difference will one more kidnapping make?"

"No." Her eyes softened with hurt. "I'll not have you commit some other act for which you'll spend your lifetime paying. You said once that your heart was as black as tar, but it doesn't have to be."

She reached out through the emptiness between them, her fingers lightly brushing his cheek. "Forgiveness is yours, Trace, if you will reach out and claim it."

Entranced, he stared at her, almost able to ignore the mocking voice inside that wondered why she persisted to care for him. Didn't she know Duncan was dead? And Captain Mariveux and his innocent daughter and countless seamen wounded in the cannon shot from the *Jacques*. Rachelle lived far above the isolation of his sin. He *had* reached out for forgiveness and found it beyond his grasp.

Standing, she crossed the distance between them and knelt at his feet, one hand resting gently on his good leg. "I do not regret one moment of my time with you. I sorrow for your pain and Duncan's death, but God worked in the wilderness." Her dark eyes shimmered with light from the window. "He helped me find my heart . . . and it will always belong to you, Trace Bettencourt."

Before he could respond, she rose against him, touching her lips to his, then kissed him with a hunger that belied her outward calm. Her touch flamed through his veins, burning his soul, and then she pulled away, squaring her shoulders before she opened the door and stepped through the doorway.

She didn't look back.

▾▲▾▲▾Rachelle knew Lanston would be waiting in the vestibule. She closed the door behind her, then leaned against it as her strength and determination faltered. Enduring the wounded look in Trace's eyes when she refused him had been the most difficult trial of her life, but she had persevered. And won.

Lanston studied her, wounded dignity in every lineament of his face. "Was it a sad parting?" he asked, a touch of mockery in his voice. "Will the good captain survive without you?"

"Well enough," she answered, standing upright. She walked toward him and gestured to a sheaf of rolled parchments in his hand. "Are those the manumission papers?"

"Yes." His dry smile flattened. "One set for Virtue, one for Fala. All signed and perfectly executed. I've just returned from the magistrate's house."

She wanted to sigh in relief but settled for taking the documents from his hands. "I'll see that they receive these. When are you providing papers for your prisoners?"

"You asked for a doctor, and the papers will take a few hours at least." His voice went dry. "When would *you* like them released? After all, you're paying for them."

"Send for the doctor, prepare the papers, and release them before dark," she answered, tucking the parchments beneath her arm. She folded her hands and looked toward the wide doors, anxious that the Indians be well away before sunset. She couldn't guarantee their safety if they remained within the city after curfew—too many Charles Towne citizens were quick with a musket and slow to ask questions.

"Yes, dear." Apparently reconciled to the concessions he would have to make in exchange for her fortune, Lanston opened the door leading to the street, then disappeared.

Rachelle bit her lip, hoping these measures would be enough to keep the Indians safe. She could do little after tomorrow, and she could do nothing if the Indians lost their manumission papers. Trace was right about Lanston's lack of honor—his virtue extended only to the limits of his purse. And once her purse was legally joined with his, she'd have no power over him whatsoever.

Lanston must have set to work with a will, for three hours later Rachelle saw that all her demands had been met. A pile of manumission papers lay curled by the barracoon door, and the physician had made a cursory inspection of the captives, even agreeing to set the French prisoner's shattered leg and broken wrist. Rachelle had not dared to enter the office while Trace screamed in torment, but waited in the vestibule, closing her eyes against the sound of his pain.

The day was nearly spent by the time the frightened Indians appeared in the inner doorway, their eyes sparking with fear and confusion. "Come," Rachelle said, taking the proper manumission papers from Virtue, who stood in the foyer and sorted them according to tribe and family. Rachelle gave each head of household his papers, then led them to the main door and out to the street. "Go back to your homes."

She stood in the sunlight, rejoicing over every soul that passed and grateful that the injured ones were able to walk. Apparently Lanston's slave hunters had not bothered to transport those who could not stand, healthy and ambulatory, upon the auction block. Whether they had killed the more seriously injured ones or merely left them behind—she shivered, unwilling to consider the implications.

The rattle of a horse and wagon broke the silence of the street, and Rachelle's heart lifted in another small but satisfying victory. This wagon would take Fala and Trace to safety, and part of her would go with them. And in the days ahead, when she felt sorrow as a huge, painful knot inside her, she would remember that she had trusted her heart to two people who loved her. She was loved . . . and knowing that made all the difference.

Stepping out of the stream of Indians, Fala appeared at Rachelle's side and slipped an arm around her waist. Rachelle lowered her head onto the taller woman's shoulder, then idly brushed back a silken strand of Fala's hair. "Take care of him," she said, swallowing the despair in her throat.

"Mademoiselle Rachelle—"

"No." Rachelle cut her off, abruptly standing straight, then checked the parchments to be sure she had the right one. "Here," she said, placing the precious paper in Fala's hands. "This makes it official. No one can ever enslave you again, do you understand? This paper says that you were once a slave, but you have been redeemed. Keep it with you always. Never allow anyone to tell you that you are not worthy—that you are not free."

Fala's head bowed and her shoulders slumped as she accepted the paper, but her eyes shone with gratitude when she looked up at Rachelle.

"Here's your cursed wagon," Lanston called, hopping down from the driver's bench. For a moment the sight reminded Rachelle of Duncan upon the bench of the wagon they'd taken to Roxbury. Fala must have been jarred by the same memory, for Rachelle felt her friend stiffen beside her.

"Rachelle—," Fala began, her voice shattered.

"Duncan would want you to go," Rachelle answered, her hand at the small of Fala's back. She firmly pushed her toward the wagon. "So get up there. I'll have Lanston bring Trace—the captain—out in a moment."

Several Indians gathered around the wagon, hope gleaming in their eyes, and Rachelle nearly shooed them away, thinking they would slow the pirate's flight away from town. But Fala was a generous woman, and Trace a self-appointed rescuer. Neither of them would be able to refuse someone in need, and Rachelle knew she couldn't speak for them. Not anymore.

She leaned back against the wall of the building, noticing that the gray clouds had blown away. A blaze of gold and crimson now lit the western horizon, contrasting exquisitely with the deepening azure of the eastern sky. Against this tapestry of living light the jagged edges of the forest stood out in dark outline, a fortress to which the Indians would have to flee.

"Excuse me, ma'am."

Rachelle turned toward the deep voice. An Indian warrior stood before her, one she had never seen in Ezhno's village. Despite the cold, he wore no shirt, only a breechclout and leather leggings. An elaborate series of striped and triangular tattoos adorned his powerful shoulders and forearms, but his face was clear and without paint. His head was completely shaved but for a small spot on his crown, and dark hair sprouted from it in braids like the snakes of Medusa.

She felt shocked by an elusive thought she could not quite fathom. What had he said to her—*excuse me, ma'am?* What sort of Indian spoke like that to a white woman?

Surprised and somewhat thrilled by the warrior's behavior, she gave him her attention. "I beg your pardon?" she asked, noticing that his mouth had bent in a cynical twist as she studied him.

"From the others—" he gestured over his shoulder toward Ezhno and a group from that village— "I hear that you were searching for the Seewees."

"Not exactly," she murmured, perplexed by his perfect intonation. This man had spent extended time with the English, for none of the other Indians had mastered the language so fluently. "We were actually searching for a particular man."

She nodded, about to dismiss him, but a dazzling thought lit the recesses of her mind. *An Indian who spoke English? And who knew about the Seewees?*

She looked up at him, resisting the urge to grab his thick arm and demand answers. Her eyes took in his age, his height, his appearance. He was at least forty—the right age—and looked like any Indian—brown hair, brown eyes, golden skin bronzed by the sun. . . .

"Excuse me, sir." A tremor of mingled fear and anticipation shot through her. "If I may ask—what is your name?"

The Indian turned away, distracted by a woman's call for help. Rachelle stared, her blood pounding thickly in her ears, as he lifted the woman's little girl and placed her into the wagon. The Indian woman smiled her thanks, climbed beside her daughter, and locked her arms around the little girl, her eyes wary and watchful as the shadows on the street grew longer.

"My name?" The Indian's face creased into a sudden smile as he turned back to Rachelle. "The Iroquois call me Akule, He Who Looks Up."

"So you're not Yamassee or Seewee." Rachelle caught her breath, struggling to sort out her thoughts. She knew so little about the Indian tribes. "Or Oneida."

"No."

It's not him. Rachelle flinched with disappointment while the Indian looked at her, his gaze bright with speculation as she hastily thumbed a tear from her cheek.

"Are you all right?" he asked, his voice calm, his gaze steady. "Perhaps I can help."

"I don't think so," she answered, the sob in her throat erupting in sudden laughter. "It's just that—well, the last few weeks haven't brought anything I expected." She sniffed and wiped her nose with the back of her hand, feeling suddenly childish. The gleam of her mother's ring caught her eye, and she smiled through her tears.

"You see this?" She managed a choking laugh as she tapped the circle of gold around her finger. "This was my mother's wedding ring. She gave it to me as a symbol of my family credo, and I've been trying to live by it. But it isn't working. I'm supposed to live boldly, faithfully, and, um . . ."

She glanced away, then hung her head. She felt exhausted, as hollow as her voice sounded. *"Mon Dieu,* I can't even remember my own guiding principle. No wonder I can't live by it."

"Successfully," the Indian murmured, an echo of entreaty in his voice. *"Fortiter, fideliter, feliciter."*

She looked up. His eyes had grown large and liquid, and he abruptly stepped backward, the calm expression on his face shattering.

Rachelle blinked, startled by his response. Surely—no, it couldn't be. Her father was probably a million miles away. Perhaps that credo was a common one; a million other families could have adopted it.

Then why had the warrior gone pale? A drop of sweat ran down his jaw, though the chilly air held the promise of frost.

A thrill of frightened anticipation touched Rachelle's spine. "My name," she whispered, feeling her blood rise in a jet, "is Rachelle Fortier Bailie."

The Indian's face seemed suddenly molten; his eyes swam, his cheeks flushed, his mouth quivered. But his eyes did not leave hers for an instant.

"I am known," he answered, his voice husky and golden and warm as the sun, "by a different name in each tribe. The Iroquois call me Akule; the Wampanoag call me Askuwheteau; the Oneida call me Kaga. But to my mother and father and wife I was known as Mojag Bailie."

Rachelle's heart leaped into her throat as fear, uncertainty, and desperate hope surged within his eyes.

"Yes," she whispered, struggling to maintain her fragile control. "I am Babette Bailie's daughter." Tears welled up and overflowed, full and round, down her cheeks. "You are my father."

For a moment neither moved, both of them caught in the deadlock of uncertainty and shock. Then Mojag Bailie reached out and pulled Rachelle into his arms, pressing her to his chest, his heart pounding against hers.

"I praise you, Father God," he whispered, his hands entwining in her hair, his breath warm upon her cheek. "What could I have done to deserve such a blessing?"

▼▲▼▲▼Mojag breathed in the scent of the woman he held in his arms and felt his head spin in a dizzying delight. This child, this woman, was so much like Babette! If he had only known she existed, he would have moved heaven and earth to find her.

As this girl—*his daughter*—wept in his arms, Mojag whispered words of thanksgiving:

> *"Who is like unto you, O Lord, among the heathen gods?*
> *Who is like you, glorious in holiness, fearful in praises,*
> *   doing wonders?*
> *You stretch out your right hand,*
> *And bring my own to me.*
> *I will sing unto the Lord, for he has triumphed gloriously.*
> *The Lord is my strength and song,*
> *My soul magnifies the Lord,*
> *And my spirit has rejoiced in God my Savior.*
> *For he has regarded the humble state of his servant:*
> *And generations shall rise after me and call me blessed.*
> *For he that is mighty has given to me a great gift;*
> *Holy is his name.*
> *And his mercy is on them that fear him, from generation to*
> *   generation.*
> *He has shown strength with his arm,*
> *He has scattered the proud in the imagination of their*
> *   hearts.*
> *He has put down the mighty from their seats*
> *And exalted them of humble status.*
> *He has filled the hungry with good things;*
> *And the rich he has sent away empty.*
> *He has helped his servant,*
> *In remembrance of his mercy."*

Rachelle's weeping grew silent, but he could feel her uneven breathing on his neck as he held her close.

"Father?" she asked, lifting her face to meet his gaze.

"Yes?"

"Nothing." The warmth of her smile sent a shiver down his spine. "Just—Father."

Mojag drew his treasure closer into the circle of his arms, awed and suddenly struck dumb by the magnitude of God's gift. Though he could no longer speak, his heart sang with delight.

▼▲▼▲▼ Furious at his temporary vulnerability to Rachelle's demands, Lanston walked through the shadows at the back of the cells, one hand holding his handkerchief over his nose, the other prodding a sick straggler with his club. For the most part, the Indians had filed out in an orderly fashion, but a few of the older ones were taking sweet advantage of his generosity.

Though his spirit recoiled at the thought of the financial loss he would suffer for this afternoon's dealings, by this time tomorrow night he would have more than recouped his losses. He'd have not only Rachelle's money but her life as well, and he'd make her pay for the frustration and humiliation of this day. Of course, he'd have to be careful how he punished her, for a single careless bruise would set the tongues of Charles Towne to wagging, but he knew ways to make a woman suffer. He'd used them before on his mother's maids, and they were surprisingly effective. Now not one of the slaves had the nerve to even peep in protest when he pulled them from the shadows of the slave quarters.

The old Indian finally shuffled out of the cell, walking with stiff dignity toward the doorway. Lanston took one last look, then made a face at the smell of the place. No white man even belonged in the cells; by all rights his slaves should have been here doing this bit of work. But he didn't want witnesses. His father would eventually find out that Rachelle had committed this bit of chicanery, but by then the old man would be well comforted by the thought of fifty thousand pounds sterling.

Lanston left the cell, slamming the iron door behind him in frustration. Several thousand pounds had just ambled away from his grasp, and the cause of his generosity stood in the doorway that opened to the street, bidding the Indians adieu like a hostess saying farewell at a fancy dress ball.

He froze in midstep, startled by the sight that met his eyes. One of the slaves, a supremely savage-looking Indian, stood next to Rachelle with his arm around her shoulders, his lips pressed to her hair.

"A pox upon him!" Bristling with indignation and anger, Lanston strode through the doorway leading to the vestibule, raising his club even as he called curses down upon the whole lot of heathen barbarians. He caught a glimpse of Rachelle's wide eyes, the startled Indian's half-turned head; then a steely hand caught his arm in a vise grip.

"Drop the club." Trace Bettencourt's voice was soft, but the venom within it was unmistakable. Half-hidden behind the door that separated the vestibule from the prison cells, the pirate had caught him unawares.

Lanston hesitated, wondering if he could maneuver in such a way as to bring the stick down upon the pirate's head, but the heavy door stood between them.

"The animal is mauling my wife," Lanston muttered, his voice hoarse with frustration.

"Leave her alone," came the sharp reply.

Lanston released the club; it fell to the floor with a faintly wooden sound.

Rachelle stepped out of the warrior's embrace and looked at Lanston with something faintly triumphant in her eyes.

What? In silent anger that spoke louder than words, Lanston stared at her, yearning for the moment when she would be his. If she had sought to embarrass or humiliate him, she could not have managed it more thoroughly if she'd embraced and kissed a hundred heathen savages in a parade through the streets of Charles Towne.

"Lanston, dear," she called, her voice bright and artificial, "about our wedding tomorrow—I can invite my family, can't I?"

"Your family is dead," he snapped, his anger a scalding fury in his belly.

"Not all of them." She waved her fingers in a delicate, teasing gesture, the gold of her mother's ring gleaming in the faint light. "You remember my father, the English minister? If I can find him, I'd like to invite Reverend Bailie."

He glared at her, seething with mounting rage, unable to understand this madness. Had she truly gone insane from the horror of her ordeal? It wouldn't matter—he could marry a mad woman as easily as a sane one, and he'd have public sympathy on his side when he put her away.

He took a deep breath, forcing himself to calm down, and decided to play along with her little game. "What do I care whom you invite?" he asked, suppressing his anger under a mantle of indifference. "Invite the Lords Proprietors of the colony—the more the merrier."

Clasping her hands beneath her chin, she gave him a smile of purest sweetness. "I was hoping you'd say something like that." She reached back to slide her hand along the filthy savage's arm and brought the man forward, through the doorway.

She paused, letting Lanston boil; then her black eyes impaled him. "Dearest Lanston, I'd like to thank you for helping me." The cold edge of irony cut through her voice. "Your little hunting party trapped more than you intended. This man is my father, the Reverend Mojag Bailie."

Lanston stared, certain he'd misunderstood. But the Indian's eyes—mirror images of Rachelle's—were dark and deadly earnest, his face as handsomely sculpted as her own.

"I want him to come to the wedding," Rachelle went on, blithely ignoring Lanston's silence. "He will give me away, of course, and sit beside your parents at the wedding dinner. And everyone in Charles Towne will want to meet him, for it's not every day that a father and daughter are reunited by the efforts of an eager groom."

How could it be true? Lanston had known Rachelle's father might have an Indian ancestor, but *this*—this man was a heathen, wild-eyed, shaved-headed, half-naked, tattooed devil with not a shred of civilization in either his deportment or appearance.

In one glance Lanston noted the man's set face, his clamped mouth, and his fixed eyes—without a doubt, the *Indian* believed Rachelle spoke the truth. He studied Lanston, lifting his head like a cat scenting the breeze. He must have intuited Lanston's intentions, for his jet black eyes began to glitter like a snake moving toward a paralyzed bird. His hands clenched at his side, eager to defend the daughter he'd never known.

Lanston staggered backward, as much from the force of the man's personality as from sheer fright. This was no English minister; this was a complete, unredeemed savage! Rachelle was a *half-breed*, little more than an animal. He couldn't take a half-heathen into his arms, and not even for a million pounds sterling could he honor her with his name.

"Get away!" His hand trembled as he pointed toward the road. "Get out of my sight, all of you, before I return with my pistols."

"Come." The Indian turned, taking Rachelle's hand and leading her to the wagon.

"Not without him," she cried, pointing past Lanston. With a start, Lanston realized that the cursed pirate still stood behind the door. Lanston stepped aside, too stunned to offer resistance.

"Quickly," Rachelle called from the wagon bed, tucking her petticoat under her legs as the Indian helped the other men lift Bettencourt into the wagon. "We've no time to lose."

Lanston waited until the last of them had passed out of his building, then he slammed the door, blinking in horror until he heard the whip crack and the pebbly sound of wheels churning against the road.

Finally, as silence fell upon the barracoon, his heart began to slow to its normal pace. He shuddered convulsively, wondering how to spare his parents this awful revelation. He'd tell them that Rachelle had run away, that she had lost her mind—anything but the truth.

Thank God above, Rachelle Bailie was on her way out of his life . . . for good.

Night had spread her sable wings over the city by the time the wagon turned from Chalmers onto Church Street. The full moon had risen in the west, casting strange shadows across the road. Fortunately, Rachelle thought, glancing ahead, the moon shed enough light for Fala to see the trampled dirt track of the road that led northward from the half-built fortifications around the settlement.

Rachelle crouched in the wagon bed, scarcely able to believe the events of the last hour. Trace lay stretched out next to her, breathing heavily but alive. Mojag Bailie, *her father*, walked along-side the wagon, one hand protectively resting upon the wagon rail, the other guiding one of the Indian children who walked in Mojag's moonlit shadow, as if he were some sort of guardian angel.

He is their guardian angel, Rachelle thought, tears blurring her eyes as she studied her father's face. *He walks with them; he lives among them; he is one of them. No wonder my mother loved him . . . and no wonder she couldn't live with him.* She smiled, not trusting herself to speak. Babette Fortier had never been one to deny herself physical comforts for very long.

She blinked away the tears and smoothed her petticoat as confused emotions and thoughts tumbled in her brain. Mojag Bailie seemed more Indian than she had expected, but his appearance had worked to her advantage back at the jail. His arrival and savage aspect has saved her from a life of misery and marriage with Lanston Wragg, and for that alone she should be grateful. He was her *father*, and after a long, exhausting search, he was finally at her side—but she had no idea what she was to do with him.

What did any daughter do with a father? *Grand-père* had been only a faint shadow of a father figure, and he had always kept her at arm's length. She had admired him, respected him, and wanted desperately to love him. . . .

As she loved Mojag Bailie now. In the space of a few moments he had captured her heart with his words, his courage, and his strength. If later he felt it necessary to leave her to continue his work among the Indian tribes, she knew she would carry that love with her as a reassuring shelter from the storms of life. And he would always *want* her near. One look into his eyes, dark with longing and wonder, had convinced her of that.

Fala made quiet clucking sounds as she drove the horse, a soothing accompaniment to the soft song Virtue hummed at the back of the wagon. Rachelle turned and looked toward the road ahead. They had reached the northern boundary of the city and were passing the section of wall that fortified the perimeter. One day, the council members had assured the residents, Charles Towne would be a secure walled city, but that time had not yet come.

Tonight Rachelle breathed a sigh of relief, grateful that no wall yet existed. From this day forward she would be much more concerned with getting people *out* of Charles Towne than worrying about who might get *in*.

Fala did not hesitate but drove the wagon deep into the woods, her back straight as a rail as she handled the reins. Moonlight sifting through the trees formed strange silvery hieroglyphs upon the occupants of the wagon, and Rachelle searched the flickering shadows to check on her patient. Trace seemed to be at rest, but the flesh of his hand burned with fever when she lifted it to her cheek.

"Trace?" she murmured, her adrenaline level beginning to rise. What if he was seriously ill? She had no medicines, not even water with which to cool him.

His eyelids fluttered like the heartbeats of baby birds, then opened. "I'm here," he replied dully, in obvious answer to her question. She pressed her hand to his head, then looked over at

her father. Mojag's eyes had already turned toward her, as if he'd
been expecting her call.

"He's feverish," she said, sobered instantly by the frightening
possibility that she might have saved Trace Bettencourt's life
only to lose him to fever. Agues of several types had raged
through Charles Towne at various times, killing swiftly, ruth-
lessly, efficiently. Barbados Fever had once paralyzed the port so
completely that only the death carts moved through the streets,
calling from house to house, heaping the dead one upon another
for mass burial.

"Tell the woman to stop the wagon." Mojag's voice carried a
unique force, and as Fala pulled back on the reins, Rachelle
noticed that all of the walking Indians stopped, too, turning
toward Mojag expectantly. He climbed onto the wagon and
began to speak in the Indian tongue, his voice echoing with
depth and authority. Rachelle had no idea what he said, but she
drew Trace's head into her lap, smoothing his dark hair away
from his damp forehead. When she was certain he slept soundly,
she looked up and watched her father.

Mojag Bailie spoke slowly, gesturing with his broad hands,
pointing in the direction of Charles Towne, then moving his
hands toward the west. The Indians listened as he talked, but
Rachelle studied him, eager to imprint his features, his very soul,
upon her heart. In the shifting moonlight Mojag seemed all
face—his features luminous and golden, his countenance so rar-
efied after all the years of service that now only his soul seemed
to show. He spoke with the graceful air of a man who is at home
in many worlds, and a masculine force enveloped him, a great
presence born of certainty. Rachelle felt herself blushing in pleasure and suddenly realized that what she was feeling was pride.

Babette was right. Mojag Bailie was a good man.

At length, Mojag fell silent, and the only sounds were the
whisper of the wind and the creaking of the horse's harness.
After a moment, Ezhno spoke, his voice rising above the crowd.
Then another man answered. One after the other, various men

offered their opinions, and Rachelle realized that these warriors were speaking for their tribes.

When the last man had spoken, Mojag lifted his hand in salute and murmured words that sounded like a benediction. He closed his eyes when he had finished speaking, and the Indians began to move away, silently, through the woods.

"Where are they going?" Rachelle asked, leaning forward as much as she dared without disturbing the sick man in her lap.

"West." Mojag climbed into the wagon and sat beside her, then reached out to stroke a damp curl from her face. "They know these woods are no longer safe. I wouldn't be surprised if the man we left at the barracoon attempts to round them up again on the morrow, papers or no papers."

"Why—" Rachelle bit her lip, afraid she might ask too personal a question, but the smile in his eyes gave her confidence. "Why were you among them? Reverend Eliot told us you were going to find the Seewees."

"You found Joseph Eliot?" The warmth of his smile echoed in his voice. "So you have been searching for me?"

Rachelle nodded, her heart too full to speak.

"Ah." He gave her a look that was pleased, proud, and vaguely possessive. "You'll have to tell me all about it. But first—" He leaned over the backboard of the driver's seat and gently told Fala to follow Ezhno and his people, who walked just ahead on the wagon path. "They will lead us to water for our friend here," Mojag said, gesturing toward Trace as he smiled back at Rachelle. "And I have some herbs in my pouch that will ease his pain."

He turned around and folded his arms, nodding toward Rachelle. "Tell me, Daughter," he said, his deep voice simmering with barely checked emotion, "how and why you came to find me."

Rachelle looked at Virtue, who sat at the back of the wagon, her dark eyes wide with wonder. "It began when Mama gave me the ring," Rachelle whispered, noting the look of pain that flashed through Virtue's eyes. "Right before she died from pox." She glanced at Mojag, but his eyes were flat and unreadable in the moonlight. "And then I found her journal and read about you. And I knew I would have to find you."

Mojag sat silently, his arms crossed, his face alternately twisting in compassion or lifting in a smile, as she told of meeting the Eliots, escaping the *Gordon Hawke,* and learning the Seewees' sad fate. She wasn't sure how long they traveled as she talked, but the stars had begun to fade behind a sky of dark blue velvet when she began the final chapter of their story. As she described the situation that had existed between herself and Lanston Wragg, Mojag's normally genial expression clouded in anger.

"God is indeed good," he murmured, when she finally stopped talking and looked up for his reaction. "You must forgive me, Daughter, but I did not know you existed. But even though I did not know, God has kept his hand upon you, guarding you, keeping you safe." His dark eyes surveyed Trace Bettencourt's sprawled body. "And I think God sent this man to you, so we must take care of him."

The wagon lurched to a stop, and Rachelle looked behind her, startled to see that they had come upon a winding river.

"Let's get water for that young man," Mojag said, leaping out of the wagon with a grace and agility that belied his years. "'Tis the least I can do for the one who saved my daughter."

▼▲▼▲▼ "Mademoiselle—" Fala stood beside the wagon with her gaze cast down, her long lashes hiding her eyes. "Since you are here to care for the captain, I choose to go with my people."

Rachelle looked up in surprise, startled out of her concern for Trace by Fala's soft statement.

"They are my people." Fala awkwardly gestured toward the Indians who splashed and drank at the riverbed. "I belong with them. You said I was free to choose."

"You are." Rachelle's mouth curved with tenderness as her surprise gave way to understanding. "And I pray God will go with you."

Fala hesitated, then reached out to embrace Rachelle. Without another word she turned and resolutely walked toward Ezhno and his people.

"Will she have a difficult adjustment?" Rachelle asked, turning toward her father. Mojag sat beside her in the wagon, his eyes upon the feverish captain. "She's lived with us for so long."

"She'll be all right," Mojag answered, a half smile crossing his face. "She's following her heart."

At that moment Trace stirred, aroused either by the water Mojag had dribbled on his lips or by the wet cloths Rachelle had stripped from her petticoat and pressed to his forehead.

"Who are you?" he snapped, regarding Mojag with a blank animal eye. His eyes searched until they found Rachelle's. "What is this? Where are we?"

"You're with me, Captain," Rachelle answered, placing a reassuring hand on his chest. "We're in the forest north of Charles Towne, and the Indians have led us to water. You have a fever—you're probably feeling a little delirious."

"Not so delirious that I can't think straight." Trace thrust out his good hand. Clinging to Mojag and Rachelle, he pulled himself up, then shuddered as fresh rivulets of sweat and water ran from his forehead.

"Rachelle—" his blue eyes came up to study her face—"you are in more danger now than ever. You surprised Lanston Wragg, that's all. Give him time to think, and he'll find a way to take your grandfather's money and you, too. Would you like to be sold into slavery? I wouldn't put it past him. If he thinks you're Indian, even half-Indian, what's to stop him from coming after you?"

Rachelle froze, a wave of apprehension sweeping through her, but Mojag's hand quickly covered hers. "I may look like an Indian," he said, his voice velvet-edged and strong, "but my blood is not as Indian as my heart." His eyes moved into Rachelle's, and he smiled at her as if she were a small child. "Shall I tell you the history of the ring?"

"Yes," she whispered, her thoughts fiercely concentrated.

Without being asked, she slipped it off her finger and placed it in his palm.

"I never thought to see this again." Mojag sank back against the side of the wagon and traced the golden circle with one finger. Smiling as if he thought of friends and people far away, he lifted his eyes to the brightening sky and began to tell the story.

"As I understand it, in 1587 Jocelyn White married Thomas Colman. This ring served at their wedding; it had belonged to Jocelyn's mother. Jocelyn and Thomas had a daughter, Regina. Regina gave birth to a daughter, Gilda, fathered by a Powhatan warrior. In the same village—Ocanahonan—Audrey Bailie had a son, Fallon, who later married Gilda. The ring was Gilda's wedding ring. Boldly, faithfully, successfully they wed when all the world stood against them."

Mojag paused, his eyes wide as though mesmerized by some marvelous dance taking place in his head. "Gilda and Fallon had twin sons, Daniel and Taregan. Daniel died in his brother's place, and Taregan took his brother's name and a Pequot woman for his wife. This ring joined him and Dena as they wed."

"And then?" Rachelle asked, fascinated.

"Dena and Taregan—who was then called Daniel—had a son and a daughter—my sister, Aiyana, and me. Aiyana married a man called Forest Glazier; they live in Natick, a village of praying Indians. I married Ootadabun, who gave her life for me in King Philip's War."

His expressive face became almost somber as he lifted the ring and peered at it. "With this ring I later married Babette Fortier, who came into my life as unexpectedly as snow in summer."

Rachelle and Trace sat in the quiet of the night shadows for a long moment, respecting Mojag's memories.

"So Rachelle isn't a half-breed because you aren't full Indian," Trace finally said, frowning as if he had found it difficult to follow the twisting family tree.

"No." Mojag exchanged a smile with Rachelle, then shook his head. "I am five-eighths Indian. I would stand in any English court—after putting on proper breeches and a frock coat, of course—and swear that Rachelle is not a half-breed. The slave traders could not hold her."

His questing eyes turned toward Trace. "Does it matter to you?"

▾▲▾▲▾ Trace shivered, not certain he had understood the question. Did *what* matter to him? Rachelle's ancestry? He couldn't care less who or what had lived in her lineage—he was quite sure that a harlot, a drunkard, and an infamous crooked merchant had sprouted from somewhere within the roots of his family tree.

"Rachelle's safety matters to me," he said flatly, looking up into the sharp and intelligent gaze of the man who sat across from him. He closed his eyes, surprised that this journey had ended as well as it had. He had wanted to deliver the girl to her father, and he had, though he had no idea how he'd managed to do it.

"And now that I have seen the mademoiselle safely to you," he said, wiping his hand across his damp forehead, "I should return to my ship. We are heading north, no? Ocracoke is not far. If you would be so kind as to deliver me to the coast, I can hire a trapper to carry me from—"

"But your ship has left you," Rachelle interrupted, her eyes flashing with alarm. "They were supposed to meet you three days ago, and you weren't there!"

"Mademoiselle," Trace said, completely aware that Mojag watched him with a sharply assessing gaze, "I am certain my men arrived at the appointed time. When they did not find me, they would make preparations to careen the ship, knowing something had detained me. They will put the *Jacques* in the shallows and scrape the barnacles from her hull, taking up to a week, if necessary."

He shrugged, noticing that her eyes had filled with infinite distress. She was remembering their conversation in Lanston's office. She had told him she loved him, that her heart was his, and though he had been glad to hear it, her heart was a gift he could not accept.

He closed his eyes, glad that he had not revealed the depth of his feelings for her. He had not wanted to burden her with the truth in the event of his death; he certainly did not want to burden her now that it appeared he would live. A pirate—an outlaw—could not afford to be distracted by romantic notions.

He waved aside her concern, deliberately misinterpreting it. "Do not worry, mademoiselle, every ship needs to be careened occasionally. There is a hidden inlet where the *Jacques* will not attract attention."

She flinched as though he'd wounded her deeply, and Trace looked away.

"So you'll be running again?" Mojag asked, shooting Trace a twisted smile. "Like Jonah, off to sea instead of obeying the voice of the Lord?"

"That's not fair." Trace lifted his uninjured arm and tried to shift his weight. He wasn't very successful, and his movement sent spasms of pain from his knee up his leg.

"I'm not running. I'm returning," he muttered through clenched teeth. "My place is with my ship, Mr. Bailie. I've taken more than two weeks to help your daughter find you." He waved a hand between the two of them. "You have each other now. So take Rachelle away from Charles Towne and be happy."

He pressed his lips together and groaned, pained as much by the conversation as by his physical distress.

"Rachelle," Mojag said, his voice resonant and impressive in the dark, "take your maid and leave us. I must have a private talk with Captain Bettencourt."

Rachelle stood and gestured to Virtue, then climbed out of the wagon. As she walked away, she glanced back at Trace with an expression of unease, as though she were abandoning a drowning man. Trace resisted a momentary impulse to call her back, but she and Virtue moved away, vanishing into the night.

He and the minister were alone. Silence fell between them,

broken only by the sound of the Indians' distant voices and the wind in the pines.

"Trace Bettencourt." Mojag took a deep breath and stood upon the wagon bed, planting his feet with battleship solidity. The forest around him was dense with blue shadows and the promise of dawn.

Mojag's face, resolute and strong, shimmered in the moonlight with a delicate dimension of sensitivity. "The Spirit of the Lord bids you to stop running," he said, his eyes shiny as if with dreams. "Whither shall you go from his Spirit? Or whither shall you flee from his presence? If you ascend up into heaven, God is there. If you make your bed in hell, behold, he is there. If you take the wings of the morning and dwell in the uttermost parts of the sea, even there shall his hand lead you, and his right hand shall hold you."

Mojag fell silent for a moment, applauded by the fluttering evergreens and the quiet sigh of the river. Even the Indians, whose voices had filled the woods a few moments before, seemed to listen in silence.

"Aye," Trace said, hot tears filling his eyes, "God haunts me. I know he follows me everywhere, for I can feel his presence. It is his forgiveness I have never felt, though I have often sought it."

"Why shouldn't he give it to you?" Mojag's stentorian voice rumbled through the forest. "'The Lord is merciful and gracious, slow to anger, and plenteous in mercy. He will not always chide: neither will he keep his anger for ever. He hath not dealt with us after our sins; nor rewarded us according to our iniquities. For as the heaven is high above the earth, so great is his mercy toward them that fear him. As far as the east is from the west, so far hath he removed our transgressions from us.'"

Trace turned on the minister in a sudden flash of defensive spirit. "Don't you think I've heard this before? I know everything you're saying, but nothing changes the fact that I do not feel forgiven. I've committed serious sins, Reverend Bailie—malfeasance and mutiny and murder. I've begged God to forgive me, to cover me in his grace and allow me to make a new start.

Yet I rise from my knees with the same shadows on my soul, the same price upon my head."

Trace's outburst startled Mojag, but now the minister's face settled into lines of satisfaction. "You are well on your way to forgiveness," he said, his voice soft. "The admitting of evil is the first beginning of good. What you need, my friend, is to make confession."

Trace snorted. "I'm not Catholic."

"This has nothing to do with Catholicism." A flash of humor crossed Mojag's face. "This has to do with pride. Sometimes a brother or sister can make God's presence and forgiveness real to us. All believers are part of the royal priesthood Christ ordained."

Trace sat back, momentarily rebuffed. "I don't understand."

"Sometimes," Mojag went on, lowering himself so that he sat directly in front of Trace, "we privately confess ourselves in the dark, but our sins remain hidden. Fed by the pride that forbids us to humble ourselves publicly, our iniquities fester in our souls. But if you confess yourself to a brother, your sin is uncovered and brought out into the light. Though God's forgiveness is genuine whether you seek him privately or publicly, the heat of the light destroys pride . . . and may help you find the peace you are seeking."

Trace sat very still, feeling his brow furrow. Rachelle had said Mojag Bailie was an unusual clergyman, and this was the most unorthodox teaching Trace had ever heard. But it made sense. Perhaps pride had held him back. He had been so conscious of his position as captain, as a leader of men, that he'd never been able to speak openly about his guilt to anyone—until Rachelle.

"All right," he said, after a long moment. "How do we do it?"

"You talk to me." Mojag smiled with beautiful candor. "And I listen."

Trace nodded, finding grim satisfaction in the man's wisdom. This minister had undoubtedly sensed the emotional currents running between Trace and Rachelle. Once Trace unlocked the

secrets of his past, Mojag would be happy to send him away . . .
far away from his daughter.

"All right." Trace let his head fall back and stared at the
slowly brightening sky. "It all began when I was ordered to
scourge a young boy. . . ."

▼▲▼▲▼ The rising sun licked a golden paste over the
woods, giving the forest a gilded dignity that faded even as
Rachelle watched. Virtue lay asleep next to Rachelle, quietly snor-
ing in a bed of pine needles. Mojag and Trace had been sitting in
the wagon for over an hour. Though she heard the deep rise and
fall of Trace's voice, she could not catch his words.

*Heavenly Father, almighty God, grant Trace the peace he seeks. And
give my father your wisdom.*

The sound stopped, and during a long moment of silence
Rachelle crept forward. Trace now hunched in the wagon with
his head bowed, and Mojag had risen to his knees. His broad
hands rested upon Trace's gleaming hair; his face looked toward
heaven. His mouth moved in words Rachelle couldn't understand, but she saw Trace's shoulders shaking as Mojag prayed.

Did he weep with sorrow or joy? She crept closer, wanting to
be near if Trace needed her.

"The fear and pride that clung to you like barnacles cling to
others also," Mojag was saying as she walked toward them.
"You are not alone in your sin, nor are you alone in forgiveness.
Break free of your guilt, Trace Bettencourt. The cleansing grace of
God flows to you."

Trace lifted his face, opened his eyes, and Rachelle saw tears
running down his cheeks, glittering like jewels in the sunlight.
She ran to the wagon and climbed in, crawling to his side as he
reached out for her.

As Mojag sank back to the wagon bed, a contented smile
upon his face, Trace buried his face in Rachelle's shoulder and
shed the tears of a free man.

▼▲▼▲ Feelings—his, Rachelle's, Mojag's—hung thick in the air like smoke, but Trace could not speak. He lifted his head, opened his mouth, but he'd developed a habit of repressing his feelings; he had cut himself off too many times.

"Trace Bettencourt," Mojag said, seeming to follow Trace's thoughts, "God has forgiven you. Now you must forgive yourself."

For some shapeless reason Trace thought of Duncan, the hot-tempered, sweet-natured Scot who had unwittingly cut the cord linking the men of the *Jacques* with the rest of the world. He was gone. Now Rachelle held his hand to her cheek, her tears burning his flesh worse than any fever.

Out of loyalty to his friend, Trace had gone willingly into exile. Why couldn't love for this woman bring him into freedom? If she could love him, knowing what he was and all he'd done, perhaps Mojag Bailie was right.

Today there were no shadows across his heart, for his soul had filled with a fathomless peace and the light of freedom. It was time to grant forgiveness . . . and accept love.

"Rachelle—" He pulled out of her embrace and sat upright, then looked at her, his eyes probing to her very soul. "I told you once to search your heart. If you will do it again and find me there, know that I will always love you. If you would take me as I am, I would give my life to you."

Placing her hands upon Trace's arms, Rachelle felt her heart constrict with happiness. "You once said," she murmured, her eyes watering in the early sunlight, "that when I could give you a new name, a new face, and a new soul, you would be good enough to please me."

His vivid blue eyes narrowed at the memory, but he did not retreat from her steady gaze.

She smiled, trying to still the wild pounding of her heart. "I like your name, Trace Bettencourt, I would not change your face or a hair upon your head, and I believe you have found healing for your soul. I will take you as you are, and I would give my life to you in return."

She felt her heart skip when Trace looked toward her father. "Excuse me, Reverend—do you still have her mother's ring?"

As if on cue, Mojag extended the small golden circle.

Trace reached out with his good hand and plucked the band from Mojag's palm, then offered her a small, shy smile. "Would you, *cherie*, wed me? Would you have me as your husband, knowing what I am—and all I have been?"

His blue gaze moved into hers, and Rachelle felt her heart turn over in response. "I know you for a God-fearing, honest, and true man," she murmured, leaning toward him. "And yes, I will marry you, Captain Trace Bettencourt." Lifting her hand, she slipped her finger through the golden circle.

Despite his fever and pain, Trace gave her a blissful smile. Putting a hand to Rachelle's waist, he drew her to himself and sighed when she slipped her arms about his neck.

"Well." Mojag slapped his hands on his knees, apparently well satisfied to find his daughter and give her away in less than twenty-four hours. "I'm a minister, after all. I suppose we can make it official whenever you like."

"Not yet." Trace raised his hand to caress Rachelle's cheek, damp with tears she couldn't remember weeping. "I won't marry her with a price upon my head."

Rachelle released a laugh that was half a sob. "I don't care, Trace."

"But I do." Still holding her, Trace looked to her father. "Confession is good for the soul, Reverend, *oui?* I'll go before the governor of Carolina and confess to my piracy—they say he's offering pardons for all who will swear to steal no more."

"He'll want restitution to be made." Mojag's expression took on an inward look. "And I've no money to speak of."

Rachelle smiled as powerful relief filled her. "I have money." Idly, she traced the stubbled shadow of Trace's lower lip, then gave him a bright smile. "I've just learned that I have more money than I could ever spend. I'll give the governor whatever he requires for your pardon, and we'll use the rest to continue your work somehow."

She gave him a secretive smile. "You were right about so many things, my captain. Slavery is an abomination. I don't know how or where, but we will establish a place where no one lives in bondage, a safe haven where any man, no matter what his heritage, can be free."

"I'm afraid there's no place like that in the colonies." Mojag's eyes darkened with feeling. "Most people now see nothing wrong with slavery. Even the ministers have found ways to condone it. But the frontier is still open. Perhaps that would be a good place to start such a work." He looked at Trace with a smile in his dark eyes. "I'd be willing to help you."

"Thank you," Trace answered. Turning his gaze toward Rachelle, he pressed his hand to her neck, and she smiled in gratitude when her father sensed an urgent need to slip out of the wagon and water the horse.

"My *belle* Rachelle," he murmured, pulling her forward until their foreheads met. "I hope you won't mind having a husband who limps. I'm afraid this knee may not heal completely."

"Lean on me, then," she whispered, entwining her fingers in his hair. "I will stay by your side always, anywhere."

"You may have to live aboard the *Jacques* for a few weeks, until we settle things." His hand tightened upon her neck, and he lowered his gaze. "I'll explain things to the men. They're loyal, and most of them will be relieved not to spend the rest of their lives dodging cannonballs. But we may still be in a bit of danger, for the *Jacques* will be known as a pirate ship until we obtain our pardon—"

"I'm not afraid." She placed her finger across his lips, then lifted his head until she found her mirror in his eyes. "As long as we're together, I won't fear anything."

"'Twill not be the life you were born to," he cautioned, a faint note of regret in his voice.

"*Dieu merci!*" She laughed softly, pressing her palm to the back of his neck. "It *is* the life I was born to. You forget, sir, I am the daughter of a Frenchwoman and a missionary to the Indians. I was never meant for tea parties and harpsichord lessons."

From the corner of her eye, Rachelle saw Virtue's head rise over the wagon. The maid gasped in surprise, her eyes widening; then Rachelle closed her eyes and kissed the pirate who had stolen her heart . . . and finally brought her home.

▼▲▼▲▼ Mojag Bailie stretched his legs out over a boulder at the river, content to watch and wait. Already there was a warmth in the sun, a sure sign of spring to come. A delicious idleness spread through his limbs as he leaned back upon his elbows and looked down into the rippling water below.

He dropped the reins on his mind and let it wander back to another spring, a time when he had held his wife in his arms and rejoiced in her love. He must have carried the memory of Babette's face, stored like a seed in the dark soil of his mind. Last night, when Rachelle stood in the doorway and questioned him, that seed had sprouted.

He glanced down into a quiet pool beside the rock. At least a dozen minnows moved in the water, swimming with one mind toward his shadow, then suddenly darting away. Mojag's eyes focused on his reflection. He caught his breath as his eyes and face dissolved into quite a different image. Babette's face was reflected there, her blue eyes as bright as the sky, her honey brown hair curling loosely over her neck and shoulders.

"She is very like you," he told the image in the water, noting again her softness, her tip-tilted eyes. "She is very lovely, Babette." The soft lips curled in a smile; the eyes brightened and glowed. And then, as suddenly as she had appeared, she was gone.

Mojag closed his eyes, slowly bringing his thoughts back to the present. He had been struggling in his own battle with guilt, for he had not reached the Seewees in time. But God had obviously directed his steps here for a unique and thrilling purpose.

Boldly, faithfully, successfully he and his people had ventured into the wilderness. And now—he smiled at the thought—a new generation would take up the challenge.

REFERENCE LIST

Historical information for this book came from the following sources:

Anderson, R. C. *The Rigging of Ships in the Days of the Spritsail Topmast, 1600–1720.* New York: Dover Publications, Inc., 1994.

Chartier, Roger, ed. *A History of Private Life, Vol. 3: Passions of the Renaissance.* Cambridge, Mass.: Harvard University Press, 1989.

The Complete Walking Tour of Historic Charleston. Charleston, S.C.: Charleston Publishing Company, 1986.

Cordingly, David. *Under the Black Flag: The Romance and the Reality of Life among the Pirates.* New York: Random House, 1995.

Fraser, Walter J., Jr. *Charleston! Charleston!: The History of a Southern City.* Columbia, S.C.: University of South Carolina Press, 1991.

Gragg, Rod. *Planters, Pirates, and Patriots: Historical Tales from the South Carolina Grand Strand.* Nashville, Tenn.: Rutledge Hill Press, Inc., 1994.

Roberts, Nancy. *Blackbeard and Other Pirates of the Atlantic Coast.* Winston-Salem, N.C.: John F. Blair Publishers, 1995.

Rogozinski, Jan. *Pirates!: Brigands, Buccaneers, and Privateers in Fact, Fiction, and Legend.* New York: Facts on File, Inc., 1995.

Winslow, Ola Elizabeth. *John Eliot, Apostle to the Indians.* Boston: Houghton Mifflin Company, 1968.

Wood, Betty. *The Origins of American Slavery: Freedom and Bondage in the English Colonies.* New York: Hill and Wang, 1997.